IT'S A
WONDERFUL LIFE
for
Lexie
Byrne
(aged 41 ¹/₄)

IT'S A WONDERFUL LIFE

for

Lexie Byrne

(aged 41 1/4)

Caroline Grace-Cassidy

BLACK & WHITE PUBLISHING

First published in the UK in 2022
This edition first published in 2023 by
Black & White Publishing Ltd
Nautical House, 104 Commercial Street,
Edinburgh, EH6 6NF

A division of Bonnier Books UK
4th Floor, Victoria House, Bloomsbury Square, London, WC1B 4DA
Owned by Bonnier Books
Sveavägen 56, Stockholm, Sweden

A CIP catalogue record for this book is available from the British Library.

ISBN: 978 1 78530 567 2

1 3 5 7 9 10 8 6 4 2

Typeset by Data Connection
Printed and bound in Great Britain by Clays Ltd, Elcograf S.p.A.

www.blackandwhitepublishing.com

For my girls . . .

1

16 December

Merry Christmas Everybody

As I click-clack (not terribly elegantly!) across the old cobblestones towards the Brazen Head, the first few snowflakes trickle down. Listen, I'm no gazelle, it's not easy to navigate these eighteenth-century pavements in heels.

"Thank you, God!" I land on the mercifully more even pavement across the street and expend a sigh of relief, delighted not to have ended up face-first in the cobbles. Clumsy is my middle name. If there is a glass door to be walked into, a drink to be spilled or a pothole to freefall down, I'm your woman.

"You're welcome, my child," some smart-arse calls out from across the way and makes the sign of the cross with his extended hand.

"Thank you, *Father* Christmas!" I'm always one to answer back, but then I recognise him as one of the security guys at Silverside Shopping Centre, where I work.

He swaggers on from block to block, swinging his arms like Liam Gallagher himself.

"Oh hiya! It's alright for you men, isn't it, Tony? You lot don't have to perform balancing acts on a bloody night out," I shout

I

over, one straight palm cupping the side of my mouth, the snow sleeting sideways past me.

"Don't be blamin' men for yer footwear now too, we liked yiz barefoot chained to the kitchen sick, remember? It was yous who didn't agree!" He stops, throws a very pronounced wink at me. "Only messin' with ya, have a good night, Lexie! Merry Christmas!" On he swaggers.

"Same to you, nice to see you." I pat down my blunt fringe because this wind is playing havoc with it.

"Come on," I rouse myself, head down as I totter on. I'm on my way to a birthday party and, if I turn up in my usual attire, trainers and jeans, it will look like I don't want to be there (which I don't, but that's not the point). I've had to stuff my bloated self into my fancy frock and hoof on my "going out-out" cream knee-highs. Yes, I'm pre-menstrual, but I'm also built well, so I've been told – not sure about genetics as I'm an only child, so I've no sister to compare thighs with!

White twirling flakes pirouette down from the low, dark sky and I stick my gloves out to catch them. A glimpse of my watch face under the yellowing flicker of the streetlamp tells me it's almost nine o' clock. Out here, the Dublin city streets are quiet; it feels like I'm the mysterious, always-single, lost out-of-towner in a Hallmark Christmas movie (a not-so-guilty pleasure of mine!) until my phone rings at top volume, disturbing this winter wonderland.

"Oh please be you, Adam!" But see, I'm not single! I have me an Englishman. And I implore the bloody universe that this is him ringing me!

Lifting the tails of my blazer, I pull the phone from my dress pocket. Dolly Parton sings my chosen ring tone of 9 to 5. I check the caller ID.

"Yes!" The relief is palpable.

2

It's him!

Adam.

My lovely, extremely hot, long-distance lover.

"And about time too!" I hiss but frustratingly can't activate the finger slide with my woolly glove.

"Shit! Hang on, Dolly!"

She tumbles out of bed and stumbles to the kitchen as I bite my right glove off, yanking an ear pod out with my other hand. Obviously, I'm not actually *listening* to anything. I don't have that luxury. I'm a woman, walking alone at night.

"Oooooh lover boyyyyyyyy?" I answer, singing that line from "Lover Boy" in *Dirty Dancing* as I fold my freezing five-foot-seven inches into the sheltered entrance of Kilroy's chipper on the corner. Ducking, I just about avoid colliding with the glittery Christmas paper chains that swoop low. Oh Adam's well used to me throwing *Dirty Dancing* references into our conversations; it's my favourite film of all time, you see. The first time I saw it, I was sweet sixteen and thought that true love and raw sexual chemistry was out there waiting for us all. Guess what, ladies? I wasn't wrong!

"Heeeyyyy, he-hey baby!" He always plays the game, bless him. But three little words are all Adam Cooper has to sing and I literally go weak at the knees. I still get that animal thrill, that raw alchemy from speaking to him, never mind getting naked in bed with him! It maybe took thirty-nine-and-a-half years, but I did finally get me my Johnny Castle.

Standing in tight against the sea of tiny blue mosaic tiles, the aroma of fat, sizzling chips drenched in salt and vinegar wafts up my hungry nostrils.

"Well? News?" I blurt, turn my thumbnail sideways, nibble nervously at it.

"One sec, just moving out of the staffroom, coverage is crap as you know."

"Okay." I steel myself to be strong, I can't sound desperate (which I am at this stage!). "Take your time."

Please *don't* take your time. Can I tell you something else? Adam was supposed to be with me in Dublin tonight, but he had to cancel. *Again*. It's becoming a common theme. He texted late yesterday afternoon, seconds after I got all the shopping in having spent the night before on my hands and knees scrubbing my apartment! He had to fill in at work, and I was gutted. It's been over a week since I've heard his voice but nearly three months since I've physically *seen* him. Adam is a very busy man. Ah look, I'd known this from day one but it's beginning to feel like I'm midway down the priority-ladder of his life. I gotta tell ya, this long-distance relationship stuff is getting more and more complicated every day.

But we are meant to be. This I know. It was an *instant* connection with us. That Baby and Johnny first dance to "Love Man" after she carried her watermelon. I felt just how she must have felt. Floored. He hit me with a door, I fell backwards on my arse and then it was boom! An undefinable feeling. My body flooded with intense physical attraction when I looked up and saw him. It was his dark messy hair, his thick stubble, his strong jaw, that tight silver feather chain around his neck and that well-worn black biker jacket.

Then he spoke to me, and I was hypnotised. Difficult to explain without sounding cringe. We sat at a late-night bar drinking wine and talked for hours – about everything, left no stone unturned, it was all just so easy and beyond exciting. He was genuinely interested in getting to know *me*. Adam made me feel like the most beautiful, most interesting, funniest girl in the world, and I'd never felt that in my life before, ever. I ignored the "be-a-good-girl rule book" and slept with him that first night, and not for a second afterwards did I feel like it

4

was a one-night stand. Our connection was everything they tell you about love at first sight: the dopamine, the norepinephrine collided, they exploded in both of us like wondrous fireworks. Simply put, I couldn't get enough of him.

"G'dnigh'." A robust man startles me as he shuffles past. Adam's still moving through the hospital – I can hear the background noise as I lower the phone.

"Ni-night," I throw back under Shakin' Stevens singing "Merry Christmas Everybody" from the speaker above me and stifle a yawn. I wish I wasn't so bloody tired lately and already I hate myself for not wearing a softer bra because this criss-cross, underwired bastard is digging into my poor unfortunate C-cups.

"Jesus," I hiss, tugging at the wire to try and free my hormonally inflated boobs from their barbaric constraints. I detest having to get dressed up, I'm never comfortable. I'm a cosy attire, Netflix and takeaway woman. Why can't the world just let me be me?

The man who's just left the chipper shakes the brown paper bag, folds it open and steam engulfs his weathered face. I'm in a hot potato trance as he lifts a long golden crispy chip in the air. A grunt of envy rolls around my mouth. I'm absolutely starving even though I had a meatball marinara and a rocky road before I left work!

"You still there, gorgeous?" Adams voice in my ear.

Oh! Shit! See how easily distracted I am by carbs? What can I tell ya?

"I'm here!" I speak into the receiver, stepping out to the edge of the high concrete step, the snowfall coming down lighter now.

"Ah, thought you hung up on me . . ." his deep, husky Cotswolds accent serenades me.

"Hung up, you say? I'm hung up on you alright!" I'm unashamedly in love with my forty-four-year-old soulmate.

5

However . . . nothing in life is quite so perfect, is it? Adam isn't without his complications. He's divorced, it's messy and he has a teenage daughter, but adorable Freya is not the reason for the *however*. Our problem is his ex-wife, Martha. She's still besotted with him, borderline obsessed, I would say, lives across the road from him and hates the fact I even exist. They have shared custody of Freya, but if Martha had her way, or gets her way, they'd still have a shared life.

But now he's all mine and soon – hopefully – he'll be here for Christmas.

2

16 December

All I Want for Christmas Is You

"WE HAVEN'T SPOKEN ALL WEEK, I miss your voice!" His tone is silky, still slightly panting.

"I know, me too, texting just isn't the same. You men are brutal at it, sorry but it's a fact!" My stomach flips just talking to him; I can just picture him in his work uniform.

"Correct and all my fault, as always!" He groans. "Jesus, when will I stop apologising to you? I don't deserve you."

I want to scream: *When are you coming over to Dublin?* But I hold strong.

"Don't be silly, no one deserves me!" I joke, and he laughs in reply. "I was just sheltering on the Quays, it's started to snow in Dublin. It's beautiful."

I gaze up to the sky and a flying white flake finds my eyeball in a direct hit.

"Aghh!" I yelp.

"You okay? What's happened?" he reacts worriedly.

"Snowflake went in my eye!"

"Hardly a stone!" he chuckles.

My eye runs water. "It's stinging so bad! Mascara-in-your-eye pain. You've no idea, Cooper. Ow!"

I'm no doe-eyed, natural beauty, so I rely on my eye makeup, a nice liquid cat eye and my lashes layered with dark mascara. I brush that stuff on like I butter my toast.

"Dab the eye with the bottom of your palm, cleanest part of your hand," he advises. "Listen, quickly, I'm just finishing into shift, I'll be home by eleven, it's bloomin' chaotic here! I wanted to – oh, for Pete's sake . . ." A beep-beep-beep-beep-beep "call waiting" sounds down the line. "Ah – hang on Lexie, another call, let me get rid of it—"

"Go ahead." I balance on the step, doing a few on-the-spot heel-to-toe moves to keep warm. I screw up my face to focus on a young couple approaching the chipper. He's swinging a guitar case in one hand, a beanie hat covering his head, and she's all sorts of gorgeous, white snowflakes sticking to her black faux fur coat, leather leggings, red trilby. For a split second she makes me feel old in only that way really young, spirited-looking women can do. You know the type? Oozing independence and individuality, probably had one of those large well-worn push pin world maps blue-tacked to the back of their bedroom door growing up, with colourful tops marking the exotic countries they planned to visit.

I've only ever had one travel destination on my Lexie-bucket list – to visit:

New York City.

New York, New York, so good they named it twice.

I can't tell you how much I want to go see that city. To walk those famous streets. To look up at those magnificent skyscrapers, see the famous outer stairwells, brownstones, Broadway, Bloomingdales.

Someday.

Well, between you and me I should have been there by now. Years ago. Myself and my best pal Annemarie were supposed to go together. We'd even opened credit union accounts to save! Painstakingly planned every solitary second of our Big Apple adventure:

Freshly squeezed orange juice on top of the Empire State Building.

The New Yorker afternoon tea at the Plaza hotel.

The Tavern Burgers at Tavern on the Green in Central Park.

All the fake designer bags we could carry back from Canal Street.

Catching *The Phantom of the Opera* on Broadway, hanging around the stage door after.

Late night-cocktails on the roof top of Beast & Butterflies at the M hotel on Times Square.

And shopping in Bloomingdales purely to get the Big Brown Bag signature store carrier bag to swing as we strolled along some of the three-hundred and ninety-nine blocks of the city.

But it never happened.

And it still hasn't, because Annemarie pretends she's forgotten. The reason? She had a baby and her life dramatically changed. She lives in a world of infinite love and infinite terror. Such is her anxiety about leaving her toddler son with his perfectly capable father, she avoids any mentions of our New York trip. It's the Empire-elephant in our friendship. And I can't go without her, that's just not my style, because I'd feel too guilty.

The too-cool-for-school couple stands a few feet from me, gazing up at the illuminated menu in the window; he's whistling Jingle Bells rather impressively, she's chewing gum rapidly, counting loose change out in her hands, the soft glow from the Christmas decorations turning her pallor golden.

Adam's voice pulls me away again.

"Okay. Got rid of that call. Forgive me, it's mayhem here! Some massive punch-up at a local land development protest march near Chipping Campden apparently. I've bloody noses and bones protruding everywhere I look, a cornea left hanging out by all accounts on the earlier handover . . ."

"Ew! Sounds horrendous!" I shut my left eye in sympathy, slap my hand over it.

Oh sorry! I should have said, Adam's a triage nurse, incredible at what he does. Get this: I saw him deliver Annemarie's son when she went into early labour in a hotel room in the Cotswolds! Speaking of stressed-mom.com again – she's waiting for me in the Brazen Head – it's her husband Tom's birthday drinks and I'm late.

"Well? Do you know when you're coming over?" I have to ask now.

"That's why I'm calling, I know you're a busy woman, but can we FaceTime tonight when I get in . . ."

Just tell me now! I howl in my head, take a further step out onto the road with my finger in my ear. I do an inelegant stumble back as empty taxis with their lit-up plates whizz by me too close for comfort on these blustery Dublin quays.

". . . or are you out late-late?"

I can hardly hear him over the wind. Through the curved window I watch the man in the white coat shaking a frying basket behind the counter.

"I'll be home, let's talk later. And we'll talk about Christmas?" I bulldoze on.

Trying not to get blown over and too wet, I rest myself up inside a glass bus shelter. A cute two-point-four perfect family dressed in matching Christmas reindeer pyjamas advertise mince pies or fresh cream, I'm not sure which, as someone has graffitied a rather rude piece of anatomy over the brand. But all I'm thinking here is, *come on*, he *still* doesn't know when he's coming to me for Christmas?!

"I've got you something, I hope you'll like it," he goes on as I grip the phone tighter.

"You on a platter? In just your silver chain?"

Cheeky Lexie. But I'm not even messing.

Hurry up man! I think as I turn my back to the snowy gale, leaning my head on the glass.

Then his tone changes. "I wish I could've been in Dublin with you tonight – I'm sure Annemarie will be on your back about me cancelling *again* and that's just not fair on you – but there is nowhere I'd rather be, you know that, right? We'll figure this out . . ."

I hear ructions going on in the background, the distance sounds of an ambulance siren. I wish I hadn't told him of Annemarie's unimpressed observations about him of late.

"Ah don't worry about her! *I* understand, totally, and all I want for Christmas is you."

The young couple walk past me and again the smell of chips permeates the night air.

"So, a face-to-face later?"

"Yeah, I'd love that." But I'm gutted. Surely his staff rota is out by now so he can book his Christmas flights?

"Oh hang on . . . Was there something else I'm forgetting?" he ponders.

"Dunno?" I squeeze my finger in tighter, flattened with disappointment, stare again at the picture-perfect seasonal family enjoying mince pies.

"Surprise! Our Christmas rota is due to be signed off on tonight! Beth, the administrator, just emailed me at last. I'm sure she's fed up with me hounding her all the time, she knows how

11

desperate I am to get over to you for the holidays, the whole hospital knows! The whole village knows! I only hope this shit-show doesn't put her back trying to deal with the paperwork for all these people in A&E tonight." I can hear the excitement in his voice.

"Yes! Oh—" Hastily I try to moderate my words and tone. *Try to sound casual and less concerned, Lexie, you're not sixteen,* I chant in my head. "That's . . . um, jolly good." I throw my eyes with the odd turn of phrase I've chosen but good woman! Chillaxed! I make a fist and throw a little victory punch into the cold night air, the snow turning more to sleet now.

"I know! At last." He's breathless, on the move again. I conjure up the image of that silver chain he wears around his neck swinging against his perfect skin.

"It'll be brilliant to get the dates pinned down, so I can plan, shop for us and all that ya know? Maybe book us a table in my local Indian for the night you arrive? A vindaloo and you, what more can a woman want!" I joke oh-so-breezy-like considering I'm so excited my heart thuds with the thrill. I'm dizzy with the thoughts of having him naked in my bed for days, genuinely light-headed.

Listen, I know I should be honest and tell him I've been desperately waiting to hear from him, but Adam has so many people desperately waiting on him, both in his personal and work life, and I don't want to be another one. That was one of our golden rules laid down by me when we got together: no hassle. We committed to a relationship of no hassles. An unconventional romance. If only I'd known that two years later it wasn't as "progressive" as it sounded. If only I'd known sharing him wasn't as easy as I'd thought.

"Only if you're planning on being home, no pressure? I just got giddy when I saw Beth's email, had to call you straight away despite this shit-show here." He's so easy-going, all the time.

"No! I'll be home!" *Too eager again, pull it back, Lexie.* I fake a yawn. "Sorry, I'm dog tired for some reason these last couple of weeks – well I know why, we're slammed behind information. Don't doubt you see some terrifying sights in A&E but working in Silverside on the countdown to Christmas is truly treacherous. I'm longing for my bed."

Adam laughs in his delicious, masculine throaty, infectious way. "I'd be at your information counter every day if I lived in Dublin, watching you . . ."

"Careful, you sound a bit like stalky Sting . . ." I say as a man walking his dog past the shelter throws me a funny look, so I totter out, against the wind and sleet.

Adam laughs harder. See? He really thinks I'm funny.

"Don't come home early because of me. Enjoy yourself . . ."

I'd run over Brad Pitt to get home to you, I think, breathe and shout over the wind:

"I'm just gonna pop in, show my Botulinum-toxin-free face and be home on the last bus. Should be home by – what – huh—?"

That beep-beep-beep noise is sounding on the line, cutting in again.

"For fu—!" he snaps, his voice sounding far way again now, away from the mouthpiece. "I can't deal . . ."

"What now? The headless horseman just walked into A&E?"

Unusually, Adam doesn't laugh at my joke. The irritating beeps continue. I'm starting to shiver now and my ear is getting sore; I need to get to the Brazen Head.

"Hang on – need to know what time to call you at?" His voice is loud again, back into the speaker.

"Okay, no worries." My hungry eyes (pardon the unintentional *Dirty Dancing* pun) return to chip-man. He's up ahead, perched on a graffiti-inscribed electricity box. Chip-man's legs are strewn out in front of him, like they don't belong to him at all, one sensible brown loafer crossed over the other.

"Stop calling me!" Adam's voice booms.

Huh? I think, my teeth chattering, but before I can answer:

"For the last time. It's no. It's still no. It will always be no. That's the end of it! It's never going to happen!" Adam's voice is not a happy one, in fact I've rarely heard him like this.

Who's he talking to? But I think, *Stay quiet*, squeeze the phone even tighter to drown out the whirling breeze, trap my blowing dress between my knees.

"Hello? Can you answer me? Just stop this now, I mean it." He inhales deeply. "Please, it's hectic here and I'm still on that call to Lexie . . ."

Oh shit. I have to say it's still me. I should have jumped in seconds ago.

"Um . . . It's still me . . . Stillll Lexie." I shift onto my right foot, then my left, trying to ease the discomfort from my ankles and an overall sudden *ick* feel I have. Who the hell was that?

"Oh! Shit!" he spits.

"Shit?" I say. I don't like this, my stomach swirls like a bobbing sea trawler in a storm.

"No . . . I – oh sorry – Lexie – sorry—" He sounds alarmed.

"Who *was* that—"

I'm not even sure what he's just said or to who?

"Who were you talking to there?" And just like that, my subconscious goes into overdrive. Suddenly I'm in a small holding room with a two-way mirror and no window. Adam sits opposite me at a table, a small tape-recording device whirrs in the centre and I'm asking him what he said. He's shaking his head, he can't recall, and that's when I stand up so fast my chair topples over, I bang the desk hard, keep my hands on the table,

14

look him straight in the eye and say, "You said: *It's no. It's still no. It will always be no.*"

"Oh, it was . . . Can you hear me?"

"Yes." I'm dragged out of my worst-case scenario imagination overdrive and swallow. Is he stalling for think-time? My teeth keep chattering as the sleet whips across my body.

"Salty as the Irish sea," chip-man tells me as I walk past, I give him a thumbs up.

"It . . . It was my pain-in-the-arse sister . . ." he mutters feverishly.

"Ah-ha." I release a fast breath I didn't even know I was holding.

"Deb . . ."

"Right."

My nose runs. I need to fish out a tissue. I clasp the phone under my chin and rummage in my bag.

A pause. Neither of us speaks for seconds.

"You arguing with her?" I sniff.

"Um, yeah, kinda, she wants me to agree to – never mind, it's silly, her fortieth is coming up, she's all panicked. I'm not usually that snappy but she's really pushing my buttons today. Listen, I gotta run . . . I'll call later, yeah? What time?" Voices are increasingly raised around him in Cotswolds General. "Another ambulance just off loaded on us here out front . . . they need me back in triage."

"And I need to get to Tom's party, I'm late. Eleven-thirty?" I wipe my nose, shaking like leaf now and I pull my flimsy blazer collar up like it's going to help.

"It's just – all I'll say is you know our Deb, Lexie – dog with a bone to get her own way. She's insisting I wear a white suit and a dicky bow to her black and white themed fortieth birthday dinner . . . in Martha's house!"

"How very Bond," I say in my best 007 voice. "Better go." But I'm feeling triggered by that accidental call-swap.

"Actually, erm, there is something I do need to tell you about – Martha wants . . . ah, all this is for another day. It's a date for later . . . And, Lexie?"

No one else can make my name sound quite like he can. It's like I'm someone else, someone exotic! Adam sounds it like Leux-eeeeey. Dermot, my cheating, asshole ex-boyfriend (and reason I've just been triggered!) sounded it like Lxey. Still, when Adam says my name, my heart beats so fast I can feel it down my arms, down my legs.

"Yes, Adam?"

"I can't wait to see you." The desire drips between us.

"Really? Not getting sick of me yet?" *Oh don't, Lexie*, I chastise myself as I probe pathetically. Why am I still looking for confirmation when I know I don't need to? I trust Adam. But I flick my head to rid it of Annemarie's answer to that – back heel the high kerb with my kitten heels. Although I'd love nothing more than to chat to him all night – well, I'd love to have him here of course as planned – the sounds of crashing emergencies in the background remind me he's very much in demand.

"Christ. Never." He groans. "Speak later, gotta go!" The line goes dead as I stand alone, shivering on the freezing quays. I'm gripping my phone so tightly I realise my fingers are aching.

"Bu-bye," I say into the silent phone, as I push down this feeling of loneliness that all of a sudden washes over me.

3

16 December

Do They Know It's Christmas?

BUT THIS ISN'T ME. I'm Lexie Byrne! I'm the glass half-full gal, the eternal optimist! I give myself the pep talk.

"Cop yourself on, the man has to work and had words with his sister. No biggy! Actually, you know whose fault this is? Annemarie's!" I remind myself. "She has you all paranoid. Shake it off!"

So I do. I teeter on as fast as I can manage, hop back on the uneven cobbles, up on my tippy-toes towards the entrance of the pub. The sleet is easing as I reach the door. The very same door that brought me and Adam together. The one he hit me with! Not so much Cupid's Arrow, more Stupid's Arrow. But no matter that I ended up flat on my arse, legs akimbo, the private contents of my bag scattered for all to see; it was the greatest moment of my life to date.

I'm sure you think I'm far too gushing about Adam, but you see meeting him changed my life. Oh, not because I'd met a *man*, Jesus wept, no! I delighted in my singlehood, was loving life. But he crashed into my world and turned it upside down.

Because I'd met *him*. The *one*. When I'm with him, I'm happier than I've ever been. Yes, I have to sacrifice a lot, and no it's not easy being with a man you love this much who has another full life in a different country, but he's more than worth it. I let go of the brass handle on the door and with it all feelings of that earlier self-pity. I've a wonderful man in my life and I'm a very lucky woman. He wants to be with *me* and he's doing his best to make that happen. A nice cold fizzy beer and some Christmas cheer might just be what I need after all!

And with that in mind, I stride in the door.

"Oh, come on! You've got to be kidding me?" I protest, clamping my hand to my forehead.

The pub is *crammed*, like I lifted the ring-pull and slid inside a tin of singing sardines. A red sea of Santa hats and multi-coloured, flashing Christmas jumpers blind me. The whole bar seems to be swaying. It's just on the part of Bono's line in "Do They Know It's Christmas" and the whole crowd joins in, with a rapturous Irish roar.

"Well tonight thank God it's them instead of yoooooouuuuuuuuuu . . ." They raise the old tile roof in harmonious unison and impulsively I find myself singing along; it's involuntary and possibly written in the constitution. I wasn't expecting this crowd, it looks like the kind of night you need boundless energy for, of which I have zero. I haven't been here in ages. In fact, I left this pick-up joint two years ago when my friend Jackie left for Dubai.

Across in the main bar, a smoky turf fire burns every shade of orange. Newcomers hold their palms up to it, rubbing them together.

"Honk! Honk! Watch out!" I narrowly avoid walking smack into a tall skinny guy, with pints of Guinness in both hands.

"Crikies, sorry!" I squeeze myself sideways. Packed pubs always make me feel like I take up too much space.

"Not your fault, lovey!" His hands high in the air he carefully lowers them, steadies the pints but most miraculously he manages to be heard above the combined voices of Paul Young, Boy George, Simon Le Bon, Sting, Tony Hadley, the guitar playing of Gary Kemp and the drumming of Phil Collins with two bags of Tayto crisps firmly clamped between his teeth. He pushes on past me, so I lean my back up against the exposed old brick wall to let him through.

"There you go, lovey," I retort with a smile, his jeans hanging so low I can see the top half of his rainbow Pride boxer shorts. Perspiration is starting to slide down my back already and I wriggle out of my damp white blazer, fold it over my bag. My wrap-around dress swings just above my knees. I'm more conscious of its length now that a group of rugby players, still in their mucky kit, huddled in a circle, like they've remained on the pitch long after the ref has blown it up, all dip their eyes to half-mast. I've good legs (even if I do say so myself) and I've been brave enough to face the elements bare legged. I refuse to do tan tights – or as Jackie likes to call them, "nan tights".

"Lexie!"

"Yes!" I spin around in the inch of space I have, looking for the caller.

"Over here!" It echoes again, hard to make out over the music as I rock from side to side, trying to catch a glimpse between the massive queue that trails back for the ladies. Women in glittery dresses and sparkly sequined playsuits groaning in pain, crossing legs; one woman is actually doubled over, leaning on her friend for support.

"You're going to be okay, Caoimhe, look at me ... Keep looking in my eyes, hang in there, chicken! You're going to make it!" Men, whistling merrily, utterly oblivious, skip past, on their way out of the empty gents, still zipping up.

19

"Come on girls! It's getting serious now!" the friend of the doubled-over-er shouts in. "We're runnin' outta time out here."

"My bleedin' bladder's burstin', so it is!" Somewhere from the very end of the swirling snake-like queue.

Another one bangs on the outer toilet door. "Better not be pairs in there for the chats or I'll lose my shit!"

". . . think we're all gonna lose our shit!" a drunk girl giggles in a lopsided Christmas pudding hat.

I giggle at that. Note to self: head to the loo at least a half an hour before I need to pee. One drink then queue? Before I can formulate a plan, there's that voice again, but now it's starting to sound familiar.

"Leeexxxiiiiiieeeee! What's keeping you?! We're all over here!" A quick break in the crowd and there she is.

Annemarie.

She's jumping up and down, waving manically at me from the long seat under one of the many sliding sash windows. I heave out a sigh.

I know what's coming.

4

16 December

Christmas (Baby Please Come Home)

MY STOMACH KNOTS.

Because I know *exactly* what Annemarie's going to say to me about Adam's non-arrival.

Yet again.

"Coming!" I wave my hand in the air. *Don't let her wind you up.* Truth is, I know she's only looking out for me and, as much as I hate to admit it, I *can* see her point but I can't let her know that. But there's a niggle in my head recently that pokes me, saying: *If the tables were turned, you'd probably be telling her the exact same thing.* I push that niggle deep down.

As soon as she clocks he's cancelled again, she'll feel sorry for me. Tell me that this isn't fair on me. She will flick up one dainty, polished nail after the other, making her points.

That he isn't reliable.

That he has too much baggage.

That he's never going to commit to me.

That-that-that . . .

I take a slow breath in, blow out through pursed lips. Right, let's get this over with.

To reach the table, I need to pass through a monstrous hen party. The bride-to-be has her brightly streaked orange hair in two high space buns, her cheeks flushed with alcohol, and she's wearing a too-small white satin jumpsuit with arrows drawn on in black sharpie – ah, I see, she's meant to look like a convict. Her bouquet of plastic toy-handcuffs confirms my suspicion.

"Here! You! You look married off. Tell her not to do it! Tell her to run a mile," someone shouts at me from within the throng.

"Oh. Um—" I point back towards Annemarie. "No, I'm not – um, excuse me." I try to take a step further, but I physically can't budge.

"Run, Forest! Run as fast as ya can in that leg brace, ya mad yolk, wha'! Fair play, not easy!" The voice from the hen party steps forward, talking right at me now, her puce sweaty face peeping out the tiny hole in her pink plastic blow-up willy costume. She gasps for air.

"Ahh, I'm sure she'll live happily ever after." I try again to sidestep them but I'm stuck. Flinging a smile of confidence at the bride-to-be, I sleek down my damp fringe to mask the awkwardness. She's sucking on a wet paper straw like it's the body and blood of our Lord, Jesus Christ. Even above the Christmas chaos, it's still slurpingly loud.

"Dunno about that . . . Fairy tales are a loada bollix if you ask me!" The willie shrugs, steps back underneath the sticky-out branches of the tall twinkling Christmas tree.

Oh, don't say that, I think. *Don't you burst my Lexie bubble too.*

"Happily *never* after maybe!" someone else roars as they start to gather round me even closer.

"Cinerfuckingella . . . She got her fella!" The willy does a hip hop dance move with a rise and fall of her foreskin.

"And she wasn't even right in the head, she talked to the birds, for fuck's sake!"

"Would ya say she was on sometin' thinkin' that pumpkin was a carriage?"

"Defo. Bibbidi-bobbidi-barbiturates!"

"Running down a flight of stone steps in glass shoes?! Death wish!"

"Mad an' all as she was, she still got a prince, bu' doesn't leave much hope for us girls!" I don't know who said that as I spin my head around.

"What's wrong wit' us?"

I spin my head the other way. They seem to be multiplying!

"During the ceremony, her bridesmaids, them ugly stepsisters, had their eyes pecked out by doves!"

"Not me eyes!" the willy wails, her eyes half covered by the deflating plastic.

"And they weren't even that ugly!"

I'm literally trapped in the middle. Oh Adam, come rescue me!

"Depends on which film ya see! In them old-fashioned ones they were fairly unappealing now, Trish?"

"Were dey? Bless. The last one I saw with Lily James as Cinders, the sisters were fuckin' rides!" Trish responds.

"Ugly on de inside bu' . . ."

"Like that's the first thing a prince is gonna notice!" Trish pushes up her ample bosom with her fists, and they all howl.

But *I* believe, I almost want to protest, then think better of it. I believe in the fairy tale. In fact, I'm relying on my long-distance romance with Adam being a box-office smash, winning an Academy Award for Best Song, having a sequel, not to mention a full range of merchandise in Primark, so successful will it be!

"When's the big day?" I'm suddenly curious, so I interrupt the ravings about Cinderella's stepsies.

"Tomorrow."

My mouth falls open. She can't be serious?

"Gonna be bleedin' wrecked, amn't I? We're out since lunch. Supposed to be for one or two, cheeky Nando's hot thigh or three then home—" She rubs her eye, smudges her liquid liner. "We never made it to the chicken hut, an' I've a hundred and fifty-nine comin' to the afters." She drains the drink.

"Fifty-eight and a half!" the willie gasps.

"Shurrup will ya, Doris! I've told ya a million times! My Fergus McCabe is not a little person, he's just shorter than the average bloke, Jaysus!" From someone in the circle.

My eyes continue to be glued on the bride-to-be as she concentrates with all her might, hoovering up any remaining alcohol that's seemingly trying to escape her.

"Oh really? Should you not be getting back? Slapping the eight-hour cream on?" I have to ask because it's well after nine o' clock now and her friends really should know better.

She continues to look at me. Her mouth opens then closes again. She appears to be absorbing what I've said. She has two pointed top incisors that sit just on top of her bottom lip when she closes her mouth. I'm somehow reminded of Garfield, my old cat, and his resting face. One of her extra thick, ill-fitting, fluttery fake eyelashes has come unstuck at the edge and looks like it's trying to pluck up the nerve to jump. A look passes over her face.

"Fuck! Yer right! Here, Shiv. What time *is* it? Yer one here says I should be at home soaked in cold cream."

I turn to see who she is speaking to as Shiv steps out from behind the Christmas tree. Immediately I wish I hadn't opened my mouth. I try to move again but I'm stuck in the middle of this circle.

"No, I didn't – that's up to you . . ."

"Who said dat, Root?" her deep Dublin accent enquires as she sucks in her cheeks then blows them out. They take forever to deflate.

I do a double take, because for a second I thought she *was* one of the rugby guys.

"Her!"

"She did!"

"Blondie here!"

"Yer one with the greasy fringe . . ."

"It's not, it's wet . . ." I'm just wasting my breath on them.

Dozens of fingers point at me with fake fingernails, lengthened like mini Swiss army knives.

Shiv speaks as she comes towards me, flat footed in three-striped Adidas. She walks very carefully, as though she's balancing a stack of extremely heavy books on her head. It's the seemingly clever walk of one who would like to appear very steady and sober but who is clearly steaming-shit-faced.

"Wat's she headin' home for love, huh? It's her last night o' freedom!"

Shiv leans back against the brick wall, all casual like, and rests one foot on the wall. "Did Michael Collins head on home for an early nigh', a mani-pedi and a facial before dey shot him dead de next mornin'?"

What's Michael Collins got to do with it? I ask myself. I just look at her. She tilts her head at me.

"You waiting for me to answer that?" I lower my eyes as I ask.

"I am."

"Um . . . Well, he couldn't really . . . eh, leave—" I grimace, clasp the strap on my bag then twirl my oversized gold hoop earring. "Listen, I gotta go – I've a birthday—"

"They sat over dere, ya know!" Shiv uses her Adidas-clad foot as leverage, pushes herself away from the wall, but the move is fast, no doubt her head's fairly fuzzy from a seven-hour-session thus far, and she almost topples over. One of the rugby boys sees her fast. Instinctively, he reaches out his large hand and steadies her. Like the odd-shaped ball whizzing towards him. She composes herself, pulls a long plait out the neck of her T-shirt, shimmies her broad shoulders in the direction of a small round table by the fire. I'd thought she'd a short haircut, so the arrival of the hidden plait is a surprise.

"W-who . . . who?" I ask in the language of the owl.

"Our Irish Freedom Fighters – dey met here, in de Brazen Head. Robert Emmet, Wolfe Tone an' . . . dey fought for our freedom, an' as long as I've breath in me body I'll fight for hers. I'll fight for de freedom of all our women."

The swarm of hens all roar in applause. The rugby lad, who literally saved her face, raises his pint in the air.

"Up the Irish!" he shouts but then belches loudly. "I'll fight to shamelessly treat any one of yiz! I'm single, girls!"

"I'm not fuckin' surprised, bleedin' state a ya!" the willy attacks.

"Wasn't talking to you, dickhead," he fires back.

"That was . . . um, really moving," I manage, twisting myself lumberingly out of the claustrophobic circle.

"Well? Isn't dat right, Root? Marriage or no marriage, Root Kavanagh goes home *if* and *when* she wants!" Shiv bangs her chest, her large boobs wobble in her black and white, Gloria Steinem T-shirt.

"Amn't I right, girleens? Marriage does not the woman make!" Again the hens all whoop, splish-splash the tops of their drinks as they high five one another. Like a group of over-developed, sugar-high-thirty-somethings – why they're having a hen party when they all seem so anti-marriage is beyond me.

26

"LEXIE! WILL YOU COME ONNNNN!" Annemarie hollers like a fishmonger (which is most unlike her, I should tell you).

I raise my hand again. I've stalled for long enough. It's time to face the music.

Turning sideways, I somehow wedge myself out, hand tight on my bag strap. Oh, how I wish I was walking into Adam's strong embrace, inhaling his cologne, feeling his biceps squeezing around my waist, loosing myself in his mouth. But I'm not. I'm walking towards Annemarie Rafter. Getting closer. Dreading it.

Maybe I'm being unfair, maybe she won't mention Adam at all? Maybe she'll bite her tongue and just be glad to see me? She knows how hard this is for me, so with any luck she won't mention his non-appearance. You know, she is my closest friend, after all – and it's Christmas, Lexie, cheer up!

"Excuse me . . . Sorry . . . If I can just squeeze by?" I ask the well liquored-up office Christmas party, ties undone and cardigans unbuttoned as they try to part. Finally, I arrive at the long table.

"There you are!" Annemarie jumps up.

I give my best friend and work colleague my brightest smile. Hers falters; she does a double take. Then she gasps.

"Where the fuck is Adam? Tell me he hasn't let you down *again*, Lexie?"

5

16 December

Driving Home for Christmas

THEN I SEE IT. Annemarie is drunk! It catches me off guard because it's at least three years since Annemarie's been drunk! Not falling-down paralytic now by any means, but definitely well on. Oiled up. Her beautiful green eyes are glazed, filling up with watery, drunken sympathy as she places her delicate hand on my shoulder, squeezes it tightly.

"You have me, Lexie. Sit." She yanks my bag strap so hard she almost topples me over. I drop down onto the seat beside her. "You," she pushes her index finger into my nose, "will always have me, love." She swallows a hiccup and I burst out laughing.

"Aww. Aren't you a cutie!" I tickle her under the chin. "Sorry I'm late – I was delayed, talking to Adam." I nod my head towards the door. "It was snowing out! We might get that white Christmas we've been promised after all? Now, can I get you anything because I need some festive alcohol."

"Oh!" Her eyes dart around the pub. "He *is* here? He actually came over?" Annemarie tries to stand but her knees buckle

28

as the table edge is too close to the long leather seat. She's misunderstanding me.

"No. But *I'm* here! A very good evening to you too, my dearest friend!"

I grin as cheerily as possible and continue my running dialogue before she can get another word in.

"Adam said to tell you and Tom he's sorry he couldn't make it, he had to work . . . And yes, I know I only finished a long shift at seven, I know it was a big ask to get home and get ready and come all the way back into town for you, yet here I am!" I move my hand up and down in front of my body. "Exhibit A, my friend: showered, slap is on, spritzed in my finest Chanel, donned some heels on my aching size sixes and am ready to sing Happy Birthday at your request."

Her rose-bud mouth falls open for a moment before she clamps it shut.

"But—" I raise my hand. "—had you had the decency to text me and let me know the pub was, let's face it, a fire hazard . . ."

Her mouth opens again.

". . . I'd be sprawled on my couch in my tracksuit, makeup off, hair scraped back, scoffing a Chinese, with a wine in hand, knee deep in Patrick Swayze lifting Jennifer Grey high above his head." I gasp for a breath.

"Right," is all she says, looking confused with a disappearing smile.

I raise my eyebrows. "Had a few gins there, love, have we?" I make the sign of knocking one back with my hand.

"A few, and we'd no dinner! I was batch cooking homemade sausage rolls for Ben, so the oven was taken. Actually, I do need some soakage." Annemarie flicks her hair behind her. "But go on. Why'd you say he cancelled again?" Her dancing eyes narrow.

"Working." I shrug. "Two colleagues came down with Covid, so he had to step in. You look fantastic, haven't seen you dressed up in ages, always the most stylish! Enjoyin' the buzz?"

Annemarie does look fantastic, but then again she can wear anything. Tonight she's in a tight black criss-cross vest, draped in delicate, long, layered silver chains and white second-skin-jeans, her wild red curls tumbling down over her toned shoulders.

"I am indeed. I've missed ya, baby. Mwah!" She takes a swig from her goblet and kisses the glass. "You do know I said to Tom when we got into the taxi, I said what's the bets that Adam doesn't show up tonight. Hard to believe."

"It's a shame but – hey ho, is there no lounge staff on the floor tonight?" I'd pay fifty euro for an alcoholic buzz right now, but you'd need an armed guard to get to the bar!

"A *shame* isn't the word I'd use? But what I really don't get is why you feel you can't admit to me that you're pissed off every time he lets you down?"

"Cos I'm not," I reply, calmly.

"Now you're lying to me." She puts her hand on my shoulder, squeezes it tightly once more.

"Will you stop squeezing me, Annemarie? I'm fine, sorry if that's not what you want to hear, Dr Phil! Plus I had to come to Tom's drinks anyway, didn't I?"

And I *am* fine but the redness colouring my cheeks is telling her a different story. I drop my shoulder with a quick twist and her hand falls.

"I feel like ringing him and telling him what I think," she blurts out.

"Annemarie!"

I'm horrified because I wouldn't put it past her with a few drinks on her. Drunk Annemarie is far ballsier than sober Annemarie.

30

"Don't you dare. I'd never speak to you again." Worriedly, I twist my oversized hoops, watching her carefully.

"I won't, but I'd give anything to ask him those hard-hitting questions that you seem to want to avoid! Too scared . . ." She raises her voice over the singing crowd.

"Oh my god, shuusshhh, will ya?" I jump in, nodding my head to the table full of Tom's friends sitting around us. You also know that feeling when you want to pinch your best friend, hard? No?

Maybe just me then.

But I refrain.

She pokes her fingers into the ice cubes, picks one out, pops it in her mouth, sucks on it.

Instead I hold my finger up near my mouth in a shush sign. "It was only ever a maybe that he'd make it over this weekend."

"I bought all the ingredients for a carbonara for the four of us for tomorrow night and Graham Norton wine!" She chews down, crunching on the ice.

"Yet I told you not to. This is how it is with me and Adam, and I'm perfectly happy with things!" I hold my breath, hoping she lets it go.

"I don't believe it!" She hides another hiccup by swallowing it.

"Relax, Victor Meldrew!" I twitch.

A tip-tap on my shoulder; I turn.

"Howrya, Lexie!" Tom, Annemarie's husband, thankfully butts in. He's waving a half-drunk pint of Guinness at me, wearing a blue "Who's A Birthday Boy Then?" sash over his Christmas waistcoat with little Polar Bears on skis. His man bun sits high and coiffed. His ears are sporting those very, very large lobe holes I find hard to look directly at. If he notices Adam isn't with me, he doesn't mention it.

"Happy birthday, Tom, I've a card for you." Finding a real smile, I zip open my bag with a whoosh.

31

"Didn't think you were comin', Lexie, when it got this late, thanks a million." He extends his hand and I shake it. "It's a miracle I finally got her into town for a few festive drinks, eh?" Tom swirls the dregs of the pint, coaxing the cream that's stuck on the side of the glass down, inviting it to meet the black as he nods to Annemarie. "Look at her, relaxed! Can you believe it's actually her?" Tom makes a fist with his free hand and rubs his eye.

"It's a beautiful sight," I agree. Tom and I don't particularly have anything in common, but we work at our polite relationship because we both love Annemarie.

"Excuse me but we do have a new baby at home!"

"Ben's two, love!" But Tom laughs. "D'ya know Lexie, this one spends more time with her nose in Instagram than she does with me when Ben's asleep." He drapes an arm around his wife's perfectly toned shoulder.

"I don't have social media," I tell Tom. "Gave it up years ago, all too fake for me and just made me feel bad about myself most of the time. I prefer to stroll than to scroll." I do an over-exaggerated walk on the spot.

"Ha! Well this one is fascinated with that fake, filtered, finger-scrolling world. Always looking at your man—"

"It's – hey! – my bit of escapism, allow me that!" she jumps in, interrupting Tom, her eyes flashing a moment of discomfort, I notice.

"I was ju—" His eyes widen.

"Yes, thank you, Tom. Lexie, are you giving him his card or not? Very kind of you." Annemarie licks her lips.

"Oh yeah, it's here somewhere . . ." It's definitely in here because it cost me six euro of garage forecourt-bought daylight "card robbery" and I scribbled my well wishes on it sitting on the freezing, old rattling bus on the way in. "Got it!" I shake it free from my bag, but I've lost Tom's attention. He's shifted his

32

position, turned his back on me, helping to lift a full tray of shot glasses over our heads. When it is safely laid down in the centre of the old oak table, I hand him over the card.

"Ah you shouldn't have . . . cheers!" He accepts it but drops it down on the table. It's wet with sticky spillage. I want to say, "Oi, Tom! Careful! There's a voucher in there, a twenty-euro voucher for *All-For-U* inside." But then he'll feel like he has to thank me and that makes me uncomfortable, so I leave it. I'm not one for being thanked.

"You look stunning too, by the way!" Annemarie finishes her drink, puts the glass down then starts pulling at the neckline on my dress, exposing more cleavage. "I love this dress on you. It's sexy, Lexie!" Over-enthusiastic wink.

She rearranges my neckline even deeper then picks up her empty glass, drinks from it, but it's still empty. She really is rather drunk.

"Thanks, it doesn't owe me anything, that's for sure." I shrug.

I pull my dress back up so my cleavage isn't hanging out and crane my neck in search of any lounge staff.

"Gimme a laugh, bet Adam hasn't booked his flights for Christmas yet, has he?" The tipsy makeup-free eyes are all over me.

"My relationship isn't for the purpose of your amusement, pet." I wink back playfully.

"Well it makes for a good comedy watching it!" Uncontrollable guffaws burst from her that, despite the sentiment, I can't help but find contagious.

"Okay, funny, you've had your say, please drop it now?" I ask and she nods. "Because, heads up, I'm due my period and I'm dangerously pre-menstrual. I had two packets of barbeque Hula Hoops and dipped a peanut butter Kit Kat in my tea *before* my breakfast, ate rings around myself all day. So let that be a warning to you, don't provoke me and the hormones tonight. No more Adam bashing, okay?"

I do have PMS so I need to be careful with loose-tongued Annemarie, because when I'm like this the rage can easily slip out of her cage.

"As you wish." She raises her empty glass. "Now let's get you drunk."

6

16 December

Jingle Bell Rock

"TOM! WE NEED BOOZE! We demand to have more booooozzze!" Annemarie roars. She bangs the table, giggling so hysterically that I'm forced to lean back away from her.

Tom passes her over another gin. "This was bought earlier. We're trying to get a lounge boy, Lexie!" he projects. "Hold tight."

"I'm gasping!" I tell him, pushing my palms together under my chin in prayer pose.

Annemarie twirls her gin by the thick stem, deep in thought. "How ya doin' otherwise, Lexie? Isn't it great to be 'out-out'? God, it's been forever. Get in here, beside me." She pulls my bag from across my shoulder roughly, then balls up my blazer, knocks my hoop earring out as she slides back into the seat again.

"My earring! Would you watch the creases!" I grab the hoop under my chin and, after three blind attempts, hook it back through and squash myself in.

"Like you do look really gorgeous. You're so pretty! *Per-it-eeeeeeeeeee!*" she giggles.

"Okay, erm – thanks. And you're wearing your finest beer goggles."

But I grin at her. If I don't get a drink soon, I'm gonna crack up. I slide in closer.

"I need a cold beer in this sweatbox! It's alright for you, you were off all day, we'd a constant queue. I'm tired, my feet are killing me, I'm bloated, and craving chipper chips." I pile that on her. Then with my head to one side, I finally find the clasp and close my hoop.

"Ha! *You're* tired?" She sticks a finger to her chest "I have a baby! I'm tired twenty-four-seven, Lexie – no, not tired, *shattered* – exhausted out of my tiny mind, wiped out." She rotates the finger at her temple.

Like I could ever forget. As I mentioned, since Ben arrived into the world, Annemarie's life has been one long anxious drama saga. I wish I could make her stand back and see all the gorgeous moments and fun stuff she's missing out on through her stress and worry, but I can't and believe you me, I've tried. I've worn myself out with the trying. Suggested our New York adventures a million times for a break away, even an overnight in Dublin, but she keeps dismissing it.

She leans across to say goodbye to one of Tom's friends who is sliding into his big sleeping-bag-esque coat to leave. It's a very rare occasion she leaves the house anymore, so I'm thrilled to see her out having some craic, letting go. Her life's narrowed completely these last few years. Sometimes I don't recognise her as the girl I met and fell for immediately. When I first started in Silverside, she was always pouring over glossy travel brochures of the Big Apple. She was obsessed with New York and especially *Sex and the City* (as was I), and we bonded over our love of the show. We'd call each other after every episode to discuss the locations they shot in. Our dream was to visit the exterior of 64 Perry Street, Carrie Bradshaw's apartment. We'd coo over the architecture of the New York Public Library, the Plaza hotel and Soho House, the vibe of

36

the Meatpacking District, the shadows from the skyscrapers, the incredible looking pizzas in Two Boots Pizza Shop in Greenwich Village, the brave fashion and the speed of life.

But just before we booked our flights, on the night of her fortieth, she met Tom in a spinning whirlwind romance, and they got married within six months. Then it began. Two awful miscarriages both at ten weeks, rounds and rounds of IVF and then, finally, Ben arrived. Beautiful, bouncy, beaming Ben. But it's a marvel to get her ten miles away from him, never mind three thousand one hundred and eighty-seven miles to New York.

"God, we'd some cracking Christmas nights in here with Jackie, didn't we?" She settles herself against me again, crosses her slim legs, moving her foot to the beat of the Christmas rock.

"We sure did," I recall with a smile.

"Young, free and single, the three of us." Her foot taps faster.

"Best of times."

"They really were epic. I never laughed so much as I did on those nights out." For a moment she looks into the distance. "But I wouldn't change a thing." She turns to face me like she needs to prove she's telling me the truth as her foot stops tapping abruptly.

"You don't need to change a thing – the craic is still out there, if you'd only—"

"Everyone judges you now, though, once you have a baby . . ." She trails off.

"In the words of Samantha Jones, from a season five episode, I believe, 'If I worried what every bitch in New York was saying about me, I'd never leave the house.'"

Instantly she cracks up laughing, heaves with shaking shoulders, and I join in.

"God bless Samantha."

She wipes her eyes. Back on level ground. Maybe we can just enjoy each other's company tonight after all?

37

7

16 December

Deck the Halls

"**S**KOOSH IN CLOSER TO ME!" Annemarie commands now, wrapping her arm around my neck, as if I can get any closer. "I want to talk to you about something else, something I think you will be veeerrrrry *ex-ci-ted* about!" She swallows another hiccup, holds her neck, swallows a few more times.

Praise be! No more Adam talk. Maybe she wants us to go to New York? Maybe she's ready to leave Ben for a few days!

"Oh I like the sounds of this!" I rub my neck, unravel myself.

"See how well I know you!" she proclaims.

The ancient leather underneath me has split and is torn to shreds, rough stuffing escaping from every orifice, springs poking out in all directions up my bum crack. Unbelievably I still have no drink and my mouth is dry as a chip as I see one of Tom's pals line up shiny shot glasses in a straight row on the old oak table. I'm amused by the schoolboy cheersing and their excitement is contagious, I feel myself slipping into the festive mood at last. I'm happy to be out, in a Christmas bar (even if it is a bit loud), with my best friend. It's natural I'm looking forward to getting home to FaceTime my fella later, that's all (the chips are an aside).

"Comfy, love?" she asks as only someone who is probably less than nine stone, sharing a four-inch seat, can.

"Uh-hum. So what is this exciting thing you mention?" I say a silent prayer she's going to tell me to pack my bags, we're going to New York, baby!

"Are you finally ready for a new adventure?" She opens her eyes wide.

"I would be if I could get a drink!" I wink at her. "But go on, I am, I am!" I'm very hopeful.

"Oh hang on, I need to stash yer bag and coat."

She hands me her drink to hold and disappears under the table with my stuff. I sneak a sip. It's strong. Gin isn't my tipple, I'm a beer or wine girl, but right now I'd sip on Poitín!

I wiggle my backside into some sort of comfortable place as one of Tom's troupe waves at me from the other side of the messy oak table. I've seen this guy a couple of times before but can't remember his name. His T-shirt sleeves are straining on his grossly oversized biceps, telling me he lives on protein shakes, raw eggs, brown rice and grilled skinless chicken. Definitely not my type. Adam's not a gym robot. I'm allergic to men who spend all their free time in a gym.

It's one of those odd, fluttery-fingered waves a child might do, but I wave back, even though when I see his reaction, I get that sinking single feeling I used to have before I met Adam. You know the one? When you're out alone, and you can tell a guy fancies you but you don't fancy him back. Zero interest. Yet you're on your own and they think, well hey! You must be available for them! Annemarie emerges from under the table, her eyes darting right to left.

"Oh deadly! You guys have . . . connected!" she bellows joyously, snatches her gin back from me.

"W-what?" I'm confused, and feather out my fringe.

She bobs for the moving straw, keeps missing it as the straw rotates; if I didn't know better, I'd think the straw was taking the piss. Finally she bites it steady, then clamps her lips around it.

"Just call me the mama-matchmaker." She shimmies her shoulders happily.

"Huh?"

"Well, as you can see Mark O' Donoghue's here and I see you two are making eyes at one another!" She crosses her eyes at me, then raises her thumb at him.

"Eh, no we're not." I force her thumb down. "Why are you giving him the thumbs up?"

"*He's* what I want to talk to you about, *he's* the exciting news, silly!" She nods again to Wiggly Fingers, shouting in my ear.

"Why?"

I cross my legs, pull at the zippers on my boots just to do something with my hands. She meets my gaze and she's wearing the expression I haven't seen in her in forever, somewhere between curiosity and devilment. It's like the Annemarie of old.

"Hear me out. He thinks you're gorgeous, always asking about you, he calls you Kate Winsalot . . ."

"You can't be serious?" I raise my eyebrows. There is not going to be any bloody mention of New York, I realise with a thud of disappointment.

"Cos he's a bookie . . . wins-a-lot – get it?"

"Have you . . . set me up with this guy?"

I could kill her.

"Maybe? Is that so bad?" She pinches her nose tightly.

"What if Adam *was* here?" I shut my eyes, hold my head in my hands.

"Ah, I knew he'd cancel!" She releases her nose, sniffs deeply.

"You can't do this," I tell her curtly now.

"You're not married to Adam, for fuck's sake, and Mark's just got a biiiiiiggggg promotion at Paddy Power's. And he's—"

"—hammered?" I nod at the demonic waving baby trying to balance a shot glass on his head, so thick are his tight ginger curls, the little glass disappears.

"It's Christmas!" she defends quickly.

"I can't believe you'd do this." I heave. "Does he think I'm here to meet him? This is mortifying!"

"Whyyyyyy? He's single, no baggage, is really decent, owns his own house, is mortgage free . . ."

I'm not entertaining her, although I am surprised – no one in Dublin can even afford to take out a mortgage on a house, let alone own one outright!

"Listen to me, his granny died last year and he lived with her, so he got the house – there was uproar with his five sisters, especially the rich one in Monaco, but it's all his now." Her neck all but disappears, so high is her hunch. "And he's only around the corner from myself and Tom too! He's perfect! Ta-dahhhh." Jazz hands.

"You are drunker than I thought!" I cringe.

"I am NOT!"

I shrug. "Okay, but I've zero interest, just to make this abundantly clear." I'm breaking into a hot sweat, dripping down my back.

"You think Mark's strange because he lived with his granny, don't you?"

"Uh, no—" I try rub my back.

"Sure your Adam basically *lives* with his ex-wife if you look at his—"

"He does NOT!" I don't let her finish, then immediately ask: "And – huh? Why would you say that? Look at his what?"

"I – I . . . I dunno – I just—" Her cheeks flush.

"No, spit it out?" I urge her.

"His life in general . . ."

"Yo! Here! Lexie! We have a live one!" Tom shouts, unbuttoning his polar bears and draping the waistcoat over the back of his chair, as a lounge boy, who looks no more than eleven but must be eighteen by law, is cornered by the lads. Trapped like a wild animal in a sea of beer hunters.

"Oh my God! Hold him! Thank you!" I exclaim as though we've saved an endangered species;. I've never spent so long in a pub without a bloody beer.

"Orders! Quick!" Tom tells us, winding his finger round and round ferociously.

"I'll have a bottle of Corona with a fresh lime, please," I shout and go to reach down for my purse but Tom waves his hand.

"Get away outta that!" he tells me.

"I'll get your next one," I reply.

"C'mon people, we're gonna lose him! What do you want, Amo?" Tom holds his arms out wide, protecting the lounge boy from other beer hunters.

"Stay baacckkkkk!" Bendy-fingered Mark waves a beer mat at them.

"One more gin and tonic, but that's my lot, and ask him for a pint glass of water and ice too? Oh, here, love! Can you get us a few packets of peanuts, please? Lexie d'you want a bag?"

I shake my head. I'm one hundred per cent getting chipper chips on the way home. Large. Drowning in salt and vinegar. Dreaming of the white batch loaf cowering in my bread bin, waiting for me to squash those fat chips in, the butter melting.

Annemarie pulls a sachet of something from her slim back pocket, shakes it and pulls it apart at the seam.

"What the hell is that?" I squint at the label, clueless, hoping it's some magic potion to steer her away from this ludicrous matchmaking.

42

"Blackcurrant Dioralyte for the water, can't have a hangover. Ben still isn't sleeping through. The morning naps have gone completely out the window, I'm utterly exhausted all the time. Even when he *is* asleep, I'm up every twenty minutes, leaning over him to make sure he's breathing, I just read on the internet—"

"I keep offering to take him overnight, let you get a full night's sleep?" I interrupt her every time she says *I just read on the internet* and I'm blue in the face offering my godmother services. However, I'm delighted for the change of subject and hopeful I can slip away soon without another word about Bendy Fingers. And if there is one subject that Annemarie wants to talk about, it's Ben.

"I know . . . but I honestly don't think he'd settle for you, then his routine will be out the window and I have to stick to the routine! It's paramount. I mean Francesca, Tom's mother, was looking at me like I'd ten heads this evening when I gave her the list printed out for tonight. She said a bit sarcastically if I'm honest, '*I hove roised three children of my own On'maree and they all sur-voived*.'" Annemarie does a very impressive posh Dalkey accent. "But I told her again, I said, 'Francesca, you have to get into our bed with Ben at eight on the dot, read him BaBaBaba-Cakes three times with the Doc Mc Stuffin's stars night light, rub his back anticlockwise and let him fall asleep on the bottle, then carry him into his cot.'"

"I can do that any night."

"You don't have a cot."

"I'll buy a bloody cot! Stick it at the end of my bed!"

"Don't be silly, Lexie."

"I just think you could make life easier for yourself—"

"You're very good, you know how much I appreciated how you helped me get over my inability to breastfeed . . ."

"The word 'inability' still bugs me – you had crippling mastitis!"

43

"I failed at it, couldn't give him the best start . . ."

"We are not going over this again, you did NOT! Ben is thriving, you're an amazing mother."

"Well anyway, let's see how you cope when you have kids . . . if you . . . ever – well – I mean . . . oh Lexie . . . pet . . . you're almost—" Her head falls onto her shoulder.

I detest the look she follows this up with. It's pity meets doubt, and I neither deserve nor need it. I turn away. Tom is still talking to the lounge boy; then, with his tray dripping slops over his head, he takes his leave to fetch our orders.

"But let's not go to baby-town right now . . . what was I saying before? Oh yeah! Full disclosure . . ." She catches her hair in between her two hands, pushes it back from her face. ". . . I told Mark you were single because I really think you should get to know him. He's very keen. You gotta agree it's time to move on? Time to call it a day with Adam once and for all. It was a bit of fun but it's over now. Real life is knocking on the door."

I'm so shocked at her words, I literally fall off the edge of the seat.

44

8

16 December

Wonderful Christmastime

"ARE YA ALRIGHT THERE LEXIE!" Tom grabs my arm just as I'm about to hit the floor on my arse. I pull myself back into position on the couch, pull down my dress to cover my bare knees.

"Fine, sorry." Morto. I blush all eyes on me, I've only had a sip of a bloody drink!

"You okay? You're falling all over the place. Were you drinking earlier? On the bus?" Annemarie eyes me up as though I'm the one who's drunk!

"Eh, no. Are you high?" I swallow with difficulty.

"Huh?" Her green eyes roll with confusion.

"Finish it with Adam? Now you're trying to set me up with that idiot when I'm not even remotely single!"

"That's not fair . . . He's . . .." She scratches her head, looking confused by my reaction.

"I'm not breaking up with Adam. So you can undo your matchmaking malarkey and tell him not to come next or near me, capeesh?"

Her jaw drops and she looks baffled, but she mutters, "Fiiinnnnnnne." Rolls her eyes like a naughty schoolgirl, pulls an ugly face.

"Okay lads. Are. We. Reaaaadddddyyyyyyy?" Tom's hollers, his man bun close to unravelling completely as he raises his shiny shot glass between his finger and multi-ringed thumb. He has the look of a man who desperately needed this night out and I'm happy for him.

"Go on, Tom! Chug it!" I say just to get away from Annemarie as I see my blind-date set-up failing to wait for the countdown and lour his shot of Baby Guinness but he doesn't get it all in his mouth. Its glutinous remains drip down his orange, bearded face. Then his very, very long tongue swings around to mop up what he can. It's quite impressive, like watching one of those ads where a magic sponge works miracles on an impossible mess.

"Now then, there's a late-night party trick if I ever I saw one . . ." Annemarie elbows me, speaks through clenched teeth. "Sure you don't want to re-think him?" Then she snorts a laugh.

"Not a chance." I elbow her back.

"That's a mighty impressive tongue . . ." Another elbow.

"Don't even . . ." I elbow her again.

"He's quite the lover by all accounts . . ." she dodges my elbow this time.

"Good for him." I cross my legs, smooth down my dress.

We're both still staring at him as he takes that second to lick his index finger, moving it in and out of his mouth.

"Jesus." She whispers behind her fingers.

"Get your head out of the gutter!" I try to keep the smile from curling on my lips.

"That's utterly revolting, Lexie Byrne."

"You thought it!"

"How do you know what I was thinking?"

46

But we both start to laugh.

"Anyway . . ." I edge her with my soft hip, shuffle back further.

"Okay, I guess I jumped the gun."

"You shot it point blank range!"

"He is a catch, Jackie was mad about him, but he saw her Tinder profile was still up even after he'd been on two dates with her, and he was not impressed."

"How'd he know?"

"How indeed, good point my friend." She raises her glass.

"You need to respect my relationship, please?"

"What do you expect me to do, never comment on your love life? Because that's not me, as you well know. I am honestly so sorry about Adam, Lexie, I truly am."

"He wasn't hit by a double decker bus, Annemarie . . ." I am *utterly* exasperated.

"He's never hit by a double decker bus, though, is he? At least then . . ."

She looks at me, goes to say something but there's a shift and thankfully she changes her mind.

"Where is your booze? It's Christmas!" She slaps the edge of the table, bottles wobble.

"I can't stand this mess." I stick my fingertips into various empty bottles and pint glasses, clinking them to the edge, slide the sticky shot glasses, soggy paper straws and ripped beer mats over to make room and so they're easier for the poor lounge staff to collect. When I look up, the next tray of drinks appears with my order sitting on there like a beacon of light; I remove it and shove my wedge of lime into the bottle, lick my fingers, crinkle my nose.

"Thanks a million! You were fast!" I say to the melting lounge boy, pull up my bag and put a few euro onto his tray. Then I poke my lime wedge further on down, take a long, grateful gulp from the cold, bitter beer.

"Oh man . . . that is sooooo good!" The bubbles tickle my nose as I hold the freezing bottle up to my hot cheek. The beginnings of a headache are marching their merry way into my head, I can feel them.

"Here! I bought ya that! 'Twas my round that time," Mark shouts across the table, hands on either side of his mouth, like I'm not two feet away. His shirt is stained from the various drooling and dribbling of drinks.

"O-oh? T-thanks," I stutter, wondering if I should pop a paracetamol with my beer. Feels wrong? I twist the long neck in my hand, the brand label already soggy and half peeling off in this heat. I'm not engaging with this guy. I look down, pretending my phone has beeped and pull it from my dress pocket. I wish he hadn't bought me the beer, it makes me uneasy. I prefer to buy my own drinks anyway and I should have insisted that to Tom at the beginning. Now I owe this guy one back and round and round it goes.

"No problemo!" He screeches but I don't look across at him. "Good to see ya by the way, Lexie, but c'mere to me, why didn't you let Jack on the aul door?"

"Huh?" I shoot him a half gaze, assuming he can't be still talking to me. I feather out my fringe with a few strokes of my fingers, willing this headache to not get any worse.

"There was plenty of room!" he shouts again, scratching his unruly mop.

"Sorry? I've no idea what you're talking about." I shake my head, and notice his eyes are slightly bloodshot.

"C'mere." He crooks a finger at me.

"No." I fake a wry smile, cross one leg over the other, then uncross.

"C'mon!" He flicks his head back, crooks two fingers at me now.

48

"Excuse me," I say politely, "I'm in the middle of texting someone here." I shake my wrist that holds my phone by way of explanation, though I shouldn't need to. *Oh, go away, dipshit.*

"I'll come over to you so?" He unfolds his legs, goes to stand up.

"Don't," I say quite definitely and throw a stern look to Annemarie, who's engrossed in her fruit bowl of gin, still counting on her fingers what number this drink is. Jesus, it's a gin and tonic, not a heroin bong!

He plonks back down. "Wasn't that you on the *Titanic*, when it sank in the freezing North Atlantic Ocean, drifting off on the aul floating door?"

And he's upright again, holding his nose as though he's drowning, bending his knees as he goes up and down. Unbelievably, Annemarie looks up and laughs. Like he's funny.

"Um, no, I . . . I wasn't on board the *Titanic*." I know I'm being a cow, a real Billy Buzzkill, but I'm not here to be Mark O' Donoghue's entertainment for the night. I've never been one for the "banter", which is another aspect of Adam's personality I adore. He's funny and witty without trying too hard and is happy to be still and silent too. One of the things I love most about us is our comfortable silences. I wish this Mark guy would just go away.

"Really? Sure it wasn't you?" He creeps around to me, all stained cream chinos, exposed red ankle socks and Hush Puppies.

"Quite sure." I look up at him.

"Ah, I'm only messin with ya, darlin'!" He puts his hand on my head and ruffles my hair; I can smell his overpowering aftershave. "Sure I know ya weren't really on it! Yer very like her, that's all." He wipes his nose with the back of his hairy hand. "Here, get in for a picture for me Gram, it's Chrrisstmmasss!"

And before I can object, he's whipped his phone out and then wangled himself under me so I've ended up bouncing up and down on his knee. My head jerks back.

49

"Smile!" He squeezes my knee on that part where you can't help but laugh. Then clicks a few times and I almost fall off his drink-sodden lap before I jump up like a scalded cat.

"D'ya wanna Bloody Mary?" He mimics a drink.

Inner thought: *I want a bloody taxi.*

"Nope." I clear my throat. "But I'd like my seat back if you don't mind." I drip the words out slowly.

"What about a Woo?" He thrusts his pelvis at me.

"I'm good for a Woo thank you."

"Yer a fine-lookin' bird, ya know that? Can't believe yer still on the shelf!"

If this prick wasn't Tom's friend, I know what I'd do. My expression darkens. "Listen, Mark, isn't it? I don't mean to be rude but I'm actually not singl—"

"Okkkaaaayyyyy Mark!" Annemarie butts in, slams down her gin on the table; droplets fly. She puts herself between the two of us to save the day and his head from having my beer spilled all over it.

"I'll be back," he tells me in the voice of Arnie, like I give a shit.

"Not on my account, I hope," I grunt as Annemarie points to something in the distance.

The tired-looking lounge boy steps in. "I forgot the nuts," he says with an uncovered yawn.

"Ah thanks a million." I scoop another few euro from my purse and hand it to him as he dumps the nuts on the table. Annemarie steps back for a moment, bites open the packet with her teeth, tips it and throws a handful in her mouth. Wagging a finger at me, she throws her arm around Mark's thick neck, hiccups with a jerk and steers him away from the table. Relieved, I sip my beer and sit back in tight against the back rest, shadowed by the heaving Christmas revellers around me. I stare at my screensaver and lose myself in the picture of me and Adam, taken on our one and only sun holiday. On Burriana Beach in Nerja, last May; a bright blue cloudless skies sits above us, his arm loosely draped around my neck, his chocolate brown eyes sparkling as he smiles for the photo, his body taut and tanned, a fine line of black hair running down to his shorts.

My phone beeps. I hit the message.

Work rota's landed in my inbox. I'm heading home now! See you soon! Adam x

9

16 December

Pipes of Peace

"**W**HAT ARE YOU PLAYING AT?" Annemarie drags me away from my phone before I can text Adam back. "Huh? Mark's a lovely guy, harmless. Salt of the earth!"

My heart's racing and my palms are sticky. In an hour I'll know how long I have with Adam all to myself over Christmas. Annemarie is forgiven, I don't care anymore, I'm too happy!

"Uh-huh ... sure," I hum along to the lyrics of "Pipes of Peace".

"You're mean. I know we're all a bit sloshed, been here since seven, but the look of horror on your face, like you *haaattteeeddd* him! He was only being nice, he bought you a drink." She pulls at the swinging silver chains around her neck, untangling them.

"I didn't want him to," I tell her.

"You're drinking it, aren't you?" She picks up my bottle of Corona, swings it and foam oozes out of the bottle top.

"Ah watch it!" I grab it back, pop my mouth over the top.

"I need the loo . . ." She pats her non-existent stomach.

"'Kay," I mumble, wiping froth from my lips, clutching my phone, happy in the knowledge that after seeing that queue I've plenty of time to text Adam back. Plus later on FaceTime he'll be home alone in bed, and I'll be home alone in bed so . . . I bite my lip with that thought, rolling my shoulders.

"Starvin'," Annemarie says as she shakes the powder from the last of the bag of dry roasted nuts into her mouth, licks the remains from her lips with a smack. I watch her wriggle out and before I go back to my phone I ask, "Any nuts left?"

"No . . . soz." She dusts her hands off one another. Her long, gorgeous fingernails, all natural, painted a deep red with little white snowball dots as decorations she had done in VIP Nails on level three.

"Wow, that was fast!"

"Soakage," she says, turns sideways, then disappears.

"Where does she put it?" I ask myself, tapping my phone back to life.

I cross one leg over the other, sing along to the song. *In love our problems disappear* – ain't that the truth, I think, as I ponder on what to type back. I inch down my dress. Should I be a little naughty? Suggestive? I'm not the greatest sexter in the world but occasionally I try. He's never had a picture of my boobs drop into his WhatsApp, now, mind you – nor would I want his penis in mine! We're beyond all that.

Yay! This is going to be the best Christmas ever!! I add a Santa and Mrs Claus and a green heart emoji, press send. Then: *Have I been a naughty girl this year?* The bikini emoji is about a suggestive as I can get. I laugh to myself.

"Anyone sittin' there? My ankles are about to snap!" A younger girl painted into a silver sequined minidress on sky-high strappy wedges asks me.

"Yeah, sorry, my friend is in the queue for the loo, but plonk your bum down until she comes back?" I press send.

But she perches on the edge of the wet table.

"Ahh no, tsk . . . I was just on it, musta been thirty of us there, no loo roll, two blocked, tampon machines empty, condom one is jammed and the hand dryer's stopped working. It's a code red in there, chick." She purses her inflated lips, sympathises. "Think I better keep movin', ya know yerself once you realise how much pain your feet are actually in, you'd never get up again!"

Well, I suppose there is wisdom in that. Sometimes, you just gotta keep going, like me and Adam I think as I wave her off. On my phone, the text message bubbles bounce; Adam reads my text as I glance up.

"How the—" I mutter, shocked to see Annemarie returning. How the hell did she get away so lightly with the queue? She picks her drink back up, waves her goblet and clinks it off Tom's black and white pint. I slide the phone away, watching her less than steady on her feet. Poor Annemarie. I'm not a doctor but I'm pretty sure she's suffering from ongoing undiagnosed post-natal depression, but she won't hear a word of it. Whenever I try oh so gently to bring it up, a huge argument erupts.

"How were you so fast?" I ask her as she flops down, light as a feather.

She turns, looks at me for a second. "W-what?" Her bare shoulder rubs off me and it's freezing.

"Did you go outside?" I shiver, dropping my shoulder from hers.

"Eh, just for a quick breath of fresh air." She's also sprayed way too much perfume, an absolute pet hate of mine; I can almost taste it.

"And did you go to the ladies?"

"Oh, no, I went to the gents, held my nose and sang, 'Ireland's Call' from the cubicle while hovering, great for the thigh muscles too." She pats the backs of her matchstick thighs. "Y'know, I was thinking as I peed, you're such a great friend."

"I appreciate that." I drape my arm around her and pull her closer, enjoying that her skin's freezing cold now.

"Tell me you're not going to leave a great night out and run back to your empty apartment just to FaceTime Adam or something, are you? After making all the effort to come in? I love you too, you know." She tilts her ridiculously pretty face up at me, her green eyes full of melancholy.

"No," I manage. Shit. "Of course not." Shit. I so badly wanna FaceTime Adam to hear the plan – how long is he coming over for? I've been waiting months! And I won't lie, I want to see him half-naked, do some flirty FaceTime stuff, but I also want to spend time with her, of course I do.

"Good, because I never get a night out with you and I miss you, terribly. I miss . . . us." She rests her head on my shoulder again and I smell her scent, grapefruit and elderberries.

My mind's made up. She's my priority tonight. "Next round on me!" I tell her.

"Yay!" Drunken Annemarie has forgotten her own curfew and she's out to have some fun.

"Lemme just text Adam and tell him I won't be back. We can call in the morning," I say happily as Ruth Kavanagh comes right up to the Santa-stencilled window behind us, with her bouquet of handcuffs ready to throw.

"Would ya' look at this one?" Annemarie sits up straight, grinning madly now.

"I know! I got caught up in her hen party earlier, when you were calling me. That's who I was talking to. They're quite the bunch." I tap out a quick text to Adam.

Something's come up. Talk first thing in the morning. L x

"Yo! Over here! Henny! Throw your bouquet this way! My best friend desperately needs it." Annemarie jumps up, waving her hands like Ruth Kavanagh is a ship's beacon at first light and she's Tom Hanks in *Castaway*.

"I do not." But I laugh.

"You may be her final hope!" she yells. A few people around our table laugh hard.

"Yer grand!" I call back over Annemarie's shoulder.

"If ever a woman needed a sign, it's this one!" She hoists up her skinny jeans, digs her finger into the top of my head. "Any bitta luck she can get to march her down that aisle! It's very sad. She's delusional!" Annemarie guffaws loudly, then hiccups repeatedly.

I'm beginning to feel uneasy. The smile on my face feels frozen.

"Get up, Lexie." She pulls at my dress. "Jump up there, see if you can catch it. Help her out! She's in dire need this one." She tickles me under my chin, shouting up to Ruth.

"It's fine!" I say as the hens all stand back behind our seat ready to be the next in line, even though they all seem to hate the idea of marriage, shoving one another out of the way, playfully yet one or two not so playfully.

"This is too funny! Just what you need! Catch it and we'll send him a picture of you with the bouquet – betcha he shits himself, coz that guy is never going to propose to you." Annemarie hiccups again, tries to hold her breath.

"Huh-mmmm." Not engaging in this line of questioning, I arch my back, keeping my eye on the hen party. I'm pushing down a horrible feeling of humiliation.

"Like he neverrrrr will." She rolls her head, almost talking to herself now. Annemarie's slurring a bit and I'm sure she's barely thought about the words before they leave her mouth. But she stares at me, swirling the end of her empty gin glass.

56

"Why?" I'm not mad, I just want to know – and excuse me, but it might be another three years before she's got this freer-gin tongue.

"Most men don't re-marry after a bitter divorce, they run a mile. That's if his divorce is as bitter as he makes out . . . Because if you ask me, Adam likes his cake and likes . . ." She throws her hands out, confusing herself mixing up the saying. ". . . having all the cake! Whatever!"

"He never said it was bitter, he said it was agonising divorcing someone who's still in love with you, especially when a child is involved. But—" I stop myself and digest her words as she's distracted again by the hens surrounding our seat, continuing to hustle for prime position. The willy is trying to walk backwards but topples over, narrowly missing the sharp edge of a table.

"Woman down!" Shiv appears, three sheets to the wind like everyone else in this pub, bar me, it seems. "Help me here, girls!" A rush of hens all grapple to seize the willy and set her upright.

Then out of nowhere Annemarie says: "You do know you'll never come first with him, Lexie."

She's hit the nerve. Drilled right through it. Of course I know I'll never come first! I shouldn't come first! His daughter should always come before me. But I don't like to hear it from my best friend said like that. In that dark, told-you-so, tone.

"And he'll always have ties to that crazy ex-wife." She loops her index finger near her head.

My heart is pounding in my ears as I find a space for my finished bottle on the jam-packed table and push it back, clinking into the throng of glasses.

"And he'll never move to Dublin."

"Freya should always come first," I tell her steadily. "If you and Tom broke up or, God forbid, anything happened to you, you'd want Ben to come first, am I right?"

57

She claps her hands. "You are absolutely right, *but* even though Adam's divorced, he's living his old life, right? It seems to me like he has two lives? His family first and you last." She flicks up two fingers.

"What do you mean?" My hands are shaking so much now I sit on them.

"Don't you think it's all a bit odd . . . this relationship with his ex-wife? They spend so much time together, it's not normal, is it? Like, who does that? Like he spends more time with his ex than he does with you!" Another hiccup is swallowed.

"They don't spend loads of time *together*, they share custody of a child!"

I face her now and she gives me this look, a sort of look that says, "Now come on, Lexie," her head tilted to one side, one shapely eyebrow raised.

"Are you trying to tell me something?" I feel unravelled as the hens try to arrange themselves all around us and grab the seat tight underneath my thighs so I don't ball my hands into fists, I'm that angry.

"Oh . . . Look, never mind . . . You don't want to hear it." She gives me a drunken stare back.

"Oh no, you can't duck out of this conversation now, Annemarie. You've been hinting at something all night long, no, for months actually and now I want to know what exactly."

"Well . . . You've asked, so I'll tell you. Adam's still under the thumb of his ex-wife and that isn't cool with me, there's something going on there." She pulls at her fingertips, avoiding my eyes now.

"No! He's not. There's not. I just told you, they co-parent – welcome to 2022, Annemarie!"

"Naaaahhhhh . . ." She shakes her head ridiculously slowly as the bridal bouquet whizzes over us. We both have to duck fast, and a stampede ensues.

"Where'd it go?"

"Hold your position, Trish!"

"She has to throw it again, Doris!"

"We're over here, Ruth!"

I look up. Even Ruth looks shocked that her aim has been so completely off track.

"Fuck me! I'm seeing double. One more time," she orders.

"It's more than that, though, you need to open your eyes, Lexie." Annemarie takes three attempts to even find the edge of the table to rest her gin on.

"Meaning?" I try to sound placid, though I feel anything but.

"His *life* is in the Cotswolds, and it's a very busy life: the Coopers have their routine, a huge close family, tight-knit village life – and where do you fit in over there exactly?"

Before I can answer, there's uproar as one of the hens catches the bouquet this time.

"Fuckin' hell, Eileen, don't marry Paddy Kinsella whatever you do! That nose will genetically pass down to your kids!"

More uproar. Then I answer her: "How I fit in Annemarie, is that I am his girlfriend."

"Hmm . . . No, no labels remember? You're his 'love buddy'." She uses finger quotes. "His lady in waiting!" She throws her head back, laughing at herself.

"Why are you being such a total bitch?" The rage is out of her cage now.

"Another drink anyone?" Tom shouts at us, the lounge girl by his side now.

We don't answer.

"One for the road girls?"

We don't answer.

"Woah. I see. Well, I'm just telling you the truth, because you asked, I suppose." She stops laughing very abruptly.

59

"Please stop talking."

"*Bitch* is a bit strong, no? Look, I'm not sayin' you've wasted two years with him, of course I'm not, you've had great times when you've seen him, but let's be honest, you've barely seen him! You spend allllll your time daydreaming about him, your nights alone in your apartment, while he gets the best of both worlds. It's starting to annoy me, and it should annoy you too. Your clock is ticking and I don't think he's being fair. There, I've said it!" she barks.

"It's a long-distance relationship, I went into it with my eyes wide open. And I can manage my own clock, thank you very much!" I yank my hands out from under me.

"Eyes wide shut, ya mean!" she snarls.

"I'm leaving. You're drunk and I'm not listening to this." I feel my heart thud and anger bubbling furiously close to the surface.

"Ah don't go!" She slaps her thigh. "You deserve more, that's all I'm saying . . . Like does he want to have a family with you? I'm not being a bitch, Lexie, but your time *is* running out? The tick-tock, tick-tock is real! Believe you me!"

I reel from her words.

"Maybe I don't want kids, Annemarie! Maybe I see you and, fuck me, I don't want that life for myself – or lack of a life, I should say! You're a nervous wreck . . ."

The words tumble out before I even think. Immediately I try to take them back.

"I don't mean – I didn't mean that—"

But her jaw is hanging.

"W-woooow, r-reeeeally? Is that so?" Her chin dips to her chest.

"I'm sorry but you just keep pushing my buttons and I don't know why. I've asked you so many times to just stop . . ." I try to think of something to say to defuse what I've said. "Look, it's

60

late, we're tired, let's just park this forever if possible, but if not for another time?"

But Annemarie's switched gear. Now *she* is mad. She stands up, out of the seat. "Tom! TOM! We're leaving!" she shouts. Then carefully places her hands on the edge of the table, leans in towards me, eyes absolutely blazing, steaming drunk now, her chin wobbling.

"You want the absolute truth as I see it? He's using you when it suits him. Look at his life, Lexie, open your eyes! Check dates! Times! His excuses! It's bullshit." Spittle flies out of her mouth now. The whole table turns to look at us.

"What the hell are you talking about?" I hiss at her.

"Sorry I ever brought it up. You can't have an adult conversation with you when it comes to him. You are delusional, like some lovesick teenager! I get you fancy him uncontrollably, which by the way is only because you never see him – and guess what? You're over forty and pen-pal FaceTime lovers isn't real life!"

I stand up and face her, anger boiling.

"What's going on? Everything alright here?" I hear Tom but don't turn around to look at him.

"Right, if we're being open and honest here, allow me my twopence worth?"

"Fire away!" Annemarie swings her arm in a full circle. "Unlike you, it seems, I'm a big girl and I can handle the truth!"

"You've been an obsessive, nervous wreck for the past three years – I don't know how to be around you anymore! I can't seem to help you—"

"Is that a fact?"

"It is. You changed—"

"I had a baby!"

"I know – oh God I know, you talk about nothing else apart from babies – and poo and naps and nappies and you slag me

61

for not going out but you've the perfect family tableau and you never go outside the door!"

"Eh, I do . . ."

"Eh, when?"

"I go to work!"

"Three days a week and even in work all you do is fret and worry and stress about Ben up in the crèche. When was the last time we'd a laugh and a proper chat? You make me so anxious every day. It's like you can talk about nothing else but Ben worries! I try to help but you refuse to listen!"

"Well sorry for sharing my life with you! I'll know not to in future!"

"It's not like that." Oh shit, I wish I hadn't said that. I feel sick. Literally queasy, like I could throw up.

"Seems it is. I have everything I want – a husband, a baby, and I don't need *you* to tell me who I am, ha! *You* of all people. Lexie, waiting-at-home-for-the-phone-to-ring! I have a REAL life!"

"No . . . no, you don't, Annemarie." I try to rein it in now, before I say more things I will regret. "What you are living is a life of constant worrying, fear and anxiety . . ."

She interrupts me just as I was going to say, *And I only want to help you, let me in!*

"Jealous much?" She throws her head back and fake laughs.

This isn't her, but my temper is beyond me now.

"God, not at all, in fact I see your life and I want the compete opposite!"

"Oh, is that so?"

"Yeah, that's so."

"Well, excuse me for being a grown-up!"

"Being a wife and mother does not a grown-up make!"

"Ah, here leave it out, girls, what are yiz at? Stop it. It's my birthday . . . Yiz are bessie mates," Tom tries.

"So, you're going to go through the rest of your life hoping nurse Adam pops over now and then for a quick ride?"

"Careful, Annemarie." I swallow a lump galloping up my throat.

"What? You've said far worse to me! I could show you a few things your head would spin . . ."

"Let's just park this, okay? I'm going to go home," I interrupt her.

"To your empty *apart*-ment . . ." But her voice wobbles and Tom steps in.

"To my home, yeah."

"Tell Adam I see him," she says as Tom hands her her puffer jacket above my head.

"Time to go, Amo," he tells her, his voice somehow stern and soft at the same time.

We've both said too much and if I retaliate, this is the end of our friendship; I know that right in this moment. I pull up my blazer and drag my bag from under the table and leave. I twist and turn, forcing my way out through the still-heaving bar, trying not to bawl. I can hear Tom calling me, but I don't look back. Outside the snow is falling thickly once more and I give a gasp of silent thanks as a row of taxis await.

"Ya alright, Lexie?" I turn. Mark O' Donoghue stands behind me on the steps, a look of concern on his face. "Hope I didn't cause that? I was only tryin' to have a bitta craic with ya? Annemarie was crawling under the table earlier and she tipped my leg and gave me the thumbs up. So I was a bit confused?" He ruffles his curls.

"It's fine, it's not your fault so." I pull my bag across me, fish my purse out.

"Can I at least put you in a cab?"

"No, thanks." I point to the row. In fairness to him he walks to the top car, opens the back door for me as I follow him up and fold myself in.

"Tom's just told me you've a boyfriend in England, I thought you were single – I apologise." Him being nice to me now is only making me feel worse, and I should say something nice back, but I just put my head down as my vision starts to blur. He closes the door with a tap-tap-tap on the roof top.

I give my address to the driver, sit back and take out my phone, tap it awake. I stare at my screensaver of me and Adam in that bright sunshine. Right this very minute it all feels like a lifetime ago.

Is Annemarie right? Has he no intentions of committing fully to me? Does she know something I don't? Why would she say those things? Does he have a better, happy life in the Cotswolds? Immediately Martha flashes into my mind. She called him non-stop while we were enjoying that first vacation together but I didn't let her get to me.

I close my eyes, still fighting the tears as I recall our holiday in Nerja, when everything seemed so perfect.

10

Nerja, Spain, 6 May 2022

Somewhere in My Memory (Home Alone)

VILLA BLANCO DEL MAR was the picture-perfect authentic Spanish villa everyone dreams about. It boasted incredible sea views way up in the high hills of Frigiliana, where we spent five glorious days. All pristine white pebble-dashed, covered in wild brambles, surrounded with bougainvillea flowers so delicate, boasting wondrous shades of vivid pinks and pale violets. After making love under the cool whizzing blades of the fan over our king-sized bed every morning, we'd make our way to Johanny's, a hippy-type open beach-bar, for two flat whites, an apple Danish for Adam and a warm, gooey pain au chocolat for me.

We'd escaped his chaotic, complicated, busy, world and embraced our own wonderfully quiet, romantic, easy time together.

"Lexie!" Adam had been waiting at the electric gates of the villa as my taxi crunched up the stone gravel on that balmy Friday night. I'd had the window rolled down and my head hanging out, waving at him like a lunatic.

"Adam Cooper! Howrya! Fancy seein' you here!" I shouted. "What are the chances?"

As always, he took my breath away. His white T-shirt had worked its way free of his jeans' waistband as he walked barefoot towards me. I could see his flat, tanned stomach and the line of dark hair that led down to his manhood. My insides physically quivered. He came closer, his overgrown hair still wet from the shower and that sexy smile of his beaming across his face. As he opened the passenger door for me, I looked up from the backseat and held his eyes. We stared at each other in silence until finally he found the words.

"Oh! Gracias Señor," he blurted, then handed the driver a ten-euro tip, for which he received a "de nada" and a tip of the man's peaked cap.

"No esta bien . . ." Adam cocked a questioning eyebrow at me and I laughed. I have zero Spanish. "It's okay . . . bueno . . . I'll get her bags." Adam sauntered to the boot and pulled my little pink wheelie out, set it down on the gravel as I got out.

"Hola! Alone at last!" I stamped my foot, attempting a Spanish dance move, clicking my hands above my head. I felt utterly alive. And utterly, utterly happy.

"Hola to you too! One of my favourite things about! You pack so light." He laughed, weighing my case by lifting it and giving it a few shakes.

"You know me, I'm no Carrie Bradshaw, unfortunately."

"You talk about her enough, I feel like she's one of your friends!"

"I wish!" I clutched my heart as the spluttering old engine of my taxi faded away, leaving us in the still of the night.

"Well, here we are, Lexie, at long last." I actually gasped over the sweet sounds of the late-night crickets and the swooshing singing of the ocean below. The night lights dotted around the

66

villa shone, though they couldn't compete with the silver glow of the full moon. Adam's deep brown eyes were heavy with desire. I hoped my giddiness wasn't plastered all over my face.

I wasn't sure who made the first move for our reunited kiss. One moment we were staring goofily at each and the next our mouths were together, at first sweet and gentle then hot and heavy and hard. His arms tight around me, his fingers dancing underneath the hair at the back of my neck. I pulled his body close to me, feeling his desires.

"God, it's so good to hold you." I eventually broke for air, still raised on my tippy toes. His skin was damp and wonderfully warm to touch. The uncontrollable lust I had was a little overwhelming, especially knowing he was all mine for five long days. There was no awkwardness, not for a second. Adam felt like home, even though I hadn't physically seen him in months.

"I've missed you like crazy." He wrapped himself around me, held me so tight my ribs protested, but I inhaled him as though it might bring us even closer.

"Oh me too."

He took my face in his hands and just looked at me. Studied me. "The relief of seeing you, I couldn't sleep last night. Aren't I pathetic?"

"Total loser," I joked.

"This is the best feeling in the world. Don't worry, I'm conscious I sound like a broken record, but I really am sorry about not getting to see much of you these last few months. Especially on your birthday when the ruddy pipes burst in Rosehill; and the time after that, when it was my turn to drive Freya to Gymkhana in Norwich. I'd stupidly hoped Martha would do the right thing and swap the driving commitments, but she wouldn't budge, I'm—"

The last name I wanted to hear was *Martha*, so I put my finger over his soft lips.

67

"It's alright, Adam, I understand."

Giving me that perfect smile, he lifted me off the ground and it was a long time before he set me down. (To be fair, I had been in training for Nerja for three weeks, but light as a feather I was not!)

"Your hair's blonder?" he noticed.

"Highlights, hun," I replied with a flick of my fresh, curly, shoulder-length blow-dry.

"New dress?"

"Penney's, hun, fifteen euro." I twirled in the halter-neck polka dot on my high red wedges.

"That's quite the tan you already have?" He held his leg up against mine, and even though it was pretty well-covered in dark hair, his thighs were pale compared to mine.

"Cocoa Brown, hun, free sample." I jutted one knee in an Angelina Jolie pose, rested my hands on my hips.

He stood just grinning at me, slowly shaking his head as though he was still amazed that he was with *me*. It was the greatest feeling ever.

"I've been sacrificing hot deli-counters, chippers and chocolate oranges, so I'm gonna gorge myself this week!"

"Well, good thing I've got two bottles of white chilling in the fridge: Pinot Grigio, your favourite, and a Marqués red is breathing. I took the liberty of buying long crusty French baguettes, Parma ham and cheeses . . . and crisps, obviously!"

"These are the reasons I . . ." I left that sentence hanging, shrugged my bare shoulders through my halter and, instead of saying those three little words, I made a heart shape with my hands.

Adam didn't throw the love word around willy-nilly, so I decided not to either. I'd said it to my ex, and this time, I vowed, I would treat those three special words with the utmost respect.

To think the first time he'd said those words was on the night we almost broke up, at Deb's engagement party, only a few weeks after we'd met. He'd had a bit to drink, and I'd been accosted by Martha in the ladies, where she told me she wanted him back and that I was standing in the way of her family getting back together. She'd warned me off him. Or at least tried to.

"You do know I can't get you out of my mind, not even for a day. You're in here all the bloomin' time." He tapped a finger to his temple. "It's great but also pure torture that I can't come home to you every night, curl up on the sofa with you and open a bottle, binge Netflix."

"Oh, I know."

"I can't relax like this . . ." He looked down to the ground, exhaling a slow breath as though expelling the burdens of his head. "Not the way I do when I'm with you. I love how you see the world, you're so different to everyone I know. This . . ." He'd dug his finger into his T-shirt, then pointed to me, then back to himself. ". . . all feels so different but completely right. And I know I haven't told you this, Lexie, but you're the—"

This was the moment I'd been waiting for, quite literally all my life. I held my breath. Our perfect Hollywood moment washed over me, and . . .

Like a distress siren, his phone rang out and shattered the moment.

"I mean I – want to—" he stalled.

"Oh go ahead, answer it," I said, sounding patient yet feeling anything but.

I wanted the moment to be perfect and if that meant waiting, I could wait. He dug the noise out from his back pocket, the blue light illuminating his happy face, but it immediately clouded over.

"Martha?" I said instantly, but I smiled. A fine-fat-fake one it was too. Five minutes into our reunion . . . and there she was.

69

Mrs Cooper. His ever-present ex-wife.

"Yeah . . . It is . . . Shit – sorry." He scratched his head. "I can't – I mean she won't – what I mean is, there's this *thing* she wants to do – it's utter madness, as usual from her – I don't know how to say this exactly, but she wants . . ."

But the ringing was pissing me off.

"Oh just answer her." No surprises she wanted to do something that was utter madness. Repeal the divorce probably! Get Property of Mrs Martha Cooper tattooed across his perfect peach-like-arse. I pictured her, no doubt in some pearly white Lycra gym wear, roller blading out of hot yoga or whatever heated twisty torture she did for that body. And look, I'd have been more than happy to have a civil relationship with Martha, even a friendship, but she hated me on sight. What's a girl to do?

"No, I'll turn my phone off if you like? I told Freya if she needs Dad or if there's an emergency, and she can't get me, to call your phone, is that alright?"

"No, don't do that, that's silly." Last night's blow-dry still bounced freshly as I shook my head, despite the heat of the night. "Just see what she wants?" There was no use in getting angry, not at him, anyway.

"You sure?" His brown eyes looked relieved.

"Of course. Tell her Leddy says hi!" I winked jokingly and he half-laughed, unsure. That was the name Martha had insisted on calling me. Martha knew very well my name was Lexie. I'd like to say I couldn't really blame her for disliking me, but I didn't break them up! He was miserable and filed for divorce years ago. Life moved on, it was just that Martha didn't get the memo, or at the very least refused to read it!

"Thanks. I'll just be a minute, leave your case and go on in . . . Open then wine!" He swung away from me, accepted the call, took the three granite steps as one and jumped down towards the pool area. Reluctantly, I watched his body get further away from me, till he was down to the far end by the yellow spongy sun loungers, phone pressed to his ear. One bed already draped with a Great Tew Rugby Club towel, a small brown bottle of Spanish beer and sun cream on the table. Not that I'd have wanted to hear their conversation – but if I had . . .

I strolled on towards our beautiful villa and that cold bottle of white wine, replaying Adam's words to me before Mrs Cooper had so rudely interrupted us.

Mrs Cooper. That really shouldn't be her *name anymore, should it?* I wondered as I stepped into the cool white marble kitchen and poured a large glass for one.

*

"This is you, love?" I start in the back of the taxi as the snow pelts down and the wipers swish busily to clear it.

"Yes, thank you." I fish out the fare, pay and tip the driver.

The violins soar and the Tabernacle Choir sing "Somewhere in My Memory" so melodically from Christmas FM on the car radio; from one of my favourite Christmas movies, *Home Alone*.

"Merry Christmas, love," he tells me, tucking his fare into the glove box, slamming it shut and adjusting his Christmas hat.

"Same to you." I haul myself out and up to my apartment, shutting the hall door behind me so that the glass pane rattles. I go straight to my bedroom and collapse onto my bed, never feeling more home alone than I do right now.

11

17 December

The Little Drummer Boy

"*ADAM COOPER*," MY PHONE'S DIGITISED VOICE TELLS me as I
stuff my face into my silk pillow, kick the heavy tog duvet
to the floor.

"*Adam Cooper.*" It repeats the name amid its ringing. I had a
crap night's sleep of hot hormonal tossing and turning.

"*Adam Cooper.*"

"Ohhhh ssssttttooopppp—" It doesn't.

"Wake up, Lexie."

I blindly tap my hand across my floating side table for the phone
and knock my pint glass of water all over my sheepskin rug.

"Lexie! For fu— you clumsy – gah!" I fling myself out and
whip up my phone just before it gets a soaking too, then pick up
the pint glass.

The phone stops then starts again; this time I look at the
screen.

ADAM COOPER WANTS TO FACETIME.

"Oh no chance, buddy . . . You can't see me like this. Bloody
typical Lexie luck! I'm waiting months to hear the plan for

Christmas and now he has it I can't fecking answer!" I hit my head lightly with my clenched fist, go grab a towel from the bathroom, come back and dry up the water. My eyes feel caked with mascara; no doubt I've a better panda eye than Dublin Zoo can boast. Squinting a look at the time, I see it's five past ten. I climb back into my warm bed and rest my elbow over my eyes, still shattered.

"Sshhhhiiiitttt," I moan, "you can't be this tired? You have to get up." I'm due in Sir Patrick Dun's nursing home at midday. Today is the Book Club that I started. We finished Maeve Binchy's *Light a Penny Candle*, and it's taken us three months. Big Farmer John, one of the men, said he missed those days!

"Miss the comradery, the sneaking of the black stuff in Jim Cullen's back shed. People all lookin' out for one another, community, ya know? Homemade fruit cakes with a dash of sherry!" He chuckled and danced his feet out of the wheelchair foot rests.

So I'm bringing a sherry fruitcake from Faye's Frosties, my local bakery, and the residents are looking forward to it. No way I'm letting them down. I'm extra close to a few residents, especially Máiréad Farrell. Oh, I've more than a soft spot for Máiréad (as I know she has for me!) and I've been really worried about her lately, she isn't well. I've some Vic's Vapour rub I bought for her to take in with me.

"For the soles of me aul feet," she told me, folding money I didn't want to accept into my palm. "Never a borrower nor a lender be, Lexie."

Swinging my legs back out, I squeeze my toes into the soft fur part of my rug that's still dry and coax the rest of my body to follow suit.

"Oh no! Annemarie!" My eye pop wide open.

The memory hits me like a runaway train.

73

Now this overwhelming sleep fog is lifting, I recall in horror the fight we had last night and drop my head in my hands. The memory freight train of the pub choo-choos at breakneck speed through my brain, then crashes to a halt with a devastating realisation: what if we never make up? What if we can't get past this?

"Ffffuuuuucccckkk."

I hate conflict, especially with Annemarie. I slump to the kitchen.

"Morning Jimmy." I give a wave to my overgrown Yukka potted plant. "You're both too old for this shit, Lexie." Filling the kettle I tell myself, "Grown women don't fight like this."

Listen, Annemarie and myself have had our fair share of arguments, don't get me wrong. This isn't an isolated incident by any means, but this was closer to the bone than we've ever come. While I wait for the kettle I go into the bathroom and brave a look in the mirror.

"Oh. Come. On." The Doc from *Back to The Future* stares back at me. I lean my forehead against the glass. Two black panda eyes. I've that red blotchy look. Flaky skin on my chin. Brushing out my unruly curls, I twist my hair on top of my head, secure it with a scrunchie, wash my face and pat on a bit of Astral to quench my parched skin, and plod back out.

"I'm going to have to FaceTime Adam back looking like this," I tell Jimmy as the kettle clicks off. Turning on the radio, I lean against the kitchen counter and sip the tea I've made. The Little Drummer Boy is there, pa-rum pa-pum pum.

"I've my own guilt drum in my head, thanks very much . . ." I switch it off, welcome the sound of silence. My phone beeps again from my room. I head back in.

Call me? U okay? Adam X

Just before I can type back a message, the FaceTime starts up again.

ADAM COOPER WANTS TO FACETIME.

I hop into the bed, sit up straight. Pinch my cheeks in my best impersonation of Scarlett O' Hara and hit accept. Here we go! How long have I got him to myself for?

"There you are! Hiiii! Got your texts last night, have fun?" His face fills my screen, the light parching the colour; he looks as white as I feel.

"Hey," I warble. "Well? Tell me?" I cross my fingers up high so he can see them.

"Ohhh! Too much fun?" Jokingly raises his eyebrows up and down, towelling his brow with a small white towel.

"No. There was absolutely no fun!"

"No fun? Sorry to hear that." He throws the towel.

"I assure you it was a torturous night out from beginning to end."

"Damn! Was hoping you and Annemarie had fun."

"Um, no."

"Did she have another go at you for me cancelling?" His dark eyes look concerned.

"Meh, well . . ." I stifle an unexpected yawn. "Sorry! I can't seem to get enough sleep these days."

"Anyway, no biggy, I just started to worry a little when I couldn't get you this morning before my run. Late night then I'm assuming?" He squints down the lens.

"I look that bad?"

"No, that good! You know I adore bed-head Lexie." He moves away from the window, holds the phone up high, and finds better light; I can see him clearly now. In his rustic kitchen in Rosehill Cottage, his old, unique, protected house in Great Tew, copper pots and pans swing above his head. In grey jogging bottoms, and not much else, sweat glistens on his bare chest, dark hair stuck to his skin. I squeak involuntarily.

75

"That's better, I can see you now. I wouldn't say I look good at all! I'm not dying, drank very little."

"Oh?" He props the phone up on the windowsill now, I see all the exposed beams and hear Spangles, his cute little dog, bark.

"Good boy! Into bed," Adam commands with a click of his fingers, and the fluffy little black dog does a few turns, curls up in his wicker basket across the room. I watch Adam throw two large spoonfuls of coffee into his French press. He throws the scoop into the old ceramic sink.

"Hoped to chat to you before I hop in the shower. I've a mad day today. Soooooo? Go on . . . guess how long I have off?" He raises his cup. My eyes fight to keep eye contact. He glances down at where I've just been looking. Holds my gaze with those brown eyes crinkling at the sides. Adam's laughter lines are possibly my favourite part of his face.

"How long?" I gasp at last, holding the phone so far away from my face the muscles in my shoulder begin to ache. Trying to find my best light! Outer Mongolia might be the best location!

"Are you ready for this?" He raises an eyebrow.

"I sure am!" I cross my toes.

"Drum roll please!" he taps his fingers on the back of his phone.

"*Dad?*" I hear Freya calling as Adam does a double take, I can only see his ear now.

"Tell me!" I implore. "How long? When are you coming? Adam?"

"Huh? Hang on," his ear tells me. "What's going on Freya? I though you said midday?"

"*No, Daaaaaad! We're ready now!*" Freya's voice gets nearer.

"Um – I-I'm gonna have to call you back," his chin announces.

"Oh!" I move the phone closer to my mouth, speak right into

76

the speaker. "Just tell me what are your Christmas plans? I'm out all day—"

But before he can answer . . .

. . . I hear *her*.

"I brought high heels on the off chance we go to The Moritz for a late supper after the fashion show? Some soy salmon and . . . oh, who are you on to?"

She steps in front of the camera.

It's Martha.

12

17 December

Jingle Bells

TRYING NOT TO PUT TWO and two together and get thirteen, I push Martha's smug face out of my mind as I climb the spiral staircase inside Sir Patrick Dun's nursing home for today's book club. I love this building on old Grand Canal Street; it calms me. Once a distinguished school for physicians, now the smell of corned beef and cabbage wafts through the halls. Makes Annemarie gag when she comes with me on occasions to help out, but I actually find it comforting. Reminds me of my granny. Instils warm memories. But try as I might to distract myself, Martha's nagging voice cuts through and overloads my brain because still I await Adam's Christmas plans with me!

"Leddy? I mean Lexie! Why is that stuck in my head, sweetie-pie? Oh you do look tired!" Martha came so close to the camera I could see just how *perfect* she looked even at that ungodly hour. Seriously?

"I'm only back from the village run with Dominic! I haven't even showered, guys," Adam told them, whipping the phone away.

"Hi Lexie!" Freya's cute face, two French braids on each side, peered down the lens to me. "Still in bed, lucky you!"

"Gotta call you straight back," Adam told me, and the screen went black.

I waited as long as I could, but he never called. Again that feeling of being so far away from his day-to-day life crept over me as I showered and left my apartment.

I turn left now at the top, pass the picture of Anne Young, the founder of the first Irish school of general nursing. If I had a penny for every nurse here who tells me I should work in geriatrics, I'd be rich! It's true, I do love working with older people, especially the patients who suffer with dementia like my granny did. I just find they can somehow relate to me. I have patience and understanding and I'm a great listener, but mainly I've more time for just chatting than the nurses who are rushed off their feet!

"You've a gift, Lexie," Kevin McEvoy, the owner of Sir Patrick Dun's said after he called me into his ground floor office late last year.

"I dunno about that." I pushed the circular coffee pod into the machine, and it whirred to life.

"Ever think of training?"

"In the gym?" I was appalled.

"No." He smirked, handing me the milk from the fridge. "To work in residential care for older people with dementia? We could really do with someone like you here."

"Wouldn't you need a degree? I didn't go to college, Kevin – barely scraped through my Leaving Cert."

"There are a couple of brilliant short courses available. Then in-house training here?"

I shook my head, but the seed was planted. I think about it often. Too often.

"Hi Lexie," Ciara, one of the assistant helpers, starts me back to reality.

"Morning Ciara, are they all set?"

"You bet! All waiting for you. Máiréad didn't look well enough to get up; however, she dragged herself out of the bed for you. She's got such a soft spot for you, Lexie."

"I know, and I have for her, too soft!" I raise an eyebrow.

I thank Ciara and head straight towards the TV room, where my book clubbers are waiting. Finishing the end of the peanut butter smoothie I bought for the walk in, I drain it, toss the plastic cup into the recycling and push open the door.

"Lexie!" the happy cry rings around the small circle.

"Book Wormers!" I slap on my best smiling face. All negative thoughts of Martha, Adam and Annemarie immediately disappear from my mind. Poof!

"Fruit cake?" Margaret Kilroy spots my Faye's Frosties plastic bag before I can put it down.

"You bet! *Sherry* Fruitcake! The best: dried fruit, nuts, spices, soaked-in-spirits cake there is. Will I slice it and make us all hot tea before we begin?"

They all clap in approval, so I take off my coat and start to slice the cake. The room is decorated in red fairy lights and a small fake tree blinks on and off in the corner as Jingle Bells plays on an old CD player.

"Are ya alright, Lexie, yer a little pale, pet?" Máiréad asks from the chair opposite, her feet up on the La-Z-boy recliner.

"I'm okay . . . More importantly, how are *you*?" She definitely looks off-colour.

"Ach, I'm still above ground . . . Is it your man that's botherin' ya? Your Adam?" She crumples a well-used hankie between her fingers.

80

"It's a woman actually . . . The ex-wife of my man." I plate thick wedges of the cake onto paper plates, turn back to her. "And I had a row with my best friend over it." I lick my baby finger, gather some of the fruit crumbs and pop them in my mouth.

"The best thing about best friends is being able to fight with them and they never hold it against you. Isn't that right, Margaret?" Máiréad looks across to her.

"'Tis, Máiréad," Margaret replies.

"Ah I insulted her, I wasn't nice. I regret it all!" I walk around and hand out the plates, giving Máiréad the first one.

"Real friends don't get offended when you insult them. They smile and call you something even more offensive. Did she do that?"

"Kind of," I say to Máiréad and laugh lightly.

"Well then . . . Now why don't ya take her a nice slice of this fruit cake when we're done?" Margaret asks me. "Make her a pot of tea?"

"There's nothin' tea and cake can't fix!" Máiréad smiles.

"Yeah, that's exactly what I'll do. Thanks girls! What would I do without you?"

They're right! I need to offer a sign of peace. I cut two chunks, wrap them in tinfoil and slip them into my bag, but will she accept my apology?

13

20 December

Last Christmas

THE FRUIT CAKE AND TEA TURNED OUT TO BE A BAD IDEA.
Ben was cutting that back tooth and screamed blue murder
in his highchair the whole time I was there, making Annemarie
even more stressed pretending not to be bothered by his yelling
and drooling.

"Pick him up?" I'd told her.

"God no! You'll accuse me of running this bizarre, old ladies'
afternoon tea."

The sheer mention of afternoon tea immediately took both
our minds to the Plaza hotel and our New York trip that probably will never be – and that made things even more uneasy! I
unclipped Ben's straps and picked him up, much to Annemarie's
relief, soothed him then left.

I was so distracted by Martha's sudden – and most *unwelcome* –
appearance three days ago, but there was a simple explanation, as
I should have known. Martha was in Adam's kitchen because they
were taking Freya to her school's charity fashion show, and she'd
needed the loo before they set off. Adam had been dreadfully

apologetic when he called after I got home, exhausted, from Sir Patrick Dun's. But I was okay about it: he has an ex-wife, she exists and is the mother to his daughter, so I expect to see her now and then. Yes, I could have said, *but she lives across the road why didn't she use her own loo?* But that would have been pathetic of me, right?

"Oohh-woahhh, ahhh-ahhhhhh . . ." I hum along now as George Michael purrs out the opening bars of "Last Christmas" for the thousandth time in Silverside. I'm giddy with excitement. Adam is finally booking his flights this morning!

Thumbing in my password, I see one new message, hit the screen like a torpedo then shake my head.

"Gah! Feck off," I mutter; it's nothing but a text from my local discount store, Dealz or No Dealz, informing me shop damaged Terry's Chocolate Oranges are half price. In fairness I'm the one who subscribed to their discount text alert list. But alas, it's the dark chocolate ones, not interested.

But no flight details from Adam yet. He wants to surprise me with the length of the stay, so I'm still not sure how long he can stay for but he's due to arrive 23 December. He knows I love a surprise, I've told him how much I *love* surprises, but this is torture. I need to dive into *Preparation Lexie Byrne* and have her all rumpy-pumpy-ready. I'm leaving all my grooming as near to his arrival as possible. My leg hair grows faster than a hunting cheetah! Mostly I'm bursting to fall into bed with him, wrap myself around him like a rasher on a ham – and not leave the bedroom for the whole Christmas. I want to devour that man!

Wrapping an elastic band around the gift cards, I stuff them back into the top drawer, slam it shut with a bang of my bottom. I sing along with George, delighted to be leaving this shopper's hell soon. With only four days left, the place is thronged with panicked citizens whose online purchases won't arrive on time.

You can spot them a mile away. Dazed and confused. Zombieing their way around unsuitable shops, the look of dread in their bloodshot eyes. They thought they'd done enough, bought it all, only to be Amazon-denied at the final hour.

"Right, grab my jacket, will ya?" Annemarie's voice.

"Huh?" I spin.

"Marco's, I'm assuming?" Her tone is colder than the season but at least she's speaking to me! It's been a full-on cold war between us for days now, despite me trying my best to make amends. I'd hoped we could just brush it under the olive-branch-fruit-cake-carpet, but it wasn't that simple.

"Yes!" I say. Instantly I decide it's best to be the bigger person – sure, I can get her coat, that's what a good friend would do. "Are you? Coming with me?"

"I suppose I just have to get over it, don't I? You did bring fruit cake and forgiveness on your part." Her eyes have deep, dark circles underneath. She doesn't look at me, just dips them and twirls her sapphire engagement ring on her finger. Maybe my overly kind tone is working after all, because she suddenly seems *almost* rueful.

"Listen, Lexie, we were both wrong. Agreed?"

"A hundred percent!" I feather my fringe with my fingers, glad she's said that because I'm not taking full responsibility.

"And we're both trying to get over it . . ."

". . . and we always do," I jump in, carefully.

"Hey! The line starts this way." Annemarie purposefully distracts from the conversation, waves her hand to and fro as she's telling a queue-skipping-customer laden down with bags.

"Bu' I only wanna gift voucher!" the woman shouts across at Annemarie.

"We all only want vouchers, love!" a man at the end shouts up, rolls of glittering Christmas wrapping paper poking out of his

84

bags. "And yet the irony is no one really *wants* vouchers! They're a rip-off! You're much better off putting cash in an envelope!"

"Okay, thanks for that," I try to defuse his rants.

Pulling Annemarie's padded puffer from the peg under the counter, I drape it over the back of her stool.

"Thanks, Lexie," she says to me, stuffing another gift voucher into another envelope and stamping its use-by date on it so it can't be rubbed out by pen. Removing the grips in my bun, I hold them between my teeth, discharging each one as I slip them into my pocket, then shake out my curls.

"Where's August?" Annemarie holds her hand up to the next customer. "Just one moment please, we're just waiting for our lunch cover."

"She's late." I slip into my coat, pull my scarf tightly around my neck and step out to look for August. I catch my full reflection in the shop window of the Happy Ring Home jewellers across the way. Independently owned, the shop's small window is decorated with hundreds of beautiful, sparkly, tiny gold gift bags and golden twinkling fairy lights. While my polyester attire doesn't exactly scream Her Royal Mariah Careyness, I've donned a Santa hat and cut green tinsel to wrap around my blazer cuffs. Ideally, I'd like to wear it around my waist but the work pieces aren't that long and, as Jackie used to say, "We shouldn't feel bad, there's a good reason they didn't call it *thin-sel*, hun."

Jackie lasted in Dubai less than a year before she broke up with her sweet-natured, tee-total boyfriend, Namad, citing the perfectly acceptable fact that she "wanted a much bigger buzz outta life than he could give" and, from what I can make out, she's got one. Her new job is managing the N17 Irish bar in New York. I miss her terribly, she was brilliant craic and always gave it to you straight.

85

"Here she is!" I spot August, our ridiculously appointed manager, coming up the escalator. She begins her saunter across the floor towards us, in leopard-skin corduroy dungarees, three-quarter-length Christmas socks and sliders. As always, she's slurping on a frappasomething, her oversized headphones suffocating her multiple-pierced ears.

"Sure about Marco's, you don't fancy a Chopped café salad?" Annemarie's eyes still don't meet mine.

"No, definitely planning Marco's. I'm absolutely starving. That smell of sizzling bacon wafting down from the Long Haul Café BLT's is killing me. Why am I so bloody hungry all the time?"

"It's the cold," she says in her mammy voice.

I lean back on the wedge heel of my ankle boots to watch the handover exchange between Annemarie and August. I wonder can I coax Annemarie to share a plate of chips, in a peace treaty move?

"Anything. I. Need. To. Know?" August shouts, not bothering to remove her headphones.

"Basic manners?" Annemarie returns with a fake smile, to which she receives an enthusiastically sarcastic thumbs-up.

I hum along with the music, trying to keep the Christmas spirit up despite the non-festive atmosphere between us all and roll on some clear gloss.

"See you at two," I throw to August, gripping my phone in my hand. As you can tell, I'm becoming border-line Glenn Close waiting on these text flight details, but it's nerve-tingling, anticipating, heart-stopping excitement.

While George is crooning overhead, I'm visualising Adam chasing me through the snow, just like in the Wham video, our bodies tumbling together as we laugh. My snowsuit uber flattering. His messy hair is windswept, his stubble heavy on that perfectly chiselled jaw above those soft lips that lean over to meet mine . . .

Annemarie leans on my shoulder and sings into my ear. Her words are just like the song, except that she holds the word *fool* way too hard for my liking while looking pointedly at me.

Is she actually fucking serious?

My little Christmas bubble bursts.

14

20 December

Stop the Cavalry

"WHAT'RE YOU DOING?" I recoil swiftly, swallow the lump rising in my tight throat, feeling my face go puce again.

"W-what?" Her smile slides off and she looks genuinely confused by my reaction in the moment.

"Why on earth are you getting another dig in when we're just making up?" I curl my thumbnails into the palms of my hand.

She steps back, drapes her jacket over her arm. "I'm not! Oh come on, that was totally tongue-in-cheek, Lexie, my icebreaker! I thought you wanted to move past all this? Forget it?"

"I do . . ."

"I was only trying to lighten the mood. This . . ." She extends her free arm, makes a big circle with it above both our heads. ". . . is how we roll. We take the piss out of each other? Or did I miss something?"

She's right. It is how we roll. No. That's only half true, it's how we *used* to roll. I don't know how we roll anymore. We used to laugh all the time, take the total piss out of each other, been known to "lady-leak" once or twice, so funny were our nights out. But that was a while ago now, certainly before Annemarie had her first miscarriage. Life took a very serious turn for both of us after that. It was devastating to watch her pain. I felt it too.

"Okay . . ." I try to let it go. I have to.

"Come on, I'm messing? Remember? Fun?" She focuses her eyes on me now, her flashing Santa earrings swaying, her blue giraffe-print bulging baby bag slung over her bony shoulder.

"It just felt like another dig, that's all, please be sensitive?" I smile, twirl my hoop earring.

"It wasn't. Perhaps you're a little . . . paranoid? Still due?" We stand apart to let a double buggy swing through us.

"Perhaps, but I just want us to forget all that shit and carry on as we always do? It's the season of goodwill. Tra la la la la la LA LA LA!" I conduct an invisible orchestra.

"I've been miserable-la without you." She giggles, pulls the brown tortoiseshell claw clip from her long red hair as she shakes it out. As always, I can't help but admire the glossy shine she always gets.

"Me too." My stomach rumbles.

"I'm just curious because we haven't been talking. Has Adam booked his flights, yeah?"

"Yup . . ." I click my tongue as I only half-lie, jump back out of the way, narrowly avoiding a kid whizzing by on heelies.

"Oh that's great!" She ruffles her hair.

I'm not exactly lying to her, but for some reason I feel the hairs on the back of my neck stand up.

"How long is he coming over for?"

"I dunno yet, eh . . ." I fish an imaginary eyelash out of my eye.

She doesn't have to say anything, but her change of expression annoys me.

"I look forward to cooking for you both over the Christmas so."

"Us too." I stub the toe of my wedged boot into the flooring.

"Now I sense you're hangry, as am I – gimme five minutes, just need to run up to the crèche to check on Ben." Annemarie drops the enormous baby bag of shit she doesn't need, pulls on her puffer, throws the bag back over her shoulder and jogs off on her spindly legs before I can say I'll come.

"I love him and he loves me and he *is* coming, so there. Ha!" Childishly, I stick out my tongue at her retreating back. The song fades to an end, George's undercover man torn apart, just like my happy little Christmas bubble. I quickly check my phone.

No new messages.

What is keeping him?

Still I await the mothereffing Christmas plan.

15

20 December

Happy Xmas (War Is Over)

I FLOP DOWN ON THE BENCH ACROSS FROM INFORMATION. My stomach rumbles loudly again; I put my hand across to silence it. Thankfully the war seems to be over between us but I've already decided I'll make any excuse I have to, because I don't want to do dinner at Annemarie's with Adam. Deep down I know it will result in Detective Annemarie Rafter quizzing chief suspect Adam Cooper on his intentions. I don't what to deal with that stress.

I hold my phone in my hand; I know it hasn't beeped, so I shut my eyes and conjure him up. When he'd returned from Martha's phone call in Nerja, at least ten minutes later, he was hot and bothered.

*

"It's so hot out there, still, at this hour," he said, putting the champagne flutes on the old oak dresser, wiping his forehead with the back of his hand and pulling his white T-shirt off over his head with one hand over his left shoulder. And it was. It was too hot.

All of it.

All of him.

He found me sitting on the bed, legs curled under me, sipping on that chilled glass of Pinot Grigio, like a more adult version of the Little Mermaid. I'd slipped out of my polka dot dress and rested on the crisp snow-white sheet, sucking in, in the red lacey set that had cost me a small fortune. Above me, the large string-operated fan was whirring blissfully, doing wondrous things with my blow dry.

He gave a small moan at the sight of me, then collapsed onto the bed beside me.

"Did you lose your dress?" He pretended to do a double take.

"Just disappeared, like that." I clicked my fingers. "Whoosh!"

"It's possible I wished it off you so much it actually happened?" He brought his hands together and pushed his damp hair back off his face, making his chiselled jaw even more pronounced.

"Your wish came true?" I took a sip, swirled the cool wine in my glass, doing absolutely nothing to cover myself up. The sexual tension in the air was close to suffocating us both.

"Christ Lexie, I need to be with you." He caved, dropped his voice. He ran his warm hands over my shoulders, massaging them in such a way that I quickly put my glass down before I lost control of my motor functions.

"I hear ya." I nodded and we sank into one another, months of pent-up passion finally releasing.

"I dream about this moment . . . I almost don't want to do it because I want it so much . . ." He pulled his head back, lifted his chin, the small feather on his tight chain swinging near my nose. "But how can I stop myself?"

I arched my back and thrust my hips into him – there was no holding back. He stripped me of my barely-there underwear and held me close, our two hot bodies as one, then oh so slowly he found his way in. It was always pure passion with Adam. Almost too good to be true.

"Is that good for you?" he whispered in my ear.

My voice stunned into silence, my body seizing up in glorious electrical feel-good-shocks, it was all I could do to scrape my nails down his taut back and gasp.

"So good." I squeezed him tight.

"Lexie . . ." he repeated over and over, and when we were both done, we kissed, for ages, stopping only to breathe and stare into one another's eyes. I'd have kissed him forever on that hot Spanish night.

"I still can't believe my luck that I found you," he said as we folded into one.

"Or is it fate?" I pulled the white sheet up over me.

"I don't believe in fate."

"I do."

"You think we were destined to meet?" He leaned up on his elbow, my eyes on the curl of his bicep.

"I think I do. I was done looking for love. Me and my almost forty years were gonna try travel, see some of the world. Then bam! This Adam Cooper guy hit me with a door on a night I did not want to go out."

"Maybe, definitely the best mistake of my life." He kissed me again, hard and passionate, like it was our first kiss all over again.

I had felt the questions coming. I wanted to push him, on us . . . Ask him was he happy with the way things were, the meeting up when we could rule? But it was our first night on holiday, so I stopped myself and, believe it or not, we fell asleep, before the red wine that was breathing, before the crusty baguettes and cheeses – just so content to be all wrapped up in one another. As one. Apart from the mind-blowing love-making and no dinner on the first night, true to my word, the rest of our Spanish trip was all culinary pleasures and relaxation after that!

We stuffed our faces with seafood paella on Burriana Beach, washed down with sweet fruity sangria. The red halter polka dot Penney's sundress I travelled in went back in the case after day two, no longer fit for wearing . . . (Or no longer fitting was another way of putting it!) Hair piled up on my head in a messy bun, chlorine or sea-water soaked most nights, mostly makeup free, (bitta mascara, I'm not that brave!) I chilled in comfy shorts and vest T-shirts. We sipped Bailey's coffees as night caps, as the Spanish night faded away into reds and golds in the sky, and we made love in every part of that villa. As always, Adam made me feel like the most beautiful woman in the world. I didn't even wear a sarong with my swimsuit!

There was only *one* downside.

Yet again.

Martha.

I wish I'd had taken him up on his offer to turn off his bloody phone, because "Martyr Martha" never stopped calling him! It blew my mind, but I bit my tongue. He'd taken her calls in far parts of the villa, or if we were on the winding streets he'd let go of my hand, duck into a gift shop. I never pried. But on the last day when his phone rang and we were out on a boating excursion, sailing on the calm blue waves, I asked him to turn it off. He was immediately agreeable:

"Yes, of course! I'm sorry, I thought you wanted me to answer her, that's why I was. She keeps running all sorts of nonsense by me – decisions about Freya she can totally make on her own. Phone is going off!"

But I couldn't stop thinking about it.

Why was it necessary for him to have to turn off his phone just to escape his ex-wife? They'd been divorced for years. Was she ever going to let him go? Move on? Leave us alone? Then we saw a dolphin out at sea and something clicked in me. I watched the beautiful grey animal glide, bobbing up and down in the ocean. Then I said to myself, to hell with Martha Cooper, and let her glide off my back like the water on that dolphin. I forgot all about her for the last day.

Well actually, *two* downsides.

The other was saying goodbye to him at Malaga airport. He walked me all the way down to the Aer Lingus gate, the mountaintops glinting in the morning sun. We sat on hard-backed seats near the long terminal window. For the first time since I'd met him, it felt suddenly strained because I was fighting back tears. He wasn't. I didn't expect him to be. I just didn't want our holiday to be over. So I sipped on my bottled water and stared out the window that looked onto the runway.

He shook his wristwatch into place on his wrist, glanced at it and said, " I'd better go, Lexie, I'm all the way over the other side and my British Airways flight is boarding in fifteen."

"Go." I smiled brightly, stood up. We kissed.

He left.

No new plans.

Nothing about when we'd meet up again.

Oh, I knew we would! I didn't for a nanosecond doubt Adam loved me, but I just had this sinking feeling that he had somewhere to be, someone to go home to . . . and I . . .

I did not.

He had someone he couldn't wait to see, of course he did – Freya. Even as I helped him shop in the Duty Free, it suddenly, out of nowhere, began to hurt. Of course it shouldn't have, I know that, I'm a grown-up. I knew what I was letting myself in for, but

I'm just telling you the truth. As he walked away swinging his yellow Duty Free bags, containing presents of a large Toblerone, massive bag of mini Dime Bars, bottles of Bailey's and a pair of really cute sterling silver star-shaped drop earrings I'd helped him choose for Freya, I was more than aware I had no one but Jimmy, my Yukka, at home. And while Jimmy needed me, it wasn't quite the same. Of course I had Annemarie, and all the people I cared about in Sir Patrick Dun's, especially Máiréad. It just stung when he flew one way and I flew the other.

Then, when I landed in Dublin, the doubts really started to creep in. Very unlike me. I was so low when I got home to my empty apartment that I called Annemarie and, as always, she was great. She came straight over, laden down with wine and takeaway food, and wiped my lovesick tears. We watched *Sex and the City* box sets, all the Big episodes. I could relate to how Carrie loved Mr Big so much yet didn't get to share her life with him. Annemarie came over almost every night for the next month to keep me company. We took Ben for long strolls into St Stephens Green, we fed the ducks, ate Super-Size McDonald's (something Annemarie never does!). Sometimes we stayed out until it was still bright at ten o' clock at night and Ben was sound asleep in his beige bugaboo. Then we'd push him home, not saying much but knowing we had each other, knowing I had her and I was okay again after a few weeks.

"Hey! Hey Lexo Dexo! How's the new bloke treatin' ya?"

With a panicked jolt, my eyes spring open.

16

20 December

Home for Christmas

I START ON THE HARD BENCH. Sit bolt upright. Sweet suffering
Jesus, *he we go.*

It's my awful ex-boyfriend, Dermot, Head of Security, slithering
towards me like the lizard he is. I still find it hard to believe but
we were together four years – until I found out he'd been cheating
on me with every new employee in the centre. Hence his parting
gift of leaving me forever triggered when my trust is questioned!

"He's amazing." I look up briefly, then put my phone in my
bag, delicious dreaming done for now. I used to put up with his
gaslighting and wandering eye. But urgh, I cringe at my foolishness
now!

"Amazin'? Watch that! Yer lookin' well, Lexo."

"I know." I paint a smile on, pull my rose-tinted Vaseline from
my coat pocket and smear some on my lips.

Go away asshole.

He fiddles with the knobs on his talk radio. Static hisses. Adam
and Dermot are as far removed as two men can be. They are
Barack and The Donald.

"Up to me tits in thieving bastards all day." He throws his eyes, clips the radio onto his bubble jacket like he's Superintendent Ted Hastings in *Line of Duty*.

"Well at least you've a big pair." I grin, dip my eyes to his chest area.

"There're no tits!" He uses his fists to lift his man boobs. "They're pecs, from the gym. Hard work has gone into them, I'm benching ONE SEVEN FIVE!" He looks horrified.

Good.

"Oh . . ." I widen my eyes. "They look like boobies . . . Sorry Dermot, I thought maybe, since you like women so much that maybe . . . you were going down the route of change?"

"Are you off yer head?" He steps back, pulls at his too-black, dyed goatee.

"Once was, obviously."

"If things don't work out with the Brit, ya always have my digits." He makes that noisy, snorting, back of the throat hocking thing he does.

Before I can stick my two fingers in my mouth as a response, Tony, the security guard, runs down the escalator towards us, out of breath.

"Howrya, Lexie!" he pants, resting his hands on his knees. "Two young fellas attempting to rob the Christmas tree, Dermot, come on! They've a chainsaw."

They take off. Dermot shattered my confidence and it took me a lot of hard work on myself and a real man like Adam to bring me back. Okay, obviously Adam isn't without his faults. Who is? Ha! Certainly not Martha, who still thinks they will re-marry, barefoot on a beach in Tahiti with Michael Bublé singing "How Deep Is Your Love" while swinging in a three-piece white suit from a wicker swing seat.

"Merry Christmas, Lexie!"

I dart a look to my right. "Máiréad!" I clap my hands. Jumping up, I move to her; she's being pushed towards me in a wheelchair.

"What are you doing out?" I wrap my arms around her, take in her gaunt face and slightly shaky hands as she clutches her bag on her lap. But as she tries to answer, her breath goes against her and she starts a coughing fit before she can answer. To give her a moment, I grab my bag off the bench and throw it across my body. Slowly, she stops coughing.

"How . . .?"

I look up at Ciara, on chair duty, but before she can answer me Máiréad says, "Kevin took me and Margaret Kilroy out for the hour, to buy a few bits . . . I wanted to get out coz I needed to see you and get a wreath."

It takes her a few minutes to catch her breath again. I kneel in front of her. Máiréad has no family and used to put in her days roaming around Silverside before I got her into the nursing home.

"Okay, be careful, it's cold and you're not well."

"Ar'ah, I'm grand. Are you still coming to visit us before Christmas day?" Máiréad rummages up her sleeve for a tissue.

"I am."

"Did the fruit cake work?"

"You know, I think it did." I purse my lips as I see Annemarie finally coming back down the escalator. About bloody time! Lunch hour will be over soon.

She blows her nose loudly, returns the used tissue up her sleeve without noticing my grimacing. "I . . . I have a little something for ya, ya see . . . I've been—"

"I'll see you before Christmas day, I promise. I've a little something for you too." I rummage in my bag, pull out a fresh packet of tissues, hand them to her. "These are not your Christmas present, don't worry."

"Lexie, can ya do somethin' for me?"

"Sure."

She tugs at the diamond ring on her wedding finger. I noticed the ring before but, knowing she'd never been married, I hadn't asked. She turns and twists it, and it gets stuck on her bulging arthritic knuckle.

"Careful," I say, wincing.

"I got it off last week and last night with a bitta butter – hang on, it's comin'." Her tongue pushes out her bottom lip and it slides over the knuckle and off. "Can you get it polished and cleaned for me?" she asks, wheezing.

"Sure, we can both go and leave it into the Happy Ring Home if you like?" I point across to the jewellers.

"No, I need to get back to me bed, you'll take care of it for me, won't you?"

"Yeah sure, I'll bring it in with me when it's all done? They'll be up to their eyes as it's so near Christmas, but I'll ask them to do me a favour. I'll tell them it's for a very special friend."

"You're a good girl, Lexie. I've the money in my locker in a little brown envelope to pay for it, don't forget to get it when you come up next, I'll put your name on it."

"Don't be silly, let me get it done for you – my treat?" I hold the ring up to the glass roof, and it sparkles as it catches the winter light. "It's a beautiful ring, Máiréad."

But the arthritic finger shoots up.

"Never a borrower . . ."

I join in, ". . . nor a lender be."

"Ready?" Ciara leans on the handles of the wheelchair, her name badge clacking off the metal handles. "Kevin said half an hour and back out to the bus."

"Don't forget me . . ." Máiréad turns her head to look back at me, and as they move off Annemarie appears beside me. "Or the brown envelope."

"I won't." I watch her go and make a mental note to spend a full day with her before Adam arrives. If only I'd spent more time with her than Dermot, I'd have been a much happier, confident person. I'll never make that mistake again.

17

20 December

Swinging on a Star

"WHAT TOOK YOU SO LONG?" I ask, turning to Annemarie.

"Um, he was asleep . . . Now let's go eat, we've only half an hour." She stuffs a homemade Tupperware of weird-looking green shit into the front pocket of the bag.

"I though he didn't go down till half one?" I say.

"I know! Right?" She shakes her head, her red hair bouncing like she's in a L'Oréal ad. "They don't listen to me! They aren't sticking with my routine."

"They know what they're doing, they're professionals, remember?" I say softly.

"But I . . . I hoped I could get a few spoonfuls of homemade broccoli and sweet potato into him there before his nap like I do at home . . . I batch-cooked, was up till one o'clock doing it, he'll be starving . . ."

"They do feed him perfectly well, Annemarie, he's not in Mountjoy prison." I try not to laugh. "Despite the fact you asked Aveen to chew up his sausages in her own mouth first before she fed them to him."

"You know he nearly choked on a bit of cut-up sausage once!" she suddenly flies at me.

"Alright . . ." I hold my hand up.

"It's not the same as what I make for him. You know he was born premature . . ." she pants.

"I do. I was there when you delivered him, remember? But he's a perfectly healthy little boy. Come on!" I grab her arm and frog march her towards the exit.

As we walk through the centre I let her ramble on about her homemade green goodness. We pause just inside the revolving doors, by the rows of poinsettias, to let security bundle two young fellas out. I admire the beautifully decorated Christmas tree that is being pushed back into place by Tony. It towers in silver and red bows, the strong pine scent floating on the warm air conditioning. Above us an electronic Santa drives his sleigh, the reins moving slowly and reindeer legs dancing as they move. I'm hypnotised by fairy lights twinkling on and off . . . on and off . . . on and off.

Then we step out and the icy air hits us.

"Ow. T-that's cold!" I heave. "Share a side of chips, extra salt, lashings of vinegar?" I shove my hands deep into my pockets.

"No, thanks." Annemarie pulls on leather gloves.

"Why?" My gloves are at home. As usual.

"Why what?" she asks.

"Why won't you share a side of chips?"

"Because I'm – I don't want to – I'm too . . . heavy." She turns to me, suddenly fighting tears.

"You're too w-what?" I feel my jaw drop.

"Let's just cross the road." She clears her throat, points to the green man. "I don't need a Lexie-lecture."

"No, seriously, how can you think that?"

"You don't see me naked." She blows her cheeks out.

"I don't have to!" I step in closer to her, link my arm through hers tightly.

"Look, I know I'm not overweight or anything – it's just this post-baby belly hangover I need to shift, that's all . . . and . . . well . . . I ate all those Quality Streets earlier then I started on the tin of Roses. I wish people would stop giving us sweets as a thank-you present!"

"I know. They're all so mean. Bastards."

"I'll eat, Lexie, I just don't want a load of fatty chips! Is that alright with you?"

"Perfectly alright, Annemarie."

"You're still my BFF, right?" Annemarie puts on a squeaky baby voice, pretends to joke.

"Sure am, homie."

"Despite us being mean bitches to each other."

"Ah, we were honest bitches . . . Sometimes the truth hurts." I smooth down my fringe with the palm of my hand; it needs a trim.

We both let that settle.

"And despite me being a bag of nerves and all over the place all the time?" she adds.

"Despite it all," I say calmly yet astonished that she's admitting it for the first time.

Annemarie has struggled horrendously on her baby journey: conceiving, pregnancy, delivery and mothering. I'm not dissing that for a second. She suffered those two devastating miscarriages, rounds and rounds of unsuccessful IVF, not to mention Ben's sudden arrival. The whole birth took more out of her mentally than I ever knew. The abstract fear that traumatic situation evoked has never left her, and despite me begging her to get some trauma counselling, she's refused.

"I know I'm always all over the place, you're right." She smiles weakly at me, clutches her baby bag tightly.

"So am I . . . with Adam. So what? We're lucky to be able to be all over the place together. Our common theme, Amo." I use Tom's pet name for her, hoping that'll dissipate the tension in the air.

"Lexie, about Adam, I do wish I hadn't said . . ."

"Annemarie, if I don't shove that Santa Baby sambo into my cakehole in the next five minutes, I'm gonna cry."

"You got it." She laughs and her eyes light up.

"Forget about it, I have. If you want to talk about anything, you know Lexie Byrne is always here. Just please look after yourself too?"

"I will." She links with me again and pulls me close to her.

"Now. Let's go, you can watch me stuff my festive face enough for both of us!"

We march on through the biting wind in companionable silence. But deep down I'm fearful for her as I pull open the door into Marco's warm, festively decorated café. As I signal for Annemarie and her oversized bag to go ahead of me, Dolly sings out in my bag. I dive in, my head actually in the bag, and grab my phone.

It's him.

It's Adam. He must have booked his flights!

Finally, a Christmas miracle!

18

20 December

Santa Baby

"IT'S ADAM!" I SHOW MY JOYOUS FACE TO ANNEMARIE. "At last! Hiiiiiiii!"

I shove my finger into my ear to hear him clearly. Stumbling over to the crib by Marco's less-than-see-through Perspex window, I search for a bit of space. Me being me, I clumsily bang into it and knock over two of the three wise men.

"Hey ba-by!" his voice echoes.

I clasp the phone between my ear and neck and stand the figurines upright, calming down an infuriated older man with my hand.

"They're fine," I cover the mouthpiece as I assure him. "They've been through worse."

He blesses himself and goes back to circling his horses in *The Irish Field* newspaper.

"Can you talk? I know it's lunchtime?" Adam asks.

"Sure I can . . ." I shut my eyes for a brief moment. Annemarie is on top of me now; I edge away from her.

"Tell me? All booked?" I whisper so she can't hear me, shuffling away.

"Erm . . . Le—"

His voice breaks up over the static of the line. I dig my finger in deeper, nearly puncturing my ear drum. Where is he?

"You're breaking up . . ." I shout, much to the annoyance of my fellow diners.

"We're . . . b-breaking up!?" His tone rises.

"No! Fuck! No, fuck! No! I said . . ."

"Seriously, Lexie, mind your language! Is everything alright?" Annemarie's face floods with curiosity.

"Fine!" I mouth at her, then again, "It's all fine!" I shoo her away with a swing of my leg.

"Well take it outside then!" Annemarie flicks her head back in the direction of the door, then pokes me in the ribs as she hovers over a two-seater high table by the window.

"Are you nearly finished here? Looks like you are?" I hear her tell the woman bent over her empty plate as I step outside. The Dublin quays are exceptionally busy: cars inch by, lorries screech brakes and blow horns. Seagulls squawk, swooping and circling overhead. A low-flying police helicopter whirrs by. Pedestrians swerve to avoid me, clocking me with multiple Christmas gift bags.

"Hello? Are you there? Helloooooooo?" The line goes dead. "Fuck it!" I clench my fist, bang it against my forehead. I press re-dial. Engaged tone. I wait. Clutching the phone like a grey-hound with a rabbit in its mouth. I try him again. Engaged. I wait. Wrap my arms around myself to shield me from this biting December wind as speckles of white sleet begin to fall from the white sky again. I hit re-dial again. Engaged again. Then it rings!

"Hello?!"

"Lexie?"

"Adam?"

"Eh, do I sound like a man?"

107

"Annemarie? Whhhhhhat?!"

"What? Are you coming back in is whhhhhhat? I have a table here for two but I've a hoverer at three o' clock with a bowl of hot soup on a tray, a bread roll and no seat."

"Coming!" I stuff the phone back into my bag, turn back and push the door of Marco's open. Wiping the speckles of white from my coat, I see her in the corner talking to the person with the tray.

"See? Told you! Here she is!" Annemarie waves the young woman away.

"Sorry," I say.

"Seats are for people who have already purchased food," she tells me, quite correctly, pointing to Marco's big yellow sign. "Do I know you?" she asks me and I recognise her.

"I met you at the Brazen Head last weekend, yer feet were killing you and I offered you a seat."

"That's who you are! Well Karma Karma Karma Chameleon. Keep the seat, chick." She smiles as she backs up.

"Thank you!" I clasp my hands together. "We've only got a few minutes before we've to be back at work." I talk to her retreating back as she finds a free stool up at the counter.

"So how long can he stay for?" Annemarie fixes the salt and pepper, centres them.

"I don't know yet, we got cut off." I don't meet her eye as I drape my coat on the back of the chair.

"I need to go to the butchers after this, I'm going to get a small rolled and boned turkey for me and Tom. Do you like Brussels sprouts? I love them, Tom not so much, I might do mushy peas or roast parsnips . . ."

"Actually, I might come with you, need to get our Christmas dinner in too. Adam doesn't like turkey, so we're going to have roast beef." I carefully prop my phone upright on the table, leaning it against the glass salt and pepper shakers for optimum reception.

"Are you ready to order?" The waitress stands over us, pulls a tiny pencil from her waist-length, lightly pink-tipped ponytail, licks her thumbs and flips the page on her pad. "Seats are for food, girls."

"Sorry! We know, it won't happen again. Can I get the Santa Baby, please." I unravel my scarf.

"The meatball linguine please," Annemarie says, much to my surprise.

"To drink?" The waitress looks up from the pad.

"Actually no . . ." Annamarie raises a finger.

"No drink?"

"No, I've changed my mind, can I get the goat's cheese . . . No sorry, make that the beetroot salad . . . No dressing?"

The waitress scratches out the orders a little more heavy-handed with her pencil than I deem necessary and writes the new order.

"A green tea for me – Lexie?"

"Just a pot of normal tea, please."

Annemarie checks her watch.

"We don't have long."

"Coulda fooled me with all the chopping and changing of orders . . . But coming right up." With a saccharin smile, the waitress rips the page from her notebook and takes her leave.

I tip the phone. The light comes on; three bars – not too bad.

"So you'll both come to me maybe St Stephen's Day, for brunch?" Annemarie asks. "I won't do red meat then if you're—"

The phone beeps, much to my relief. I grab it, knock it over, pick it back up.

"Is it him? Ask him about brunch?" Annemarie hisses, leans across.

"No. It's a WhatsApp voice message from Jackie, I'll listen later. It's what, eight-thirty in the morning in New York? And that only means one thing: she's had a few after work and is still up."

"I'm okay to speak freely, right?" Annemarie gives me a quizzical look.

"Must you?"

"Yes."

"Go on." I sigh loudly, scratch my chin.

"I'm so curious. Do you guys ever discuss moving in together?"

"We never discuss it, no. Now, can we please change the subject? This conversation is stupid."

"I don't think it's stupid. If I wasn't asking these questions, I wouldn't be a good friend. It's why I said what I said in the pub. I—" She has to lean back as the waitress places the teas down for us just as Dolly sings again. We both look at the caller ID.

It's Adam.

"Go!" Annemarie reads the caller ID same time as I do and points to the door. I grab my coat, fling my arms in and run back outside like a stand-in in the *Matrix*, my coat tails flying behind me.

19

20 December

Let It Snow, Let It Snow, Let It Snow

"Hiiiiii! oh-f-feeeck!" cold air hits me again, this time like a blast of ice from a supermarket deep freezer as thick, white snow now falls from the sky. The temperature has dropped at least a few centigrade in the last few minutes even.

"Le – Lex – L-L – Lex—" Adam's voice goes in and out of coverage.

"Adam!" I shout as though that will make the line any clearer.

"Yes!" we talk over one another.

"Sorry, you go on!" I duck into a laneway, Lovers Laneway as it happens. "Where are you? It's noisy?"

"Just on a coffee run? Where are you?"

"Just grabbing lunch . . ."

"Where exactly?"

"Huh . . . um, across at Marco's . . ." I throw my eye to the heavens – who cares if I'm sitting on Gordon Ramsey's bloody knee twirling linguini with a gold fork and silver spoon! "What's the story? When do you get here? For how long?" I squash the irritation, just about.

What's with this mundane chit chat? Let's not beat around the bush here. I'm freezing my butt off now too.

"So . . . know . . . told you . . . rota . . . it . . . *was* . . . but . . . the time . . . finished up my . . ." He breaks up again, in and out, snippets of valuable information. "Am . . . sorry . . . can you? . . . so . . . Lexie? . . . is – okay – huh?"

"The signal is shit, Adam!" I exclaim.

"C-can . . . me . . . that o – k? For . . . is it?"

"WHAT?" I stamp my freezing feet in my wedges. The empty feeling in my stomach doesn't help. I'm positively queasy with the hunger.

"I said . . . be . . . at . . . is . . . o' clock . . ." The rustle on the line is awful, it's like a crackle of static. Then the line goes dead again.

"Give me patience!" I shout to the snowing heavens. The pone beeps. A WhatsApp. It's Jackie again. Grinning like a lunatic, arms wrapped around Damien Dempsey, the famous Irish singer, against a huge window in her bar. She's recording audio now. I retreat inside again, check the time; I've eight minutes to eat and get back to bloody work.

"A Santa Baby and a beetroot salad, minus dressing." The waitress slides the plates onto our table as I take my seat.

"Look at that snow!" Annemarie gazes out the window as my phone beeps again. I take a look at my plate and practically salivate.

"Does he know it's your lunch hour?" Annemarie says, more in sympathy than in judgement. "Eat it, it'll go cold, you've been waiting all day for it!" She folds a paper napkin and hands it to me. I can tell she'd love the same, she's practically salivating too.

Presuming it's Jackie singing "Goin' Down to Dublin Town" on a voice note, I leave the phone. Holding the little silver pot, I lift the too-hot-to-touch ill-fitting lid. (What happens to all these tea pot lids? Are they just designed to scald?) Annemarie watches me as I concentrate on giving the one teabag a good stir and squeeze it.

"You're not supposed to squeeze it . . . I read on the intern—"

"Oh, spare me the internet tea-bag-squeezers-commentary!"

"Breathe." She joins her fingers and thumbs into circles and breathes in and out.

"I watched my granny make tea for thirty-odd years. I think I can make tea without having to look up how other people make bloody tea," I spit.

"Was just sayin'." Annemarie stops, cups her hand and gathers salt that spilled on the table. She scoops it into her fist and throws it over her left shoulder.

"Here, watch it!" A guy wipes salt from his eye, as he passes with a takeaway coffee cup.

"That's good luck for you! You're welcome! Happy Christmas!"

I pour my tea, busy myself adding my milk and slurping the first strong mouthful. Annemarie holds her teabag by the string, like a puppet master, and dunks it repeatedly. So I don't have to talk I open the WhatsApp message.

But it's not from Jackie in New York, it's from Adam! My heart lurches like a plummeting lift.

SORRY!

Oh no? What is he sorry for? The bad connection maybe?

Then more texts fly in one after the other with a whoosh.

Shit reception

Oh, is that all, phew. Another whoosh.

About my trip

Oh here we go, a week please, say you can stay for a week! Whoosh.

113

I'm so sorry but I can't get over

W-what? I know my jaw has dropped. Whoosh.

Martha's come down with strep throat.

So what does that mean? Whoosh.

I have to take care of Freya. I won't be able to spend Christmas in Dublin with you.

Oh come on. I can't actually move. Whoosh.

Know you get home at 7, can I call you from the hospital? 7 on the dot?

Appetite suddenly diminished. Whoosh.

So sorry Lexie X

I don't type back. I slide the phone away.

"Who was that this time, Jackie? Was she telling you about her acting course? She only texts me when she's pissed, bugs the shit out of me . . . I said to her, don't be texting me—"

". . . Adam." I lift the ciabatta, squash it between my hands; warm brie oozes out.

"And?" She stabs a mini square of beetroot with her fork, holds it aloft.

"Yeah, he's not coming for Christmas, Annemarie." I take a massive bite, taste nothing, chew slowly and it goes down like sandpaper.

Please don't say I told you so.

Please don't say I told you so.

Please don't say I told you so.

I chant in my head.

She doesn't.

"I'm sorry, Lexie." She places her fork across her salad bowl, makes sure it's balanced, then reaches across for my free hand.

I drop my Santa Baby onto the plate. The top falls off, stuffing falls out. I hold her eyes with mine.

"It's grand," is all I can say.

20

20 December

Lonely this Christmas

I'M BEYOND DEFLATED. Not sure how many more of these disappointments I can emotionally take. The butterflies have stopped flapping and have curled their wings in tight around them.

Protection.

I trudged back to work with Annemarie linking tightly with me, a whole Santa Baby left on my plate, and in fairness to her she didn't say another word about him. She made idle chit chat about Tom's Christmas present and her recipe for turkey stuffing. We were slammed behind information with returns, gift cards and lost children, and I wished the afternoon away so I could get to seven and talk to Adam. So I can make sense of all these disappointments. Okay, he has to take care of his daughter if Martha's sick, of course I get that. However, he didn't ask me over to Rosehill Cottage instead – but maybe he will later? Maybe that's it? I cross my fingers behind my back. He knows how much I love surprises . . . Maybe I can go to him? Some hope ignites in the dying flame of my heart.

"Do you want the hazelnut swirl one? Chocolate helps everything." Annemarie waves the blue and red open box of Roses under my nose. I shake my head as she picks out the empty wrappers August insists on putting back in, which drives Annemarie up the wall.

"Leave less for me. Go on?" Shake. Shake. Shake.

"I honestly don't want it."

"Who in their right mind says no to a hazelnut swirl a few days before Christmas?"

"Me."

"I said in their *right mind?*" I know she's only trying to make me laugh, but I'm no longer feeling festive and optimistic despite her kind attempts. She unravels the purple paper; it squeaks on opening and she squashes it up in her hand, pops the whole chocolate into her mouth.

"I twy shuk ih dwn to de not." She spits.

"W-what?" I cup my hand behind my ear. She leans against the marble counter that's finally quiet and sucks like a baby calf. I wait.

"I said, I try and suck it down to the nut."

Then she crunches that hazelnut to its untimely death.

"Go on. I know you must want to say something?" I finally say to her.

"I don't! Jesus, please don't think I'm gloating because I'm most certainly not, I'm upset for you, but it is what it is – you'll come to us. Ben will be thrilled to have you . . ." She keeps her tone clear of any "I told you so" vibes.

"Might fly out to Spain to see my folks, I dunno yet," I lie to her again. Of course they'd be beyond thrilled to have me, but I'm devastated and won't be good company. I wouldn't wish my love-sorrow-face on my beloved folks and ruin *their* happy Christmas. But I can put my happy-face on here and put this disappointment to good use. My mother would see straight through me but the residents at the nursing home won't. So I'll offer my services to Kevin to help out on Christmas Day. I know Máiréad will be delighted; in fact, I may as well text Kevin now and ask if I can eat with them. There's always plenty of food and I might print out some bingo cards for the evening, buy some tins of biscuits for prizes in Dealz Or No Dealz.

"Of course, but if you don't go, I really would love to spoil you?" Annemarie snaps the lid back on the chocolates, seals it tight. She slides it under the counter as August finishes her cover shift.

I watch another couple emerge from the Happy Ring Home, newly engaged it seems; her eyes glued to her left hand, holding her twinkling diamond up to the glass rooftop, him still looking at the receipt he's pulled from the beautiful little gold bag. The sense of merriment they must be feeling, planning their wedding, their life adventure ahead. I wonder have they talked about having kids? *Oh course they have, Lexie,* I chastise myself, most normal couples do that.

*

It's not that we haven't discussed kids. We have. We discussed kids at length last October.

Deep in the crook of his arm I'd lain naked on top of the duvet in my bed.

"Just wish I could stay longer," he said, and my head bobbed as his chest rose and fell.

"Me too." Inhaled his masculine scent. Begged for time to stand still.

"We'll have Christmas together to look forward to in December."

"I can't wait." I wriggled out, leaned up on my elbow, stared into his face. He carefully curled my hair behind my ears, scratched at his dark stubble, curled his arms behind his head, his biceps hard.

"Can't believe it's been nearly two years since we met."

"Me either."

"Imagine we hadn't?"

"What?"

"Met."

"I can't."

"Would you still be single, do you think?"

"I dunno."

"I would."

I leaned across to put my cold lips on his, then he said:

"Why'd you say that?"

"I was actually happy just being single. I didn't think after Dermot anyone else would have been good enough for me. I really learned to respect myself, I broadened my mind, was going to travel when I could. I'd never have settled . . ."

". . . even though you were almost forty?"

What now? I'd immediately thought. Instead I said: "What does that have to do with anything?"

"Well I mean if you . . ." He rubbed his hand across his face.

"Go on."

Then he pushed himself up, leaned back against the head-board, pulled the cream sheet up over his manhood.

"If you wanted kids . . ."

"I might still want kids . . ."

And there we were.

In uncharted water.

Swimming against the tide.

We discussed kids the very first night we met. If we both wanted kids. Neither of us were sure. We hadn't spoke about

118

it since. Now here I was, with the man of my dreams, looking forty-two down the barrel of the last-chance-saloon-gun. This was the time to tell him how I felt.

"Do you?" He looked me in the eye.

"Do you?" I stupidly released my power and gave it to him.

"We've never discussed it properly I guess . . ."

"We kinda did a few years ago and we both weren't sure . . ." *That's all I'm saying,* I think.

"Oh yeah, we did."

He rubbed his stubble, crooked his index finger underneath his chain and moved the silver feather about. He seemed suddenly slightly stressed.

"Listen, Lexie . . . Martha is going on about wanting to have another baby," he more or less blurted the words at me.

Is he actually having a laugh?

"Good for Martha." But I grinned.

I couldn't care less if Martha had quadruplets. What about me and him? What about us?

"It's a bit more complicated . . . How do I say this – she – well, she—" He stopped, flushed a bit.

"Are we actually talking about Martha in the middle of THIS conversation?" My voice colder, I shrugged, unimpressed, and he saw it.

"Absolutely not! Sorry, Lexie." He stretched his arms above his head, then hooked them around me, pulled me in close to him. "If you want a baby, we'll have a baby."

"Well, no . . . We'd both want to have a baby?" I noted seriously.

He said nothing for a few minutes, took a deep breath and went to say something again then stopped himself. He was leaving in a few hours' time, I wouldn't see him again until Christmas and I just wanted us to be together, so I leaned over and kissed him, hard and long, my tongue exploring his hot mouth.

Case closed.

"Do you know why I'm so besotted by you?"

"My supermodel ass?" I shook it but my insides flipped.

He laughed and cupped my bare bottom left cheek with one hand.

"Of course, but I just love how free you are?"

"Free?" *What?*

"Like, you're always available," he added.

"Like free Wi-Fi?" I didn't laugh.

"Oh God, no! I'm not explaining this right, am I?"

"Not as far as I can tell."

"Free as in . . . your personality, your energy, Lexie, it's so open and intoxicating, and it adds to how I feel towards you physically. That's never happened to me before. It's on another planet, my attraction to you. Oh listen, I've had lots of one-night stands, a marriage, you know . . ."

"I think I'm going to throw up now!" I joke, put my hand over my mouth. But *Free?* I still don't understand that reference. What does that mean?

"This. What we have. I've never felt *this*. It's all of you. I see you just watching TV and I could just stare at the curve of your body on the sofa. I try not to stare but I can't help myself; or the side of your face when I sneak a peek, the height of your cheekbones, the softness of your lips, those deep green eyes you have, full of love and warmth and fun. You make me laugh all the time. It's terrible the hold you have over me . . . I feel so free when I'm with you . . . no . . . you're free spirited! That's what I meant! Free spirited!" He exhaled, like he'd just finished a race, and gave me that winning smile.

I smiled back, trying to bask in the compliments, while at the back of my head that question kept spinning: what does *free* really mean? I don't want to be free, I want to be *his*.

21

20 December

Christmas Tree Farm

"E XCUSE ME?" SOMEONE SAYS, QUITE LOUDLY.

"W-who the?" I start, still draped across the information counter; the newly engaged couple long gone. "How may I help you?" I straighten myself up, brush myself down, smile at the man at the front of the queue.

But suddenly I think: what if Martha's not really sick? What if she just wants to sabotage our first proper Christmas together!

"Fuck you, Martha!" I say out loud then immediately freeze, realising what I've done in front of a customer.

"H-huh?" he exclaims.

"Oh . . ." I turn puce.

"Charming." August laughs. "Christmas Tree Farm" is blaring on her iPhone, and she's holding a steaming mug of hot chocolate and bobbing mini-marshmallows. "I can see why my mother promoted *me* to manager."

"Can you turn off the music, August?" Annemarie shakes her head.

"No, Mrs Grinch, I'm sick of the constant loop of the same songs for the last six weeks here – I'll lose my mind, it's Taylor and she's singing about Christmas trees on a farm so it's all good." August crinkles her nose.

"Well, turn it down a bit," Annemarie tells her.

Mortified, I turn to the customer who just received the full brunt of my fury. "I-I-I'm sorry, I was miles away . . . That was an inner thought."

"That's quite alright. What size are you, sweetheart?" The small man removes his John Lennon style specs, hooks the arms down the front of his V-neck on his third attempt, to take a closer look at me.

"Pardon?" I ask.

"My wife . . . She's a lady with curves in all the right places, like your good self. I saw a dress you see, but . . ."

"I beg your pardon but that is most inappropriate." Annemarie, as always, jumps to my defence.

"It's alright." I nudge her with my hip out of the way. "I don't know what size I am – I don't do sizes."

"The phone's ringing," August states the bleedin' obvious.

"August! Get off your own phone and answer the work phone!" Annemarie barks at her, and she rolls her eyes but does what she's told. August is only our manager because her mother, June, used to have the job, but June is now heading up the new Customer Service Silverside website and neither myself nor Annemarie wanted the position. Basically August is manager in all but word.

"I'm on my hot chocolate break," she says.

"Well, we're busy, would you mind just being a decent human being for a change and answering the phone for us?"

"Would you mind not eating all the good Roses and then wastin' them?" August eyes her up and down.

"What's that even mean?"

"Ask Sally-Ann the toilet attendant, why don't ya?" August pulls a face, sticks a finger in her mouth.

"W-what?" I lean in between and answer the phone. August must be on the edible gummy bears again. "Hello, Silverside Shopping Centre, please hold," I say, slamming the hold button to a blinking red, as I see Annemarie whisper something into August's ear.

"What the hell are you two rowing about now?" I hiss under my cupped hand.

"It's nothing," Annemarie says.

"Hello?" the man repeats.

"Oh sorry, your wife, go on . . ."

"I said, how do you know what fits you so?" he continues.

"I just look at the clothes and hold them up to me . . . muscle memory maybe."

I'm drained now as August lifts the hatch and slams it shut.

"Just going to the *toilet* before I head off on me mini break," she says, unnecessarily loudly. "I'll be back at six for the late shift. Leave some Roses for me, why don't ya." She gives Annemarie a pointed look, her mug between her hands.

"But I thought you were a vegan!" Annemarie shouts at her back.

August turns. "I don't eat dead animals but I do eat chocolate, I'm not fuckin' stupid!"

"Is she off her head?" I look to Annemarie. "What was that about the toilet and her big act?"

"I've no idea, I spray too much perfume by all accounts! Like, gimme a break."

I can't say August has a point but she so does.

"Would you come down to Threads," the old man continues as if none of this behind-the-counter drama had just occurred, "that's the shop, and take a look for me?"

123

"Are you on the eggnog?" Annemarie asks him, tip-tapping her snowball-painted fingernails on the counter.

"Listen, miss, if I come home with a voucher again my life won't be worth livin'. If I pick a dress too small, can ya imagine the carnage that will cause? That'll be even worse! All hell will break loose. It's a very dangerous time for us men, buying clothes as Christmas presents . . . All I want is her to think I put a bitta effort into it this year, and for her to like it. I've been warned: I got her a gift voucher for here and a gym membership to Curves last year . . ."

"Oh." I grimace.

"Jesus Christ," Annemarie chimes in.

"That's what she said, I mean every time we passed the bloody place in my taxi she'd say: *'I'm going to get a membership for Curves'*, every bloody time, so what did I do? I listened to her, like she asks me to do, and I go in and I pay silly money for a membership and d'yiz know what she did? She threw it at me!"

"Come on." I lift the hatch and head off with him to Threads. Because on the way back I plan to nip into the ladies and have myself a good old-fashioned, healthy, ugly cry.

22

20 December

Baby It's Cold Outside

I STEP DOWN OFF THE BUS AT TEN MINUTES TO SEVEN into the relentless biting cold. The traffic was awful, and the snowfall is still coming down heavy. Thick, fluffy balls of whiteness twirl under the illumination of the yellowy streaked streetlamps. It should be pretty and wondrous but such is my disappointment I can't see the beauty just now. It's all to perfectly, picture-postcard Christmassy and I won't have that after all. Slow, ponderous tears now start to fall and I allow them as my nose runs and I audibly gulp the sobs out.

Walking through the open gates of my apartment block, I hold my leather bag up over my head as a makeshift umbrella. I'll wait for Adam's call at seven then I'm climbing into bed with my hot water bottle, a bowl of popcorn and cheese sauce, re-watching *Dirty Dancing* and pulling the covers up over my head. This is not how I planned the first night of my Christmas holidays. I'd bought some extra red and green bows trimmed in gold stitching for my tree, a nice bottle of wine, ingredients for a spaghetti bolognaise – I mean, I got *fresh* basil, for Chrissake.

"Ha." I sob through a laugh, feeling utterly wiped out. The snow hits my face and I drop the bag, throw it back over my shoulder. No point. My mascara runs down my face and my curls limp to lie flat and straight in the dampness.

I look like I feel: a damp squib.

All the adrenalin drips out of my system like a leaking tap. Can't think about the future because it's not looking good and I know that I must face up to that. I've so many questions for him but I'll let him speak first. I'm not the type of person to blame. He has responsibilities in a different country, I get it. But I have needs too. As I key in the door code, suddenly I hear a noise. I freeze. It's coming from the long, tall bushes that line the apartment blocks driveway, separating the apartments from the housing estate. A click. Pulling the glass door faster than lightning, I slam it behind me and turn. I stare out the glass. A large shadow emerges. It gets nearer. The shadow bangs on the glass. Hard. My heart pounds in my chest.

I scream.

"Aghhhh! Fffffuck off! Go away! I'll call the Guards!" I wave my phone. "SOS! Help! Hellllpppp!" I yell, dropping my bag turning to the staircase in case anyone's heard me.

"Le . . . L-Lex-! Is it you? Is—" Low muffled words come back at me.

"W-what!" I spin. It's so black out, all I can see is a dark shadow. "Dad?" I stick my nose to the glass.

"It's not . . . it's me!"

Louder now. I stick my whole face into the pane, contorted in concentration.

And only then do I hear it.

The voice.

It's him.

It's Adam!

"A-Ad-dam?" I scream into the glass.

126

He's here! But how?

"Is it you, Lexie? It's hard to tell with your face pressed into glass like that?"

"ADAM!" I step back, squeal again, like a deranged One Direction fan.

"Everything alright here, petal?" a deep country accent echoes. Twisting, I see a kind-hearted old man, in his dark robe and well-worn slippers, virtually backless with the wear, as he takes the industrial brown carpeted stairs carefully. He winds the one strip of grey hair he has back over his head.

"Erm – yes . . . I—" I wipe my dripping nose with the back of my hand. Oh my good God the absolute state of me! Stupidly I point to Adam at the door. I'm still rooted to the spot.

"Ei'll break yer fuckin' neck for ya, pal!" Suddenly he makes a run for the door, way sprightlier now than you'd ever imagine.

"No!" I start, wag my finger.

"Lemme at him!" He's at the last step. "I boxed for Kerry in the under-15s championships when I was a lad, ei'll take his head clean off! Ei'll bury him!"

"Noooo! Sorry! It's fine . . ." He reaches me and I put my hand on his velvet shoulder. I squeeze it as Adam jumps back, falls over something and lands flat on his face.

"Argh!" I hear from him.

"Oh shit!" I flick the silver latch down, push the door.

"I thought he was stalkin' ya or somethin'? Too much of that shite goin' on . . . I've four gir'dls down in Tralee . . . Well one was born a lad but she's my daughter now too – what a woman she is, she inspires me every day despite the bullying she gets from the lads she used to hang around with – arseholes every one of them pricks! I know how to deal with these lads who think they can follow women and scare them – break their bollixes!" He rolls up the stripy gown's sleeves.

I hold my foot to the door and grab my bag off the floor.

"I – yes, you're quite right – but I promise I know him, it was just dark and . . . and the snow . . . and it was unexpected and . . . I got a fright . . ."

"Are ya sure, peteen?" He takes me by the chin, grips it tightly and lifts it.

"Uh-huh." I nod, hardly able to open my mouth.

"How can I be sure you're tellin' me the truth?"

"Well, just let me open the door fully and just let him in . . . He's my boyf—" But I stop myself. Even in this moment I'm conscious of not calling Adam my boyfriend in front of him.

I open the door.

And there he is.

Snow-covered Adam, like some kind of miraculous Christmas mirage. He holds his elbow and rubs it, but those big brown eyes of his are crinkling at the sides. Typical Adam, he has such a great outlook on life and situations, never gets fussed or stressed and always finds humour or solutions. Every nerve in my body wakes up. I tingle all over.

"You always say you love surprises, right?" He pulls a face, throws his hands up to the skies then pats down his black parka.

"Oh – I—" I can't speak.

"But methinks this one's kinda backfired." He makes a face like Wallace from *Wallace & Gromit*. My heart boom-boom-booms off my rib cage. He looks unsure but only for a brief moment, then smiles at me.

"Martha's not sick?" I shake my head.

"No . . . I'm terribly sorry, I didn't mean to frighten anyone. You always go on about surprises, so I took you at face value."

"Bloody right!" I run and throw my arms around him. Despite his sore elbow, he lifts me off the ground, swings me around like some Supermarket Christmas ad photo shoot and we kiss. Oh I'm already lost in his mouth, his smell, his touch as I hear:

"I believe ya so . . ." The old Kerry man chuckles and slides away.

When we can't breathe for a second longer, I gently pull away.

"You're mental . . ." I say.

"You can't say mental anymore, remember?"

"Okay you're nuts."

"No, no, no to nuts." He wags a finger at me.

"Crazy?"

"Jury's still out."

"Bonkers?" I clasp my hands together, prayer-like.

"I think we can do bonkers!" I put my hand up for a high five and he meets it; we laugh. A woman walks up to the door, laden down with shopping bags, wrapped gifts barely staying in the bags, so we step out of her way.

"Feeling Christmassy now, right? It's a night for the fire." She smiles as she passes and goes towards the lift.

"Totally." I return.

Then Adam leans across and puts his cold lips on mine again.

"At last! Let's go inside, shall we? I can't believe I'm actually here! That was the hardest secret to keep!" He holds his palms up to the falling elements, his parka covered again in white snow.

"Is it snowing? I hadn't noticed." I do my best awful Andie McDowall whispery moment in *Four Weddings and a Funeral*.

He laughs out loud, as do I.

Adam Cooper, the ridiest ride in the whole world, really thinks I'm funny.

"Come on, Lexie."

He takes my hand in his and, as happens every time, a bolt of a thousand watts shoots through my body. He's here.

He's really here!

23

20 December

A Winter's Tale

PUSHING THE JUNK MAIL ALL THE WAY through my letterbox I hear it thud and turn the key. On opening my apartment door the warmth hits us. Thank goodness I'd set the heating for six o' clock. I don't normally, as it's so expensive these days, but like I said, this evening I was treating myself to my luxurious Lexie Byrne, festive night in. He steps in and I kick the door closed behind me, rattling the glass pane. We go straight down my long, narrow hallway.

"Ooooh, feels so cosy, just need the bathroom." He rubs his hands together, ducks into the bathroom.

"Please be clean, please be clean, please be half-clean even," I mutter. I'm sure it is; my bedroom might be a tip but I'm very hygienic. Flicking the light on in my living area, the high wattage bulb illuminates the small room. First things first, me and my candles. Annemarie says it's like one of those exclusive spa rooms my living room, with my expensive scented candles. They are my pleasure, and I won't say guilty pleasure because why should I be guilty about treating myself to some nice candles when I work so hard?

Reaching into my glass bowl, I pull out my long candle lighter and trot around lighting my many scented Christmas candles.

"Guess who's here, Jimmy?" I whisper, shimmy my shoulders, feeling the soil in my fingers; he needs a drop of water. "Adam!" I hiss. "Adam is in the loo!"

Throwing my bag over a high kitchen stool, I fill a cup with water and give Jimmy a drink. I bend down, turn on my Christmas tree lights. They twinkle on and off in deep reds and glazy whites as I inhale the fresh pine scent. It's only a small tree but it's real and I love it. Underneath, a dozen gifts are all wrapped and tagged neatly in Will Ferrell *Elf* paper, all stacked high on top of one another. I love to buy for people. I've gifts for Annemarie, Ben, Adam, Freya, Máiréad, Ciara and some more of the nurses at Sir Patricks Dun's, my neighbour underneath me whose real name I don't actually know – I just know her as "underneathy". It's just a bottle of wine because underneathy has my spare key and I need someone who is home at lot and she's never outside the door. I did introduce myself to her when she moved in but she just held the door open enough for her head to pop around, said, "Hi, lovely to meet you," and never offered her name in return!

"You need to go look in the mirror!" I talk under my breath and see I left my breakfast dishes to drip dry before I left for work this morning, but also toast crumbs on the countertop, the marmalade still clinging to the knife. Turning the hot tap on, I drape my yellow dish cloth under it, squeeze a dollop of washing up liquid on it, ring it out and run it swiftly over the countertop and my kitchen table.

Adam returns, smoothing his shirt down. "Ah the place looks great. Can you come to Rosehill Cottage to decorate mine? I'll hide all the washing!"

"Anytime," I say (and mean it!). "Just lemme know the date," I add rather pathetically then think, shite! I've also a load of washing all over the bed and I've yet to see myself in a mirror! My eyes must be smudged panda-like (without the cuteness) from all my silly, unnecessary tears, and I've been perspiring all afternoon since his text in my polyester uniform.

I do a double take. Only now I clock his suitcase.

"Is that what you fell over?"

He nods, rubs his elbow then the back of his head.

"You hurt?"

"No . . . but wasn't exactly the way I'd planned the surprise."

"More Mr Bean than Mr Big," I acknowledge.

"Good one." He laughs, slides his silver feather across his chain.

"Sorry, I overreacted."

"Not as much a that old man did. I thought he was going to beat me up!"

"I'm not sure an old man could beat you up, Adam . . ." I raise my brows.

"I'm not violent, Lexie, I'd never hit an old man who was hitting me for his own good reason. I never got to tell you Frank got into an actual punch-up with my friend Dominic last week – you met Dominic?"

I'd met them both; it was a tough call.

"I hope Dominic won?" I only half joke.

Frank's married to Adam's sister Deb, a loud-mouth farmer from Co. Clare who tells terrible jokes all the time and is rudely insensitive.

"Well I had to step in, literally hold Dominic back. Frank was slagging him about his balding hairline, which Dom is highly sensitive about."

"Frank has no filter."

"No, but Deb says he doesn't really mean any harm, he just speaks before he thinks."

132

Yes, he does, I say, but only in my head. If ever there was a perfectly matched bitchy couple, it's Frank and Deb. I pull off my scarf.

"Actually what *was* that Deb was hassling you about on the phone last week? Her fortieth party or something, wasn't it?"

"Hum?" He crinkles his nose. "I can't remember . . . anyway Deb said I—"

"For how long—" I interrupt this family saga not a moment too soon. He holds out his cupped fist, turns it facing upwards, flips up his index finger, then the next, then his ring finder, baby finger, thumb.

"Five days." He grins, waving his hand in the air.

"Oh my God, really?" The relief I feel is overwhelming, proper quality time but as I quickly do the maths, I work out he's leaving on Christmas Day. No, surely not? He wouldn't leave me on my own on Christmas Day? Maybe he's taking me home with him? To the Cotswolds!

"But that is Ch—" I stop myself in the nick of time.

Another surprise, Lexie! Don't bloody ruin this one too, for crying out loud!

24

20 December

Mistletoe and Wine

"**F**OR REAL?" I SAY AGAIN.

"Really and truly." Adam flops back on the sofa in his parka and distressed-brown-lace-up-ankle-type-man-boots and can't help myself, I pull my coat and skirt up to my knees so it doesn't encumber my movement and I straddle him. Feck fixing my face, it can wait!

"Oh-ho, I like this Lexie move . . ." His hands cup my bum as I kiss him slowly all over. I start on his cheeks, that prickly feeling from his dark stubble against my lips, up to his forehead, back down to his mouth. He moans. I moan. He smells of Sauvage by Dior, I bought it for him for his birthday. It's unmistakably masculine: cedar, sandalwood and mint.

"Oh, I've missed you." He buries his face into my neck, pecks me with butterfly kisses. I shiver and thank my lucky stars I sprayed some Charlotte Tilbury Scent of a Dream tester earlier; at least that's what I *think* the girl at the makeup counter told me it was called on my way back from helping Dan (that was the man's name!) pick a dress for his wife in Threads. A very nice black A-line dress if you don't mind, with long sleeves, with a thick, linked gold chain and earrings to match. He wanted to tip me, but I wouldn't take it and we agree to put the tenner in the Christmas Children's Appeal charity box.

"Wine!" I finally remember my manners.

"No mistletoe?" He looks up at my ceiling.

"Not necessary." I pout a few air kisses.

"Let me get our wine. I'm sure you want to get out of your work clothes?"

"I'm sure you want me to," I snigger.

"Give me some credit I'm not an animal . . . yet!"

Up he gets, off the couch, bends down, onto his knees.

"I bought you something, not giving it to you yet, though . . . Think you'll like it, as least I hope you will . . ." He zips around his grey suitcase and flips it open. "Also bought you a last-minute gift today, which I hope will be to your liking!" He rummages through a few bags inside as I peer over his body. A small black bag, a small gold bag, a long narrow box, a red glittery bow on top another huge, long package and a green plastic M&S bag. He pulls that out, removes a bottle of red wine and a meal deal for two.

"Go on, I'll pour some wine."

"Is it the pulled beef?" I enthuse, removing my coat, pausing on the last button.

"Sure is. We have slow-braised pulled beef with porcini mush-rooms wrapped in a butter puff pastry," he reads from the box, rocking back on his heels. "And . . ." He sticks his hand back in.

"Don't!" I fall to my knees beside him.

"Voila! Lexie Byrne's favourite!." Better than the Holy Grail itself, he holds two chocolate melt-in-the-middle puddings in the air.

Victorious.

"Oh come on, man! You're amazing!" Struggling all the way out of my wet coat, I throw it over the stool and get down on my knees again beside him. I want to peer into his case but I stop myself.

"I wish I had—" But I interrupt him and his brown eyes dip.

"Gimme twenty minutes. Stick a needle on vinyl, I bought some great new albums since you were here in October. There's Fleetwood Mac's *Rumours*, Richard Ashcroft and a bulk of Christmas albums I got on sale when Golden Discs was being taken over. I haven't even got through most of them yet, but definitely some classics in there."

"Can't believe I haven't been here since October . . . It feels like longer and I know it's not been easy, that's why I thought this surprise might be better? Give us both a lift. But bloomin' heck, then Deb started winding me up, as only sisters can do, when I was waiting for the flight in Birmingham departures, calling me to say no woman would like THAT surprise, that I should come straight home and—"

"Well, I do! I love them. Especially this one."

Shut up, Deb. I'd say now Deb has been hoping we'd break up. I don't really like to recall the meetings I had with all his family, they did not go well. I'm pretty sure they all think I'm a lunatic.

He smiles and stands, all six foot one of him – right here, on my beige fluffy carpet, in my small living space, and for a moment it's so easy to picture him here, for good. It makes me sigh with longing, with all that hope and tightly bundled-up pain I've been hiding for months.

It really *has* been hard.

"God, Adam, I've really missed you . . ." I swallow a gulp. I feel like I should pinch myself to make sure he's actually here.

"Not as much as I've missed you."

"It's hard, isn't it?"

136

"Well . . ." He winks at me and breaks the ice and we both howl.

"You know I was actually in Silverside when I rang you. Knew you'd be on lunch, so I popped in to get us dinner. I was crumpling this plastic bag over the phone to make a crackling noise. I'm sure people thought I was nuts . . ."

"Adam, naughty . . ." I wag a finger at him.

"Not nuts . . . No, I mean I'm sure people thought I was bonkers." He raises an eyebrow.

"Overruled."

"Phew. I actually saw Annemarie going into the ladies, I ducked behind the electronic advertising board, sure she'd seen me! Thought I'd better wait until she went back down in case I bumped into her, but she was in there forever and of course, just as I moved, she emerged; I ducked again, she just waved into the crèche and went down the escalator . . . Oh man, it was so hard knowing you were so close to me. Then I thought, shit, what if you don't go straight home, what if you go out after work? That's why I had to call and send the text to make sure. I needed you to come home. I couldn't sleep last night. I was literally too excited."

"I was about to curl up in bed and cry myself to sleep!"

"Oh no, don't say that." He looks horrified.

"Joking!" I'm not really but instead I say, "Totally joking! Right, I'll just hit the hot jets, make yourself at home." I grab the coats and my scarf. "Be right back, lover boy!" I flick my blonde curls, lean on the door frame and bend my leg in a Maureen O' Hara move.

"I'll never be sorry . . ." He does his unbelievably impressive impression of Patrick Swayze from *Dirty Dancing*.

"Neither will I," I say back in my velvety Baby voice. We both giggle as I disappear from his view, and then the blind panic

137

ensues. Shit! I'm nowhere near ready for him. I break into a jog to my bedroom, stuff the coats in my wardrobe, leaning on the current occupants to make room. They aren't happy.

"Shit! Shit! Shit!" I hiss on a whisper.

"Where's your corkscrew?" he calls.

"On the side of the sink," I call back.

I'm anything but Adam Cooper bed-ready! I was purposely waiting to book my "tidy-up" of my nether regions and buy some new undies tomorrow, not as expensive as the summer ones, a nice matching set, somewhere affordable. My underwear never lasts five seconds with Adam so it's a waste of money and I'm not one of those women who treats herself to luxury underwear just for herself, or just in case of an accident. Always found that odd. As though you were waiting to get hit by a car. Bad energy. Careless karma. If I'm going to get run over, I seriously hope the last thing the doctor is looking at are my knickers and if they *are* looking at my knickers instead of my injuries, I want them to be dishcloth grey!

Of course my bedroom is a tip! Grabbing all my dirty laundry (work shirts mainly) off the bed, I shove them underneath. Pull my white duvet up. Fluff the pillows. Shake out my Christmas throw from its plastic zipper bag that I was saving for Christmas Eve, drape it neatly across. I've been so flat out in work I've literally been falling into bed. My dirty bowl from last night's lazy Koko chicken noodles supper is still on my dresser. He'll think I'm a pig.

"Well, if the trotter fits, babe," I mutter to myself.

I hide that in my bottom drawer.

"Shit! Speaking of clean knickers?" Sliding on my still damp rug under my window like Tom Cruise himself in *Risky Business*, I yank open my stuffed drawer and rummage through it.

"Where are my Stella McCartney's?" I've three pairs, black, nude and red, I got in a pack in the sale last year at 75% off but I can't find one pair! Who's been stealing my knickers? Is bloody "underneathy" sneaking in when I'm at work? *Don't be stupid, Lexie*, I think, *you know they are in the bottom of the linen basket that you never remember to empty*. Settling for a new, mini-rise white cotton pair that are too small and have hardly been worn, I wriggle into them, pull the green wrap-around dress from the hanger, hold it to my nose and smell it – did I wash it after the night in the Brazen Head? I can't remember? It smells of fresh fake lavender, oh great! I reach across for my smells-like-Jo-Malone-isn't-really-Jo-Malone from the dresser and spritz myself. As you can probably tell, I love this dress, it's been my saviour on more than one occasion. Another half price get at Silverside in Threads. My nails are shellacked a dark grey to match my toenails. We're home all night so I can go barefoot.

"Where's my razor? Christ if he feels these legs, he'll think I still have my work tights on!" I whisper as I dart across the hall into the bathroom undoing my tie.

"Won't be long!" I call out.

"Take your time!" his voice echoes around my little one-bed apartment.

"I should be more prepared for visitors, I guess! I just can't keep a tidy home the way my mother used to."

"You listen to me, I don't want to hear that from you, YOU can." Another immaculate Johnny Castle impression.

"I used to think so," I call in my broken-hearted Baby voice, and we both crack up.

He'd gone home after our first date and watched the film over and over which, to this day, I think is the most romantic thing he could ever have done for me. When he throws a Johnny Castle line at me, it makes me feel like he'd do anything for me. I've no clue if he actually likes the film, nor do I care because all I care about is he cares enough about me to feign the interest.

I shut the bathroom door.

"Operation sexy Lexie is underway," I say to myself, like I'm on one of those make-over shows where they show the before and after. Stepping into the shower, I pull the glass door closed and I hit the button to welcome the hot jets.

"He's here!" I clap my hands but don't let the palms meet. "Everything is fine, he loves you." Scrubbing my hair with my best coconut oil shampoo and conditioner, I lather on the body wash and get to work on my areas of forestation.

25

20 December

White Christmas

BING CROSBY'S WONDERFUL, SOFT MELODIC TONES fill the air as I open the living room door. Adam leans against the table he's set. He's sipping a glass of red, reading the back of the Bing Crosby Hits vinyl cover. In that split second before he looks up, I feel it again, how right it feels for me to have him in my apartment, but out of nowhere a nagging in the back of my head immediately tells me this will probably never be.

He looks up.

I audibly gulp at this realisation.

". . . and may all your Christmases be white . . ." Adam murmurs as he points to my window.

"What? I swallow, hard.

"Look." But thankfully he's too distracted to notice my expression as he winds up the Venetian blind and I gasp. Fluffy snow is coming down thick and fast, twirling and spinning like my stomach, sticking to the ground in a blanket of whiteness.

"Just for you." He grins, his eyes crinkle.

"Oh, come on! Too perfect," I manage.

"You're too perfect."

"Ah go on outta that." I release the nervous energy in a cheeky grin.

His eyes take me all in. "You look absolutely gorgeous."

I tiptoe over to him and accept the glass he's offering.

"Why, thank you." Little curtsy. I let the anxiety go.

"Wine was still a bit chilly so I stuck the bottle on the radiator for a warm-up."

I take a sip.

"Mmmmmmm." I hold my index finger and thumb together, kiss them. "Magnifique, but please, allow me to assist. I shall open the microwave door, it's the least I can do." I pull the little handle, and the light flicks on. He's here and that's all that matters right now.

He laughs. "I was going to have it on the table for you but I know you like to have a little aperitif before to unwind?"

"Sure do."

"Shall we sit?"

We move to my two-seater couch, sit at the same time but I turn and lean with my back against the elbow rest, prop myself up. Drape my bare legs over his. On his hard, thigh muscles, through his well-worn jeans.

"So how's Freya, is she all set for Christmas?" I ask.

"She's great. It's all Billie Eilish at the moment, a Kindle, surprises . . . which I hate as I've zero clue. I actually managed to buy her a few bits in Silverside this morning."

"Ah you could have had my discount and I could have helped."

"Never mind." He twirls his wine glass.

"I forgot to ask, did she like the earrings I picked with you for her at Malaga airport?"

"Uh-huh." He takes a drink, warms the glass with the long stem between his fingers, slowly swirls.

You lucky old stem, is what I'm thinking.

"How hungry are you?" I ask him.

"Why?" he looks up.

"Like can you wait . . . I dunno . . . an hour?" I pull the tie on the wrap-around dress and it falls open.

26

20 December

It's the Most Wonderful Time of the Year

"JESUS, LEXIE BYRNE, when will I ever have enough of you?" Adam rolls off me, sweating and panting.

"Um, never, hopefully!" I gasp in small pockets of much-needed air. "At least that's my plan!" I pull the duvet up from the floor where we'd discarded it to cover my modesty. Oh I hear you, gate, horse bolted, etc, etc.

"I love every inch of you, every part of you!" He breathes heavily, flips onto his back, puts his hands on his glistening chest. His eyes close and his lips draw into a contented smile.

Listen, I'll level with you, I haven't got the best body in the world, I know that – but he seems to think I have! I've boobs that must have fallen out as one time they were very close. I've uninvited cellulite and thighs that could keep a shepherd warm, but when I'm with him I don't feel anything but desired. I feel he desires all of me. I turn him on. Me. Lil' ole, over-forty, can-scrub-up-well Lexie Byrne. With all my insecurities and regular shopping centre job.

I lie back beside him. Throw my leg over his. Run my finger through the speckles of hair on his still heaving chest. When we've caught our breaths, he props himself up. I let my fingers dance over his curled bicep. He gently moves my damp hair from my hot face.

"You're so beautiful."

"Don't I know it." I turn my eyes in together, stick my top teeth over my bottom lip.

"And funny." He laughs; a real, free, hearty laugh. "No one makes me laugh like you do, I swear, you're really funny . . . really funny . . ."

"What do you mean, I'm funny? Funny how?" I turn and eyeball him.

"Well you know . . . Just how you tell the story . . ." He looks suitably uncomfortable, playing our *Goodfellas* game – you see I'm Joe Pesci to his Ray Liotta – one of his favourite films, which I've watched a dozen time so I can quote it back to him.

"What? Let me understand this, maybe it's me, I'm a bit fucked up maybe. Funny how? Like what, I'm a clown? I amuse you?" I sit bolt upright, boobs wobbling, eyeball him and, still in my best Joe Pesci nasal-squeak from that infamous scene, I go on, "How the fuck am I funny? What the fuck is so funny about me? Tell me? Tell me what's funny?" I bob my head and catch my breath.

Adam laughs so hard he has to sit up and hold onto his side, his eyes watering. He grabs a tissue from the box of scented ones on my floating table.

"Oh man . . . funny . . ." he repeats, then he takes his two hands and pushes his hair back; his biceps curl. "But. Lexie . . ." His expression slowly changes as he links his fingers behind his neck.

I feel a bit dizzy all of a sudden.

He exhales with a puff of air through pursed lips. "We need to talk . . ." His eyes don't blink.

"H-huh?" My throat goes dry, heart plummets, stomach lurches.

Time stands still.

Tick tock.

Tick tock.

He's going to dump me.

This wonderful life . . .

It's over.

27

20 December

The Power of Love

*P*ULL YOURSELF TOGETHER, LEXIE, MY BRAIN KICKS IN. In my head a terrifying dialogue is taking place. *Deep down you knew this was never going to last. Dermot cheated on you for a reason. Look at Adam? Look at you? Do you deserve him? He's Naomi Campbell level of perfection. You're the wild card at Wimbledon. He is finishing it. You knew this was coming. Annemarie tried to warn you. Don't go to pieces. Don't embarrass yourself. Find your dignity. Cop yourself on.*

"It was a joke, *Goodfellas* . . . I mean I know I'm a bad actress, but you were laughing, I won't give up the day job, eh . . ." I know it's not that but it's all I can think of to say.

He makes a sudden move.

Inner dialogue: *Please don't leave me!*

But he doesn't get out of my bed. Instead, he leans on his hands to manoeuvre himself up, lays across me without dropping any of his weight onto me. His intense brown eyes focus on mine. Not a laughing crinkle at the sides to be seen. I'm sure he can feel my heart pumping like a pneumatic drill. What's going on here?

147

"And it was a great performance Lexie. I love that you get me, love that you take interest in what I love – and share the experience with me . . ."

Softly he rests his lips on mine, gently probes his tongue to open my mouth, and he dips in and out, circling his tongue in slow movements. I'm so confused I don't kiss him back. I need to ask what is going on, but as he pulls away, he speaks softly, "Love that you see the good in people first, love that your glass is always half full, love your positivity and vitality." He rests his forehead on mine.

"Need to talk about . . . w-what . . .?" *Oh you pathetic loser.*

He lifts his head back, kisses my forehead, small sharp butterfly kisses, nuzzles my ear. I shiver. What if I never get to kiss this man again? I feel nauseous.

"A-Adam?"

"Hmm?"

I lift his chin and again drown in those deep brown eyes with those long dark eyelashes, the silver feather dances.

"You just said, 'But. Lexie . . . we need to talk . . ." Verbatim. The words are circling my brain. Like a crossword puzzle. How do I solve the meaning?

"Yeah, we really do." He pushes himself off me and gets up. "This can't wait any longer." I watch his toned, naked body move to the bedroom door. The sinew of muscle in his broad back. The peachy curve of his bum, the skin paler there than everywhere else on his body. He leaves the bedroom, goes into the living room.

"Hold it together," I whisper into the duvet pulled right up over my mouth. *Should I get up and get dressed?* I suddenly think, but before I can move, he returns with a square blue plastic folder in his hand. All the while I'm still lying here like a child on a time-out.

"I hope you don't mind but I took some photos when we were in Nerja?"

I'm so confused and dazed by the sheer nakedness of him as he speaks these words. I can't work out their meaning.

"P-photos of w-what?" Jesus, is he going to blackmail me? Put my nakedness on the deep dark web? *Who'd want to pay to see you naked, Lexie, come on.* My senses awaken, like someone has waved a line of snuff under my nostrils, bringing me back to reality.

"Your passport."

Makes much more sense. But, Jesus, is he some kind of catfish man? What the actual fuck is going on?

"W-why? Why would you do that?" I make the move to get up now. I fish for my red silk dressing gown at the end of my bed, find it in a crumpled ball, slide my shaking hands through the puff sleeves, pull the belt tightly across me.

"So I could do this."

He puts his hands on my back and eases me back down, slides his cool body in beside me and hands me the blue folder.

"Open it." He pulls at the chain twisting the feather between his finger and thumb.

"Okay." I've no idea what to expect as I open it. Is it me spreadeagled on his bed in Jury's hotel, Christchurch the first night I met him and we had sex? Is it me in his own bed? Is it me at all?

"Hurry up!" he rushes me.

I pull out two pieces of printed paper. Hold them up to my eyes then put them back down before my eyes will allow me to look. Look back at him. A slow smile is creeping along his lips, those laugher lines on show.

"Read!" He folds his hands together, kisses me again then gently pushes the paper back up to my face. My hands are

149

still shaking. It takes me a minute to focus. I read. Then read again.

It's a boarding pass.

It's *two* boarding passes.

PASSENGERS:
LEXIE BYRNE
ADAM COOPER
21 December 2022
DUBLIN to NEW YORK (JFK)

Departing Dublin:	06:55
Arriving NYC JFK:	09:50

I'm utterly speechless. He hands me another piece of paper. I drop it on the duvet. It's on headed paper.

FITZPATRICK HOTEL, 687 LEXINGTON AVENUE,
NEW YORK
THREE-NIGHT STAY
MERRY CHRISTMAS, LEXIE BYRNE
ADAM. X

"Well . . .?" He bites his bottom lip.

"W-what?"

"Oh God! I've done it again . . ." He facepalms.

"We're . . . we're going to – to *New York?*"

NEW YORK?

NEW YORK??

NEW YORK???

Christ, the relief is palpable. In fact it is oozing out of my pores. I can't even digest the fact I'm going there! I'm still thinking, *He didn't dump me!* We could have been going to pitch a tent in some mucky field in Leitrim with no toilet facilities in gale force winds, and I'd still be this excited.

"Oh Adam!" I prise his hand off his face.

He nods. "On your bucket list, right? See? I listen! I've been planning it since the night you first told me of your love for New York. Sur-prise?" He grits his teeth, waves his hands.

"I don't know what to say except this is amazing." Stupid hormonal tears flood my eyes. I don't recall ever telling him about it and instantly think of Annemarie and our promise to go together; I'd obviously never told him *that* part, and I can't now.

"Oh don't cry!" He shakes his wristwatch down into position, checks it. "So we've got . . . eleven hours."

"No?"

"You not see the dates?"

"No." I sniff.

"We fly out in the morning!"

"No!"

"Yep." He hands me a tissue.

"Adam . . ." I stare at the papers again, then blow my nose rather inelegantly. I'm properly speechless. You know when I said I find it uncomfortable to thank people, this is one of those *exact* moments.

"Are you sure you're happy?" He tilts his head. "We're going to spend Christmas together in New York. Surprised?" He runs a hand through his hair, a flash of confusion in his eyes.

Still I can't find the right words.

"I'm doing my very best with the surprises . . . to make up for . . . the disappointments . . ." He suddenly looks so vulnerable, like a little boy trying so hard to make me happy.

"Oh. My. God!!!" I scream. There we go! That will do it! Good girl, Lexie!

"I. Know!" he screams too.

"This is too much . . ." How much did this cost him?

"Nothing is too much or too good for you, you mean everything to me." He leans over and kisses me; so powerful is his kiss that I lean back onto the bed, and he moves his body to lie on top of me, taking the brunt of his weight on his elbows. The move only serves to accentuate the muscles in his arms, the feather swinging slowly.

"Thank you so much," I say, mopping the tears.

"You're most welcome," he replies, taking me in his arms and holding me so tight. When we let go I can see his eyes are burning with passion.

"I'd move here in a heartbeat – to Dublin I mean, if I could . . . If things were different, you do know that, don't you?"

I nod and realise I'm still physically shaking. My whole body is shaking with the want of him again. I swallow. Run my fingers through his hair, hold it back from his beautiful face. Tightly.

"I know . . . at least . . . I – mean I could move to . . ."

But he interrupts.

"I've never felt like this, it's the best feeling in the world. I'm scared to change a thing." Adam plants small butterfly kisses on my forehead again, moves down to my neck and I moan. His voice joins mine in chorus. Moves to my ear lobe and, as he begin to softly nibble it, the words just come out.

"I love you so much . . . maybe too much . . ."

But I don't think he hears me as I pull the belt from the robe and arch my back.

28

21 December

It's Beginning to Look a Lot Like Christmas

I'M MORE THAN READY FOR THE BIG APPLE! I can hardly believe it. Lexie Byrne is going to New York City! It's finally happening. The excitement is electrifying! As much as I wish I could have gone with Annemarie, I have to just enjoy the experience. And I will. Dublin airport is bustling with passengers heading home for the holidays: people sit on cases in every corner; queues for check-in are snaking back for miles. Adam insisted on buying me some Chanel perfume, my favourite, and we ate breakfast fit for a king and queen. We devoured a huge selection of hot-from-the-oven fresh pastries and strong coffee.

The rush to get ready for the trip was real. I left Adam soaking in my tub, listening to a podcast on the history of Manhattan as I packed. Mainly jeans, jumpers and boots. Then, anxious and a more than a little guilty, I'd called Annemarie.

"Guess who's here?" I asked her.

"Santa?" she replied with a laugh.

"Close . . ."

"The Tooth Fairy?"

"Cold."

"Who?

"Adam!"

"W-what? No way? Oh! I'm delighted for you guys!" She'd sounded genuinely thrilled for me.

"Thanks! I think I'm still in shock, Annemarie. He wanted to surprise me." I took a quick breath. "And guess what else, guess? He's flying me to New York tomorrow, for Christmas!"

"Oh. Oh. Right – New York? Oh. Wow." Her voice got smaller. "Is that okay?"

"Yea." Her breath wheezed, her voice smaller still.

"But we'll still go together someday?" I said in hope.

"Of course we will . . . I didn't mean to sound . . ."

"Won't we? Say we will? Just name the date!"

"Ben is roaring up there, that bloody back tooth still isn't cutting through, I better go. I'll text later. I really am happy for you. Enjoy every second of . . . New York." She hung up, but I felt a real tug at my heart strings.

Life has changed. It has moved on for both of us. Ben changed Annemarie completely and utterly, and falling in love with Adam has changed me too. We just need to find a new way around our friendship.

"Do you think people really do it on a plane?" I ask Adam now as we relax on high stools, watching the passengers of the world pass by. With our cases checked in, I feel more relaxed. Actually, Adam has been more of a panicked traveller than I'd expected. When we were in the sloth-like queue inching to check in and he needed the bathroom, he told me more than once to watch his case. Like I was going to move up a space and leave his case behind me. Then when the airport guy was tagging the bags and pushing then onto the conveyer belt, he made him double-check the JFK tag. He clocked me trying not to laugh and told me that on more than several occasions airlines had lost his luggage. That he'd never got them back.

"I can't really see how myself?" He stands up, pushes his stool back, the sliver zips on his well-worn leather jacket rattling.

I nibble on a piece of warm, brown bread – we've a long road ahead, and I'm still hungry! Adam has started to move, bending his knees while stretching his two arms out straight.

"What are you doing?" I laugh.

"Taking up the toilet space, not much room left for you?"

I watch as three women, sipping on early morning Bucks Fizz, practically salivate.

"What if I'm on top of the toilet cistern?"

"There is no cistern?"

"Is there not?

He shakes his head. "Let's really think about this."

He sits back down, slips out of his jacket. He's wearing a black shirt, top two buttons open, black jeans and black runners.

"And all because . . ." I said to him this morning when he came into my kitchen for an early coffee and just as I expected he got my Milk Tray man reference.

"Let's think this mile-high thing through, Lexie."

I'm still stuffing the last of the thick nutty brown bread into my mouth. "If I eat any more of this delicious bread, I won't even fit into the plane seat, let alone the toilet!"

He shuts his eyes. "Okay, okay, I can see it. You do it."

"Do what?" I swallow it down.

"Picture an airplane toilet."

Jesus, I think, *I'm trying to enjoy my yummy food.*

"Door closes, straight in front is the toilet. It's flat, not many inches off the ground, it does have a lid that closes, that could act as a makeshift seat, turn—" He turns. "It's that tiny metal sink with holder for paper towels and that's it. I could I suppose sit you up on the sink, the toilet is too low, so I'd never get my knees to hold out as I, ya know, did my thang . . . But on the sink maybe I could manage you?"

"I wonder, do they have like mile-high club cards, the more you have the ride on a plane, the more points you get?"

"Not must thrusting space, but if I kept my movements small—" He raises his index finger "—then maybe we can join the mile-highers?"

"Not great for the person who uses the sink after us, is it really?" I pull a face, pop a fallen nut into my mouth.

"More coffee?" He lifts the tall silver coffee pot.

"Please." I extend my empty cup, he re-fills.

"We have a panicker," Adam says, "at ten o' clock!"

Twisting my head over my left shoulder, I see a man running like the clappers towards the board. He stops under and his eyes dart to find his flight, clocks it and breaks into an awkward run towards his gate.

We cover our mouths and laugh.

"Last call for Aer Lingus flight EI553 to JFK New York, boarding now at gate twenty-two, could all remaining passengers make their way to gate twenty two, immediately please." The announcement rings out over our frivolity.

"Bugger! That's us!" Adam screeches.

29

21 December

Rockin' Around the Christmas Tree

"**S**HIT! IS THAT THE TIME?" I CHECK THE CLOCK.

"My case! Come on." He leaps up.

"Never mind your case – our Christmas in New York!" I screech.

We grab our hand luggage and sprint towards the gate, right past the man we've just been jeering at. I've never run on a travelator before, but I feel as light as I've ever felt in my entire life. Like I could jump in the air and glide over all the other passengers. Usain Bolt, I am feeling you.

"Keep running!" Adam hollers behind me.

We disembark and I almost topple headfirst on normal non-moving ground.

"Ah for fu—" Adam stops, drops his rucksack and bends over, his hands cupping his knees.

At gate twenty-two, mounds of people stand in the queue. People are questioning the Aer Lingus ground staff behind the desk.

"No one's even boarded yet!" He exhales loudly.

"Some have?" I point to people who are already behind the boarding gate.

"Well there's definitely some sort of delay to the flight," he says as we trawl the area looking for seats, of which there are none free. Annoyingly, some people have used seats to store their luggage. Eventually we find a free table between two seats filled with Duty Free bags and we plonk down, sharing it.

"Look like it's going to be a while, do ya wanna drink?"

Do I. I nod eagerly. I thought he'd never ask.

Adam rocks around a beautiful white Christmas tree to the kiosk and while I know the wine is pure muck from these paces, it'll do. Needs must and all that.

"Is this for New York?" a woman in her heavily accented American drawl asks me. "JFK?"

"Yes, looks a little delayed," I tell her as she ignores me and I watch her squeeze through the waiting passengers, towards the desk.

"Black coffee, extra hot."

I start. Adam hands me a coffee.

A COFFEE.

"No wine?" I quiz him.

"It's a bit early, no?" He shakes his watch down, checks the face and twists the cap off his bottle of sparkling water.

"S'pose?" It's wine o' clock in New York, I think! I do like a nice pre-take-off drink. I'm not the world's greatest flyer, so an aul nerve settler is usually required. In fact, Annemarie was going to buy a bottle of Prosecco in Duty Free for us to sip on at the gate, I remember now.

Adams squashes onto the table beside me, all six-foot-one of him, and drapes his free arm over my shoulder. I lift the lid and blow. Pfft, no need – it's lukewarm at best. Adam puts his water

158

on the ground, holds it between his runners and leans forward, his phone hanging out of his back pocket.

"I keep telling ya, you're not in Great Tew now where everybody knows your name, this is Dublin and phones get nicked on a daily basis, even when you're actually talking on it!"

"I'm a big boy." He slides his phone on.

"I'll say."

He side-eyes me. His screensaver is of Freya, dressed up as a penguin for Halloween, or, as she says, Guy Faulks. I sip another mediocre mouthful. I intend to dip into my minimal savings to buy him a few meals out. I'll definitely get something for Annemarie in Bloomingdales just to get the shop bag for her! I won't be able to shop for myself, what I have packed will have to do. Right now I'm in my brown leather jacket, faded jeans, cream suede pixie boots and red off-the-shoulder angora sweater. My hair's tied up in a high, bouncing ponytail and I'm fresh-faced apart from mascara-wanded eyes and a good liquid liner cat eye.

"It's minus four in New York!" He shows me the weather app on his phone as I dislodge his heavy arm.

"How *are* we going to keep warm?" I stroke my chin, wizard like, and he laughs as I pull my own phone from my bag. Logging into my bank app, I check my funds. I tut. I'm by no means flushed. I spent a lot on Christmas presents and obviously I hadn't budgeted for an unexpected New York trip but I'm okay. I'll get by.

"What'll we do first?" Adam asks, shifting his weight on the hard plastic table.

"Check in to the hotel . . . Get in . . ."

". . . to bed?" He laughs.

"You took the words right out of my mouth . . ." I sing.

He sings the reply to me, even higher, and we laugh again. It's beyond easy with him, sometimes.

"But seriously, we only have a few precious days, we need to plan."

"I've a few places I've always wanted to see in New York."

"Go on?"

"Ellis Island."

"Ellis Island?"

"Yeah, did you see *Brooklyn*?"

"No."

"Oh you have to watch that with me. Ellis Island was America's largest immigrant inspection centre. During the famine and beyond, over three and a half million Irish people passed through. Steeped in our history."

"We'll do that And the Plaza hotel?" he says.

"Nah." I have to lie; I need to save that for me and Annemarie.

"The John Lennon star in Central Park?"

"Yes!"

"And the Dakota Apartments?" he adds.

"Absolutely. Broadway? *Wicked*?"

"Can we not?"

"No musical?"

"Not for me . . ."

"Annemarie and myself always planned to go see *The Phantom of the Opera*, it's the longest running musical on Broadway."

"This is our first real hurdle." He shakes his head, purses his lips.

"It was only a matter of time." I play along, drop my chin in my hands.

"I was hoping for a baseball game? Yankee stadium."

"Say it ain't true, baby?"

"How about we just find a really cool bar, order a couple of beers and a bucket of chicken wings?" He brings his face in close to mine, our lips inches apart.

"Blue cheese or barbeque?"

"Blue cheese every time."

"Bliss." We kiss.

I plan to buy Annemarie loads of little keepsakes – whet her appetite to actually come with me the next time. Maybe we can go in the summer? When she feels more relaxed?

"I want us to have a serious talk over Christmas – actually, I took the liberty of pre-booking a few restaurants just to have them there, they are all twenty-four-hour cancellations so we'll take a look on the flight and see what we both like, yeah?"

"Sounds good." *Serious talk?*

"I've a Thai in Greenwich Village that has insane reviews on TripAdvisor . . ."

What kind of serious talk?

". . . and the oldest Chinese in Chinatown that boasts Woody Allen as one of their regulars."

"We'll be avoiding that one so." I curl my lip.

"Yes, on second thought, let's forget about that one . . ."

"Honestly, Adam, I'm more than happy with whatever you've booked." I replace the lid on my coffee. I should have gone back with it. It probably cost him close to a fiver. It's one of our biggest pitfalls as Irish people: we are useless at complaining. How often have I sat in a hairdresser's close to tears, looking at my reflection in the mirror and the hairdresser has asked:

Happy?

Fantastic! I've said, paid with a great tip and cried my eyes out all the way home.

A family passes us pushing a trolley piled high with cases, almost running over our feet. A mam, dad, son and daughter. I watch them for a moment. The dad is just like the son, with shocking spiky red hair, both in Dublin GAA jerseys, the mam and daughter both sporting short haircuts and matching pink Cath Kidston backpacks. The mother stops and pulls out two purple juice boxes from her bag. She navigates the tiny clear straw into the hole, hands it to her daughter, then does the same with another one for her son.

"I wonder what I'd be like as a moth—" I start but before I can finish Adam's phone rings. Even before he looks at the caller ID, he makes a groaning sound.

I turn away. I've no doubt who it bloody well is. Who it bloody well always is. Instead I look up, focus on the giant, shiny bright red sleigh dangling above our heads. Rudolf out front, right where he should be and his red nose flashing on and off, on and off, on and off.

"It's Martha!" His face clouds.

"No shit, Sherlock." But I force a wink. Looking back down, I'm still seeing red flashes; that decoration should come with a warning – like his ex-wife!

"Sorry, Lexie—" He stands, the phone ringing in his hand.

"Take it over there." I wave him towards the window. I'm not letting Martha ruin this moment, no siree! How she is the mother to such an easy-going girl like Freya, I'll never know. Freya accepted me from the get-go. I've only met her physically twice – once at Deb's engagement party and once when Adam took us to London. Actually the second time it was slightly odd, because they obviously shared a room in the hotel and I was on my own in my own room on a different floor. I understood it, of course, but at times felt like a bit of an outsider; no faults of theirs, I just felt it. But we were all together, getting to know one another, and I guess that was the whole point of Adam arranging the trip. Slowly, slowly catch a monkey, as Jackie said when I told her. We went to see some Marvel movie and ate stacked cheeseburgers, fries and Oreo milkshakes in Five Guys, and it was a lovely two nights. On the last day, as we were leaving, when Adam went up to pay the hotel bill, she asked me:

"Do you think you and Dad will get married someday?" Her eyes shut tight, almost in a wince, almost as though she had been primed to ask the question and needed to bring home the answer.

How do parents do that? How do they involve their children in that way?

"Honestly, I don't know, Freya." I poured the rest of the raspberry lemonade into our glasses as we sat in the bright reception area.

"Will you have a baby?" She nibbled on her thumbnail.

"I'm not sure." I looked her in the eye.

She looked over her shoulder at Adam. I just knew for sure this was something Martha put her up to.

"But no matter what happens with me and your daddy, you have a mammy and daddy who love you so much, never forget that! You are the apple of your daddy's eye, and your mammy's. And all that huge family you have of uncles and aunties, your village, and hopefully a new friend in me?"

She checked for Adam again, tightened the bobbin holding her low ponytail that was plaited down her back, then pulled herself in tight to the table, almost winding herself.

"I need to tell you something, Lexie. My mum wants to have another baby," she whispered, her eyes wide. "My brother or sister. Did you know that? Did Dad tell you? Do you think that's okay?"

"Of course, I think it's a fabulous idea!" I said.

"You do?" Her eyes were wide like saucers, as if she couldn't believe I'd be so cool about it. Well, it wasn't like Martha's life or her body were any of my business!

"Of course, she's still a young woman."

"I thought you'd be hopping mad?"

"No." I smiled at her warmly.

163

"Dad is furious! I overheard them, Lexie, I was in the garden, and Dad was hopping mad at her: he said over his dead body would she have a brother or sister for me, and Mum said he had no say in it and Dad said he bloody well did and—"

"Everybody ready?" Adam returned, proffering two red lollipops, sucking on his own one. "Compliments of the hotel."

I accepted the lollipop, unsure how to take in what Freya had just said.

Why would Adam care if Martha had another baby?

30

21 December

You and Me and Christmastime

"WHAT? CAN . . . CAN YOU – W-WHAT? Slow down, Martha!" I'm pulled back to earth as Adam walks back to me and kicks over his water bottle. Its spillage makes a wet trail across the floor. He stumbles a bit, moves away again, over to the window where I can see our Aer Lingus Boeing having the last of our bags loaded on. I sit forward on the plastic table watching him as he paces, up and down, up and down. What the hell is going on now? I wonder as he nods a lot, checks his watch, runs his hand through his hair and then, finally, he starts walking back towards me, phone still jammed into his ear. I immediately stand up. I can tell by his drawn face it's not good. A cleaner is approaching and I wave him down for the water mess in case someone slips on it and gets hurt.

"It's alright Martha, let me just tell Lexie here and I'll see you in a bit," I hear now.

See her in a bit? Huh?

"Shit." He scratches his head, messes up his hair, closes his eyes and pinches the bridge of his nose. He slides the phone away, takes my lukewarm-coffee hands in his. "Thanks mate, sorry about that," he says to the cleaner mopping up. "Appreciate it."

"Adam?"

"Shit, Lexie? You're not—"

"What?"

"Freya's had an accident . . ."

"Oh no!" I pull my hands from his and they find my mouth. "Oh fuck! Is she okay?"

"It's alright, it's okay. The Revel, her pony, threw her – well, it's not great . . . Martha said they have her in a neck brace as a precaution, just to be sure, she's in A&E in the Cotswolds awaiting X-rays. And her right knee seems to have taken a bashing . . . Thanks again, mate," he says as the cleaner moves away with his gear.

"Oh the poor thing . . . Jesus, that's awful. She must have got such a fright."

"I'm going to have to go."

"Where?"

"Home," he says.

"Home?"

"Yeah." He nods.

My finger jabs my own chest. "To my apartment?"

"No, home to the Cotswolds."

It takes me a second to understand, then:

"When?"

"Now."

"Oh. Okay."

"I have to go be with her, Lexie, Martha says she's hysterical, asking for me all the time, she says she really needs her dad . . ." I just notice that his hands are shaking. "But you go . . . I'll fly out

166

to meet you tomorrow once I've checked she's okay and talk to our doctors."

"Oh. Oh." It's all I can manage.

"I'm sorry."

If I had a penny for every sorry . . . Immediately I want to pinch myself. *Don't be such a bitch, his daughter's hurt.*

The announcer ding-dongs, breaking the silence.

"Good morning. Aer Lingus flight EI553 to JFK, New York is pleased to announce the rest of the boarding is now re-opened. Apologies for the delay, we had a small technical issue with the aircraft. We are boarding the rest of the passengers in rows 1–20. Anyone travelling with young children . . ." I stop hearing.

We're not going to New York.

"That's us. I booked us the front seat so you wouldn't have anyone in front of you, I know how much you detest people putting their seats back on a plane."

"There's just insufficient space . . ." I trail off.

"Right . . ." He seems to be waiting for me to say something.

"But we are going?" I'm so confused.

"No, you're going."

"I – I'm not going to New York on my own."

"Please, Lexie . . . my case!"

Is he actually having a laugh?

"Um, *our* cases . . ."

Jesus wept.

"Lexie, it will be a huge mess if we have to get them to take our luggage off, all these people have been delayed already. I'll be there before you know it. Trust me?"

I'm lost in those big brown eyes and the strong jawline once again.

People pass us boarding the flight now.

"I'll just fly home, get someone to collect me at Birmingham and take me straight to the hospital. I can speak to our guys on duty, see what's happening, comfort her, I'm sure she'll be fine, she just had an awful shock . . . I'll jump the next available flight to JFK, I promise you."

The look in his eyes softens me. Don't get me wrong, I'm horrified by Freya's accident, it's absolutely awful for the poor little thing, but I can't help feeling deflated.

Instantly, though, I cop myself on. There is a young girl in hospital, of course she needs her father!

"Of course, go! You must. Sorry, I—" I nod furiously.

"Oh, thank you!" His relief is palpable. "Honestly, you're the best." He zips up his parka high under his neck, picks up his rucksack, flings it over his broad shoulder.

"Text me when you land?" he says.

I nod.

"I'll make it up to you."

I nod.

"I'll forward all the hotel's booking emails to you . . ."

I nod.

"Just jump a cab to Lexington at JFK, Fitzpatrick's Hotel, Irish owned and run, you'll be right at home there."

Again, I nod.

Then I start to think.

"B-but I don't have any dollars? For the cab? Or—"

He drops his bag to the ground, rummages, gets out his wallet and gives me two fifty-dollar bills. "All I have," he say apologetically, swings it back onto his leather clad shoulder.

I know I'm forty-one and a quarter but suddenly I feel like a little girl again, very lost. Very alone and helpless all of a sudden. I don't like this feeling at all. I've worked so hard on myself to be independent.

"I love you, Lexie." He doesn't say the words very often but oh when he does. He leans across, kisses me and from the corner of my eye I see a woman, in a sweatshirt dress, who just can't take her eyes off Adam.

"Boarding rows one to twenty . . ."

I pick up my own bag, duck my head and secure it over my body. It's bulging with bottled water, perfume and makeup. I feel like I'm in a dream.

"See you tomorrow, can you manage both the cases at the other end? Get a trolley. You know what my case looks like right? Grey, it's slightly . . ."

"I know it," I say a little defensively. Christ, he seems more worried about his case than leaving me to fly miles all alone to a strange city. And this is the moment I choose to blurt:

"Adam, am I going back with you to the Cotswolds for Christmas Day?"

31

21 December

Have Yourself a Merry Little Christmas

"W-w-what?" HE STUTTERS, his face scrunched up, his body half-turned to exit from me.

"I was just wondering, you said five days ..." I do a five-fingered wave. Oh, what am I saying?

He looks more than a little confused. "We're going to New York for Christmas?"

"But – yeah – we won't be there for dinner, on Christmas Day?" *Shut up Lexie!*

"Well no, I fly home for Christmas from New York."

"Oh. You aren't flying back to Dublin with me?"

"No . . . Is this a problem? I really have to go here." He repositions his bag.

"Are you working on Christmas day?" I know I shouldn't but I have to ask.

"No Lexie, but Freya—"

"I thought Martha had Freya this year?

"She does, but I want to see her on Christmas Day – is this really . . ."

"Last call for passengers on Aer Lingus Flight EI553 to JFK New York, now boarding at gate twenty-two . . ." The queue of people has suddenly disappeared. It's just me and Adam.

"Can we talk about all this in New York?" He scratches his stubble, shifts the rucksack onto his other shoulder again.

And yet again, I nod.

He turns on his heel, face down in his phone, no doubt getting online to Expedia to fly home to the Cotswolds. I wait a minute but he doesn't look back at me before he disappears up the escalator.

"You do know you'll never come first with him, Lexie, like ever." Annemarie's words ring like a dinner gong in my head. That whole conversation plays out. I can clearly see Ruth Kavanagh the convict-bride-to-be, unclipping the handcuffs from her bouquet.

I walk up to the gate slightly in a daze at this turn of events, and hand my boarding pass over. The air hostess scans it and asks me something.

"Pardon?" I'm still holding the boarding pass in my hand.

"Passport?" She leans back to the late stragglers arriving now behind me, pitches her voice higher. "Can you have your passports open, please? We're behind schedule here and don't want to lose our runway slot. It's a very busy day."

"Oh." Another Lexie Byrne rummage as more people grunt behind me. I find it, show her the picture of me that looks like I'm on the FBI's 100 Most Wanted List, it's that awful, and I'm free to go. I think I hear her telling me to have a good flight. The gateway rattles and gravitates under my feet as I trudge towards the door of the plane. Feeling utterly alone, I stare out the window of the jet bridge at the other airplanes docked. Which one is Adam going to get on? I show my boarding pass again at the aircraft door.

"Good morning. Welcome on board." The flight attendant peers at my boarding pass. "Row A, seat 1, right here." Her friendly, pretty face smiles at me in her immaculate green uniform, with a shiny Shamrock brooch, and *Leontia, Cabin Crew* written on her name badge. I knew my seat was here because Adam told me as she points right to Row A.

"Thanks a million." I smile back, my legs still feeling like jelly as I click open the overhead compartment. My jeans are stuck to me. There's very little space, so I remove my phone, water bottle and purse, and shove my bag into the tiny slim space left at the side. I don't even have a book! All those plans I had for this flight with Adam, holding his hand at take-off, resting my head on his strong shoulder for some shut-eye as we soar, watching the monitor at the miles were clocking up. Just having him beside me for seven non-interrupted hours was all I wanted. Despite being in the Cotswolds, London and Dublin together, we've yet to share a flight.

"Excuse me, sorry," I say to the man in the aisle seat. He doesn't get up, though he looks up from his paper and smiles warmly. Bending my legs is difficult as my jeans hug the knees tightly. I shuffle into my window seat, very glad for Adam's free seat between me and the man. I'm not in the mood for hours of polite chit-chat. I sit in, put my items in the stringed compartment for now and click my belt, pull the seatbelt strap as tight as I can, and tip my phone to life.

Annemarie's gonna love this.

32

21 December

Blue Christmas

*A*DAM'S GONE HOME, I TYPE. I need her right now. When the chips are down and all that. Although I know we haven't completely recovered from the fight we are trying and we will get past it, we're that strong.

The dots bounce.

WTAF? With a blue and yellow scary eye emoji.

Freya's had a horse-riding accident but I think she's alright, might have broken something though but hopefully not too serious, he'll follow me out tomorrow.

The dots bounce and bounce.

The poor thing! That's dreadful. Will I come and get you? I'll get Tom's van? Stay in mine for a few nights? Fire's lit, tree is finally up! Will make Baileys Coffees?! With the coffee and all the alcoholic drink emojis.

I'm sitting on the plane! I add the plane emoji so she doesn't think I'm THAT upset! Emojis have a way of detracting from the text. Scrambling the meaning somehow. Reaching up, I twist the cold-air nozzle on. The relief I feel is wonderful as the cool air rains down on me. I hadn't realised I was so hot. So damn queasy.

The dots bounce again.

You're not going to New York on your own????

I am.

Quick bounce.

That's nuts.

Immediately I see Adam. I shake my head.

Just for one night.

The dots bounce.

Oh he's unbelievable! Sorry but this is not on! Angry orange face emoji.

I don't know what I was expecting. Maybe it's too soon since the fight after all. Why can't she just be supportive? Tell me everything will be alright. Be a friend!

I don't type back.

The dots bounce again.

Why don't you go stay with Jackie?

"Jackie!" I shout, drop my phone on my lap, clap my hands.

"Yes?" the voice to the left of me says, and the row of seats jerk.

"You're Jackie?" I turn and ask the older man.

"Last time I looked, anyway . . . Jackie Kiely. I prefer Jack, but everyone calls me Jay."

I smile at him. Well, if this isn't a sign, I don't know what is!

"You, my dear, have a unique look." He dips his thick, black-framed glasses down his nose, studies me as I wriggle out of my leather jacket and adjust my off-the-shoulder angora jumper.

"It's called shock, Jay," I say, folding the jacket under my seat, and actually laugh. It feels like I've been holding my breath for an eternity.

"Well it certainly suits you, dear." With a precise move of his thumb, he slides his frames back up.

I pull at the netted magazines. Maybe I'll buy shit I don't need and put it all on my credit card. I know I need to stop over-reacting, pull myself together and cop on. I'm a lucky girl, flying off to New York to surprise my dear friend and I'll see Adam tomorrow.

"Travelling alone?" Jay asks, resting his *Irish Times* newspaper on his well-ironed yellow slacks as he carefully crosses one leg over the other, pinches up the crease. A shiny, pointed, laced patent shoe bobs up and down, revealing a glimpse of a rainbow-coloured sock.

"Uh-huh." I smile back.

"Me too," he says, "and you are?"

"Lexie."

He picks up his broadsheet, shakes it out. "Well, Lexie, if we go down, we'll go down together, my dear." He returns to his folded page as I only half-laugh in flying fear and look out the window again. Last night's snowfall didn't stick and has turned to that awful grey melted slush that I hate.

"Ladies and gentlemen, welcome on board this Boeing seven three seven flight to New York JFK. The flying time today is approximately seven hours and thirty-five minutes, and we have a good tail wind behind us . . ."

Jackie Miley.

I squeeze my head back into the little white cover on the soft headrest as the aircraft jerks and moves back. How did I not think of her immediately? Shock, I tell myself! I peer out as we slowly taxi to the runway then stop and take our place in the queue for the skies.

She is exactly what I need. A great big happy dose of Jackie in the Big Apple. I check the time and as I spend far too long working out the time difference calculations of when precisely I will land in JFK, disembark, get through passport security, collect the cases, transfer by cab, check-in and get another cab to the N17 to surprise her – I am sucked back by sheer force into my seat as the Boeing accelerates at ferocious pace down the runway. Faster and faster and faster still until her nose lifts, her wheels come up off the ground and the engine noises roar together.

As I grip the seat rests for dear life, Jay turns to me and says:

"Did you know the first sixty seconds are the most dangerous as we take off? Count to a hundred, if you're still counting at ninety-nine, chances are we got up safely." Jay shuts his eyes behind his glasses.

"Thanks for that, Jay," I utter.

"Yer welcome."

I shut my eyes tight and start counting.

33

21 December

Christmas in New York

NEW YORK, NEW YORK! SO GOOD THEY NAMED IT TWICE! I'm actually here! Manhattan seems too like the movies to be true. Snow is piled up on the sides of the road but the sky is frosty blue right now. Strangely, I've the strongest feeling of déjà vu I've ever had in my life as my yellow cab spins me towards the city that never sleeps. Big lights will inspire me, right? Damn right! I had time to make sense of all this on the flight and I feel like a weight has been lifted. Now I just feel free, and excited Adam will here soon, but still sad Annemarie isn't with me. I truly wish she was.

"We're a fixed-rate at fifty-three dollars, ma'am, we never discussed?"

"That's fine," I shout over the predictable honking of horns and shouting out of windows as we hit a traffic tailback. Inching slowly now. Like I said, I never told Adam that New York was on mine *and* Annemarie's friends-bucket-list, and there was no reason to make him feel bad; he couldn't have known. It's a bucket-list tick but it's bittersweet, and I do want to come back here with her – just us two, the way we used to be, when she feels stronger and more at ease about leaving Ben alone with his dad for a few days. I stick my nose to the taxicab glass as we edge towards the skyscrapers; germs or no germs, this is one view I'll take my chances for.

The flight was lovely actually: I fell fast asleep not long after take-off and only woke when my nose recognised the hot aroma of food. People complain about airplane food but I had a lovely little tinfoil treat. Some sort of coated chicken with gravy and potatoes. Jay politely passed, instead pulling a very impressive ready-made fruit bowl from his seat pocket in front. He had strawberries, blueberries, raspberries, mango, pineapple, all the healthy stuff. We made polite chit chat and I was glad of the distraction to be honest.

"Business or pleasure?" I asked him as I held my plastic knife and fork so close, they clipped off one another to get them inside the little carton of ingredients.

"Both, dear, well . . ." I watched in utter awe as he deskinned a kiwi with his long thumbnail. "I'm searching for someone . . ." He used his thumbnail to scoop out the fruit and ate it off his nail.

"That's impressive." I nodded.

"Many years working late into the night and hunger would strike, I had to be inventive. I can peel an orange in my pocket with my gloves on, some might say! Har. Har. Har!"

He actually said the words har har har in his laugh and before I could ask him what he did for a living:

"My job takes me to the streets of New York to find my lead for *Maybe She Did What She Wanted*."

"Oh." I waited for more, clueless as to what Jay was talking about. Stabbed at my chicken, couldn't get the knife in, so I forked a pea.

178

"I've done all of Europe, I simply can't find her."

"Oh." Still no clue what he was on about. "Who is *she*?" I tried.

"She is raw, new, electrifying." Another scoop of kiwi.

"Riiigghtt," I said, moving onto the mini almond cake, picking the one almond off the top and popping it in my mouth. "You have a significant other?" I changed the subject.

"Of course I do, dear; he's a writer, he writes from our basement. Poetry, mainly. Beautiful uplifting ones. I don't see him too often. I do me and he does him. He does not have to do as I do."

"I see." I sucked on the almond.

"You do see dear, the thing about relationships is they should have freedom, don't you agree?"

"Don't get me started on THIS topic." I ate the cake in one bite and ranted to Jay about my life with Adam and Annemarie's take on our relationship for the rest of the flight.

It was good to vent to a stranger.

34

21 December

Sleigh Ride

"WHICH FITZPATRICK'S, MISS?" The taxicab driver looks at me in his rear-view mirror through the Perspex glass, his red Yankees baseball cap on backwards, slurping on the biggest cup of something from Dunkin' Donuts I've ever seen.

"Oh. There's two hotels?"

"Uh-huh. One on Lexington and one near Grand Central station, miss?" He struggles to set the cup between his legs as he clicks open Google Maps on his phone mounted to the dashboard.

"Oh, shit. Hang on?" Pulling my phone out of my leather bag, I open Adam's email. I read down. "Lexington Avenue," I say, acutely relieved that I know what I'm talking about even though I'm utterly clueless. I'm in New York on my own and I don't feel scared! I'm a woman-sized version of Kevin McCallister. I just feel like, crikey the world is a big place.

And your world is so small, that inner voice whispers.

Skyscrapers get nearer.

Towering.

My own life does feel very small.

Uninteresting.

But the radio blasts out "Sleigh Ride" and I sing along, looking out the window.

Christmas feels real!

My phone beeps, and I jump on it.

You pick up my case alright? A x

"And I'm fine thanks . . ." I mutter as I type back.

In the cab, both cases in the boot, on way to Fitzpatrick's, how is Freya???

Dots bounce.

Just bruised thank God – sorry am running – all over the place!

Oh thank goodness, I think. But poor Freya, I'll buy her something nice in Bloomingdales too.

Text me later? He adds two green love hearts.

What does that mean?

When is he coming?

Is he still coming?

Jesus, I think, this relationship is like a broken record!

Did you book your flight here yet? I press send but it remains undelivered and once again my excitement bubble bursts.

Pop.

Pop.

Poppidy pop.

35

21 December

Home for the Holidays

THE RED CANOPIES AND FLAGS ARE FLYING MERRILY as we pull up outside the hotel. I'm still like a deer in the headlights as I take in Manhattan. I hand over the two fifty-dollar bills in my possession, but the driver holds on to my change, his eyes on me the whole time.

"Plus six per cent toll, miss."

"Oh and tip!" I need to keep the price of a bottle of water until I find an ATM. "It's my first time, what's the going rate?"

"Twenty per cent, miss." He removes his cap and scratches his bald head.

"That's fine." And then he hands me back thirty dollars and jumps out to help me with the cases. I get the distinct impression that without a tip, he wouldn't budge. Fair enough. I stand outside Fitzpatrick's, on Lexington Avenue, and soak it all in like a sponge. The buildings, hustle and bustle, the Christmas lights, the deli's, the yellow cabs, the traffic lights up high, Wendy's, the flying flags. *I made it!* I think with a grin as the porter holds open the door for me and helps me inside.

"Welcome to Fitzpatrick's hotel," the smiling girl on reception, with the whitest teeth I've ever seen, greets me. She sits on a high-backed chair in her smart uniform behind a well-polished mahogany desk as I take a seat on the soft leather one facing her. Already this hotel feels like home away from home. I can feel it's Irishness.

"Hi there!" I give her the booking reference and the porter puts our cases on a shiny gold trolley. As she tip-taps away on her keyboard I look around. The lobby is cute and busy, with a small bar at the side. People come and go. It's festive décor minimal but stunningly classy. Garlands surround the lobby, decorated in tiny red bows and golden flaxen fairy lights. The reception hosts glass lanterns housing red and green holly and dozens of acorns.

"Oh, it's so Christmassy," I say out loud.

"Thank you. Alright. Here we are, so you are in our suite."

"Suite!" I'm gobsmacked.

"Yes, ma'am, Mr Adam Cooper has reserved a suite, is that correct?" She straightens up in her chair to see if anyone's behind me. I'm nearly sorry Adam isn't here because I know what look I'd see on her face. Jealousy. It never ceases to amuse me. My bad.

Now I'm fighting embarrassment. "Yes, I'm afraid he has to follow me out tomorrow, we'd a bit of a family emergency," I quickly explain, pathetically enjoying the idea she thinks we're a married couple.

"I understand, if we can assist you with anything during you stay with us, please don't hesitate to ask."

Taking my plastic key card, she points me to the lift and although I can't help but wonder, *How did I end up here on my own?* I know it's not his fault! These things happen. I'm dating a man with responsibilities. But still my head spins. I need a hot shower and some grub, and then I'll go surprise Jackie. I fire a quick text to Annemarie and to my parents.

Arrived safely, will text later. x

Then check if my earlier one to Adam was delivered.

It was, I see, and before I can react the lift pings and the gold door slowly opens back. The porter stands directly across at the door of the suite with the trolley. I step out and read his name badge, JP.

"Thanks a million, JP."

He opens the door for me with a tap of his card and flash of a green light. I step inside our suite. The cream carpet is soft, cushioned beneath my feet and the first thing I see is the big super-king bed with a soft, light-red leather headboard and a deep red throw over the starched white sheets. A long window welcomes me over to the view as New York City sprawls below me. My heart explodes at the view. There's a smart dining area and in the spacious bathroom a sunken bathtub I can't wait to dip into, feck the shower, I'm taking a soak! JP watches me amused as he leaves the cases by the wardrobe. Then it hits me!

"JP, shit! Tip! I'm really sorry, I have to get used to this." Again I rummage.

"That's up to you, ma'am, if you like you can tip me at the end of your stay?"

"Oh? Would that be okay? That'd be better for me and I promise we will tip you properly!" I say as he tips his badge.

"If I'm not here on check-out, you can leave your gratuity at reception for me. Again, my name is JP. You have a good day."

The heavy door clicks closed behind him. Suddenly I feel very alone, again. My feeling are like a rollercoaster, I'm that up and down. I take a slow, deep breath.

"Well, well, well Lexie Byrne, here you are, New York City," I shout out loud now, throwing myself on top of the beautiful bed. "And just think, in a few hours Adam will be here."

I look up at the ceiling, kick off my ankle boots. The room fills with silence. It feels too big for me alone.

Then I whisper to myself:

"But you are alone."

I lie down on the bed, put my palm under my cheek and turn on the pillow to look out the window, across the New York skyline.

"He has to put his family first," I tell no one.

Below, the New York traffic honks and hollers. It doesn't do enough to drown out the deafening silence that answers me.

"Still, it's not easy being on the outside."

A heavy dark cloud floats past above.

"But you always knew that," I whisper.

The cloud covers the afternoon winter sun. I sit up suddenly. I swing my legs over the side of the bed. Walk across the room. This time I talk loudly, directly into the mirror mounted on the wall in front of me.

"But I don't think you really did until this exact moment. You can never trust the plans you make with him, or the hopes you have for the future. He can't give me all of him. It's not his fault. It's just how it is. But Annemarie is right. I think I need more now. I'm not sure this is enough for me. Or fair on me." I rub the condensation with the palm of my hand where my breath has fogged the mirror. Then I pull off my socks and pad across the carpet to the bathroom for a long soak.

It's time to put Lexie first again.

36

21 December

Christmas Lights

I HEAR JACKIE MILEY BEFORE I SEE HER. Peeking out from behind the large pillar, I see her leaning on the faux marble bar top. I'm in better spirits. I've had a long soak, scrubbed myself with delightful-smelling free hotel mini bottles, put on clean jeans and a cotton shirt, and I ordered a cheeseburger and chips to the suite. Adam still hasn't read my WhatsApp and I told Annemarie how I was feeling in a lengthy, truthful phone call, and this time she was far sweeter, understanding and caring. We are back on track at last! That's the most important thing.

"I'm sure he's caught up at the hospital, and remember what that coverage was like when I was taken in after I had Ben? Sketchy at best. I've no doubt he will be there tomorrow, love. You can talk to him about how you feel then. Sort it all out. Just be honest. You deserve to know his intentions at the very least. It's been two years, I think you've been patient enough and I don't mean wedding bells, I just mean sharing a life."

I lay back in the bubbles. "Thanks, I feel terrible for feeling so sorry for myself, what a cow."

"Not at all, you care a lot for Freya, it's not that . . . That isn't how you roll, you put everyone before you all the time."

"Annemarie, I am so embarrassed and sorry about saying I didn't want your life . . ."

"What about me being an anxiety-ridden wagon?" She laughed.

"That too."

"No, I needed to hear it."

"Ah not like that."

"I started it, I got on your case about Adam. I was drunk, you were right, I threw up when I got home. And you know what, Tom agreed with you, I need to butt the hell out and let you live your own life. I just love you so much and I'm so lucky to have you—"

"Oh and me too, I'd be lost without you and I appreciate the concern, I truly do." I sat up in the bath, pulled the plug.

"Now go have some craic with Jackie . . ."

"Annemarie?"

"Hm?"

"I won't do all the things that are on our bucket list – here I mean, in New York. They are the things I want to do with you."

The line was quiet as the water whooshed out.

"Really?"

"Promise."

"No freshly squeezed orange juice on top of the Empire State Building?"

"No."

"No New Yorker afternoon tea at the Plaza hotel?"

"No."

"No Tavern Burgers at Tavern on the Green in Central Park?"

"No."

"No fake designer bags from Canal Street?"

"No."

"No *Phantom of the Opera* on Broadway, hanging around the stage door after?"

"No."

"No late night cocktails on the roof top of Beast & Butterflies at the M hotel on Times Square?"

"No." I step out of the sunken bath.

"No Bloomingdales?" She gasps.

"Oh I'm doing Bloomingdales!" I wrap the luxurious white fluffy towel around me. "I must. Even if it's just to hand you the Big Brown Bag bag with something small in it."

"You don't have to do all that for me," her voice breaks.

"I know—"

"Please just enjoy New York, don't think about me."

"But I want to."

"I'll get it together . . . Get myself together." Somewhere far away from me, her voice wobbles. "It would mean the world to me for us to go together . . . what we've always planned."

"Maybe in the summer? When Silverside centre closes for the annual painting job? Three days?"

She said nothing for a while. Then:

"And Lexie, just tell Adam that a girl needs more security, that's all it is. He needs to know it's harder for you . . ."

"I will."

"When you see Jackie, tell her I said hi."

"Will do."

"Tell her Mark O' Donoghue is going to hit her up next month, he's over then."

"Lucky her." I only half joke; Mark was very kind to me at the end of the night.

And there she is. Chatting animatedly to an older man in a poncho who is sat up at the bar nursing an amber whiskey glass between his hands. In the corner a traditional Irish band are setting up. There's sawdust on the floor, resting on top of it are bodhrans, fiddles, tin whistles, guitar cases and a drum set with a huge shamrock painted on the front of the kit. Otherwise this bar is quiet at this time of the early evening, just a few student types scattered about, reading or on MacBooks or with AirPods inserted, no doubt far away in some podcast world. I lean my head around.

". . . so ya don't spend all yer earnings in here Mick . . . Maybe ya bring some home? Wha'? It's not rocket science! I don't want Kathleen back in here ranting and raving that I'm serving a drunk!"

A huge smile erupts on my face at the very sound of her voice. I realise just how much I've missed her. I tiptoe across the sawdust and watch her for another moment behind one of the many exposed red brick pillars that are mounted everywhere in the N17, wrapped in Christmas tinsel and fairy lights. Jackie's wearing black dungarees, with a skin-tight long-sleeved white T-shirt underneath. Her hair is kind of a peroxide blonde shade, piled up on her head in a messy bun that somehow looks perfect on her. Her pixie cut is well grown out now. She is just ridiculously pretty and full of self-confidence.

Her head moves and I jerk mine back behind the pillar, almost pulling the red tinsel off. I settle it and put my hand over my mouth to stifle a giggle. I wait a few moments before I peek back around; she's now facing toward the curved window, her back to me. Yellow cabs spin by one after the other. I step out, click the top button open of the high neck on my leather jacket. Lift my wide-leg jeans so the damp ends don't gather sawdust. She's completely oblivious as she wipes the countertop with a white cloth, a tea towel of the American flag slung over her shoulder. The curve of the window frames the frantic pace of Christmas in Manhattan.

See Adam has me pegged, I just realise. I absolutely love surprises, I realise once again as I make my move. I step out.

"A gin and orange, a lemon squash and a Scotch and water please!" I shout out mine and Jackie's favourite saying, from Mr Wareing, a disgruntled guest in the famous *Fawlty Towers* episode.

"Who the – what the fuck-a-duck?" Jackie spins around, clutching her heart. The tea towel flutters to her chest area and she grabs it. For a nanosecond, she looks like she's seen a ghost then her eyes glint, she slaps down the tea towel on the counter with force, runs towards me and just as Basil Fawlty does in the famous episode, she grabs me and frog marches me out the door!

Outside it's bitterly cold but we don't feel it as we try catch our breaths. My legs are actually crossed and we are howling, laughing on the bustling Manhattan street. Jackie's actually crying she's laughing so hard, we're both doubled over.

"Stop it! Oh Jesus, Lexie Byrne, me stomach hurts, hun . . . ya mad yolk!" She wipes her heavily kohl-lined, baby blue eyes.

"Oh stop, so does mine," I can't even straighten up yet. I have to hold my cheeks to stop the painful ache.

"Get off the sidewalk, bitches!" a woman yells as she passes around us with her miniature dog in snow boots. I freeze.

"Shut yer hole!" Jackie shouts after her. "Never see two old friends laughing, ya miserable aul biddy? Don't mind her, hun." She leans her hands on my two shoulders. "Now, not sure how me knickers are still dry but what the actual mother of all fuckers are ya doin' in my bar, Byrne?!"

"Long story." I heave. "God, I needed that laugh." In fact I can physically feel the stress releasing, my shoulders drop, I rotate my neck.

"Lexie Byrne, that was the best thing ever! Seriously, fuckin' brilliant, hun. I really am nearly after pissing meself, though."

Jackie holds her ribs, winks at me, wraps her arms around me again.

"Oh, it's so good to see you!" I wipe my eyes.

"Here, let's go inside, me nipples are bleedin' freezin'!" She rubs her boobs with both hands and jumps up and down. "I can never get used to the nipple cold here after bein' out in Dubai."

"After you," I say as she holds open the old wooden door by the harp-shaped brass handle, and we go back inside. Despite the daytime smell of a pub lingering with toilet bleach and sweat, the warmth is welcoming.

"I'm nearly lost for words and ya know me, that'd be a first – bu' serio, what are ya doing here and why in the fuck-duckin' hell didn't ya tell me you were comin'?" Jackie pulls herself up on a high stool at a high round table, pats the other stool for me to sit. I take off my jacket and bag, drape them on the stool.

"Jackie? There's a customer?" A heavily accented New York voice travels across the bar.

"Gimme ten minutes, Mick, can ya jump in behind? One of me best pals is over from Dublin!" she calls over to the man sitting at the bar who she was talking to when I came in.

"Me boss." She shakes her messy bun in his direction, pulls a vape pen from her back pocket, inhales, pulls her white top free from her neck and exhales the vape down it.

"Oh. I though he was a customer."

"He is." She laughs with her head back up now. She picks up a little black square N17 napkin from the wooden box on the table, unfolds one and blows her nose. "The best one unfortunately, on his days off."

"I see." I grimace as we both turn to see Mick now behind the bar, a glass up to the optic, pouring himself something from a clear bottle.

191

"He's a lovely man, but he's too fond of the jar . . . bit like me before I came here." But before I can comment she continues, "So come on? Spill! What are ya doin' here?" She throws her hands out wide. "And look at ya? Ridey as always! Ya look brilliant, Lexie!"

"Dunno 'bout that . . ." I pull at the skin under my eyes.

"Them natural lips of yours that look done, I can never get over. I caved, got a little bit done—" Jackie shoves her index finger into her top lip. "—in Dubai, but didn't like it. I looked like I'd had a bang of a baseball bat to me lip. One of me mates said I looked like I'd food stuck in it."

Laughing, I take her hands in mine.

"Jackie, you're so beautiful you don't need anything."

"Ahh hun, thanks. I miss ya, miss Dublin and everyone in Silverside, like ya wouldn't believe. But I love it here, it's given me everything I've been searchin' for, I can't tell ya. How long are ya stayin'?"

"Just three days."

"Here, sorry, me bleedin' manners! Drink?"

"No, I'm okay actually . . ."

"Are ye here on yer Tobler? On your Toblerone? On yer own?" she quizzes, and I can see her head starting to work out the logistics and the possible reasons. Just the mention of the word *Toblerone* brings Adam to my head and our Duty-Free shopping for Freya.

"Yeah. Well . . . for tonight anyway, I think."

"When did ya get here?"

"Few hours ago." I stifle a yawn.

"Oh, righ'." Jackie crosses her arms, looks at me straight in the eye, tilts her head to the right.

"Yeah."

"Are ya havin' a breakdown, hun?" Typical Jackie: she does not beat around the bush.

"No."

"A break-up?" Tilts her head to the left.

I watch the band sound check, *one-two, one-two*, while I consider that question. "No." I know I don't sound convincing with the inflection in my voice.

"A boob job? Them C cups of yours are grand!"

"No! I'm not having a boob job."

"Tummy tuck?"

Now I'm insulted.

"No!" I suck in.

"Will I mind me own business so?" She uncrosses her arms, pulls the strands of hair that hang, crosses her legs.

"No, I'll fill you in . . . but it's nothing bad, I'm just tired I think, and don't want to waste time moaning, I wanna catch up with you!"

"Sure yer up early, long flight, I know meself."

"It's so good to see you." I can't help beaming across at her. Jackie is pure gold.

"Lemme get us two hot chocolates, hun, yeah?"

"That actually sounds lovely," I say as Jackie hops down, pushes her high stool back in and jogs back to get the drinks. My hand goes straight into my bag on the back of the stool and I check my phone. It's two in the morning now in the UK and I haven't heard a word from Adam since I was in the taxi from the airport to the hotel. I'm assuming he's arriving tomorrow. But who knows?

"When you assume, you make and ass out of you and me," I mutter to myself, my mother's favourite saying, as the lead singer soundchecks into the mic.

"One two, one two," the red-headed guy in the band says. He adjusts the mic in the stand, pulling it up higher. Two earpieces hang around his neck. "One two, one two, one two."

He gives a thumbs up now, and pushes the earpieces into his ears.

"Oh Grace just hold me in your arms and let this moment linger . . ." His sweet voice echoes around the bar. So sweet. So melodic. I wasn't expecting it. A shiver shoots up my spine.

"Extra cream? Crushed Oreos?" Jackie roars over him. I shake my head to both, too embarrassed to shout back "yes please to both" because of the weird lump forming in the back of my throat.

"With all my love, I place this wedding ring upon your finger,
There won't be time to share our love for we must say goodbye."
The music soars.

I'm not sure if it's the jet lag, the patriotism, the sentiment of the untimely, vicious dying love between Grace Gifford and Joseph Mary Plunkett, but completely out of character for me, I burst into sobbing, flowing tears.

37

21 December

Silent Night

"**A**H, HUN! WHAT THE FUCKIDY FUCK'S HAPPENED? I knew there was sometin' up with ya!" Jackie's over to me like a flash with a tray of hot chocolates and mince pies dusted with caster sugar. I'm mortified. I look down at the sawdust, wishing it could swallow me up.

"Nothing." I sniff.

"Nothin', me hole." She sets the tray down, grabs a few of the little square napkins, hands them over to me.

"It's yer man Adam, isn't it?"

I nod, try to stop the sobs. This is ridiculous.

"He dump ya?"

I shake my head 'cause I can't stop the heaving.

"Is he ridin' someone else?"

I shake my head, blow my nose.

"Not that I know of." Stuff the tattered napkin up my sleeve.

"Ya seen him on Tinder?"

"No."

"Gay?"

195

"No, definitely not gay." I manage a snotty laugh.

"Right, I'm headin' home an hour early and your comin' with me. I'm due out at half eight for me class but Mick can manage until Sharon arrives, I'll call her to get her arse in early. I filled in for her after her divorce party across in Brooklyn last week. She owes me one. Gimme two minutes till I call her, fling yer leather on, hun . . . We'll fix ya, don't worry about dat. Jackie Miley knows all the tricks. And ya know what dey say about men, don't ya?"

I shake my head, scoop my hair back into a low ponytail.

"Be as picky with your men as you are with your selfies." She winks at me.

"Honestly, I'm overreacting, I have no idea where that outburst came from! I'm so embarrassed!" I'm more composed now. "Think it was the song and the jet lag, I just felt very emotional."

"Hang on, hun." Jackie jogs back behind the bar again, this time picks up the phone receiver that's mounted on the wall. I can't believe I've just done this to her. I did not want to burden her with my problems. She clasps the phone under her neck and ear as she taps away on a computer. She hangs up, says something to Mick, who looks over at me and waves. I wave back, stand up and zip up my leather, click the top button closed.

"Righ', she'll be here in a minute, Mick can hold the fort. Let's go chat, hun." Jackie links her arm through mine.

*

I'd heard New York City was cold at Christmas, but this is a different level of cold. It's absolutely bloody Baltic! My nose starts to run like a tap as I reach for one of the fresh napkins I put in my back pocket. I pull the collar up tighter on my neck as we wait for the lights to change outside the N17 bar. Even the different crossing signals excite me; everything here is so new and magical, it's just the distraction I need to pull myself together.

"I'm just up off 56th – it's so handy to the bar job and my classes. It's a grand spot, I got really lucky, as I was tellin' ya on WhatsApp."

"Oh that girl, Portia?" I recall.

"Yea, it's a sub-let. Portia, the one I was tellin' ya about, she actually owns it, or as I say *Pour-Cha* . . . She's a jammy bitch, a millionaire's daughter, her da sells yachts! Wot! Wot! Yacht! Yacht!"

I laugh, our arms entwined as I snuggle closer into her for body heat.

"Imagine dat? My da sold fish from the stinking boot of his ancient rusty Ford Fiesta! We're nearly the same, but, righ'? Six degrees of separation between the fish and the boat, amn't I righ', hun?"

"That's what they say."

"And anyways, fuckin' nightmare for me since last night. Pour-cha came in and told me she was going to the Cayman Islands until June to find herself, and unless I can find someone else to sub-let with me for the next six months, I'm out on my ear. No one wants six months sub-let."

"Oh no, really? I'm sure loads do?"

"Well there's another problem, and I will really be in trouble, because I can only afford to do my classes because I have this place so cheap. You do not want to see the last hovel I lived in."

"What's the other problem?"

"Lady Woof Woof." She shake her head.

"Huh?"

"Problem is, I need to find someone who's in New York for six months and who isn't scared of bulldogs!"

"Huh?" I say again.

"That's Pour-cha's dog, Lady Woof Woof, she's a bulldog! She's at her step-dad's in the Hampton's at the minute, Pour-cha's ex – they have shared custody! Listen, the lives of the rich, don't even ask! Anyway she'll be back tomorrow and she's part of my deal: I take care of her, feed her, clean up her shit, but she has a dog walker that comes in twice a day too; trips to the nail salon, she eats fillet minion, but she's temperamental bitch to say the least."

"Aren't we all? Try the colleges?" I suggest.

"I have, pinned notices everywhere, seems no one wants to live with a bulldog."

Jackie pulls up the hood on her coat, it's covered in white fur so her face all but disappears. It's like talking to E.T. The lights change and what sounds like machine gunfire rattles the signal and we cross. I jump every time a horn sounds, which seems to be every ten seconds.

"Relax the cacks, hun!" she tells me. "Your pot herbs are gone."

"My?"

"Nerves . . ."

"Ah, it's just so loud," I say.

"Isn't it bu'? Loud and lively and real." Jackie stops, so I stop. People push past. So many people. A young guy hands me a flyer as Jackie shadow punches.

"Doesn't this city make you feel alive, Lexie? Like really alive?" She takes a long breath in through her nose and the cold air rises with it as she exhales. "Like 'ere ya can do any'tin'."

"You know, it *does* make me feel alive." We walk on. Skateboarders rumble past us, wheels spinning noisily, and people hand me more flyers every two steps.

"Why are ya takin' dem?" She refers to the mounting pile of flyers in my cold blue hand.

"Well they're handin' them to me." I shrug.

"Bu' just say no."

"Right."

"It's okay to say no!"

"Right."

"You in particular never say no, you certainly never complain, you don't even like to be thanked, for fuck's sake."

"It sounds stupid when I hear you say it out loud, but you're right."

"I know I am. Remember the room we had in that hotel for Annemarie's hen in Wales?"

"Will I ever forget." I grimace.

"It smelled of wee, had stains all over the wall and you wouldn't complain."

"*You* did." I remember Jackie at the desk kicking up a massive fuss that her room had a broken shower and a window that wouldn't open at all.

"I did, and I got a new room. But you said nothin' and went out and bought a load of Glade plug-in air fresheners at your own expense."

I actually laugh at my stupidity.

"See? That's what this city has taught me. Look at me, hun?" She stops abruptly again, this time in front of a Pret-A-Manger. The aroma of coffee beans permeates the cold evening air and in the window display Mrs Claus is drinking coffee. I watch her electronic arm raising the paper cup to her lips and back down again in a fluid motion.

"I'm looking."

"Yer not! Yer lookin' at Mrs Claus. I always wonder what her name is? I mean we know he husband's name is Santa? What's her name?"

"Dunno." I'm hypnotised by her red and white dress, her small gold round glasses, her rosy cheeks and smiling face.

"Helloooooo?" Jackie waves her hand in front of my face.

I focus on her. "Sorry, it's the realistic arm movements."

"Who was I at home?"

"Em, Jackie Miley."

"That's right. D'ya know who I am here?"

Christmas shoppers and commuters bustle past, some talking loudly on through their Bluetooth earphones. I don't know how to answer her because I know she sometimes felt inadequate or lesser than when she worked with me. Oh, not because of our job but because she came from the inner city, her mother had a problem with alcohol and her dad worked hard to bring her and her four brothers up. Jackie had a Northside Dublin paper-round at fourteen and she had to use a fake ID to get it. She didn't get to finish school because the household needed money.

"I'm Jackie Murphy-Miley. I'm someone else. Isn't that deadly? C'mon!" She links me again but keeps talking. "You need to explore the world, hun. I see meself in you when I was workin' in Silverside. It took a lot for me to brave the leap to Dubai, and in fairness it was Annemarie who told me to go for it. It wasn't the place for me, but all risks lead to somewhere else, righ'? If I hadn't gone to Dubai, I'd never have met Aonghus in McGettigan's Irish bar out there and he'd never have told me about Pour-cha and the house and the N17 job. It was all meant to be – here, turn onto 59th street, hun."

We turn onto a different block. I honestly feel like I'm in a movie because there it is – Bloomingdales!

"Oh my God! Look." I stop, point to it, stare at it, can't believe I'm inches from it.

"Ya wanna pop in?"

"Do I!"

I actually gasp as I walk up to the famous flagship shop front on the Upper East Side, all lit up for Christmas. The top half of the brown building is completely covered in thousands of tiny fairy lights, and three red circular wreaths light up the doorway. As yellow cabs pull up outside, I enter through one of the many doors side by side and gasp again as my feet find the famous black and white chequered flooring, makeup after makeup counter girls smile at me.

"Would you like to try . . ."

"Can I ask, have you tried . . ."

"Welcome to Bloomingdales, have you tried . . ."

"What are ya after?" Jackie pulls me past the perfume bottles in the girls' outstretched hands, scrolling through her phone, oblivious to my delirium. I wave my hand in apology to the counter assistants.

"Mainly just two Biggest Brown Bag bags for me and Anne-marie to carry around Silverside. I haven't much money for shopping. This time!"

"Well there's nine floors, hun, all chock-full of designer clothes, beauty, home décor, shoes and handbags . . . and you just want two brown paper bags? I dunno, maybe socks?" Jackie tries.

"Perfect!"

Jackie Googles the floor, and we take the elevators up. I'm speechless with the moment, then I find my words:

"I just can't wait to get back here with Annemarie and do it all properly." I tell Jackie as we step off the elevator. Another floor to beat the last in its stunning Christmas decorations.

"You mean Adam?" Jackie probes.

I think. "No I mean Annemarie."

I buy us both a pair of Happy Socks. The cheapest socks they stock. Only eighteen dollars each. They are the Watercolour Friends style. Pink toes, blue spots, yellow hearts and two little girls holding hands.

"May I get two bags?" I ask the friendly counter assistant.

"Absolutely? Gifts?" she enquires.

"Yes."

"Well let me wrap them, ma'am."

"Oh for fuck's sake," Jackie warbles under her breath, her back turned on the counter, as she checks her watch. I watch in awe as the sales assistant wraps them individually in delicate red tissue paper, seals them with a circular Bloomingdale's sticker and pops each of them into a coveted Big Brown Bag bag.

"Are ya ready? We're running outta time for a bite and a chat."

"Oh – sorry, okay." I didn't realise she was under time pressure, I hoped we could hang out all night. "Let's go."

"As I was sayin'," Jackie picks up right where we left off as I swing my bags by the paper handles. "Life isn't all about eight hours sleep every night. Eating smashed avocados, drinking gallons of bottled water, popping this vitamin and that vitamin, hot yoga and avoiding the craic . . ."

"Who avoids the craic?" I won't let that one go!

"Everyone these days." Jackie stops, juts her bottom lip out and does a little foot stepping on the spot dance. "Oh noooo . . . I can't have a glass of wine on a Monday night, it's bad for me, worse for women then for men of course . . . and oh no, I can't stay out late at night – it's dangerous and bad for me . . . and oh noooooo I can't take a toke on that joint because it's bad for me . . . and oh no I'm not married with a baby and I'm forty and now no one will want me." She makes two fists and pretends to rub her eyes. "Boo fucking hoo to them all, they aren't livin', hun. The ones who THINK they're gonna live life for the longest, joggin' an' liftin' weights, eatin' like Popeye, sweatin' buckets until they feel like their hearts might explode in their chests, they aren't living at all, and that's the sad part."

She links with me again and we turn yet another corner.

"Don't get me started on wellness. I despise that fuckin' word. Wellness is makin' people sick! All this abject fear of not being healthy, it's so unhealthy!"

"I agree, everyone's listening to some expert or another, right?" I add.

"Exactly, and it's all bullshit, Lexie."

"Ah, try telling Annemarie!"

"She still Googling every little thing?"

"Yup."

"My granny was a hundred and one. She never exercised – well, she walked to the shops cos she'd no other way of bleedin' gettin' there! She ate buckets of salt on her meat and mounds of butter on her potatoes, drank a brandy or two every night, lived her life her own way. Live life your way, Lexie."

She steers me around yet another corner and I actually see the famous smoky steam coming up from the underground.

"Look!" I say, giddy with excitement, rummaging for my phone. "Get me with the steam! I have to. Oh my God, this is unreal! It's an iconic New York pic. Annemarie will freak!"

I pose with a jut of my hip and Jackie clicks off a few, laughing at me. I take a swipe into my messages before I put the phone away to see if Adam's been in touch.

But this time I don't expect to see any messages.

And I'm right.

38

21 December

Bells Are Ringing

"COME ON!" JACKIE SHAKES HER HEAD as I stand transfixed by the silver plaque of Studio 54.

"Studio 54, Jackie! I don't believe it."

"It's upstairs at the old studio . . . it's cool but a small bar above what used to be the famous nightclub. No wild parties anymore."

"I don't care, I'm standing here where it once all happened. Think who walked on this very spot I'm on to pass through the doors? Diana Ross, Jacqueline Kennedy Onassis, Cher, Truman Capote, Andy Warhol! History, what an adventure it must have been."

"I know. It's true but life should be your own adventure! Some people just don't get that? Blows my mind, hun. It was why I wanted to leave Dublin in the first place! Ireland has become such a do-gooder. Too much of, 'don't do this' and 'you can't do that' and 'you really shouldn't' – pretty much everything that's any way enjoyable is bad for ya. I don't give a shite how many Dry January's you do or how many friggin' vegan dinners ya inject, how many juices you drink, you're still gonna die, hun."

"Charming." But I laugh and we move on, trudge the streets.

"You agree with me though, right? And why is it, do you think, it's always women who suffer the most from the world's propaganda? We're always on diets or secretly dyin' our grey hair or being persecuted and bullied into looking younger. Because we think men and romance validates us. BULL-SHIT! Turn."

We turn down another street, onto another block, and I walk with my head in the air – gasping again at the height of the skyscrapers that surround me. Hundreds of glass windows in steel that stretch up for miles and miles – reaching high into the jagged New York skyline. People rush into buildings, hail cabs, cars crawl along bumper to bumper, and I'm the happiest tourist in the world just watching it all. All this life, all this anonymity. The buildings are stunning, all browns and grey, some pointed, some flat, some smaller, some taller. Traffic lights seems to start every couple of feet. Pedestrian crossings like piano keys go on as far as my eye can see. There's a Prada store, Elizabeth Arden, Victoria Secret, Michael Kors, so many beautiful shop fronts. It's like I'm on a movie set everywhere I look.

Then some kind of flashing makes me look down and straight ahead. This time I really am in a dream. I blink, blinded by the lights. *Times Square.* Towering advertisements flash is the brightest colours I've ever seen. Reds. Greens. Oranges. Pinks. Yellows. People rush by. Christmas songs play from every shop doorway.

Jackie sees my wonder. Has she walked me this way on purpose?

"See? Life. And it's for living, Lexie, this isn't a rehearsal. Today might be your last day. Make *yourself* happy! That's what I've learned, and all this—" Jackie waves her hand. "—New York has taught me that in more ways than one. You get one shot at this. Grab what you enjoy, while you can."

Her words ring around my head as I look up in wonder and pure joy. Am I putting all my eggs in Adam's basket? Should I be relying on Adam to make me happy? Shouldn't he just be a *part* of my happiness?

"You'll be back, really explore it, but gotta keep moving."

I'm reminded of that girl again, the one in the Brazen Head who was going to sit but was too afraid to take the weight off her feet or she'd never get back up. Who gave me her table in Marco's because I'd been nice to her. What goes around comes around. I feel like I am supposed to be here, in New York, walking into Times Square. Like I wished it so hard it came true. Like I deserve this moment. Turning my head, I take in the familiar yet unfamiliar sight. Like a virtual reality. So much to do and see and sell on every flashing board. Jackie moves me on, steers me across the busy road, where a queue for pretzels and hot dogs snakes away from a small van and a man serves people with a whistle.

"Doesn't this city just make you feel like you can do anything in life? No closing times, not like Dublin. No gossiping, it's too big; New York welcomes everyone and anyone. You're starving at three in the mornin'? No problem, there's always a burger cookin', waitin' for ya, hun."

"Look at it!" I point to another Irish bar, O' Shea's. She ignores me. What is it about being in another country and seeing your own flag above a public house that makes you so giddy?

"People here all have the same chance as everyone else of doing exactly what they want."

"Well you could've worked in any bar back home?" I say but with a sure feeling that something is coming.

I know why none of this has been said over WhatsApp voice memos, the real reason she opened this conversation while walking. I know Jackie Miley well enough, more than eight years now, and some of our most honest, most important chats have been while walking to and from Silverside shopping centre.

She likes to walk and talk. It's how she feels most comfortable communicating.

"I coulda, but the job is only a means to an end. Lexie?"

"Yeah?"

"I wanna be an actress."

"Stop!" I exclaim.

And we do. Again. On the edge of this sidewalk on a side street that's now much quieter. The honking seems further away. Just a lone man pushing a shopping trolley full to the brim with what looks like traffic cones and old rolled-up carpet, making noise as he approaches, the mini-wheels screeching, and then he passes.

"Serio . . . It's all I've ever wanted to be, honest, hun." She back heels the curb in her cowboy boots.

"You've never said?"

"No. Cos ya know what people are like back home, they'd have ripped the absolute piss outta me, sayin' I just wanted to be famous and all that shite and that is not what I want. Plus there were no opportunities for someone like me. It's the same heads on Irish TV every show they make, for fuck's sake! But I want to be on stage. You can't dream big workin' behind information in a shopping centre in Dublin. Once me brothers all had jobs, I knew I had to give it a shot. I saved enough out in Dubai to get here and pay for my acting classes."

"Oh I was wondering what classes you were on about."

"I'm an acting student, Lexie." She positively beams at me.

"I think you'd be brilliant." And I mean it, I really do.

"Oh I am! I started the night course on my three nights off with Mick Mellamphy, he's the artistic director at Origin Theatre Company, and he says I'm really fuckin' good Lexie! Like when I'm doing it . . . acting . . . I just feel so at home, like it's where I'm meant to be." Jackie's blue eyes shine.

"I can totally see you as an actor."

207

"Actress!"

"Oh! I thought it was all PC to say actor?" I smooth out my fringe with the palm of my hand. The PC world terrifies me. I'm always afraid I'll say something wrong.

"No, an actor is a man! The patriarchy has taken enough from us, they aren't taking that word too. I am an *actress*."

"Fair enough," I say.

"So go on then?" We walk on, arms linked again.

"What?"

"I've spilled, so you spill?"

"What do you mean?"

"Lexie, you hate getting the bus home on your own! There is no chance you flew to New York on your Tobler without very good reason!"

"Adam was supposed to be with me."

"I was afraid that was the case . . . And why isn't he here?"

"Freya? I've told you about her, his daughter? Well she fell off her pony just as we were about to board, so he had to head back . . ."

"Obviously," Jackie tells me.

"Right, I know . . . but I was still . . . hurt . . . I know that's selfish . . ."

"It's not at all, bu' why did ya come on yer own?"

"His case was – I mean our bags were on the flight and look, he'll be here tomorrow? I didn't tell you I'd be here as I had no idea until last night! He surprised me and I was so flustered with looking for my passport and packing, I forgot, to be honest. We only have two nights now . . ."

"He's comin' all this way for two nights?"

"Yeah."

Jackie puts her hand on my shoulder as we stop outside an old brownstone house. Stone steps run up to the large double casement windows as Jackie zips down her coat, puts her hand down her white top under her dungarees and pulls out a long blue string. Attached to it is a key. We walk up the steps.

"I feel like Carrie Bradshaw!" I heave.

"She should be so lucky! I'm gonna open a half bottle of wine, make us a cheese, ham, tomato, onion toastie on rye and you tell me all about it, hun, yeah?" She checks her watch.

"Well at least let me go to the shop and buy some things? Some wine? Some chocolates?"

"I will in me hole! You're my guest, I'm only delighted to see you. My home is your home. My cheese is your cheese, and my wine is your wine, cos ya know why?"

"Why?" I have to swallow another lump. My emotions are all over the place, what is wrong with me?

"Cos you'd do the same for me."

"Thanks, Jackie," I blurt as we stop at the door, never more grateful for a true friend in my entire life.

39

21 December

Christmas Island

JACKIE DID HER HOME A DISSERVICE by calling it a "place". It's an out-of-this-world New York brownstone! All high beams and minimalist furniture. Like something you might see on a design show. Old leather armchairs, mahogany as far as the eye can see. Scattered books on small glass tables, with bent iron reading lamps. I can see why she wants to get that lodger asap so she can stay – I wouldn't want to move out of here either. Ever.

As I walk around in awe, my phone beeps. Six new messages. I start. With shaking hands I scan through them – they are all from Annemarie. All worried about me, in fairness to her. I fire her back a reply on WhatsApp that I'm fine and with Jackie, but the circle turns and it won't deliver.

"Have you Wi-Fi?" I call after her as I follow her into the kitchen. Jackie shakes the copper kettle and fills it with water, places it on an old black Aga that takes up half the space. Copper pots and pans of all shapes and sizes sway above her head.

"Jackie loves life, all uppercase, no spaces."

"Cheers." Now the shock of seeing all those notifications has passed, I can't help wondering why the hell Adam hasn't texted me.

"Did ya listen to my voicemail? Damien Dempsey was in! Sit down on a stool there at the kitchen table, take a load off, as they say in America." She points to the only two stools that sit around an old beer barrel with a thick glass top that I'm assuming is the kitchen table.

"Sorry, I did, I meant to text you back. Was he nice?"

"Legend."

Jackie busies herself rattling presses and cutlery drawers and popping bread in the toaster. I know I shouldn't but I input the Wi-Fi and go straight into Adam's WhatsApp so I can see when he was last online and if he's read my message.

"What the—?" He was online half an hour ago, why hasn't he messaged me?

"You take butter, don't ya?"

"Little bit, please," I say as I feel something odd on my ankle, where my skin sits between boot and trouser leg.

"What the—?" I look down and see this squashed-up, snuffley face looking back at me. "Shit! Jackie!" I haul my feet up, wrap my arms around them.

"Lady Woof Woof! No!" Jackie clicks her tongue, and the little dog scarpers.

"I thought she was away?" I tense.

"She must have been dropped back, that means her minder will be here soon. I'm actually very fond of her." Jackie clicks again and the small, dumpy dog pads over to her.

"There she is . . . my little Woof Woof, don't tell but here ya go." She dangles a piece of ham, and the little dog goes up on her hind legs and takes it as Jackie picks up a note on the counter. "Aha, her dog walker will be here at nine." Jackie goes back to preparing our food and I stare at my phone, willing it to beep. It doesn't. Just as I'm about to ask Adam why he hasn't texted me at all, Jackie returns, now barefoot, balancing two plates expertly over each inner arm.

"Get that intaya Cynthia!" And she hands me across the most delicious-looking, crusty, cheesy ham and onion toastie on rye bread I've ever seen, and suddenly I'm ravenous.

"Mayo?"

"No, Dublin."

We're that in-tune we hock out a timely laugh that doesn't deserve much more than a groan.

"But. Yes! Please." She pads over the maple floors to the press, returning with mayo, mustard, ketchup and salt. "Now, I've a bottle of red and I've half a white, I think. I've definitely beer and pretty sure I've vodka?"

"Oh, I'd love a glass of red, Jackie, thank you." Off she goes again to the gold-plated cool-drinks trolley in the spacious hallway under the painting of the Statue of Liberty, wine glasses hanging off it. She uncorks a bottle and lifts up two crystal glasses.

"The perks of the rich, eh?"

"Oh my God, this is soooooo bloody good!" Rudely, I haven't waited, as I pull at the string of white melted cheese off my chin, the ham doorstep tangy with a mustard seasoning and the onion finely chopped. I accept the glass, noticing mine is almost full to the brim and hers a rather small measure.

"I know right? Pour-cha still has her shopping delivered! I know it's mental . . ."

I resist but again Adam hits my memory.

". . . but she told me to just use it all up, less hassle than cancelling her standing order, so she says. By all accounts she went sailing for a month, around the coast of Italy, they did *The Talented Mr Ripley* sailing tour for the rich! So I basically eat an' drink for free, all me money goes on the rent, acting lessons and headshots."

"Oh I'd love to see your headshots?" I say through a mouthful of toastie. "Mmmmm . . . Oh this a good vintage!" I sip the wine, swirl the glass.

"Where are ya stayin' again?"

"Fitzpatrick's."

She nods bites into hers. "Which one?"

"Manhattan."

"So will I see ya again before ya head back?" she chews.

"I hope so, we'll drop by to say hi either tomorrow or the next morning, I'm sure?"

"Yiz don't have to? It's a flying visit."

"I'll try," I wipe my mouth with the linen napkin, kick off my own boots.

"So then . . . what's the real problem, hun?" Typical Jackie: enough of the small talk.

"Well, like I was telling you, Freya . . ."

"I get it, his daughter had a fall and he had to bail on the trip, but that's not it, righ'? That can't be it. I know you; you'd have insisted he go take care of his kid, there's more to this story than that?"

"Annemarie thinks he's never going to commit to me."

"It doesn't matter what Annemarie Rafter thinks – what does Lexie Byrne think?" Jackie swirls her drop of wine, so I do the same with my over-filled glass.

"Well there was never a commitment promised past 'we see each other when we can'."

"Sounds alright to me."

And then I say it out loud. For the first time to someone other than myself.

"But I want more."

213

"Ohhhh." She takes another bite, studies me. "I didn't know ya were that serious about him?"

"I am."

"Shite."

"Why do you say that?" I implore.

"Well, correct me if I'm wrong, but hasn't he a mad ex-wife?"

"Yes."

"And you said he'd never leave that Cotswolds place he lives?"

"No."

"So?"

"So?"

"Why don't you move in with him then, shut the ex-wife up for once and for all?"

"He hasn't asked me."

"And d'ya think he will?"

"I dunno." I lick my index finger and pick up some loose onions off the plate, pop them in my mouth.

"You think he just likes it casual like this?"

"No, I think he loves me, we love each other, it's just . . . Annemarie thinks he's too much baggage, she says I'll never be his number one."

"And that's harsh." Jackie wipes her mouth, her eyes finding mine, probing now for my reaction to her question.

"I think so, it's like Annemarie seems to think he planned his life so that he has the best of both worlds," I tell her.

"In what way?"

"Well, that it's him who gets to pick and choose when we see one another because we have to work around him and his life . . . She never stops harping on about how I'm not being treated right by him, it's soul destroying." And yet again my bloody eyes start to fill up! This is utterly ridiculous!

"Annemarie sounds like she's being a bit bitchy at the moment, Lexie." Jackie undoes the straps on her dungarees, so they fall down and she shifts her weight into the middle of the stool, getting more comfortable. "And ya know I'm fond of her, not like I am with you, but she was always nice to me at work."

"Ah no, she isn't bitchy . . ."

". . . let me finish. Before I left for Dubai, Annemarie was great craic, don't get me wrong, and she also told me a few home truths before I went. I didn't actually agree with them, but I took them on the chin. She asked me if I was an alcoholic because I was in the Brazen Head a few nights a week, but I wasn't."

"Jesus." I hold my head in my hands. *Fucksake, Annemarie,* I think, *can you not stay out of everyone's business?*

"Ah listen, I'm a big girl, I can take it. She was doing another round of IVF and she was very, I dunno, angry?"

"Oh that she was." I nod. Annemarie's hormones were off the charts when she was going through IVF, the poor thing.

"And listen, I was lonely and unhappy, so I did drink too much . . ."

"I didn't know you were *unhappy*?"

She waves a hand dismissively, indicating it's all in the past for her. "Ah there was nothing you could have done, I needed to make the changes myself. However, since Annemarie got married and had her baby, I think she's a little jealous of your life, Lexie, especially when you met that absolute ride, Adam."

"No . . . She's my best friend." I shake my head. I don't want to be thinking about Annemarie like that, and I can't help coming to her defence despite everything that's happened over the last few days.

"Seems to me like Annemarie is madly jealous of you and Adam, that's all I'm sayin'."

I shake my head. "She really isn't," I say. She has everything she always wanted – Tom and baby Ben – she doesn't want my life at all.

"Well, how come I saw it then? Right after you met him, the week before I left with Namad for Dubai, we were in Silverside, you were all goo-goo gaga over Adam and I saw her face. She'd come in for a visit with Ben, he must have been two weeks old, we were all in the food court having enchiladas and I watched her watching you and I saw it, the green-eyed monster. An' ya know why?"

"No, you're wrong." I drop my napkin across my clean plate.

"You know why?" she repeats.

"Why?" My voice is small now because deep down I'm fearful Jackie has a point.

"Because she was used to you being single, being there for her, and she's terrified you're going to fuck off to the leafy Cotswolds, become bosom buddies with Kate Moss and become the greatest stepmother since Kurt Russell." Jackie steals a look at her watch again.

"I dunno, maybe you're right but . . ." I trace my finger around the pattern on the plate. "I just don't think she trusts his intentions to fully incorporate me into his life, that's all," I finally admit.

"And do you?"

"I do . . . I mean, he tells me he loves me . . . Okay, he doesn't tell me all the time, but I like that! I like the words to actually mean something when they're spoken, those three words are so throwaway these days, he said it as he left Dublin airport . . ."

"Is he gaslighting you?"

"Definitely not!" I lick my fingers one by one. "I had a Dermot, remember, I know a gaslighter when I see one. Annemarie keeps telling me to open my eyes, that he's never going to commit,

216

to check dates, all this mad stuff, but it was me who set the boundaries in the first place, I said that we'd see each other when we could . . ."

"But that's not how you feel now?"

"No. I wish to God it still was, it was all so much easier, but no, I'm going to need more and that's not fair on him, I don't think he can give it." I push my plate back and open the top button on my jeans, sigh with release. "I think that was the best sambo I've ever eaten?" I tell her truthfully.

"I do make a good aul toastie."

"By the way, Mark O' Donoghue wants to hook up with you when he's over in a few weeks," I raise an eyebrow at her.

"I've no time for men, Lexie. Not right now. He's a nice enough fella but my life's too full doin' me."

I nod. "Ya know, I think Annemarie's suspicious of Adam's life with Martha, it's like she knows something I don't, it's weird."

"Is she stalkin' him online, d'ya think? Do you?" She tilts her head at me, winks slowly. "You can tell a lot by a person's social media."

I stretch my hands over my head, could care less that my belly is exposed to Jackie, she's seen it all before. We used to swim together on Monday nights after work, until Jackie got barred for diving in and landing on an old lady (she was fine, she even laughed!).

"He's not on social media, nor am I, as you know."

"Lexie, Lexie, Lexie . . ." Jackie twirls her glass. "*Everyone* is on social media, hun."

217

40

21 December

We Need a Little Christmas

"I'M NOT," I POINT OUT. "I closed all my accounts, remember? Like four years ago. I hated the green button brigade, all those nosy old school friends who never posted a thing but gladly sucked up everyone else's lives, drove me mad!"

"Share or get off the pot, am I righ'?" Jackie says.

"Too right! And Adam's never even had any – well, he had some TikTok account a couple of years ago but it was only to keep an eye on Freya, but that's it."

Jackie shoves the last bit of toastie into her mouth, chews rapidly and takes a sip of the wine.

"Righ', hun. I think we need to do this . . . To see where we're at with this Adam fella? See why Annemarie's up your hole so much?" Jackie lifts our empty plates and gets up, dumps her plate loudly in the oversized ceramic sink. "More wine?" She proffers the bottle at me.

"I'm grand for the moment, thanks," I say, noticing she isn't drinking much at all.

"Where were you, say – oh I dunno – last weekend, Lexie?"

"Why?" I mumble as I sip. I watch as she takes a MacBook from the granite counter and comes back over to the barrel.

"Cause I bet my shrivelled-up foo-foo that I can find *you* on the internet."

"Jackie!" I wince. "Ew."

"Soz." She shrugs. "Truth, though, and ya know me? I'm mad for an aul ride but I've just been at my acting classes, learning monologues and zero shifting opportunities. Anyways, let's find ya!" She flips it open, wipes the screen with her cupped fist, and her fingers tap tap tap in her password.

"No chance," I say, with a sincere shake of my head.

"So where were ya lately? Have ya been to the Brazen Head?"

"Yeah, actually for Tom's birthday, the sixteenth of December, I believe?"

Jackie types, her fingers dancing and I sneak a look at my phone. Still no reply to my delivered message over an hour ago. How odd? How annoying!

"Ha! I see ya!"

"No, no you don't?"

"In yer green wrap-around number from Threads, again I see! Jeez that dress doesn't owe ya anythin', Lexie! Yer chatting to some big cock?"

"W-what?" I reach across but she jerks the machine away.

"And there's Annemarie. Jesus, she's so thin! There's not a pick on her!" Jackie practically touches her nose to the screen.

"H-how?" I grab for the Mac, turn it to me.

And there I am.

In The Brazen Head.

Mother of God!

On Twitter. Hashtag *RuthKavanaghsHenHilarity*

"That is mental!"

Adam again. *Bonkers, Lexie!*

219

"So, whaddaya say? You wanna dig around a bit into Adam's life?"

"I dunno."

Do I?

My heartbeat races.

Yes.

Yes, I do.

"Go on." I gulp.

"Follow me." Jackie moves through to the huge leather couch. "Grab the wines."

I do as I'm told but say: "Your glass has like a sip in it?"

"It'll do me. Watch this." I sit down beside her, curl my feet under me. She sits cross-legged with the computer balanced on her lap.

"Okay, so he has a kid, Fred, yeah?"

"Daughter, Freya."

"Same thing, how old?"

"Fifteen."

"Okay, maybe not the gram . . . Defo not Facebook, oh! You said she's a TikToker?"

"She was . . . but that was two years ago when she was mad into Niall Horan, now she's into Billie Eilish, does that matter?"

"Freya what?'"

"Cooper?"

Why is my mouth starting to go dry? I reach for the wine, but I can't stomach that all of a sudden, in fact I've heartburn starting to kick in. I ate that sandwich far too quickly.

"Can I get a glass of water?" I ask her.

Jackie just flings her thumb over her left shoulder, so engrossed is she in what she's looking at, as her short nails click clack the search terms into TikTok.

"Bottled water in the fridge, but filter in the fridge also, whatever you prefer?"

I go to the fridge and pull out a bottle of Pellegrino, twist the cap, and drink some from the neck.

"C'mere will ya, I need ya to spot her."

I sit back down beside her and watch her type in FREA COPER, a pile of accounts all flash up, all different ages and races.

"It's F.R.E.Y.A. C.O.O.P.E.R."

She moves the cursor, adds a Y and a O. Then she scrolls. "Any of these her?"

I shake my head. But then my eyes nearly pop because I see her! "That's her!"

Jackie stops scrolling. "Which one?"

"*FreyaCotswoldsCooper2010*, back up!"

Jackie backs up, clicks on the profile. "Yes! It's public!"

"What's that mean?" I feel a bit gross spying on Freya like this.

"Means we can check all her posts?"

"I feel like we're doing something wrong."

"We're not, it's public! It's an open account for all to see *but*, most importantly, we can see who likes her posts . . ."

"I don't care who likes her post?" I swig the water from the bottle, my heartburn is scorching me.

". . . and stalk them." She rubs her chin.

"Why?"

"Because they just might have an Insta that we see your Adam on . . ."

"Oh, I doubt it . . ."

But Jackie is a woman on a mission. Her head is buried in the screen. It's frightening, how much she can glean from an internet stranger just through their profile; I would never have thought of even looking.

"That ex-wife." She snaps her fingers at me. "C'mon, what's her name, what's she called?" Jackie grabs a pen from the glass side table and turns over a *New Yorker* magazine.

"Martha."

Jackie writes down Martha's name. "Still Cooper?"

"Yeah." Which is desperate, if you ask me. Can you blame me, considering our history?

"Odd."

Then we lean in, both our noses almost touching the screen as Jackie scrolls through Freya's TikTok. My eyes dart all over the account. Mostly silly dances and lots and lots of horses.

"Go back up!" I say, my index finger standing to attention.

That's when I see them.

Adam, Martha and Freya, all doing some dance. I lean in closer. All in sync, but it's not the dance that's bothering me, it's the drop-star earrings we bought in Malaga in the summer. My stomach lurches.

Not in Freya's ears but in Martha's!

"Aha! Liked by MrsMarthaCooper1," Jackie says, her finger jabbing at the likes on the account.

Her account handle makes my stomach lurch like I'm about to be sick. "Let's try find Martha's account?" My voice breaks.

"You okay?"

"Yeah." Another swig of the water.

Jackie clicks on MrsMarthaCooper1 and we find her Instagram account.

"Now c'mere to me, ya might not like what ya see on this, hun. Just warnin' ya."

"Scroll, Jackie," I demand.

"Jesus Christ Almighty," Jackie says almost immediately as we both stare at Martha's account, our mouths wide open.

41

21 December

Where Are You Christmas?

ALMOST EVERY GRID ON MARTHA'S INSTAGRAM ACCOUNT is a picture of her, Adam and Freya. I think I might vomit.

"Ya okay, hun?" Jackie holds my eye.

"No." I swallow loudly.

"That's Adam, right? I remember his face now, a ringer for Cillian Murphy."

"He's . . . He's in all her pictures . . ." I put the bottle of water on the glass table after three missed attempts.

"Well they're all family ones in fairness to him, hun . . ." Jackie mutters, but she's looking at the pictures with a very disapproving expression.

"But in one of Freya's I saw, I mean Martha was wearing earrings I thought he bought for Freya . . . I picked them out, Jackie . . ." When we were on holiday.

"Did he say they were for her?"

"Well, no . . . But I *assumed* and when I asked him the other day, he kinda clammed up now that I think about it. He bought them for his ex-wife, Jackie." I'm incredulous.

223

Jackie just spits out one word. "Cock."

"I want to see them all!"

The photos are all Insta perfect, the Cotswold Christmas Fair last year where the three of them are dressed in matching red reindeer jumpers. The Christmas I was supposed to come, our first Christmas as a couple. Am I kidding myself here with this guy?

"What date is that one?" I point to another one of them above it, in the kitchen at Rosehill, Freya in her horse-riding gear, cream jodhpurs, a black jacket and riding boots, and Martha's holding up two red rosettes, as Adam looks on, beaming.

Because I know the date well.

It was my birthday.

The night he said the pipes burst in his cottage and he couldn't make it over to see me! I'd bought all the ingredients for a korma chicken curry, bought the fancy wine, splashed out on new linen sheets, had the blow dry, scrubbed the place on my hands and knees. It had cost me. I'd sat in and drank a bottle of wine on my own, ordered Chinese and watched *Dirty Dancing*.

"D'ya think he's back with her?" I have to ask.

"I dunno. D'ya think he's even divorced, hun?" Jackie replies.

"Yes! Of course! Jesus, Jackie, I met Martha, remember? She cornered me in the ladies at the Moritz hotel at his sister's engagement party, told me she wanted him back, but he's not in love with her, he . . . he just isn't, I know that much for a fact." I really do.

"Has she maybe just worn him down so, hun? Things change."

"I don't know." I shut my eyes, swallow the stinging heartburn in my throat.

But I intend to find out.

"Keep scrolling."

Picture after picture of the happy family.

224

"What a prick, the fuckin' head on him? These pictures tell a very different story to an unhappy divorcé, Lexie, you do see that, right?"

"Okay, please, can we stop?" I lean back and shut my eyes again. "I don't feel right doing this, I feel yucky. I can't believe what I'm seeing." My stomach lurches again and a wave of queasiness rolls over me. With every cell in my body, I feel totally *grossed out*.

"Does he never mention family shit, huh?"

"He does! But never Martha. Well, never in any type of positive way."

We are holding on a picture of Martha cutting a cake at Freya's birthday, Adam behind her, his hand on her shoulder.

"Shut it off."

"As you wish." She slams down the lid.

"Adam is a good guy. Better than good, that's too small a word."

"Right. So, you love him, then just ask him what's the craic with his ex-wife and what are his future plans? It's all a bit too ick."

"What if I scare him away?" I hear myself and instantly hate myself.

"Grow a pair a fuckin' balls, Lexie Byrne!" Jackie checks her watch.

"I'm trying! Do you have to be somewhere? I feel like I'm keeping you from something," I finally ask. She's been checking the time a lot this evening and, although I need her here, I'm getting the uncomfortable feeling that I'm in the way.

"I do, hun. I've an acting class to get ready for, I've pre-paid and they aren't cheap! We've been prepping our monologues for a month for tonight, it's a big one . . . Been working on it mindlessly in the bar for weeks, trying it out on randos. I got word that someone's comin' in to see us tonight. Someone important.

A big casting agent! Wanna come? Support me?" Her eyes light up and I can tell she wants me to come.

"Sure," I say. I can't go back to the hotel room alone now anyway, not after seeing all that. I need to clear my head.

"Cheer up Lexie, did ya not hear a word I said on the way here?

"What?"

"Everything happens for a reason, hun."

I pull my boots back on, grab my jacket and bag, and follow her out of the apartment like a zombie. I want to believe her, really, I do. But what reason could there possibly be for something this horrible to happen to me?

42

21 December

Santa Claus Is Coming to Town

IT'S HARD TO BE MISERABLE AT CHRISTMASTIME in New York. The bright lights really do inspire you, I muse as I walk towards Broadway linking Jackie's arm. All the high, flashing illuminated signage, *Wicked, Phantom, Chicago, Jersey Boys* – row after row of incredible artistry. *I'm stronger than this*, I think. I can't expect a man to complete me. I know this. So I have to get on with my life, yes I'll wait for his explanations. There is no point in my jumping to any conclusions because, despite what my eyes have seen, I know deep down Adam loves me, but can I do this relationship?

I also know I need to find me again, not get completely and utterly lost in this man. Annemarie is right. I have been sitting at home hoping for a FaceTime and praying he can come visit; I need to let Lexie free again. What will be, will be.

"Ya alright?" Jackie asks me.

"I am. I've decided to just park all that shit for tonight and just enjoy being with you . . . whom I adore," I add, grinning.

227

"Ahhh, hun." She leans her head on my shoulder for a second.

"Broadway!" I can't help myself: I swing around the nearest bus stop and kick my heels together as yellow cabs spin past us. Jackie laughs.

"Come on, ya mad yolk!"

The actors' studio is as off-Broadway as you'd imagine. All heavy black drapes, plastic tiered seating and a soft floor. A small, white, fake Christmas tree twinkles with gold, bulbed Santa faces.

A tall, beautiful, thread-like Black girl stretches in a skin-tight onesie.

"Evenin', Jackie love!" She sticks her head through her matchstick legs in a good ole Cockney apples-and-pears accent.

"Hiya, Billie," Jackie responds, "how did the call-back go?"

"Awful." Billie is still talking through her legs. "They emailed brand-new sides the morning of, killed myself to get them right, then I arrived to a room of blondes!"

"Fuck off?" Jackie seems to understand all this.

"In the room I said to Jim, I said, has the character brief changed? He said no but it was bullshit."

"Oh balls, sorry Billie, you'd have killed that part."

"Don't I know it." Billie pops her head up now and we move on.

"I didn't bother introducin' ya, Lexie, cos I know you how much you hate small talk."

It's true.

"Is there yoga here too?" I whisper to Jackie as she leads me up the rickety steel steps with five rows of plastic seats to each side. I flip up a chair and sit fast before it bangs back down.

"No, she's warming up?"

"To act?"

"Yes, to act."

"Okayyyy."

228

"LILLYLALLYLILLYLALLYLILLYLALLYLILLY-LALLY," Jackie suddenly roars, the back of her tongue bouncing as it hits the roof of her mouth.

"Fuck me!" I jump, catch my finger in the side of the seat. "Ow!" I suck it.

"REDLEATHERYELLLOWLEATHERREDLEATHERY-ELLOWLEATER," she expels new words now, discarding her white coat on the back of a seat, doing star jumps on the non-secured steps as the whole row bounces with a clatter.

"What are you doing?" Is she pissed? We had less than half of a glass of wine between us and massive toasties!

"OOH AH PAUL MCGRATH! I SAID OOH AH PAUL McGRATH!"

A couple of actors at the back join her in the famous Italia '90 chant. Is this some kind of cult Jackie's in? Trying to get me into? Nothing would surprise me about Jackie Miley. A dark box of Scientologist expats? I search for the light of the exit, my eyes darting, terrified.

"I know what you're thinkin'. Oh Adam where art thou?" Jackie sniggers, bending an elbow over each shoulder, pressing it down with the opposite hand.

"That's my addition to our vocal warm-ups. Deadly, isn't it? Really warms up the lips." She purrs, bends to one side as Michael Douglas straight off the set of *The Kominsky Method* enters the black box, in an Oscar-winning teacher's swagger.

"Michael Douglas!" I stab her in the ribs.

"It's not! You're turnin' into me! It's Harry Hathcrowe, our teacher, an' he's amazin', Lexie. Watch and learn, hun." Jackie hops down the three-metal step, more relaxed and at home here than I've ever seen her anywhere – well, maybe when the Brazen Head did Happy Hour on a Sunday afternoon, but other than that. She joins the ten other people on the blue plastic matted floor.

At last I get some me time. I pull out my phone – no coverage! Not a single bar? God damn it!

"Turn off yer phone, Lexie!" Jackie calls up to me, doing some sort of folding snake move, up and down and up and down.

"Why? There's no coverage?"

"Ah we all think that, but it comes and goes sporadically, so you have to turn it off altogether or put it on airplane mode."

"Okay!" I swipe. It's not like Adam's going to text me now anyway, he's fast asleep. I find my setting and slide onto airplane mode.

"Sit!" MD says, and they all drop to the mat like wounded drunks. I slide my phone onto the floor underneath my seat like a good girl. I'm the last person that likes to be called out and humiliated. As if it's all been perfectly choreographed the actors all fold their legs and sit upright, some cross-legged, some hugging their knees close to them, some leaning back on their hands.

"Tonight we will find our truth. This is the night we have been preparing for . . . for months, this is the night we find our inner souls . . ."

"Amen," someone says, and I laugh. Loud. It wasn't meant to sound that loud, but it echoes around the black box. All the eyes turn to me. I turn it into a cough.

"Sorry, swallowed my chewing gum." I raise a hand in the shadows.

"Settle, please, people . . ." MD paces the group in his bare feet now. "Tonight you will show me inside of you, who you are, how you can transfer that to your character. I want truth, I don't want . . ." He jumps high in the air on the spot, his feet slapping down on the rubber mat, his head swivelling. "Ac . . . *ttttiiiinnngggg*."

How long is this going to take? I really need to see if Adam's texted me any news. Okay, I'm trying to forget him as much as I can, but I can't completely. Maybe I can sneak out, say I need the loo and hop out onto the sidewalk (see, I'm a New Yorker already!) and check my messages? Then text him? Or is that too much? Is he asleep? Maybe by Freya's bed? Am I an absolute nuisance to him right now?

"Breatheeeeeeeeeeee . . ." MD heaves.

No, of course I'm not. Annemarie and those Instagram pictures have me paranoid. He'll be here tomorrow and that's the way I'm looking at it. That's what I'm willing. Adam will be in Fitzpatrick's hotel tomorrow. Then the door opens and shadowy figure creeps in. The door bangs and they all stare.

"That's it!" MD shouts. "No one leaves or enters this room until we are done! You know your order." He claps his hands. Dust particles dance in the air as someone flicks on huge blinding lights hanging from bars in the ceiling. Something happens. A hush descends. Necks are turned and twisted, bodies are hugged. They all take a seat in the front row. Except Jackie. She rotates her neck, stretches her arms above her head, kicks off her shoes and, bending, pulls off her socks and stuffs them into her shoes. Adjusts the straps on her dungarees. Someone gets up and moves her shoes off the blue rubber floor for her.

Jackie circles, like a caged lion, and I watch on, fascinated.

"In your own time, Irish Jackie," MD says and walks backwards to the front row, where a student flips down the seat just in time and he flops back, his satchel clasped in his grip.

The spotlight finds Jackie.

Suddenly I'm terrified for her. What if she's shit? I wince as she paces for a few seconds doing strange breathing. Moving her lips around in shapes. *Oh God, this is torture*, I think. Then she finds the centre of the floor. Stands bolt upright as though she's just been possessed by the devil himself and stares right at ME. In my face. I dare not breathe.

"I keep things in. Things. Emotions," she says slowly, but precisely.

Is she talking to me or acting? I can't tell.

"My emotions . . ."

She *is* talking to me. Why is she saying this in front of everyone? I stand; the seat rattles. I sit again. Then she moves, just a small step back. Before I can answer her, tell her I'm here for her no matter what, she speaks again.

"I know that's probably not a good thing. Life has made me that way, I guess. I have a tendency to show no emotion when I am feeling emotion. I just have a hard time opening up to someone. I get closed off. I feel that being emotional in front of someone kind of makes me very vulnerable and weak, and I have a hard time with that. You know, being in that state of vulnerability, it's not a place where I like to be because I feel like I'm not in control. When I'm not in control, I get anxiety."

She put her two hands out in front of her; they're visibly trembling. I'm rooted to my seat. I *think* she is acting. She nods slowly.

"Whenever I truly loved anybody and opened myself up to them, they have always stabbed me in the back. I have a hard time with that, trusting people. It can be anyone . . . friends, family, boyfriend. I'm not sure if I truly trust anyone in my life. It's sort of a protective shield I've put up, and it only gets stronger with time. I do desire to be more vulnerable, but at the same time I desire to stay protected. I feel torn. Every time I do take a risk, I get hurt. Not sure if I should keep taking those risks."

She stands very still, then a fat teardrop forms and drops from her right eye. She doesn't wipe it; she lets it crawl down her face. Takes a moment. Heaves an unsteady breath and seems to be dispossessed of whatever took over her body and mind. Steps forward again and takes a little, slightly rushed bow.

"BRAVO Jackie!" I stand up, clapping like a Lexie lunatic. "Oh my God! You're brilliant! You're Miley Fucking Streep!"

43

21 December

Stay Another Day

MY HANDS ARE STILL GOING LIKE THE CLAPPERS.
They all stare at me. Whoever is working the spotlight turns it on me, practically blinding me.

"Miss Lexie?" I hear from the back, from far up behind me. "Is that you?"

"What the actual f—?" I hear from Jackie on the floor.

I spin, shield my face with my hand in a salute type move from the dazzling spotlight. "Who said that?"

"It's me dear!" The spotlight swings, can't quite find its target, then it does. Settles.

"JAY?"

"Yes?" Jay answers from the back seats.

"No way, Jay!"

Jackie's voice is half concerned, half irritated. "What are you doing, Lexie? Are you alright, hun?"

"No . . . I met him on the way over! Jay Kiely, is that you?"

"That's my name, don't wear it out, dear." Jay Kiely, my Aer Lingus flight companion, laughs, a fountain pen clamped firmly in between his aligned teeth.

"What is going on up there, Jay?" MD rises.

"Apologies, Harry ole chap, please continue, bit of a nothingness." Jay Kiely waves his clipboard.

"Who is this geezer, Lexie?" Jackie calls from the floor, moving towards me. I can see she's upset, probably thinks I've ruined her big moment, but I didn't mean to. I'm devastated!

"I'm so sorry! You blew me away! It's no one, we flew over together from Dublin, just met on the plane. I'm sorry, I thought you were just amazing! I totally forgot it was you, yet it was totally you. I had no idea you were so talented. You should be so proud of yourself, because I am so proud of you!"

"If you might allow the rest of the class to perform, miss?" MD asks me, the sarcasm dripping from his tone.

"Sure, sorry, I'm new to all this, sorry everyone," I mumble, hunching into my seat. So much for not being called out in front of the class!

In fairness to the other actors, they all smile at me and reassure me it's fine. The rest of them do their thing but no one is nearly as good as Jackie. Not even close. She is the Meryl Streep of this room and there is no question about that. When they finish, they head for the showers (mad, I know!) and I scoot up the rows to Jay Kiely.

"This is ment—" I start but Adam in a tight white pec-hugging T-shirt floats into my mind's eye.

"Rather bizarre, dear."

"—nuts." And again. Adam swims.

"That woman, who performed *Protective Shield*. A friend?"

"Who performed what now?" I curl my lip.

"The piece, her monologue . . . it's called *Protective Shield* by Joseph Arnone, the messy-bun-headed one, black dungarees, eyes of steel."

"Oh right! Wasn't she amazing?"

"Hmm . . . Lovely depth, good control, the right look . . ." He clicks his tongue. "Just might be a tad too old? How old is she? Not that her real age really matters?"

"Tad old for what?"

"For *Maybe She Did What She Wanted*, the play I'm casting? I'm sure I mentioned it?"

"Oh . . ."

"Yes? I think I did. I mentioned I was street casting on this junket, did I not? In vulgar reality TV terms, it *actually* means 'on the street' but for us thespians it means drama classes, off-Broadway plays, the staff at Abercrombie & Fitch, expensive sushi restaurants. We are looking for our Julie, it's a Broadway play; it's a dark look at a broken marriage, a young alcoholic wife from the deep South. I wonder how she is with accents?"

"Brilliant!" I say. "Oh my God, Jackie can take off anyone, you'd want to hear her do Posh Spice." I laugh. "Dayyyyyvuuuuuiiiiiid-dddddd . . ." I laugh again.

"Well, shall we three go for a nightcap?" He slides his fountain pen into a little slot on the side of the clipboard.

Jackie's going to literally wet herself when I tell her this.

"Sure." I twirl my hoop earring, trying to appear calm. Wait until Adam hears this, he thinks Jackie is brilliant. He only met her once at the Brazen Head, but you only need to meet Jackie Miley once to know she's brilliant.

"Let me just chat to Harry for a few brief top line comments, he'll be in for a little commission if we cast Jackie – great name by the way – meet you at the call sheet pinboard in ten?" He moves off with a spin on his Cuban heels.

"Great," I say as Jackie heads back to me, her hair slicked back and wet. Before I can mention Jay, I say:

"You can't go out in minus two degrees with wet hair?"

"Dad? Is that you?" She does an about-turn, and the floor squeaks beneath her.

"I'm not messing, you will catch your death. Okay, I just heard myself. Listen Jackie—"

"I always do," she interrupts me, "I've been leaving here with sopping wet hair for over a year now. I'm still above ground." She stamps her feet.

"Jackie—" I try again.

"Look, you're new to New York, we walk everywhere here but we'll get a warm cab if you fancy a pint? Grab a bite and see the band tonight in the N17? Roddy's playing later, he's always at me to drop in on my nights off. Not one to blow my own trumpet, he has a soft spot for me, but like I said romance is the last thing on my mind, ya know hun?"

"Jackie!" I've tried at least three times to get a word in!

"Dat's me name, don't wear it out!" Playfully she pokes me.

"Will you listen to this!" I outstretch my arms, plonk them on her shoulders.

"Are you droppin' the V's?

"The what?"

"The Valium's?"

"No! Shurrup!"

"Ya sure? Ya seem a bit out of it? All that cryin' is so not you. I know when I used to take the odd one I'd be all Zen, but I hear it can have the opposite effect on some people, they go all cuckoo, like . . . you?" She makes little circle with her index finger at the side of her temples.

"That man tonight, back there." I jut my thumb behind me. "He's a casting director for a big play on Broadway and

236

he loved you! Like L.O.V.E.D. Y.O.U. He's taking *us* for a drink!"

"Shurrup yer face right now, Lexie Byrne!" Her eyes nearly pop out of her head.

"I'm serious and you are seriously talented, my friend!"

"Oh my God, he's the one Harry was telling us was coming! The big agent!"

"I know! Honestly you blew me away!"

"Told ya, didn't I?" She winks, straightens herself. "Harry told me the very first night I was leaving, after the trial class that I had . . ." Jackie props her left hand on her left hip, curves herself at an impressive angle and clicks her fingers on her right hand. "*It.*"

"Well, he wasn't fibbing."

"Where shall we go my dears?" Jay Kiely rounds the end of the black drape as though he knew we'd be standing there, just the two of us.

"N17?" Jackie says quietly, and I'm surprised at how professional she is. You'd never tell she's buzzing with the excitement. Calm as a cucumber. I throw my bag over my shoulder and, as we walk to the exit, I have another one of those eureka moments.

I'm in New York City, alone. Well, Jackie's here, but my lover isn't . . . And all of a sudden, I'm okay with it all. All of a sudden, I feel really alive. There's more to Lexie Byrne than any man. Always has been, always will be.

44

21 December

Away in a Manger

THE FAMILIAR HUM OF THE RIVERDANCE UILLEANN pipes greets my ears as Jackie holds open the harp-handled door for us. Inside the N17 it's hopping. People are Irish dancing on a makeshift stage, sawdust rises, glasses are being raised in toasts. I reef off my jacket and throw it over my bag.

"My round!" I say to Jay, Harry, MD and Jackie. "What'll it be?"

"Shall we share some fine red grape?" Jay Kiely says.

"Perfect." Harry thumbs it up.

"I'll drink an'thin'," Jackie says. "Far corner. Go!" Jackie makes a ducking and diving move through the crowds to a recently vacated table and dives over it, literally drapes herself across it. I laugh at her lunacy as I step into the bar queue. The Riverdance builds and my feet tip tap, and I realise I'm smiling like a maniac.

I'm happy.

I'm truly happy right now. And it's got nothing to do with Adam. I savour the moment. This isn't an epiphany – I already knew I was happy in my own life. I don't need to marry Adam or leave my life and move to the Cotswolds. What have I been thinking? I just need to do more with *my* life! As soon as I sit, I'm going to text him, tell him not to come out here. He should stay home with Freya, that's where he's needed most, and I'll see him in the New Year. I still want him, physically, more than I can ever explain, the desire is unabating, but my senses are more awake now. I must find my own happiness outside of him too.

I need to take a leaf out of Jackie's book. Ha! Those are words I never thought I'd say. But it's the truth. Maybe Kevin in Sir Patrick Dun's is right, I should do that course in dementia care for the elderly. Do something with my life I really want to do.

I get hustled up as someone leans on me from behind.

"You look like a girl who's on the naughty list?"

I turn. A tall, well-built man in a Lakers T-shirt stands behind me, much too close. With every sway of the crowd he pushes against me.

"Hope not," I say and as I try to make some space between us something clicks in me. An image of Mark O' Donoghue flashes before my eyes and although Mark did little wrong, I know that, suddenly I'm angry about all the "Mark" types who've overstepped the mark with me. It's not that this guy is doing anything different that hasn't happened to me in a bar a hundred times before, but this time I'm going to address it. Let him know. Speak up.

"You're rubbing off me there, mate." I hold his eye, my head turned over my shoulder.

"And you like it?" He winks, tugs at his V-neck, tongue probing his back teeth.

"No. I really don't." I stare at him. "Now back off."

"Oh." He moves back.

Empowered, I turn back to the bar and, as timing would have it, I'm next in line, so I say:

"Bottle of house red, four glasses, please!" I manage to catch the eye of the bartender who watched my exchange and he gives me a knowing smile.

"Had myself a good divorce party a few weeks ago, good for you." She's speedy with the drink and tray and as I make my way over to the table, Harry jumps up to help. The Riverdance from the band is powerful: from somewhere on that makeshift stage comes the loud click of a hard Irish dancing shoe. I sit thankfully on a small straw-topped stool; Jay Kiely unscrews the wine cap and pours an exceptionally civilized micro drop into each glass.

"Ah here Jay! Yer lettin' our good name down!" Jackie holds the glass up to her eye. "Any other nigh' I'd be laughin' at yer measures!"

She turns to me. "Guess wha'?"

"Wha'?" I mimic her accent.

"I've an audition in the mornin' for Julie, in front of Michael Scotta, a famous English director for the lead role in his new play, *Maybe She Did What She Wanted*. Jay Kiely here, is one of the biggest casting directors in the world, and you, Lexie Byrne, are my lucky charm, you brought him to me." Jackie looks like she might cry with happiness.

"No, you did it all yourself," I tell her. The two men put their heads together in conversation and we lean back.

"Can't fuckin' believe this is happenin'?" She purses her lips into an O and exhales very slowly. "Even his real name is Jackie."

"I know and I believe it's happening." I raise my glass. She puts hers down.

"I'm not drinking this, I need a clear head."

"Is this an apparition?" I joke, throw my eyes to the heavens my arms out wide.

"When you really find what makes you happy. Nothin' else matters."

"Oh! Adam! Shit! I just need to text him something quickly!" I rummage in my bag for my phone. Can't feel it anywhere. Tilt the bag this way and that. Dump out all my shit onto the table. It's not there.

"What are you doin'?" Jackie piles all my stuff up.

"I don't have my phone?" I tell her.

"Ya really shouldn't be carrying yer passport in yer bag Lexie!" She holds it up to my face.

"Oh shit, thought I left that at the hotel." I'm still searching, madly.

"Relax, check your jacket pocket?" She rummages through the pile.

I shove my hand into every pocket that I can find.

"No! It's not here." Oh no, this is all I need, you know that lost phone feeling, it washes over me.

"What's up, dear?" Harry asks.

"I've lost my phone!" Then a flashback. I'd put it on the ground when I turned on airplane mode. "It's on the floor at the actors' studio! Harry, I need to go back. My boyfriend is supposed to be joining me in New York and I need to text him . . ."

"Want to send him a message from my phone to his social media accounts?" Harry offers.

I shake my head. "He's not on social media . . ."

"Ohhh, what's *he* hiding, dear," Jay Kiely replies on point, but I ignore him.

"Surely the man has email?" MD asks.

"He does but it's an NHS one, he only has it in work, not on his phone."

"It's not my place to open I'm afraid. Lorne, the caretaker, opens and closes, union rules, and it won't open again until eight in the morning for mime and movement classes."

"Balls!"

"Sure he won't be here till tomorrow anyways? Look, you look bleedin' wall fallen hun, all of a sudden. Mr and Mrs Jet Lag have ya by the nips! Come on back with me, crash out in the spare bedroom and I'll walk ya over in the morning before my audition, and stick ya in a yellow back to Fitzpatrick's, yeah?"

"I was just going to tell him if he hasn't left yet not to bother, to be with his daughter. I think that's probably what he really wants?"

"I'm sure he wants to be with you, Lexie." Jackie stuffs all my stuff back in my bag and tips my elbow for me to rise.

She is bang on; jet lag has suddenly knocked me for six.

"We're gonna get back, I need sleep for tomorrow, and to learn my lines. Wish me luck, Harry, and thanks again, Jay."

"Break a leg, Irish Jackie." Harry raises his glass.

"Chin, chin." Jay clinks his glass off Harry's.

We pull on our coats and make for the exit.

"C'mon, hun, I'll put a hot water bottle in yer bed, you need to sleep."

"I do," I tell Jackie, and once again I link my friend closely. Soon enough we're back at the brownstone, and before I fall asleep, I can't help but think; *Well, I suppose now he knows how it feels when the person you love doesn't text you back.*

45

22 December

Christmas Without You

SIPPING HOT CINNAMON TAKEAWAY COFFEES, we pass a huge group of carol singers outside the Starbucks. Christmas hats bobble, and buckets are shaken, as their voices soar, sweet and clear on this cold New York morning. Jackie and I are approaching the side door of the studio as she pokes me.

"Here's Lorne now." She blows into her lidless coffee as Lorne comes across the icy sidewalk, with careful steps and a jingle jangle of keys. He's a large man in a brown uniform and a woolly hat that makes him look strangely childlike. Jackie explains our predicament to him and, with an impressive shifting of keys, he inserts the right one first time.

"Thanks a million," Jackie says. "No one feels right without their phone, do they?" Jackie being Jackie makes polite chit chat with Lorne.

"Wouldn't know," his gruff tone comes back, and he pats a small navy box strapped to the belt on his waist.

"What in the name of Jaysus is that?" Jackie squints.

"My pager. Only way people can contact me. Life's too short and too beautiful to go around with your head stuck in a screen and your fingers feeding your brain image after image all day every day. Too much information."

"That's the whole world now unfortunately," I admit.

"Not my world." Lorne turns the old lock. "Be the shepherd, not the sheep." He pushes the big steel door wide open with his foot and instead of acknowledging he is speaking the truth I nearly knock him over as I run in, leaving Jackie standing with him along with his words of unheard wisdom.

Inside, I drop down to my hands and knees and crawl along the row I was sitting in. No sign of my phone. I feel around the less than clean floor for it, I can't feel anything. I need a torch.

"Ow." I've hurt my back now. I sit on my knees, rub the bottom of my back. "Jackie!" I holler, still grabbing the base of my spine.

"D'ya get it?" I hear her. "Lexie?"

"Here?" I shout from the floor.

"Tell ya one ting, if we were doin' the Scottish play, I'd be shittin' meself right now!" She laughs and a light shines from her hands. "I can't even ring it for ya, it's on airplane mode." Then I see it, sitting in a groove between two seats.

"Yes! Got it!" I wipe it with my hand and swipe it to life – twenty-eight per cent battery – and I slide it off airplane mode. We run to the door.

It beeps and beeps.

"It's him!" I tell her.

"Tell him you don't want him to come now, quick!"

"It's not like that! I do want him, Jackie . . . I'm still in hopelessly in love with him, I'm just trying to live life on my own terms now too."

Since last night, I've been back and forth a hundred times with my feelings. I want him. No, I don't want him to come here now.

But I love him. And he loves me. But he's not being fair. Yes, but I want more than we agreed. Argh! My heart can't make up its mind.

"I was thinking in bed last night, nodding off, while you shouted your lines . . ."

"I wasn't shoutin', I was projecting – big difference."

"Whatever. Do you really think Annemarie has been stalking him too? Because she kept saying to me 'open your eyes' in that fight we had about him, the one I was telling you about last night?"

"Yeah, hundred per cent betcha she is!" Jackie snaps her fingers. "But maybe she's just lookin' out for ya so, I take back what I said about her being jealous. Bless her. She was good enough not to tell ya. Yid never have thanked her for it. Kneel? Kneel? WHY SHOULD I KNEEL."

"What the fuc—" I fall back on my arse with the fright.

"Sorry, it's a line for my audition this morning, I just wanted the feeling, the sentiment. You kneeling there on the ground, desperate – I can channel it later."

"I'm not desperate," I say.

"Can ya see yerself?"

"Okay. Still shit coverage even by the door, come on." I stand up, still holding the bottom of my back.

Outside, the New York air takes my breath away as I open Adam's first WhatsApp.

Where are you? A X

I'm in New York. Shocker, I text, and the response comes in quickly.

Holy shit.

SO AM I!!! A X

46

22 December

When Two Become One

"THERE YOU ARE!" HE'S SITTING UP AGAINST the red headboard in a white T-shirt and grey tracksuit bottoms holding a glass of water, the open bottle beside him on the side table.

"Hi," I say, breathless, and throw my bag over the side of the chair as he puts the water down on the table and pushes himself up off the bed.

"Well hello, Lexie!" He grins madly.

"Oh I'm so sorry!" I pant.

"It's fine! Don't worry. I think I'm going to stop with the surprises now, though, I should have texted you." He laughs, rotates his neck, walking towards me. "How was Jackie?"

"She's great . . ." I'm still panting. It doesn't help looking at him now. Jaysus, but that T-shirt is *tight*.

"Did you run here?"

"I jumped out of the cab as soon as I recognised the road and ran the rest of the way. "How did you get over here so fast?" I ask.

"It was always my plan, to just made sure Freya was okay. It's not going to surprise you when I tell you Martha completely overreacted. Freya was more than shocked to see me run into A&E – she hadn't asked for me at all!" He rolls his dark eyes. "Anyway, once I was happy, she was fine, I got her blessing to leave and went straight back to Birmingham airport. An about-turn really. I was lucky with easy Christmas traffic and flight availability."

"I'm so happy she's not too badly hurt." I did guess Martha was trying to sabotage our trip. "But why didn't you text me? Like, keep me updated?" But I say nothing about her, bite my bottom lip.

"Like I said, I think I'm gonna re-think my love of surprises after this, it was stupid of me!" He rubs his dark stubble and has the decency to look remorseful. He really does look like he made it here as fast possible; like he hasn't even slept at all.

"Oh Adam." I put my cold hand on his cheek; he doesn't flinch, just covers it with his warm hand. "Don't say that, I love surprises, maybe just not so many in a row?" I laugh now, relief at seeing him here washing over me. I can try and think my way out of our connection as much as I want, but when I'm with him, I'm in ecstasy. Every time I see him in the flesh I get butterflies; I wish I didn't, but I do. I'm head over heels for him.

"I got so lucky with a flight home to Birmingham, literally got the jump seat not more than ten minutes after I left you. Traffic was super light to Cotswolds hospital, Deb collected me, I saw Freya, argued with Martha and turned straight around, Dominic dropped me back to the airport, hopped a flight to Paris, then a connection to New York. I was probably only hours behind you. I assumed you'd be in bed so, trying to be all romantic yet again, I thought it be better I just arrived rather than give you a running commentary in case you were asleep. I know you said you've been shattered lately what with the run-up to Christmas in work?"

Old Lexie would have said, "Never mind me, *you* must be wrecked," but this time it's not enough to forget about the questions I have building up inside me. Enough is enough; we really need to talk openly and honestly.

New Lexie – New York Lexie – instead says, "No. I'm fine. It's been a fabulous twenty-four hours! I'm in awe of this city! But what are the chances I wouldn't be in the hotel room when you arrived?" I shake my head.

"At first, I got a terrible fright, and your phone was off, so I called Annemarie eventually . . ." I see the eye roll, but I don't ask; I don't have to, I can only imagine the earful he got from her. ". . . and she told me you had gone to meet Jackie for the night, so I just crashed out then."

"Ahh man." I can't help but laugh. It's like the Love Gods are against us, it really is.

"It's totally understandable! In fact I was delighted you were having fun with Jackie!"

"It was amazing to see her, I've missed her so much, she's such a loyal friend, I forget. I need to do better." I take a step away from him, kick off my boots, slide them into the bottom of the wardrobe. I need to get The Talk started, but anxiety is clogging up my throat.

"That's great . . . Now c'mere."

His dark eyes bore into mine as I walk back across the soft cream carpet towards him.

"You're sure you're alright?" He asks and I nod.

For the first time I see his case is wide open on the floor and has been rifled through, its contents tumbling out. The precious case he was more worried about than me . . .

"I'm so glad Freya is okay, I left my phone in Jackie's acting studio . . ."

". . . in where?" he interrupts.

"Oh you've no idea of the drama, I'll fill you in on all that later. But Adam, can you sit down for a minute?" I sit, pat the bed and he comes to join me.

248

It's time. I've got to say it, I can't put it off any longer.

"I was planning to text you last night, to tell you not to come to New York. It's too much on you, you're trying to keep too many people happy . . ."

"Huh? But you make me the happiest." His eyes open wide, searching for my meaning, and his words come out almost in a whisper.

"I know I do, I know that, this isn't me being difficult or paranoid at all. But I'm just saying you've so much going on . . . right now . . . I know—" I trail off.

Inner dialogue: *Tell me the truth. Is there something going on again with you and Martha?*

"But you're worth all the effort, I hope I make that clear? I try . . ." He wraps his arm around my shoulder, pulls me close to him. He smells of his aftershave, all oaky and manly and once again my insides are electrified.

"Is *everyone* worth all your efforts, though?"

His eyes meet mine. We hold contact. Deeply.

"What does that mean?"

"I just think you have too many people you have to make big efforts with." I know I'm making no sense. The right words aren't coming out right.

"Are you okay?" His fingers stroke the back of my neck. Feathery touches that make me tremble.

"I'm fine, honestly, it's just your life is so hectic, so full?" I manage.

"I know, I'm sorry Lexie . . . It's just . . ."

I hold my hand up, interrupting him and take a deep breath.

"And mine is a bit empty . . . And our relationship has exposed it . . ."

"You're mad at me?" His dark eyes dip and I watch the silver feather, tight around his neck sway gently. His arm drops from my shoulder, down by his side.

249

"Oh, I'm not mad at you Adam . . . but I am confused."

"Right. Well let's talk, yeah? Let's talk this all out? Everything." He wills me to say yes, I can see it in his drawn face all of a sudden. "I know I'm complicated to date . . ."

"Okay." *Oh Lexie, you fool.* I squeeze my fist into little tight balls. Why can't I spit it out?

"Great!" He expels a sigh of relief. "Can I suggest something?" I nod.

"Let's go and get some food, yeah?" He tilts his head.

"Sure." I'm not hungry and I'm not sure what I'm even *feeling* right now. I need to stay strong. That is the power this guy has over me!

"But I do need to change my clothes," I tell him.

Thank God I had a quick wash up in Jackie's, and she did some cute sideways French braids on one side of my hair while our sausages were under the grill.

"And I better get dressed," he says, looking down at his joggers.

That seems like a sensible plan, so we both nod.

"Let me jump in the shower." I slip out of my cotton shirt, throw it over the vanity table.

"Can I jump in with you? I need one too." He reaches one hand back and drags his white T-shirt off over his head.

Listen, how can I say no?

Why should I say no?

Physically I still want him desperately, every part of me desires him, so I nod and undo the buttons on my jeans. He watches. I take them off and stand in my black bra and pants. Still Adam watches.

"Let me make it up to you, Lexie." Slowly he moves to me, loosens the drawstring on his grey jogging bottoms and they fall to the floor. He steps out. Typical Adam, it's all smooth naked foreplay.

"Um . . . okay." I gulp as he heads past me into the shower room, and I hear the gush of the jets of the water. "Oh man." I facepalm. *We'll talk over food*, I tell myself. I'm lost in a haze of deep desire.

As always, I never feel self-conscious when I'm with him, so I walk in to join him. He is standing, totally naked, in the oversized, grey-tiled bathroom, holding the frosted glass shower door open.

"Jesus," I say completely involuntarily.

"Adam's fine." But he chuckles, and I see suddenly it's more of a nervous laugh. Like how he laughed when we almost broke up the night of Deb's engagement party. It's a side of him I rarely see. I usually get the happy, confident side. He's rattled by my conversation.

"Mr Cooper? Where are your underpants, sir?" I joke to get a laugh out of him, then his eyes change, full of heavy lust, as I unclip my bra and step out of my pants.

"Christ, Lexie, every time . . ." He holds open the shower door and we step in.

The hot jets soak us instantly, so powerful is the shower. I stand with my back against the tiles, and he leans his strong torso in.

"I'm sorry – fuck." He throws his hands up. "Why am I always saying sorry to you? Don't worry, I hear it too . . . I sound pathetic," he says over the noise hitting the tiles. The water beats off his face and he wipes his eyes with the back of his hand.

"It's okay." I can barely breathe. I suck in my stomach and arch my back. I'm too far in now. I want him too badly. All my doubt and fears ebb away in this most erotic of moments. I'm in a hotel shower, in New York City, with the man of my dreams. To hell with tomorrow, Lexie Byrne is going to live in the present. But I do know what I need to say.

Later.

Right now we just look at one another, really look – no words required.

Now's not the time to tell him I'm pissed off or mad that he still sees his ex-wife. I knew he still saw Martha, probably every day. But it had never really bothered me until I actually saw them all together.

"Hmm," Adam moans.

I move close to him, drape my hand around the back of his neck and pull him in tight.

Roughly.

Our naked bodies touching. His face and lips wet as I put my lips on his, and we kiss like teenagers, hard and hungry, our tongues probing, barely able to breathe.

"Lexie, I love you so much." He plants soft butterfly kisses all over my face, then moves down to my neck. His words beat to the rhythm of the water and my head rolls as he nibbles my ear and just when I can't take another second of this insatiable want, he lifts me into his arms, props my back tight against the wet, slippery tiles.

"I know you do," I say as two become one.

47

22 December

Endless Christmas

WE FELL INTO BED AND SLEPT FOR HOURS, spooned up tightly together, breaths synchronised. Now I can't hear him over the noise of the hairdryer. I press the little green button down.

"What did you say?" I turn on the little four-legged mahogany stool in my hotel white fluffy branded robe.

"I said, I could watch you drying your hair forever." He's towelling his own hair, still naked, perched on the edge of the bed, his toes curling into the thick carpet.

"I can send some filthy hair-drying photos to you?" I curl my lip, perform a biting impression and he smiles at me. A great big Adam smile, eye lines crinkling.

"That would do it." He throws the towel on the bed.

"It'll be when you least expect it: in the operating theatre, your phone will beep and it will be me, naked, holding the world's biggest hairdryer."

Again he laughs, hard.

"You're nuts." He leans back and flops on the bed, tiny beads of dampness still clinging to his skin.

"Still a no-no, but in the privacy of our world, I am nuts about you, my friend." I raise the hairdryer slowly and point it towards him like a gun. "Now if you don't mind, I have some duuurrtttttyyy business to finish here."

He bursts out laughing again and takes his two hands behind his head, the soft tufts of black hair exposed under his arms.

I turn back to face the mirror but before I press the "on" button I ask, "So is Freya back at home, Adam? Sorry, I haven't even asked properly."

"Yeah, she's home. She's absolutely fine."

"Oh good." I pause, look down to pretend I'm busy entangling the long chord on the dryer, but slyly ask, "So why was Martha up the walls?"

"Like I said, she totally overreacted, she was at the stables with Freya when it happened and she was at the hospital when I got there."

"Oh, I'm sure she was glad to see you." I twist the dryer in the air.

"Uh-huh," he says, but as I glance in the mirror, I see him lean up on his elbows and dip his head. His eyes fall to the floor, and he runs a hand slowly down his face.

It's time to ask more. I must ask right now why he's in all his ex-wife's Instagram pictures, but more so why he lied to me about why he cancelled on my birthday to come see me? But somehow this just isn't the right moment. Is it because he brought me here? I honestly do not know. So I click the button back up and the hot air blasts out, putting a stop to the conversation. Running my fingers through my curls, I twist them into shape. When my hair is dry, I slip out of the hotel robe and join him under the thick duvet where he's now thumbing through the complimentary *What's On*.

"I hope you're hungry because I'm famished?" he says.

"I'm starving now! I had a sausage sambo with Jackie but that was for breakfast."

"What will we eat?"

"I'm easy."

"Somewhere fancy?"

"Hm, I fancy something spicy."

"But you don't like spicy food?"

"I know, odd? It must the New York smells floating all around the city that has me all foody adventurous like. Honestly, I'm a different person here."

"Let's see what we can get." He kisses me on the head, and I reluctantly move as he sits up and folds himself out of the bed. He walks across the suite and takes his phone from his open case. I'm still shattered – this jet lag is a killer – and I could easily conk out again, but I can sleep when I'm at home! A good glass of bubbles will help me.

"I'll have a Google." He throws himself front down on the end of the bed and I just stare down at his perfect backside.

"I mean a McDonald's would do, you know me?"

"No chance!"

"Or bar food downstairs?"

"Nope. I want to treat you. Get up and get yourself dressed, Lexie Byrne. As ole blue eyes would say, we're hitting the town, baby."

I stretch, my bare legs rubbing up and down the beautiful, high-cotton count threaded sheets. The thoughts of having to get "going-out" ready is not appealing to me.

"Well, will I dress in my one nice dress or hop back into my jeans?" I throw the quilt back.

"Nice dress, and I'll throw on my white dress shirt." His head is still buried in his phone.

"You brought a dress shirt?"

255

"Well I didn't know what to bloody bring!"

Oh man, his white dress shirt. Christ on a bike, I can't deal with this man's sex appeal.

He shifts to the very edge of the bed. "I didn't get to tell you this yet, but I was offered a promotion in at work if I want it – more money, too."

"Oh, great. But—"

"Yep – but more hours . . . We'll discuss that over dinner too." And before I can even answer he shouts: "Aha! Here we go, how about the Spicy Back Door Pepper, it's only two blocks away from here? Looks delicious!"

"Book it." I say in as enthusiastic a voice as I can, as he types away. If he decides to take this new job and work more hours the decision is already made for us. We're over. I take a deep breath. Tonight will reveal all. This could well be the last supper. I summon inner Lexie strength.

From my case I pull out my little black dress and my newly bought sexy lace underwear that he has yet to feast his Cotswolds eyes on.

"Booked for twenty minutes' time, let's go, my girl!" He raises his arm and like a professional darts player aims his phone directly into his open case. It lands without a sound on top of his clothes.

"Nice throw, Eric Bristow."

I wriggle into the black dress and turn for him to zip me up, which he does, pull on my tall cream suede boots with the kitten heels and sit back on the bed as I zip them up. He pulls on the white dress shirt and black jeans, and I watch as he folds himself into his leather jacket.

Strutting back in the bathroom, I wipe the still steamy mirror.

"Sorry you had to witness that rumpy pumpy," I say into the mirror, dab some cover stick on, apply a nude lip and run a smudgy dark olive kohl pencil in my eyeline and along my lid.

"Voilà!" I curtsy to him as he stands in the doorway.

"Beautiful, as always." He folds his arm, his hand on his hip, and I link mine through it.

"Shall we go to dinner?" he says in a posh voice uncannily like Hugh Grant.

"Key card?" I ask, nodding.

"Check!" He taps his bulging inside pocket, tugs open the soundproof bedroom door and we step into the dimly lit, poinsettia-lined hallway.

A couple steps out from the lift, each with a baby carrier strapped to them. "Have an awesome night, you guys," one of them says to us.

"Thank you, Merry Christmas," I reply.

"Happy Holidays," Adam corrects me without correcting me.

Adam is still a little nervy looking. Does he know I've been spying on him, I wonder? Maybe dinner out is the perfect time to bring it all up after all, both on unfamiliar territory.

"You okay?" I go ahead and ask him, gazing into his brown eyes. His laugher lines crinkle as he leans down and kisses me.

"As happy as a man can be." He replies as the lift pings to open and we step out into the warm, welcoming Christmas lobby. I'm fine, I really am, I tell myself. Adam hasn't done anything too wrong – yet – as far as I can see but I know the trust has been questioned and I know I'll keep checking Martha's Instagram forever more and I can't live like that. So I'm all prepared at last to ask him:

What are his intentions.

48

22 December

Hark! the Herald Angels Sing

THE SPICY BACK DOOR PEPPER is all sorts of New York atmospheric. Dark, moody red lighting and linen clad circular tables. A dark green Christmas garland surrounds the room, draped in curving patterns from the rafters. Tall, incredibly slim, red candles flicker brightly on every table. The chair backs are all decorated in red shiny bows. A pianist in the corner tinkles Christmas carols. It's picture perfect.

"Adam!" I bash him on the back as we stand at the glass reception desk behind the gold-plated *"please wait to be seated"* sign. "Is that Sarah Jessica Parker in the corner?" I'm sure I see her, but the table is far away.

"I couldn't be sure." He tells me, with his hand cupping his mouth. "But if it is her, are you going to go over?"

"Don't be stupid! I'd just want to look at her shoes! And ask how she managed to be a smoker but kept it to one a night? One! Took me years to get off them! Every time I see her having a relaxed puff in re-runs of *Sex & the City*, the craving comes punching back at me."

"Okayyy." He takes my hand as the maître d' checks our reservation, smiles a bit too brightly at Adam (see, they all fancy him!) and we follow him as he expertly criss-crosses the room towards our table.

"This is you." He whips a lighter from his white dinner jacket pocket with a black satin trim and re-lights a fresh candle. He then lays two small, soft padded leather menus on each of our place settings.

Adam pulls out my chair for me and I sit into the soft, spongy leather.

"Oh it's gorgeous here," I say, diving on the menu. I take a read, as he pours us both a glass of water from the table jug. I have never had a problem with my appetite, no matter the circumstances. It is full of delicious dishes and immediately I see what I want. Thai red curry. Very unlike me, but the belly wants what the belly wants.

"I know what I'm having." I drop the menu, squint over at SJP's table and he laughs.

"Love going out to dinner with you. Martha—" He looks like he's said a word that may get him cancelled. I can't help but laugh.

"Go on! You can say her name. I'm not that bothered by her!" I lie.

"No, I didn't mean – I was just going to say she was a bloody nightmare, barely ate anything, and yet spent so long looking at the menu, all the *will I? will I? or will I's* – only to order the same salad every time after all that."

"You can tell by looking at her she's a salad." I shrug my well-fed, happy shoulders.

The single red candle separates us and the light does make him ever better looking.

"Good evening, folks, may I tell you tonight's specials?" A waiter appears as we nod in perfect timing.

259

He tells us all about the Thai samosas the chef has prepared for starts, but Adam and I aren't starters people, we are mains and desserters all the way. We give one another a knowing glance.

"The special main course tonight is a spicy Phad Khee Mao—"

"A what now?" I interrupt without meaning to, Adam smiles at me, sips his water and leans back.

"It's a funky dish made popular by the Chinese people living in Laos and Thailand. In Thai, khi mao means drunkard." Our waiter laughs.

"Right, sounds like my kinda dish, love the sounds of that," I tell him.

"It's absolutely mouth-wateringly delicious, if you like a touch of spice? Ours has peppers, onions, spring onions, green beans, carrots, sweet basil and that good kick of chilli."

"I'm sold." I raise my hand. "I'll try that please, no starter for me but thank you."

Adam scans the menu. "I'll go for the Singapore noodles, please."

The waiter tip taps with a soft-tipped pen on his tiny iPad as we give our drink orders. As soon as he leaves, we hold hands across the table.

"Hitting you with a door was the best shot I've ever taken," says Adam.

"It was a wallop. I mean I coulda sued, whiplash!" I rub my thumb across my index finger, making the money gesture. He laughs. It never ceases to amaze me that Adam really thinks I'm funny and I never even have to try.

"I'm in love with this place," I hiss across at him. "If I forget to tell you later, I had a really good time tonight!" I feed him that line.

"How is it, in all my years, I've never met anyone like you, you're always a glass half-full . . ."

". . . not always." I don't let him finish as I let go of his hand, flatten my fringe with my hand. "I wasn't the greatest company for Jackie to be honest, empty glass was I!"

"Oh? How come? Thought you'd have had a blast together?"

"No and I feel bad now. We should've had a great aul time together."

"What happened?"

The waiter arrives backs with the drinks on a beautiful gold-plated antique tray. He carefully places two doilies on the table and deposits the drinks on top. A separate glass with mini tongs is filled with blocks of ice for Adam's Jack Daniel's.

"I was upset," I continue after the waiter's walked away. "And I have to tell you why."

"Oh. Okay." Adam drops two ice cubes in his whiskey; his hands seem gargantuan in size as he holds the tiny tongs from the tumbler of ice.

"This isn't like me . . . and I don't know how you're going to react." I take a small sip of the wine; glorious room temperature and tangy in flavours. I have to speak my truth.

"Go on." He takes a drink, carefully puts the glass back down, fiddles with the silver feather tight around his neck. The top two buttons of his starched white dress shirt are open, and his summer tan still visible all these months later, under the speckles of dark chest hair.

"I'm utterly mad about you, you know that, but I have to be true to myself, so I have to ask you a few questions – set my mind straight?"

"Fire away." Reaching up, he pushes his messy hair back off his face.

"Jackie showed me Freya's TikToks and then Martha's Instagram account." I watch him closely but there is no major reaction, just a light gulp as his actual Adam's apple contracts.

"Okay?" His eyes narrow. He leans his white elbows on the table between his silver cutlery.

"I just – it's all very – well it appears online as if you're still together?"

"Who? Me and Martha?" His eyes pop wide open, and he sits up, ramrod straight.

"Yeah, you're in every one of her picture posts."

"You've met Martha, Lexie, you know she still holds a . . . hope for us?"

"And is there?"

"What? Oh, come on." His thumb leans on the prongs on the fork so that it moves up and down.

"It's just her social media would imply that you are still together, or at least back together."

"No!" His jaw juts as he firmly shakes his head. "No, no, no, never!"

"Compliments of the house." The waiter puts a sourdough baguette with olive oil and balsamic dips between myself and Adam.

"Oh, thanks, mate." Adam says, giving the waiter a polite, British smile that doesn't reach his eyes.

"Can I get some sparkling water actually, please?" I ask. I need something to do with my hands and I'm worried I'll just keep hold of that glass of wine – or yank my fringe off from the nerves.

"You really aren't yourself – water?" Adam shakes his head.

"I'm still dehydrated from that flight . . ."

We both look at the sourdough.

"Go on," he says.

I tear a piece off.

"I meant go on about Martha," he says as I dip the dread, pop it in my mouth.

"Oh, I will. Taste this, it beats Annemarie's lockdown sourdough and that's saying something."

"How *is* Annemarie?" he asks as I reach for my napkin and wipe my mouth. Is he trying to get me off the topic now?

"Fine," I said a little too dryly. "I wasn't done with the Martha Instagram chat but why'd you ask like that?"

"Like what?"

"You really hit the *is* . . . You said how *is* Annemarie?"

"I thought we were talking about Martha?"

Jesus, I hate that woman's name.

"I'll come back to it. Spit it out?"

"Annemarie? Well I think she may have an eating disorder."

"Huh?" I'm completely thrown.

He puts on his professional, A&E nurse face: "I'm concerned. I thought she was very gaunt when I was over in October and although she cooked loads and ate more than the rest of us, she spent a long time in the bathroom after – I know because I was bursting to go but didn't want to go during dinner and I had to wait for her to come out, and when I got in . . . Well, I work in a hospital, I can smell vomit a mile away."

"Jesus! You think she had food poisoning?" I make a face.

"No, Lexie," he says, still using that patient, kind voice. "I think she made herself sick. She saw me standing there when she opened the door, and I saw the look in her eyes. Fear I'd heard her make herself sick. And funny enough when I saw her go into the ladies' room at Silverside she was an awful long time in there too."

"No?" Bread all but forgotten in my hands, I try to process what he's just said.

"Have you noticed any odd behaviour around food?"

"It's Annemarie! I mean, she always has food issues. She had all the fertility diet stuff to deal with then all the pregnancy diet

263

stuff, then the new-mom diet stuff . . ." I'm trying to think back over the last few months and a sick feeling of dread curdles in my stomach, her telling me she was too fat to share chips with me in Marco's, her guilt over eating the chocolates that customers bought for us. Jesus, I hope he isn't right. "I dunno, she's thin, though, you're right."

"Too thin."

"I can't believe I haven't noticed this, call myself a friend? I'll talk to her as soon as I get home, the poor thing. I know how stressed she is. I've been asking her all year to go see a doctor – I'm going to insist now!"

Has she been throwing up after eating and I have been so self-absorbed I haven't noticed?

Great job Lexie, great best friend you are, I chastise in my head.

We finish the bread and dips as we listen to "Oh Holy Night" on the piano keys and I think of the argument about the Roses she had with August and August telling her to talk to Sally-Ann the toilet attendant. Surely, she's not bulimic? I mean, I'd know that, right?

The mains come and I'm a little preoccupied trying to think off all the times I've shared food with Annemarie. Had she disappeared soon after? Something pops into my head as I grind some black pepper. A few weeks ago, the night of our row. She had ordered those big bags of nuts in the Brazen Head. Shortly after she ate the whole bag, she'd said she needed the loo – all the tonic waters in her gin, she'd told me – but she hadn't got into that long queue and now that I think of it Annemarie would never use the gents'. She's been cold, she'd reeked of perfume. She had obviously gone out to throw up. How have I been so blind?

Adam eats hungrily and drinks his whiskey, but my appetite isn't great all of a sudden, so I push the delicious (yet incredibly spicy!) food around and just as I try to bring up Martha's Instagram again the pianist takes a break and we are serenaded by a three-piece Cuban band who play "Feliz Navidad" for us.

"Is it too spicy?" he asks when they finish, pushing his plate of noodles towards me.

"Not too bad, but I shouldn't have had the bread, I can't do starters." Or maybe it's something else weighing on my stomach. Like our unfinished conversation.

"Try some of mine."

So I do, I roll his noodles around my fork and pop them in my mouth.

"Delicious," I say, "here don't waste this." And he doesn't. We share the two dishes, and my appetite comes back somewhat.

When the table is finally cleared, uncharacteristically we refuse desserts, both feeling the bang of the jet lag now. But now. To finish the conversation I started for once and for all.

"So I just wanted to go back . . . to tell you that Martha's Instagram bugs me." I raise my shoulders up high.

"I do get that, but what I guess I'm not getting is why you're looking at Martha's pages in the first place?" He shakes his glass anti-clockwise, drains his whiskey.

"Because Jackie suggested it."

"And why would she do that?"

"Not in a malicious way . . ." I don't like his tone.

"You know I want things to be as normal for Freya as possible at home with me and with her mum? I've been crystal clear about that, have I not?" There's no kindly nurse voice now, that's for sure. He sounds so defensive!

"I do know that, but you lied to me about the pipes being burst in the cottage and not making it for my birthday. Martha posted from your kitchen half an hour after you cancelled on me."

265

His eyes dart, he's thinking. "There *was* a plumber there, Lexie, I assure you! Come on?" He squints at me, and I feel suddenly silly. "You know I'm mad about you? I would never lie to you."

"Okay."

"And you know I'd never intentionally hurt your feelings, ever?"

"I do."

"Can we just enjoy our night and forget Martha, please? I can't control her social media, I can't avoid getting into pictures if it's a celebration, and by God, Lexie, Martha knows how to make a celebration out of every little thing. It's Freya's anniversary of the first time she got her ears pierced, we need to mark the occasion, come over for a quick coffee! Or it's Freya's last day of school before mid-term, come over for a quick cuppa tea? Or Freya's spent all day cleaning her room, just come see it? And every time, there she is with her iPhone, clicking away, so many photos. I wasn't aware they were all on her Instagram, I don't look at it."

Suddenly he looks worn out by her and I curse Jackie and Annemarie for making me all paranoid. God, I feel a bit stupid now because I didn't want to have a row and it feels so *nuts* arguing about his stupid ex-wife's Instagram!

"You're an amazing dad, Adam. It's one of the traits I love most about you and I want you to be the best dad you can be but . . ."

"But?"

"But everyone's in my ear about . . ."

". . . commitment?" He says the word.

I nearly spit my water.

There it is.

That ten-letter word is out in the great wide New York open.

"Well yeah . . ."

He sighs and leans back in his chair. This look I've never seen before comes over his face: his eyes roll and he looks sort of pissed off all of a sudden.

"I'm trying to figure out what makes me happy, Adam, if I can't have you – I still—"

"You know I've been married, Lexie; it didn't work out because I married the wrong woman, and I refuse to make the same mistake again."

My heart sinks in my chest. My breath rushes but before I can open my mouth, he's pushed his chair back. *He's not leaving, is he?* The last mouthful of food I've swallowed is still stuck halfway down to my stomach, like my whole body's been frozen. Now he's going to dump me in the middle of a restaurant, in New York, at Christmas. Brilliant.

I breathe in slowly, with difficulty, and blink a few times. But when I look around me all I see are beaming smiles from the three older women, draped in pearls, dining opposite us.

"H-huh?" I ask them.

Then I look down and there he is.

On one knee.

Adam Cooper is on one knee.

49

22 December

Here Comes Santa Claus

PINCH ME.

With a small red velvet jewellery box balanced in the palm of his hand.

"OH. MY. GOD," I scream, really loud. Heads turn and laughter ripples around the circular room.

"Lexie Byrne . . ."

He gently opens the box and a single diamond, a classic solitaire, hits the candlelight and sparkles like . . . well, a diamond.

". . . I love you so much. I want to spend the rest of my life with you. We'll make it work no matter what, that I promise you. You are everything to me. Will you marry me?"

I can't swallow. I try and I can't, it feels like I'm choking so I jump up, my chair falls over. I'm sure there is a blind panic in my eyes because I can see it in his face.

"Lexie?!" He jumps up, grabs over for my arm as I bang myself on the chest and then I swallow. Like a pearl diver surfacing, I gasp, then roar:

"I do! I do! I do!"

The restaurant bursts into applause and I throw my arms around him.

"You scared me!" He kisses me.

"Sorry, you knew that would never have been textbook with me, right?"

"Always surprising me." He's half laughing, half crying.

"Be just my luck to choke to death as you proposed! The ring!" I implore, wave my left hand around.

"Oh yeah! Sorry!" He grabs the box from the table, and I stick out my trembling left hand as he lifts my precious ring out of the box.

"Lexie, once again? Will you marry me?"

"Bloody right I will!" I say and he slides the band on. It fits perfectly. I feel like Cinderella must have felt when that glass slipper slid on. My fairy-tale romance is living up to all expectations so why, annoyingly, is there an odd feeling in my head?

I sit back down on the chair, perch on the edge.

"Adam, I don't know what to say." I really don't.

"You said yes, I think?" He chuckles. "That's the main thing."

"Damn right I did." I'm trying to shake this odd feeling. This is not how I'm supposed to feel? What the hell is wrong with me? We will figure it all out, isn't that what he said? And I love him, so much, and he loves me. That part of our relationship is never, ever in question. He's explained all the Martha Instagram stuff.

"Look, Lexie, I know I've been dragging my feet but, like I said, I promise we'll figure the logistics of this all out, okay?"

"Yeah, I know we will." He wants to spend the rest of his life with me. This gorgeous Englishman who happened to hit me with a door on a night I did not want to go out!

"That's what this weekend was for – to move us forward. To show you I only want you . . ."

269

"Okay." But I'm dazzled by the stunning ring. "Do you think Martha will be my maid of honour?" I ask and he laughs.

"I can't wait to be your husband, spend every minute of every day with you. I do mean that."

But how can we do that? I think.

"Are you going to take my name? Adam Byrne has a grand ring to it." I make a joke because I now know what the uncomfortable feeling is. This isn't your average proposal and I know the questions I need to ask, yet I can't.

Where are we going to live?

Does he want me to move to the Cotswolds?

Do I want to leave Ireland?

Can I live with his ex-wife across the road?

"It's why I was so bloody panicked over my case – the ring was in it!" He breaks my thoughts.

"Aha. Oh right! Well that makes sense now!" I lean over and kiss my fiancé.

Oh my God, he is my fiancé. *Just enjoy the moment Lexie. Stop overthinking it all.*

"On the house." The waiter proffers a bottle of Dom Pérignon, resting in the palm of his hand and the crook of his elbow.

"How did you manage a last-minute reservation here?"

"Oh this was planned months ago, are you kidding me? This place gets booked out months ahead." He takes up a glass of champagne the waiter is offering, the foam rising, and he covers his mouth with the glass.

"Can I text my parents? Annemarie?" I ask.

"Oh of course! You don't need to ask me! Go ahead." He looks relieved and very happy with himself as he falls back into his seat, rolls up his shirt sleeves. I rummage as usual and pull out my phone, take a photo of the ring.

270

Guess who got some bling, baby? I send to Annemarie then dial my mother, who squeals with excitement; my parents love Adam.

"We knew! He asked your dad's permission when you were here in May. The night they went to play pool – it's why they were so pissed! When? Where?" My mother quite rightly wants to know all the deets. I can't believe she knew all this time!

"We don't have a date yet," I tell her, and he nods furiously. I promise we will get over to Nerja to see them as soon as we can and ring off.

"I can't believe all the stuff that went wrong on me the past few days." He scratches his stubble. "Like what were the chances? I was beginning to think fate didn't want us to be together!"

"Oh I'm so sorry for you." My heart breaks for him when I think of how hard he was trying to surprise me with his arrival in Dublin and this proposal. And I was making myself miserable imagining the worst-case scenario all the time! I lean across and we kiss by candlelight.

"There are so many logistics, don't think I don't know that. Now, shall we go back to the hotel and get to bed?" he says quietly.

"Yes, please!" I can't keep the goofy smile off my face. I just need time to think about it all. That's it! I just need to think it through.

"But you're happy?" He stands, holds his hand out to me.

"Happy doesn't come close." I reach up, take his hand, the candlelight catching the diamond in my engagement ring as we both watch it sparkle.

50

22 December

Merry Christmas, Darling

CURLED UP IN HIS ARMS after a round of celebration that blew my mind, I can't stop holding my hand up.

"Question?" I say, spreading my fingers wide.

"Yes."

"Did you tell Martha?" I drop my hand, carefully place it on his chest.

"God, no."

"Freya?"

"Not yet, Lexie. When it comes to my family, I hoped we could just keep our engagement a little secret, for a while anyway?"

And there it is. The uncomfortable feeling I have now has its reason.

Ding!

Ding!

Ding!

A secret?

A little secret?!

This is what I knew was coming, in my heart. If this is a band-aid ring, I don't want it.

But "Okay" is what comes out as I struggle to think of the best thing to say next.

"So when do you think?" I let it hang.

"The wedding?"

"Yeah?" I focus on the tufts of hair on his chest.

"Couple of years, maybe? Let Freya finish school, maybe get settled into a college?"

"Years?" I take it all in slowly and deliberately.

"Uh-huh. Dunno about you but the jet lag has hit again me, love, probably not helped by the whiskey. I'm shattered. Can we turn off the light? I can barely keep my eyes open." He yawns loudly, a double yawn, covers his mouth with the front of his hand.

"Sure." I lean out and flick the switch.

Darkness descends.

"I love you," he murmurs.

"I love you too."

But I lie there. Wide awake, my eyes wide open, seeing nothing.

Am I a stupid woman? Was I dazzled by a silly ring? Why didn't I immediately say: where are we going to live? Worst thing is, I know when I check my phone the first question Annemarie will ask is: where are you going to live? We haven't even discussed it!

But he proposed and I should be over the moon with the commitment; it's what I wanted after all. At least it was before I arrived here. I knew I'd been dropping the hints, so I know he knows it's what I wanted; and, knowing Adam, he never wants to let people down. But is this what *he* really wants? Is he ready? Is he just doing this for me?

My head's spinning but I lie still, listening to him softly snore for what feels like hours. Eventually I creep out of the bed in search for some bottled water to quench this frustrating constant thirst of mine. On my hands and knees I open the mini fridge and the light comes on just as a beep comes from Adam's open suitcase beside me on the floor. I take a bottle out, twist the cap and gulp it. Then another beep and then another. I look to the case, see the blue light shine through his white T-shirt. I sneak a look at the bed; the sheet is down and my naked fiancé snores more heavily. Carefully, I pull the T-shirt back. A text is still lit up on his screensaver.

I physically retch. Drop the water.

You can say no all you like but I'm having our baby, Adam Cooper, whether you want me to or not!

From Martha Cooper.

51

22 December

Thank God It's Christmas

I FALL BACK ON MY ARSE ONTO THE WET CARPET, hold the phone an inch closer and re-read the message a spilt second before it goes dark.

His ex-wife is pregnant with his baby.

Fuck me.

Fuck *him*.

Everyone was right. Once a cheater, always a cheater. How did I get this so wrong? I KNEW something was going on! I'm pathetic!

I scramble in the weak light of the still-open fridge for my jeans and top, find them, pull them on, then my boots. Still he snores, his arm dangling off the side of the bed.

I know what I can do.

What I *want* to do.

But am I that person?

I crawl on the floor, open my bag and feel around for my passport. I should just leave. But again I look back at my sleeping lover, his arm hanging loose over the left side of the bed. It would be so easy.

But don't lower yourself, I say in my spinning head.

I'm not able to listen to my good voice, the voice that wants to protect my self-respect; the other voice is stronger. I'd be able to see exactly what is going on.

Do it.

I don't want to, but I do.

Grabbing for his phone again, I pick it up, crawl on my hands and knees across the carpet, the phone under my arm. I stop at the left-hand side of the bed, right beside his hanging arm, and I do what I never thought I was capable of, I hit the phone to life and oh so gently I move his dead hand so his thumb print hits the screen directly where it should.

His phone opens to me.

I lean against the wall, my knees bent into my chest. I open the chat labelled Martha Cooper and scroll and scroll, message after message after message. My eyes speed-read them: she rants over and over again about wanting to have his baby. His replies are short, a lot of:

No.

No to this.

I have said I do not want another baby with you.

Messages between them as early as yesterday! Martha spamming him with baby emojis!

"Wake up!" I shout before I've thought it through. Me standing above my sleeping lover, holding his phone in his face. I've hit the torch on the phone somehow and it's so bright.

"What – what the—?" He opens one eye, the light blinding him, and he shields his face with a curl of his elbow.

"Do you think I'm some sort of fool?" The anger burns.

"Lexie, w-what?" he pulls himself up.

"How far along is she?"

"Are you sleep walking, love?" he whispers gently.

276

"Oh no, but I bet you wish I was."

I wave his phone, the blue light illuminating his confused face.

"Is – is that my phone?"

"It sure is!"

"Why have you got my phone?" He sits up fully now, goes to take it but I retract it, hold it high above my head.

"Because I want to know how long you've been fucking your ex-wife for?"

"What?" He looks like he's sucked on a nettle.

"How long, Adam?"

"I am not!"

"Oh, the immaculate conception, eh? GOOD TIMING."

"Can I have my phone back please?" He swings his naked body out of the bed.

"No."

"Have you lost your mind?"

"No, I've just found it."

"How did you – why are you in my phone?"

"I opened it with your thumb while you were sleeping."

"Jesus Christ." He hangs his head in his hands.

"'Fraid so."

"And did you get what you were looking for?"

"I did. I got all the info I was after. Ever since we went into Freya's TikTok and then found Marta's Instagram, I've been on high alert. You did a good job of playing it down, I have to say . . . Enjoy your new arrival, you make such a lovely family . . ."

"Hey now, you need to stop this – what are you—"

I shake my hips. I've lost it now. No pulling "Lost It Lexie" back.

"All those cute dances, so many – you even managed to dance the night away when your house was flooded!?"

"You're quite the spy." His voice has turned cold, cutting.

"I am. Jackie helped."

"It was flooded, believe me or not—"

"Sure."

"Gimme my phone."

"What else are you afraid I'll find? Ex-girlfriends – a Tinder account?" My eyes blaze.

He gets up. Stands in front of me, extends his hand and in his stone-cold voice says:

"Give me my phone now, please, Lexie."

"Oh you can have it, and this . . ."

I shove the phone into his chest and pull off the ring.

"Don't do this . . . This isn't you . . ."

"Isn't it?" I don't throw it, I place it gently down on his bedside table.

Softer: "No."

"Well, Martha wants to have your baby, and since I'm your fiancée maybe . . . ya might have mentioned that?"

"I did – I tried – it's never going to happen, I won't let her—"

"Ha! How dare you! Who *do* you think you are? Now get out of my way!"

"This isn—"

"Shup up, Adam. SHUT UP!" I fling my hands over my ears.

He does as I ask. I grab my bag, throw it over my shoulder and, without looking back, I open the door and head for reception. I'm getting out of here. I'm going home.

278

52

23 December

What Am I Gonna Do This Christmas?

THE RECEPTIONIST DOESN'T SEEM SURPRISED I'm asking her to book me a flight to Dublin at 2 a.m. I'm sure she's seen it all. She tap-tap-taps away on her computer keypad.

"We have a flight in two and half hours? Out of Newark? That will be one thousand five hundred dollars, 'kay?"

"I'll take it." I just about have enough to cover it over two cards. JP is at the door, and I press the last of my dollars into his hand and ask him to hail me a cab to the airport.

"No baggage, ma'am?" he looks quizzically.

"Not anymore." I attempt a joke with a watery smile as a yellow cab swerves in by the curb side and JP tugs opens the door. I know I could go to Jackie's, but I just want to go home, curl up and die.

53

23 December

Carol of the Bells

THE GLASS PANE RATTLES IN MY HALL DOOR as I kick it shut. After a long flight, I couldn't be more awake. I flick on the lights. My apartment is bitterly cold as I go to the sink and fill the kettle. While I wait, I fill a glass with tap water and give Jimmy a drink.

"So I got engaged and broke it off in the space of four hours. Typical me, eh Jimmy? But something else happened to me in New York, thankfully, I know it did. I really looked at the relationship. I really looked at *me*." I bend and pick the rapidly shedding pine needles from my carpet.

Soothing silence in reply. Jimmy always knows the right thing to say. I re-fill enough for a cup of tea and flick the kettle on. Collapsing onto the couch, I pull my phone out and hold down the side button to turn it on. I'd left it on right until I got to Newark and Adam hadn't so much as tried to text me to come back. His silence spoke volumes, so I'd turned it off.

Dolly Parton sings out in my hand. No doubt it must be him. I'd time to think on the flight, so much of it and I know I shouldn't have invaded his privacy, or bolted like I did. I should have packed my case, heard him out, said goodbye and finished it like a grown-up. In a mature way. I'll tell him that now. I gulp back the lump in my throat, look at the caller ID. It's not him. It's Sir Patrick Dun's.

"Lexie?" Kevin the manager asks in a hushed voice.

"Kevin? Yeah?" I say, dropping my bag on the counter.

"I'm sorry Lexie, but Máiréad has taken another turn . . ."

". . . another?"

"Yes, I'm afraid so, one this morning too, but we couldn't get you on the phone? The doctor's been in again just now and oh, she's in . . ." Carefully he says, "She's been moved to the white room, Lexie."

"No!" The white room is the most beautiful, serene room in Sir Patrick Dun's, but it's where patients who don't wish to go to hospital go to pass over in. Where my beloved granny passed away.

"She's been asking for you all the time. She said you were coming? We've been calling and calling . . ."

"I'm coming right now!" I throw my phone on the couch, grab my bag back up and run out the door. Outside I hail a passing cab, then I jump in. I don't need to say hurry. It's written all over my face.

Kevin meets me. I can't tell by his face if she's gone or still with us.

"Thanks, Lexie. She has no one else as you know?"

"What happened?"

"Ah she's been unwell for weeks, it's her heart . . ."

I half-walk, half-run down the corridor to the white room, sanitise my hands outside and push the door open. She lies in the bed, half a smile on her face though she looks so odd and old without her false teeth and her hair permed.

"Ya came," she croaks at me then coughs. "I – I knew ya would."

"Oh Máiréad." I sink into the visitor's chair by her bed and take her purple hand in mine; it's cold.

"Ya didn't come yesterday?"

"I wasn't here . . . I'm so sorry . . ." I manage.

"You're a good girl, Lexie." She coughs again before she brings her voice to a whisper. "I didn't want to go without saying goodbye."

My face contorts and the tears fall. She can't stop coughing. It's a hollow sound masking the beep of the small heart monitor she's attached to. I can see the pain in her thin face.

"Now stop dem tears, I'm more than ready to go." She swallows with difficulty, her lips cracked as she tries to moisten them. I look for water but there is none.

"I'd a lovely few years here, thanks to you. This place—" She coughs again. "—has been like a little bitta heaven on earth, but I'm finished now, I can't taste or walk . . ." She swallows again. "It's time to let the living live . . ."

I rub her hand softly. "Just rest, I'm sure . . ." I look around for someone; she needs water. She turns slowly on the pillow and looks at me, really looks. A brittle smile spreads on her face.

"You remind me of me in a lot of ways . . . I lost a baby, you know?"

I look at the little curly hairs on her chin because I just can't look in her eyes.

"No, no I didn't know." I keep my eyes on her chin.

"Oh she came . . . A little beauty she was." She smacks her dry lips.

I'm not sure she knows what she's saying now?

"I'm sure she was." I look at her now, bite my bottom lips so hard I'm sure I'm near to drawing blood.

282

"Kathleen. I called her Kathleen before they took her away."

"Okay." I swallow my tears; my nose runs, and I've no tissue.

"Them nuns took her away. But I'll never forget her, that little pink face and dem teeny hands, curled up in a little tight pink ball."

Another rattling cough. I rub her hair from her face. Tuck the blankets up under her.

"I wish I had kissed her, Lexie. I wish I coulda held her, so I knew what she smelled like . . . and whispered in her ear that her mammy loved her. I wished that every day of my long life without her."

"Oh Máiréad . . . I-I don't know what to say?" Is she dreaming this up? Or is this true?

She shuts her eyes for a few minutes, her breathing heavy and loud. I sit. Still. Trying to compose myself. I want to go get her water, but I don't want to leave.

"He didn't want me to go to Galway, Jim. That was her father. D'ya remember me tellin' you about the offices I cleaned?"

"Yes, I do. The big offices on Pigeon House Road. You walked there and back every morning."

"'Ts right, Jim was a big wig in them offices and despite it all we fell in love, playing snooker of an early mornin', before the staff came in if ya don't mind . . ." Her coughing now turns into a fit and I'm terrified she going to choke. But she composes herself.

There's a nurse at the door now, I see it's Alison the new girl. We glance at each other.

"She needs water, Alison," I say.

"I'll get some."

"We were very innocent," Máiréad continues weakly. "But I was only eighteen at the time and him . . . from them big houses in Donnybrook he was, and him only turnin' twenty-one, a big party planned in a fancy hotel in Bray, but his family was so ashamed, I didn't want to ruin his life, so . . ."

Again she closes her eyes. When the nurse returns with water, I try to coax Máiréad to sit up, but she can't. The kind nurse rolls a soft Q-tip in the water and hands it to me.

"You can juts moisten her mouth with it."

I do that, then sit and wait. But she's still in the memory:

"All a long time ago . . . but I was a mother. I still am. I never looked for her. I wish I had. I wish I hadn't been so ashamed." Tears swim in her eyes. "I wish the years had been different and I had been braver. I let my Kathleen down." Her cough is ferocious now, making her cry fat tears.

"I just wanted ta tell someone, maybe you can find her? Tell her I loved her so . . ." She shuts her eyes as the doctor puts his head around the door.

"Can I come in?"

I nod. Stand up.

He checks her pulse. "Okay Máiréad, okay . . . it's okay." He soothes.

Her eyes stay shut.

And shut.

And shut.

And she doesn't speak again. There is no sound apart from her sporadic panting breath. I sit again by her side, stroke her cheek and her forehead, for I don't know how long until the machine beeps. The doctor returns, he presses some buttons. The beeps get louder and louder and then are followed by a long flat noise, and I know I'm never going to speak to her again.

"She's gone," he tells me, pats my knee softly. Matter-of-factly he removes the chart from the end of her bed, pull a pen from his top pocket, clicks it and writes something on the board.

"No. No," I say. My lip quivers and I cry like a baby. "I should've have been here yesterday! I promised her, but I was taken away on a surprise trip, I was in New York . . ."

He looks rightfully confused.

"It was her time. Her heart was very weak. I told her not to go to the shops last week, but it was her wish to get out one last time."

"I hate myself." I heave as he helps me up.

"Can I call anyone for you, to take you home?"

And there it is. It whacks me in the face. She was right. Her points were valid.

And now I need her more than ever.

"Yes please, Annemarie, my . . . best friend."

54

23 December

Oh Holy Night

I'D LEFT MY PHONE ON THE COUCH where I threw it earlier, but somehow I remembered her number. I'd called it out to Alison in a shaking voice and I sit in the corridor now, nursing a lukewarm sweet tea, waiting. It feels like no more than minutes when Annemarie bursts through the doors.

"Oh Lexie!" Her face is shocked yet full of love and care. "Oh love. Come on, let's get you home." Annemarie zips off her puffer and drapes it around my shoulders. I only just now realise I left with no coat and it's freezing.

"It's going to be okay. I'm here now." And I lean into her, rest my head on her shoulder. She doesn't ask why I'm not in New York with Adam. I see her clock my ring-less finger and again, she says nothing. Just soothes me with kindness.

"Máiréad has left a brown envelope for you, it's sitting on her locker?" Kevin tells me.

"I'll come back." I nod, my teeth chattering now with the shock. Kevin pats my shoulder. I turn to look back through the

286

clear glass door to the white room where Fr Joe, the resident priest, is standing in his purple robes, beads entwined between his fingers, eyes closed, praying over Máiréad. A candle flickers, and as the door swings shut, it blows itself out.

55

23 December

Santa Tell Me

"You have to call him," Annemarie tells me as I hold Ben on my knee and he suckles on his organic apple and pear pouch. I have that feeling in the pit of my stomach like I did something horribly wrong. I feel physically sick all the time. I feel like I've totally let myself down. That woman in that hotel room is not the woman I want to be. She is not Lexie Byrne.

"No." I can't face him.

"But Lexie . . ." Annemarie puts a strong black coffee on her kitchen table and a plate of warm toast. "Well, let me call him?"

"No." I can't have her interfere.

Ben's eyes flick up to me, his eyelashes as long as a spider's legs. I kiss his forehead. Inhale his smell.

"And you're sure it said she was pregnant with his baby?" Annemarie can't keep the inflection of shock out of her voice. It's hard for me to even hear her say those words, I feel like I'm in one of Jackie's scenes!

"For the fifth time, Annemarie. Yes. I saw the text with my own eyes." I replay the moment over and over in my head. I

288

wish with all my heart I'd left with my dignity and not done what I did.

"And he hasn't called?" She twists her red curls up into a top knot, secures it without a bobbin.

"I don't know, do I, I'm here, my phone's not." I don't even want to see my phone to be honest. It's too embarrassing. If I could curl up and sleep for a month, I would.

"He hasn't called me to look for you, but I suppose that's not surprising considering I gave him a few home truths the last time he called me looking for you, then felt shite after he proposed! Me going on about you needing more of a commitment and him with a ring in his suitcase. This is so hard to believe . . . I mean he ISN'T that guy?"

"But you never trusted him?" I remind her. She was right all along.

"No! I did *trust* him Lexie, I just thought he needed to be more assertive . . . considerate . . ." She uses a plastic spoon, scrapes it in gentle movements to gather excess fruit purée off Ben's chin.

"You saw him on Martha's Instagram, didn't you?" I know now she did. It explains a whole lot. I die a little more inside. I can't believe it's over.

"You knew?" Her green eyes deepen in shade as they nearly pop out of her head.

"Jackie looked him up too."

"Course she did, I didn't think it was my place to tell you, it was his . . ." She scrapes more fruit, looks up at me.

"I suppose . . ." I gently rub the nape of Ben's neck.

"And I wanted him to commit more to you and then he DID!"

"I feel sick so sick to my stomach." I cradle Ben a little closer; the warmth and weight of his little body is comforting right now.

"I couldn't believe you threw up in Tom's van." Annemarie puts the spoon on the table, strokes my hair.

"I'm sorry again." My mortification knows no boundaries it seems.

"Jesus! It doesn't matter one bit! I'm well used to cleaning up puke after Ben's milk allergies. I've never seen someone be physically sick with upset before . . . both for Máiréad and Adam, I know, love."

"It wasn't my greatest day." I expel a half-laugh.

"Máiréad was old. She was ready, Lexie." Annemarie moves to the drawer, pulls out a knife and begins to butter the toast. I find the ritual of the scraping soothing.

"I know." I gently twist the empty pouch from Ben's mouth and raise him up, rub his back gently. "She left me an envelope. I know there's money in it to collect her ring, what do I do with the ring now?"

"Is there a note in the envelope?" Annemarie looks at me.

"I haven't opened it yet . . . She had a daughter, asked me to look for her, and I will – I—" I choke up. Annemarie rubs my knee.

"I haven't been a good friend to you," she blurts, removing her hand. "I've been so caught up in myself. Lexie?"

"Yes?" I look up at her. It's so obvious to me now: how thin she looks, as if she's been sucked dry from the inside. She is skin and bone. Worn thin, worn out. I have to talk to her about it. I just have to get her to a doctor.

Her eyes dart worriedly over the kitchen as she starts talking. "I've been making myself sick because I hate myself . . ."

"Oh, Annemarie." I drop the empty pouch on the kitchen floor.

She reaches down for it, puts it on the table and holds up a bony hand.

"I'm fine, I really am okay, and this isn't about me, but I need to explain why I've been acting like such a horrible, bitchy cow." She slides the buttery toast across the table with a spin of the plate, licks her dainty fingers.

"It's only been going on for a few weeks. Tom called me out on it and insisted I went to see Doctor Eleanor, she's been trying to tell me I have post-natal depression – just as you have, I know, I know."

"Oh, Annemarie . . ." I say again.

"The reason I wouldn't hear of it from her or you is because I want to cope but I haven't been. Tom realised I was making myself sick – as did August, I might add, and she actually, in fairness to her, sent me a really lovely email telling me she was really sorry she'd called me out on it in work, but she'd suffered with it herself when she lived in Manchester. And you, my best friend, I've been so concentrated on spying on your happy life so mine didn't seem so bad . . . I was obsessed with Martha's stories and seeing Adam in them, I think I was looking for proof of infidelity and although there was none – ever – it did feel very odd to me that they were so close . . ."

"I only care about you right now." My problems are nothing compared to this. I cannot stand to see my best friend suffering like this, I just can't.

"We're some pair!" She picks up a slice of toast, takes a big bite.

"Who ya telling!" I nibble at a crust. "But what's happening?" I point the triangle of toast at her, my way of asking about her food issues.

"I have to take control of my life. I haven't thrown up in three days, I'm on some anti-depressants, to be reviewed in three months, and am seeing an eating disorder counsellor from January. I can't tell you, I feel like a new woman already. I finally get it, you know, that this isn't my fault. I just needed to face how I was feeling and get help. And now, I want to be here for you," she says, reaching her free hand across the table to hold mine. "We'll get through this, and ya know why? Because we have each other. Tom was right, I was afraid I'd lose you to Adam. I was incredibly selfish, but I wasn't thinking straight."

I squeeze her hand firmly, though gently. "Good . . . And the making yourself sick, how have you just stopped?"

"I just stopped. Totally. You see my bulimia was never about my weight! It was about me trying to control my life. I couldn't control the birth, the breastfeeding, the sleep, the anxiety – all of this was a way of feeling in control of some part of my life. It's funny, Tom used to slag me for being on Insta all the time, but I was awake last week and I saw this Instagram video about how you only have little kids for four years, and if you miss it, it's done. You tried to tell me this since Ben was born. But that post got through to me. I gotta know that there are lots of things in life you don't get to do more than once – now obviously I can try having more than one child but I'm not . . ."

"Oh love . . ."

"No." She holds a palm up to me. "I'm not going to. It's all been too much for me . . . for us both." She fights tears and holds out her arms for Ben to go to her. "And for our marriage too. Now we have this little miracle boy." She plants butterfly kisses all over Ben's face and raises him high above her head, his chubby pink feet dangling. "I'm so lucky and I need to just stop the worrying and enjoy my baby and be there for my husband and best friend."

"I'm so happy you said that." I grab one of his little feet, kiss his soft toes.

"Don't think I don't know you've tried, so many times, but now I want you to be happy and we can't just leave it like this with Adam, there must be . . ."

". . . an explanation? Like I said, Jackie showed me his social media, well Martha's, and as you know Adam's in every picture."

"Surely, he deserves to explain himself?"

"He did. He said Martha asks him over to celebrate Freya's every little thing and takes pictures."

"Explain himself about getting this baby?"

"What's there to explain, Annemarie? When a man sticks his penis into a woman's vagina . . ." I trail off, feeling utterly queasy again at the thoughts of them in the act. My mouth actually fills with that watery sick saliva, and I swallow it down. "I think I'm going to go."

"No! I mean I've sent Tom a message, he's bringing home pizza."

"I'm really not hungry, I've just had toast!"

"Well . . . Will you have a glass of wine?"

"No, I couldn't stomach it. I just want to go home, Annemarie, I just want my own bed." I push the chair back, it scrapes off the tiles. She doesn't say "lift it!" like she always does. Instead she says, "But it's Christmas Eve tomorrow! Would you please just stay the night?"

"No. No, thank you."

"Well will you wait for Tom to come back . . . at least . . . he'll drive you, Lexie, please?" Her expression is one of terror.

"Alright, calm down, I'm okay, Annemarie, I just need to be on my own for a while, take it all in," I soothe her.

"But you'll stay, until Tom gets back?" Her eyes still full of worry.

"Yes. I'll stay but only until Tom gets back."

Lexie Byrne needs to get back to her own life.

56

23 December

Please Come Home for Christmas

"THIS IS UTTER MADNESS!" I say. I'm still completely in a daze at Annemarie's actions.

We are in the back of Tom's sailing-equipment van en route to Dublin airport!

"Don't go if you don't want to, Lexie! Amo, I told you this was a bit out there." Tom puts his arm around the back of the driver's seat and looks back at me. I have to glance up, away from the huge ear holes.

"It's called CLOSURE!" Annemarie slaps her knee in the front.

"But it's almost Christmas Eve . . ." I utter.

"So? Even more reason to see him?" She slaps the other knee.

"Honestly, I . . ." But half of me desperately wants to go.

Oh sorry, you've no idea what I'm on about, do you? Well, you won't believe this. I'm only on my way to the Cotswolds! To confront Adam! Annemarie has booked us flights and into the

294

Moritz hotel for the night, so I can go speak to him, get my case back and have it out with him for once and for all. She didn't even give me the time to go get my phone and my own clothes! She's like a woman on a major mission.

"You *can* handle the truth!" she told me when she produced the flight details on her mobile as Tom arrived back in.

"I haven't even got my phone! I won't remember where he lives! This is ludicrous!" I said.

"It's Rosehill Cottage, Great Tew, how big can Great Tew bloody well be?"

"It's not *Last of the Summer Wine*, Annemarie!"

"It's close enough! Pull in here, Tom! Here!" she yells at poor Tom as he swerves into departures.

"Thanks for these by the way, Lexie." Tom waves a Dublin GAA Air Freshener Tree at me. "I got a few from your *All-4-One* birthday voucher. The van smells like a dream. No more smelly boating paraphernalia stink in here. It's the seaweed you see, gets tangled in—"

"Not now, Tom! Didn't you say you were friendly with the waitress in the Chill Out Bar? Gracie, wasn't it? And I keep in touch with the manager, I did deliver a baby there after all remember? They keep asking me back! I still have the free weekend they gave us and I'm going to ask you to mind Ben while Tom and I go . . . soon, then we're going to New York, Lexie, just you and me! Here we go, quick – they fine you now for pulling up," new and improved Annemarie declares.

"He might still be in New York!" I cry.

"He won't be. He checked out last night. Also booked a taxi to the airport not long after you. I spoke to a JP the porter, lovely man." Detective Rafter is back on the case. "I've left no stone unturned!"

"I can't do this . . ." But I want to.

She ignores me, twists her body to look at Tom. "You're sure you can handle Ben, love?"

Tom nods. He looks happier than I've seen him in months. Then her head pokes around to the back to look at Ben goo-goo-gagaing away in his car seat beside me.

"Quite sure, babe! Me and my son will have a night and a lovely Christmas Eve day tomorrow and we'll leave everything ready for you and Santa getting in on the last flight tomorrow night . . ."

"So we land at eleven, and we'll take a taxi. I don't want you dragging him out of bed . . ."

"I'll be asleep myself, it would be Ben dragging me out. We will light the fire and chillax, play some PlayStation, that's all I want . . ."

"He won't know it's almost Christmas Eve when he goes to sleep and I'm not there, will he?" She simply can't help herself, but then she does! She unclicks her belt as Tom pulls in and turns off the engine. She shakes her tumbling red hair with defiance, pulls down the car visor, flips up the little square mirror and peers right in it as she talks to herself: "Don't be so stupid, Annemarie, he's two years old! Let's go," she says.

"Let me get the case." Tom checks his mirror, opens the door and steps out.

"So I've packed us two oversized T's to sleep in, two pairs of clean knickers and two hoodies, you can travel back in those jeans and we can us the Moritz hotels shampoos and body wash . . ."

"Your knickers wouldn't even go up my thighs!" But I laugh. I'm excited and nervous and feel sick at the thought of coming face to face with Adam after all this drama.

"Well, go commando then. It's one night, Bear Grills!"

"What if he is back with Martha and it was planned to have this new baby?" My voice quivers.

"Well, then you'll get the truth for once and for all."

"You know in New York I had this . . . epiphany. I realised you were right, Annemarie. I was absolutely sitting around waiting for a moment with Adam, glorious moments don't get me wrong, but living my life by his schedule. Máiréad told me to live life and have no regrets – is too much life not to be living!"

She is one hundred per cent right, I do need closure.

"And maybe . . ." She purses her lips, swallows hard.

"What?"

"Maybe *you* should go spend some time in New York with Jackie, ya know?" Her eyes meet mine. "I would if I was you, and that's the gospel truth. As much as it would kill me to lose you, and it would—" Her eyes start to fill up. "Oh my God, Lexie, it really would, you are one of the true loves of my life."

"Stop." I start to heave now, trying not to cry.

"I was never jealous of Adam by the way, I do think he's a fantastic man . . ."

"I never for one second thought you were jealous of *him*."

"Jackie did – she called me, I didn't tell you. Told me to not be jealous, that I'd never lose you, that she's a million miles away and she's never lost you. And she's right. I thought you'd go over to the Cotswolds and I'd lose you, but now I know that will never happen, we mean too much to each other. I talked for hours to Jackie about it, she was all like, 'Sure it gives ya a great excuse to get away from the baby and yer husband for mini breaks!' Always look for the positives, she said, and by the way I heard about her big audition for *Maybe She Did What She Wanted*! I lit a candle for her, prayed to St Anthony. So come on, a new beginning awaits!"

I fold myself out of the back of Tom's van, thank him and after they embrace quickly and she kisses Ben all over, we make our way through the automatic door into Departures. Inside Dublin airport is thronged with Christmas travellers. But miraculously we check in quickly and find our gate on the board, Ryanair flight to Birmingham, boarding at 5 p.m. It's hard to comprehend that just a few days ago I was here with Adam, full of hope and happier than I'd ever been. So much has changed in me. Again. It brings me comfort to know that I evolve all the time. That I can still surprise myself with how I live my life.

"Drink?" Annemarie asks me.

"No thanks. My stomach is in knots here. He'll think I'm certifiably mad, a total fruit and nut."

"Don't you think he'll be thrilled to see you?"

"No!"

"I do. There has to be an explanation to all this."

My heart lifts, because if Annemarie of all people is feeling positive about this situation, she really must be feeling better, and that makes one of us at least.

57

23 December

December Snow

WOULDN'T YOU JUST KNOW IT, the snow falls thick and fast as we take the taxi towards Rosehill Cottage.

"Lucky to get up Farsmouth Hill, ladies," the taximan tells us as the cab slides slightly to the left.

"Christ, what if we're snowed in?" Surprisingly, it's me who says this and not Annemarie. She is perched forward, almost between the two seats, grinning from ear to ear.

"Look out, Lexie. Look how beautiful the Cotswolds are all covered in snow!"

"I know but . . ." I feel utterly ill with we are doing. I clutch my stomach.

"I have no anxiety!" She's positively giddy as she twirls her hair on her finger.

"Well I bloody do! So you'll leave me at Rosehill Cottage and go back to the hotel in the taxi?" I say.

"Not immediately . . ." she says.

"He doesn't owe *you* an explanation."

"Oh yes, he bloody well does!"

"Oh what am I doing?"

"Owning yourself."

"I could have just gone home and rung him! You didn't need to abduct me!"

"Well, I did . . . I did it for both of us."

I stare out the window. Such a different experience as I view the scenery from the first trip. It's like worlds apart.

"Made it! Think I'll call it a night and hit the Queens pub." The driver yanks the handbrake as we pull up outside. "Our local will be giving out free Christmas bitters right about now."

"That's his car, right? He's home," Annemarie says.

And there is it, Adam's home. It's lit up like something from a Christmas blockbuster. Draped in bright golden fairy lights, as the snow trickles down sticking to the dark thatched roof. Lights woven around the bare trees in the garden, and the crooked gate, all winking at us. Smoke curls from the chimney.

"Jesus, I'm going to puke again!" I swallow bile.

"No, you're not! Pull yourself together. Now get out, ring that bell and ask him what the actual fuck is going on?"

"This is psychotic," I suddenly realise. "I'm not doing this, how did I let you talk me into this?"

"Get out and do it. You never forgave yourself that you didn't confront dickhead Dermot. Remember? You hated yourself for years after . . . you were a shell of yourself, don't forget that, Lexie. All the self-help books and all the yoga and now you have the power to stand up to him? To demand answers because you deserve them? You deserve the full truth of his life. This is your life too!"

She's right.

I do.

"He does owe me an explanation." I nod, take a long, deep breath. "Okay."

300

"I'll wait in the taxi."

I spin. "You're really not coming with me?"

"No, but I'll be here . . . if that's okay?" she asks the taximan, who nods, unclicks his belt and pushes the meter off. "I'll text David Woodcock to keep me a seat at the bar." He taps on his phone. "He's my Secret Santa too!"

"Just come to the door with me?" I plead with her.

"No chance. I'll be here. You got this, Lexie."

I take another deep breath, then I get out and slam the taxi door. The gate creaks at my arrival as I crunch my way up his driveway, spoiling the untouched blanket of perfect white snow. I cringe for a split second at my appearance: jeans, black jumper, hiking boots and Annemarie's red coat, hair tied back in a low ponytail, and I've barely managed to wand on some mascara on the plane.

I stop. Look back. Annemarie's nose is pressed up against the glass. Had she pulled out binoculars, it would not have surprised me in the least.

"Alright, Lexie," I assure myself. The curtains are drawn as I reach the front door. I hover over the bell for a minute and then, with a shaking index finger, I press it.

58

23 December

Oh Christmas Time

"LEXIE!" ADAM'S HEAD APPEARS IN THE HALF-OPEN DOOR. "Surprise!" I do jazz hands, try for the joke.

"W-what the—?! Jesus Christ, what – . . ." He stumbles back, holds the door for support.

"Lexie Byrne is fine." I grin, though my heart is pummelling out of my chest.

His face remains stone-like. "I – I – what? Oh, um, I—" He really is lost for words as he pulls the old door open wide. I gulp. He stands tall in a sharp white dress suit with a black dicky bow and shiny shoes. "W-what the hell are you doing here?" he finally finds the words.

"Nice to see you too," I say, throw out a nervous laugh, "and looking dapper I might add." *Why is he dressed like that?* Something niggles at me internally. Like I should know why.

"No, it is! I'm sorry . . . It's *so* great to see you . . . But I wasn't expecting—" He steps out, half closes the door behind him now as Spangles barks and tears down the hallway.

"Are you heading out somewhere? I'm sorry . . ." I fully take in his attire.

"No – I'm – we're – Lexie, I called and called? Where were you? Where did you go? Why did you run away like that? You didn't let me explain."

I curl my nails into my palms. "I don't know what to say about all that, it's just so unlike me . . ."

"Right? That's why I was sure you'd be back. I waited, your case was still in the wardrobe, then after about twenty minutes had passed, I got dressed and went down to reception thinking you were maybe there cooling down, and the girl at the desk told me she'd checked you onto a flight to Dublin . . ."

"I guess I just saw red." I shrug, my breath rises. It's cold out here.

"I didn't even wait for the lift, I ran back to our suite, took the stairs two at a time, packed the cases, ran out to the road and got myself a taxi straight to the airport but I couldn't see you. I checked onto the flight to Dublin, but you weren't at the gate? You weren't on that flight?"

"I was."

"No, I got that flight, Lexie, you weren't on it."

"From Newark?"

His face falls. "No. From JFK."

"Shit," I say, pull the belt on my coat tighter around me.

"Right. Of course, my luck just keeps on rolling . . ." He throws his hands up, clocks the taxi. If he's seen Annemarie in the back, he doesn't say. I need to say what I came to say.

"It was when I saw your phone . . . Honestly, I didn't mean too but I did. I got up for water, you know how thirsty I've been lately, and I saw it flash with Martha's message . . . I wasn't snooping, it was just there for me to see, just more bad timing. Maybe the fates are against us after all."

303

"Saying what exactly? Which one did you read? Which text did you see? She texts so much, so often." He sounds desperate. I notice how red-rimmed his eyes, and just the mention of Martha makes him seem more tired.

"About the baby."

He just nods. Doesn't deny it and my heart lurches.

"I did try to tell you about this baby thing . . . a few times, I—"

"Um, you didn't try hard enough." I shiver all over.

"Is that your cab?" He peers over my shoulder now.

"Yes. Annemarie made me come here, by the way, now I feel like an absolute lunatic . . ." I shiver again as the snow comes at me sideways in sheets.

"No! I'm glad you're here, and I'm really glad you're okay."

"Oh, I'm totally fine. Plenty more fish in the sea!" I grab the joke, delighted I've said that. *Hold your dignity, Lexie. Just close this chapter and walk away gracefully. Go to New York. Annemarie's right.*

"Oh, I saw that." He coughs into his hand.

"Huh?" I ask.

"Listen, I didn't know what to think when you ran out on me . . . I sat in Dublin airport thinking, Adam mate, go home, read the room. She doesn't want to marry you, mate. You've scared her away with all your bullshit baggage around Martha. But I still had your suitcase. I thought I'd leave it in the Brazen Head. I didn't feel it was appropriate to follow you to your apartment, in case you set that old Kerry man on me again . . ."

We meet eyes; his hold a glint despite the seriousness of our situation. He continues:

"But I couldn't remember the opening hours, so I Googled it, up came its Twitter account. I don't know how or why but the very first picture that came up was you, sitting on that guy's lap . . . last weekend . . ." He looks forlorn now.

"No! You're mistaken, no, no not me . . . I wasn't sitting on any guy's lap, I assure you." I'm furious at his false accusation.

"It was you, Lexie. It was definitely you. It hurt."

"It wasn't me!" I insist.

"It was *you* in your green dress sitting on a guy's knee and his arms all over you. Your head thrown back laughing. A curly-headed guy? His top stained with beer. The night you told me you'd be home on the last bus but never made it home for our call? Remember? You told me the next day you'd had an awful night because you got into a big fight with Annemarie." He's more matter-of-fact than jealous. "That was a lie, Lexie."

"Oh, Mark O' Donoghue! God no! That is NOT what it looked like. He was basically harassing me, he squeezed my knee, that's why I'm laughing, he got what for off me after that, I swear."

He just shrugs. "I just know what I saw."

"Well I saw *you* in every one of Martha's pictures on her Instagram account, everyone, it's bizarre."

"Maybe Martha's pictures aren't what they appear to be either then?"

"Maybe not . . ." My temper weans. Okay, so he's got a point, but the two situations are totally different. "It hurt seeing them but not as much as this . . . as this baby. I can't get past that Adam, ever." My teeth are proper chattering now, I'm shivering but he still hasn't asked me in.

"As this what?" he quizzes me, squint his eyes.

"As Martha being pregnant with your baby." The words stick in my throat.

"No." He shakes his head, pulls at the silver feather beneath the dicky bow.

"What do you mean, no?" I shake my head. Is he still trying to lie to me?

305

"Martha is not pregnant, Lexie." He's shaking now, wraps his arms around his chest.

"I saw her text with my own eyes!" Is he deranged?

"Oh, she *wants* to be pregnant. That much is true. In fact she's been trying for months to get me to agree to use my sperm and the eggs she has frozen for a sibling for Freya. I was going to tell you, I really was, but it seemed so idiotic, I was embarrassed and I didn't want to spoil our trip talking about Martha again . . . or my carefully planned Christmas proposal."

"Your sperm!" My mouth falls open.

"Uh-huh. Obviously, I was never going to agree to it – ever, as I've consistently told her – I was going to tell you in New York all about it, but you've met Martha, Lexie?" He runs his hands through his hair, I see his cuff links with AC on them. "She's her own woman, a dog with a bone and just won't stop at me, over and over. For Freya's sake, I try to keep my calm. Of course it will never, ever happen. I've told her the same thing, every single time she asks from day one: It's no. It's still no. It will always be no."

Oh shit, I think.

"I was trying to tell you, but every time I just didn't want to see the hurt look in your eyes . . . And I'd hoped she'd wear herself out eventually . . . You seeing her text was the last thing I thought of."

The biggest penny in the world drops. Everything's coming together now. "Freya told me this when we were in London. That her mum wanted to have a baby and you weren't happy about it at all. I told her it was fine, but that's because I didn't know Martha wanted YOUR baby!"

"The idea was put to me just before we went to Nerja in May, she drove me to the airport . . ." He facepalms. "I know how that sounds when I hear myself say it, but Freya really wanted

306

to wave me off, and as Freya was filming a TikTok dance she told me she wanted to have a sibling for her with me, that all she needed was my sperm."

"Wow." I'm utterly incredulous.

Martha isn't pregnant.

Adam isn't sleeping with Martha!

"That's exactly what I said, laughed, kissed Freya, told her not a chance in hell and headed off to departures to go see you in Nerja like an excited teenager!"

"Oh shit, oh shit to all of this," I manage, biting my bottom lip. Oh I want the Cotswolds ground to open up and swallow me whole. I am such an idiot.

"Yeah. Oh shit . . . Yet now, here you are."

"Adam it's getting cold, I better . . ." I smooth out my snow-soaked fringe with my fingertips. I'm aware Annemarie is still in the taxi and I'm pretty sure he's not going to ask me in.

"Listen, Lexie . . ."

"Adam? Who is it?"

And again.

There she is.

"You have got to be joking," I mutter under my breath.

Fucking Martha.

"W-what? Oh. L-Leddy!" Her pretty face contorts with fake ditziness. "Gah! Lexie! Why do I keep doing that? It's like I've got brain freeze when I see your face."

"Go back inside, please," Adam says, shutting his eyes tight.

I back up a few steps, the gravel crunching under my feet.

"Marsha!" I say and force a smile.

"Are you – a-a-are—" She sounds remarkably like a seal and can't seem to find any other words.

"This was all last minute." Adam nods his head to Martha. "I arrived home unexpectedly early, as you know! I wasn't meant

307

to be here for Deb's fortieth birthday. Anyway, obviously I went to see how Freya was and Martha's oven broke, she was hosting the—"

"Course it did." I tilt my head at her, but I actually laugh. I back up a few more paces, the gravel still crunching under my feet, the snow falling heavily now.

"But you're still standing in the cold, sorry! Do come in, Lexie . . . We need to sort this out once and for all."

Oh don't do this in front of Martha, I seethe inside.

I give him a lopsided grin and say, "Gotta go. Annemarie's . . . there?" I point to the dark taxi.

"Of course she is." But suddenly he laughs too.

"Well . . . the cold is getting in," Martha says.

It's then for the first time that I take in Martha's drop-star earrings again, but now I bet she borrowed them from Freya. They look childlike and silly in her adult ears. I check out her red satin V-neck jumpsuit and tiny, neat black pumps. She is effortlessly beautiful physically, but she looks slightly deranged standing as close to Adam as she can get and actually her eyes are too close together.

"So – if you don't mind." She literally tries to close the door in my face, but Adam jams his foot in.

And just like that, all of a sudden. I'm not jealous of her anymore. I feel something else.

Pity.

"Perhaps I will come in for a little while – after all he just put a ring on it and it's bloody freezing out here!" I laugh loudly and Martha's head almost falls off her rope-like neck. As quick as a flash she moves her beady eyes to my wedding finger. The relief in her face is funny as she doesn't see a ring and I have to stifle a giggle. She looks to me then to Adam, convinced she has heard me wrong.

"Great, please forgive my manners!" Adam slaps his hands against his legs. "Sorry! I'm just in complete shock at seeing you. Come inside for crying out loud, it's sub-zero out here. Get Annemarie too!" Little Spangles sticks his wet nose in between Adam's legs. "Good girl, it's only, Lexie," he whispers. "Does Annemarie want to come in?"

"Lemme check, thanks," I say. I trudge the white covered gravel to the taxi.

"Well?" Her face is contorted for the gossip.

"Martha's here," I tell her.

"Course she is," she says.

"She's not pregnant."

"Course she's not."

"Do you want to come in?" I ask in hope.

"Course I do." She opens the door and jumps out, smooths down her puffer.

We trudge back to down the gravel and just as we reach the door Annemarie says:

"I do think it's time myself and Martha had a few words, don't you?" Annemarie straightens her shoulders and together we step inside. Side by side we shake the snow off our coats, walk down the rugged stone steps into the heat of the kitchen-cum-dining area.

And immediately, I want to die.

59

23 December

Holly Jolly Christmas

THAT'S WHY HE'S WEARING THE WHITE SUIT! I remember now. It's his sister's fortieth birthday party! So that was true too. Now, Adam's kitchen is packed with people in white suits and white dresses. Like a big snowball family. The table is decorated beautifully: gold candles burn brightly and Christmas crackers are laid across empty plates. A browned turkey sits in the middle on a silver tin foil tray, with all the trimmings in glass bowls, mashed potatoes, boiled potatoes, roast potatoes, carrots, parsnips, Brussels sprouts, and about to tuck into this festive delight are Adam's family and friends.

"Oh balls," Annemarie hisses under the Christmas carols that play quietly.

"What kept you Coops – oh wouldya look who it is. The mad Irish pair! The headbangers!" Frank, Deb's husband, waves his ever-present green bottle at me. "Lovers' tiff, I can tell. Didn't buy his excuse of coming home early! Face on him like a slapped fish!"

"That's enough, Frank," Adam says.

"Oh Jesus," Annemarie on my shoulder mutters now. "It's a family Christmas dinner."

"No shit, Sherlock," I throw back, my hand covering my mouth.

"Adam, darling," his mother scolds, "you never told us Lexie was coming to Deb's fortieth dinner?"

"Oh it's worse than that. Shit. Shit," I whisper to Annemarie.

"We've done it again." She snorts a laugh now. I pinch her arm.

Oh please no, I haven't ruined another one of Deb's parties. As I turn, from the corner of my eye, I see them. Piles and piles of beautifully wrapped gifts stacked up under Adam's Christmas tree and a huge bunch of silver balloons, bobbing on a string, held down by a water balloon that says: HAPPY 40th DEB.

Adam's mother pushes back her chair and stands.

"Hello, Lexie dear, and if I'm not mistaken, you're Annemarie? I recognise you from the photos Adam showed us of you and your beautiful son."

"Hi, yes that's me, guilty as charged," Annemarie says.

"Lexie! How delightful to see you again, dear," his dad says. "We heard New York was cut short. Shame."

"Um, yes . . ." I nod, implore Adam with my eyes.

"Yes, such a pity you had to get back for work," he tells me.

"W-work. Yes. Busy. Lots of children need good gifts," I stammer.

"Massive row more like it," Frank guffaws.

"Lexie! No wayyyyy! Hiiii!" Freya bounces in, runs straight to me and gives me a huge warm hug. Martha scurries behind me, back to her seat.

"Look at you, you've taken a stretch since I saw you last," I tell Freya.

"You think?" Her blue eyes widen.

"For sure."

"Good, because Pia, in my stables, keeps calling me Shorty and she's bugging me, are you staying for long?" she asks, hopefully.

"Not this time, in fact, it's a flying visit – but next time?" I smile brightly at her.

"Sit, Freya, we're about to eat," Martha commands.

"I'm going to ask Dad if we can start messaging?" Freya says and I nod.

"I'll just grab two more chairs?" Adam says and I see Deb's face cloud over.

"Happy birthday," Annemarie says to her. "Lovely dress."

"Thank you," she replies, tugs at the polo necked, tight white woollen dress.

"No! No! We can't stay . . ." I say.

"Right." Deb pushes her chair back, champagne flute in hand.

"We had a load of buttery toast before we left . . ." I try feebly.

"Well then—" Deb looks at Annemarie. "How lovely to see you both even briefly. Shall I call Spin, our local cabs?"

"Nonsense!" Adam's mother says as Adam arrives back with two stools in each hand. "Have something to drink and a little nibble?"

"We really—" I try, feeling so out of place it's making me break out in a sweat.

"There is more than enough food here to feed an army, right sis?" Adams asks.

"I think the ladies want to leave?" Deb smiles falsely at us all.

"Yes, they've already eaten Adam," Martha pipes up behind her.

"Right then. I can't wait a single second longer, I'd eat a scabby man's leg through a gate post." Frank stands, reaches over for the carving knife and as soon as he slices the bird, I get the smell of turkey, but it's the strangest smell. That watery saliva builds up in my mouth again. Horrified, I swallow it back down, but it fills up again. I swallow. It's back. I gag behind my hand. Perspiration runs down my forehead.

"Sit." Adam practically pushes the stool under me and the same to Annemarie.

"You okay there?" Annemarie side eyes me.

"I dunno—" I mutter as Adam hands me a plate of mini sausage rolls and I pop one in my mouth to try and swallow the watery saliva down.

"Oh—" I put my hand on Annemarie's arm.

"What?" she turns to face me now. I see Frank slice and slice, in and out of focus.

"Oh God—" I heave, clamp my mouth shut again. My shoulders raise. I heave again.

"Oh! Oh! Ohhhhh shit!" Annemarie says, staring at what I know is my now ashen face. I feel the blood literally drain, but it's too late. "Get up," she tells me a look of pure horror in her eyes.

But I can't even turn in time, and I throw up everywhere, all over the dinner table.

60

23 December

I Saw Mommy Kissing Santa Claus

"JUST TAKE TINY SIPS." Adam holds the small, cone-shaped paper cup to my parched mouth.

"Thank you, I don't know what to say," I whisper. I'm well beyond mortified at this stage.

"It must have been something you ate? It's not your fault, please don't worry. Although I'd say Deb is done inviting you to her parties." He sniggers.

"It's so not funny. I only came to talk about us."

I can still see her bulging eyes and hear her shrieking echoing in my ears. I will never live this down.

"Well, you rest, let me do the talking?"

I nod, sit back, just thankful the vomiting has stopped. It was horrible.

"This can wait you know? Until you feel better?"

"I'm fine, honestly, I leave in the morning so let's just get the crux of it all, yeah?"

"I'm not sure what it is you want from our relationship anymore, Lexie?" He pulls the dicky bow loose, unbuttons the top button on his shirt, perches on the edge of my A&E bed.

"I am . . . finally," I say, reach up for the paper cup again, take another sip.

"What?"

"I want to *live* my life . . . like really live it."

"Without me?" he asks, taking the paper cup from me.

"No. Definitely not, no . . . with you but as part of it . . ."

"What does that mean?"

"I don't want to wait for you anymore."

"What does that mean *exactly*?" His eyes are full of concern.

"It means I'm going to go forward with my life. I'm going to travel and see things . . . I have plans, but I still want to be with you; I can't deny myself us, I just need to put me first. So, we are back to where we began – you understand?"

"Okay." He sits further in on the bed. He raises his index finger, he's thinking about what I'm saying.

I rest my head on the soft pillow. I had projectile vomited for forty-five minutes until Adam drove me to the hospital with suspected food poisoning. I have never been as humiliated in my entire life. I've an IV drip in my arm now and feel so much better. The weird thing is, all I had was that mini sausage roll! I haven't eaten a thing before it all day except toast. But I'm stressed, so stressed.

He stands up now: "So what about my proposal? Do you still want to be engaged to me?"

"Yes. I do." I nod. I do.

"You do? Oh really?" The relief in his eyes and voice as he drops his head into his hands. "Thank God for that!"

"But you pointed out you want to wait for Freya to finish school, so while we wait, I want to use that time to work on myself. On Lexie Byrne."

"Of course."

"So, Máiréad died . . ." I tilt my head.

"No? Oh gosh, I'm sorry."

"I was with her." Oh Máiréad. I swallow tears. Right to the end, she was so caring and generous. In all the mad dashing to Annemarie's place and then the airport, I'd almost forgotten about the envelope that Kevin kindly dropped into Annemarie's house for me.

"She left me an envelope of money and a note. Quite a sum, to be honest. Thousands that she could have spent on herself. And a ring. She had a child, Kathleen, that was taken from her, and I want to try and find her – give her what's rightfully hers, her mother's ring bought for her by her father. But first, I'm going to apply for a six-month college course, I'm hoping to get onto at NYU, in caring for geriatrics with early dementia . . ."

"You're leaving Ireland?" Any residue of laughter is wiped clean off his face as soon as I said that.

"Just for a while. I'm going to go to New York for six months to study."

He just looks at me. Then a curl of a smile.

"Good for you, Lexie Byrne." He nods. "Good for you."

"Really?" I'm so happy he gets it. Gets where I'm coming from. "And when you can, I'll expect you to join me!"

"Try stopping me!"

"Oh, Adam, they will be the best of times . . . You understand? Why I'm not going to let life pass me by while I wait for you?"

"I do. I get that."

"I knew you would. It took me a while to get it right in my own head."

"Honestly, I'll be happier knowing you're happier, I feel so much guilt all the time, trying to do the right thing by Freya but constantly letting you down."

316

"You're an amazing father . . ." I take his hands. "After New York and being with Jackie, being on my own when you had to leave me . . . rightfully leave me, I know . . . something shifted. My horizon expanded and it was great, and it doesn't mean I love you any less, I'm besotted with you! It just means at this point in our relationship, if we still want to make it work and get married in a few years, I need to do more in between, for me."

"And I think you should." He nods.

"I will and I am."

"When does the course start?"

"January."

"So soon? Where will you stay?"

"I'm going to sub-let Jackie's brownstone for the six months, it's stunning Adam, wait till you see it! Then when I get back there is a job for me at Sir Patrick Dun's – well, if I pass my course, that is."

"So you'll leave Silverside?"

"I think I will. It's time for a change. Máiréad left me enough for my course fees and some rent, I can get a part-time job in the N17, Jackie's bar."

A nurse steps in quietly on her white plimsoles, comes around the blue curtain.

"Bloods are back, Ad." She hands him a yellow page and he unfolds the sheet of paper.

"Okay? What was it? Arsenic in the sausage roll?" I laugh as his brown eyes dip lower. He seems to re-read the results.

"Am I okay?" Suddenly I'm fearful. Put my hand on my neck.

"Lexie. You're pregnant," he tells me, his expression professional. "At least ten weeks according to this."

"W-what?" I yelp.

"The blood work shows you are pregnant." His calm eyes hold my panicked ones.

"You are kidding me?"

"I'm not." Again he remains totally professional. It's like I'm talking to a nurse, not to Adam. Well, he is a nurse, but you know what I mean.

"Oh my good God." Immediately my hand goes from my neck down to my stomach and I do what every woman in the world who didn't know she was pregnant does. I say:

"But I've been drinking! I didn't take folic acid! I haven't been to pregnancy yoga!"

"Because you didn't know," he says softly. "It's very early days."

"But I'm going to New York. I've told Jackie." I can't take this in. I'm pregnant with his baby. My brain does the calculations. October. The last time he was in Dublin for that quick overnight. I'd had a stomach bug the week before . . . I'd been out of work sick, the bug must have interfered with my pill.

"It's your decision obviously . . . and after everything you've just said I totally understand if this isn't what you want but I just want to say . . ." His face flushes, he pulls at his chin, rubs his hands up and down his stubble, fiddles with the silver feather. "I felt like punching the air when I just read these results. *I'm* that happy."

A baby.

Our baby.

But do I want that?

Only you can answer that, Lexie.

Again my hand moves down to my stomach, holds its position. Adam's baby is in there.

"But what would we do?" I ask him.

"Whatever you wanted," he tells me, "you tell me, this changes everything. It's a new life, it's our baby."

"But you can't leave your life here?" I say.

His face digests this.

318

"No, but I can certainly change it. If these last few days have taught me anything, it's that I need to prioritise you . . . a lot more, and if—"

"No, that's what I don't want, you need to prioritise Freya." I throw my hands up and automatically rest them again on my tummy.

"It was actually Freya who opened my eyes. When I got home, after the disaster in New York I told her about us and she listened – then she said, 'Dad, I'm fifteen, I'll be gone off to uni in three years.' She told me she knows how much I love her and that I wasn't to let her mum boss me around anymore. She said she's seen how happy you make me and she thinks you're great. So I told her we were engaged and she was thrilled."

"Oh, she's just deadly, I absolutely love her." I mean it.

"You know . . . You can move over here to be with me? With us? I'd love that?"

"Raise the baby here?" I say.

I see his face light up, but I hold up my hand.

"With all your family? Oh I dunno about that Adam, I'd need more time . . . Or . . ." I say as he takes my hand, kisses it softly. "Or I could have the baby, keep my job, use the crèche, see you when we can . . ."

"No. No, Lexie. That's not what you want. I won't have you live a life that isn't exactly what you want. Your course. New York?" He's determined.

"Well, let's think, after we get used to the idea of us being parents!"

"So, you'll have the baby?" His knuckles are white, his hands are rolled into a ball so tightly.

"Oh absolutely," I say and laugh out loud.

"Oh my God." His eyes fill with tears.

"And . . . maybe, just maybe you're right. I can still do it all . . . all the things I've planned . . . the Lexie Byrne way?"

61

23 December

Joy to the World

"DEFINITELY MAYBE!" ADAM WIPES HIS EYE.

"Adam . . ." I start.

"But I'll move to Dublin if you don't want to live here, as soon as Freya goes off to college, you do know that, right? I can get a job in any hospital, I think, I'm good at my job. I'm also turning down the promotion as it will mean more work and longer hours, and that's not what I want."

"Let's just wait and see? I do love it here, maybe I can fit in?" I sit up straight in the bed, feeling suddenly full of energy again.

"Whatever you want," he says again.

"I can still go to New York in January, can't I? Do my course and stay with Jackie, maybe when the baby is older, I can look for a job in geriatrics? If I get my course, that is?"

"Oh you absolutely can and you absolutely are! I'll come visit lots, visit you both." His eyes dip to my stomach.

"Well this was unexpected?"

He pulls me close, and we kiss.

"The best things in life always are . . . Nearly all the best things that came to me in life have been unexpected: Freya, you and now our new baby."

320

"Like Baby meeting Johnny in *Dirty Dancing*." I can't resist.

"Exactly!" He laughs. "I love you, Lexie Byrne, life is the best with you in it."

"Where's my ring?" I ask, suddenly wanting it so much as the nurse steps back in.

"An Annemarie Rafter is still waiting in the corridor?"

"Gimme two minutes, Sally, and I'll go and let her in." Adam smiles at the nurse before turning back to me. "Oh, I have the ring, don't worry . . . but do you actually want to get married? I know you say you do, but do you, really?" He tilts his head at me.

"Definitely maybe." I laugh. "Look, it's not important to me anymore, I was focused on the things that really didn't matter, if we ever do it, like I said when we first met, maybe in the Balcón in Nerja, something quiet? After the baby? No fuss."

"Sounds ideal." He nods.

"I really feel stupid, though, running away like that. It just wasn't me! Not talking things through, turning up at your doorstep unannounced. Of course I didn't realise I was joined by the pregnancy hormones . . . Vomiting everywhere. I can't get the *Dirty Dancing* scene out of my head?"

"Which scene?"

"You know when Baby lets her dad down?"

Those lines are all I want to say right now.

"Yeah, out by the lake?" He curls his lip.

"Yeah."

"Go for it." He can't help but laugh.

"But if you love me, you have to love all the things about me, and I love you." I do an impressive Baby impersonation.

"Oh I do, Lexie, believe me, I do."

Then he kisses me softly on the lips, we wrap our arms around each other and I know we're going to live happily ever after.

Our way.

62

April, New York City

Fairytale of New York

"To us!" Annemarie raises her plastic cup of freshly squeezed orange juice as we stand beaming at one another on top of the Empire State building. At 443m up in the sky, the wind blows my hair like a wind machine.

"Well, we did it, our New York bucket list is ticked!" I say.

"Well, almost; we still have to catch our Broadway show," she reminds me, "and hang around the stage door after, get the star's autograph!"

"Shit!" I take a look at my watch. "Speaking of, we took far too long in Bloomingdales, let's go! Show starts in a couple of hours."

We suck on our paper straws as we wait for the elevator to take us back down. The gold doors open and the crowd surges as I turn myself sideways to fit in. Oh of course I'm not the glowing mummy-to-be! I'm the size of a house, have varicose veins, swollen ankles, heartburn that would reduce any man to tears, and still have three months to go! But I've spent the most incredible few months here with Jackie and the last three

322

days with Annemarie, exploring New York, eating creamy pasta, drinking mocktails and just laughing.

"TAXI!" Annemarie roars. She's taken to New York like Carrie Bradshaw herself, as a yellow cab spins in for us. "The Plaza hotel, please," she tells the driver.

I watch the New York streets whizz by with a tear in my eye. I'm going home on Sunday and will be taking my final exams online, as it's the last time I can fly and I need to be back in work after August granted me unpaid leave. My course was more than I ever expected, I adored it, and, if I pass, I'll eventually go into caring for dementia patients in Sir Patrick Dun's, but I'll have our baby first and that's the next chapter of my life.

"There they are!" Annemarie says, waving madly as we pay and get out of the cab at the end of the trail of horses and carriages. I look up ahead to see Tom chasing after Ben, and Adam and Jackie chatting on the famous, red-carpeted hotel steps.

"Hi, love." I kiss Adam, who arrived last night to the brown-stone exhausted after his week off doing up "our" apartment in Dublin. He basically baby-proofed it. I'm sure you want to hear the new plan? Well, we've decided to stay in my place for the foreseeable. It's what I want. Adam will come over every Friday night and return late Sunday night to the Cotswolds, for the next while, at least.

And Martha? Well, Adam sat her down for a long talk, told me he spelled it out to her, carefully, kindly but truthfully. That his new life was with me and while Freya would always remain his number-one priority, he had other responsibilities now too. Martha, finally seeing no way back to him, eventually agreed to have Freya at weekends and Adam has her during the week. Any weekend Freya wants she can come with her dad, and I can pull out the couch bed for her. I have Annemarie for all my other needs.

"Just waiting on the babysitter," Annemarie calls over her shoulder, "she's taking him up to the hotel room." Annemarie and Jackie hug tightly.

The sun comes out from behind a dark cloud and I raise my face to it. I owe a lot to New York City. I always knew it was a special place. I felt it in my heart. It changed me.

"Are you all set, Jackie?" Adam asks and we all look at her.

"Opening night, hun!" She pulls out her phone and we all gather around looking at the picture. It's of the sign above the theatre:

Jackie Murphy-Miley stars in *Maybe She Did What She Wanted*

We all coo at her name in lights. She nailed that audition. Jay told her she was a star and the previews all agreed. The New York critics are raving about her already. "Up-and-coming star" she's been called.

"Piece o' cake," she says but sticks out her hand and it trembles. "Shittin' bricks, but I'm so thankful to you all for being here, lads."

"I wouldn't miss it for the world," I say.

"I can't believe I'm the one to provide the final tick on both your bucket list! I've heard about this bleedin' bucket list for years when I worked in Silverside. Never in my wildest dreams did I think *I'd* be the lead in the Broadway play yiz were going to see!" Jackie pinches her nose, shakes her head.

"Or us!" Annemarie says. "Nor can I believe this is my second time in New York in a few months! You girls have just been amazing! I'd be lost without you both." She shifts her Bloomingdales bag on her shoulder, the picture of health now.

"That's what friends are for." Adam brings us back, drapes his muscled arm around my shoulder, and I place my hand across my huge bump.

"Friendships aren't about who you've known the longest, it's about who walked into your life, said 'I'm here for you' and proved it," Tom says and we all stare at him.

"That's very profound, dear." Annemarie dissolves into laughter.

Tom winks at her, waves his phone. "Right, sitter's in the lobby, let's get this little man settled for the evening. I could do with a cold beer before the show."

Tom scoops Ben up in his arms and the three of them head towards the red steps.

"Here, let me get the buggy and bags for you." Adam lifts the pram, throws the overflowing toddler bag across him and follows them.

"I've spent the most incredible few months with you," I tell Jackie truthfully as I waddle to the far side of the hotel and rest against the grey stone wall.

"Me too. I'll miss ya, but I won't miss yer snoring!" She leans beside me, sips from a bottle of water. She's hardly recognisable anymore, her hair dyed jet black and cropped into a tight pixie cut. She's been kick boxing and lifting weights and is broader and muscular. All part of getting into character (see, I'm learning the lingo!) for the lead part of Marie!

"Oh me too, but you're coming home to Dublin after the run, right?"

"You better believe it, as soon as the Broadway run finishes in six months, I'll be home to see you and bumpidy bump here. And my mam and me will be going for a pamper weekend." She makes a face, puts her hand gently over my tummy, rests it there.

"Jackie Miley having afternoon tea with Mummy? Wot! Wot!" I laugh but I'm really happy to hear this.

"*Maybe She Did What She Wanted* has taught me so much, all my research into the character of Marie has been eye opening. People are complex!"

"True that, but that's brilliant, Jackie, I'm sure your mam is over the moon?"

"Ah she is. Ya know, I think you're an inspiration, Lexie," Jackie blurts, looking down at her flip flops, sliding one foot in and out.

"Really?" I feel myself blush a little.

"You don't see it?" She looks up, eyebrows raised.

"What?"

"Look at ya, Lexie Byrne. Look at *you*! So independent, you made your own rules and didn't settle for less than. That's amazin'."

"Well, you taught me that, Jackie."

"Did I, hun?" She's only delighted with herself.

"Totally."

"If I ever have a kid, I want to bring them up to look at life the way we do now: the world is our oyster and we can fit it all in. Women supporting women, prioritising friendships, that's what it's all about."

I nod, squeezing her hand still resting on my tummy.

"Think she knows my voice?" she asks.

"I'm positive!"

"Shall we grab a coffee and a chocolate pretzel in the park?" Adam says as he returns.

"I'm gonna jump this cab to the theatre, I'm due in make-up soon, see yiz after?" Jackie crosses both her fingers, then sticks her hand out. The cab pulls in.

"Break a leg," I tell her and we hug.

"You'll bring the house down." Adam hugs her tightly too.

"Haven't got all day here!" the cab driver shouts out his half-open window.

"Relax the cacks, hun, will ya! I'm bleedin' comin'!" And with that, Jackie disappears to go fulfil her dreams.

"Did you say chocolate?" I look up at Adam, lick my lips.

"I did, my love." He leans across and plants his lips on mine. I inhale him, nodding as he takes my hand. We walk in comfortable silence, into Central Park, just me, my man and our baby bump.

As he queues at the pretzel stand, New Yorkers bustle past us and the sun shines warmly again on my face. We head deeper into the park, find a free spot and he takes off his leather jacket, lays it down for me and helps me to sit. Lots of young people are sitting around on the grass nearby, dining al fresco, and I feel the baby kick! Tiny butterfly kicks. It stops me in my tracks.

"She's kicking!" I say as he hands me a pretzel. Then quickly Adam puts his hand over my belly. Concentrates.

"I feel her!" he says.

I hold my hand over Adam's as our baby girl does a little jig inside me.

"She's dancing." Adam says and I take a minute as the word vibrates around my head.

Dancing.

She's dancing.

"That's it! I've got it!" I suddenly turn to him, a smile of delight across my face.

"The name?" He knows only too well how much I've been obsessing about her name ever since we found out we were expecting a little girl.

"Frances!" I say. "Like the first woman in the cabinet."

"Frances, that's a real grown-up name." He gives me Johnny's line and kisses me softly.

Then, ever so lightly from across the park, I hear it. The hairs stand on the back of my neck. I stick my ear out, push my index finger behind it, extend my neck. The faintest tones of the opening bars of "Time of My Life".

"Adam! Do you hear that?" I grab his T-shirt.

He nods.

I sing out loud, joyfully and shamelessly. I *have* been waiting so long, and I do have that someone to stand by me now.

"You don't expect me to sing in Central Park, do you?" He laughs, carefully peels the lid off his coffee. "I mean, I will if you want me too? You know I'd do anything for you, Lexie Byrne." He raises his eyebrows at me, his silver feather swaying around his neck.

"No, you just do you and I'll do me, yeah?" I tell him, crossing one foot over the other. Then I take a massive bite out of my chocolate pretzel. Completely content, I look up at the man of my dreams then into the bright blue sky and give a big smile of thanks to the Universe for me and my wonderful life.

THE END

Acknowledgements

The Lexie Byrne books are ultimately about the importance of female friendships.

So, to my gal pals, massive love, respect and thanks: Marina Rafter, Leontia Ferguson, Lisa Carey, Aveen Fitzgerald, Barbara Scully, Ciara Geraghty, Róisín Kearney, Amy Joyce Hastings, Naomi Sheridan, Janine Curran, Nicola Pawley, Marie Woodcock, Samantha Doyle, Sarah Flood, Elaine Hearty, Elaine Crowley, Amy Conroy, Caroline Cassidy, Fiona Looney, Suzanne Kane, Ciara O' Connor, Linda Maher . . . and anyone who due to peri-peri I may have forgotten!

I still pinch myself that I'm a part of the greatest supporters club that is the *Irish Female Authors* – thank you Claudia Carroll, Sophie White, Carmel Harrington, Catherine Ryan Howard, Marian Keyes, Anna McPartlin, Sinéad Moriarty, Hazel Gaynor, Sheila O' Flanagan, Patricia Scanlan, Vanessa Fox O' Loughlin – and the much missed, much loved, always remembered Emma Hannigan.

Thanks to all at Black & White Publishing for working with me on this, our fifth novel together!

Thanks to my Irish agent Ger Nichol and UK agent Peter MacFarlane.

For Mam and Robbie Rock Star 'Dad' Box and Margaret Kilroy.

For Kevin, Grace and Maggie, my true loves and all my extended family – but most of all, to you, dear reader, thank *you* for giving me this job I love so much!

Hi, I'm Caroline!

Hi, I'm Caroline! I'm an author of nine novels and a screenwriter, lover of wine, long summers, and very proud mammy to two amazing girls. I'm a Creative Director at Document Films here in Dublin, where I've written eight short films and am currently in development with two feature films. I'm also a regular contributor on TV and radio.

I really hope you like what Lexie did next and I absolutely love to hear from readers – so please do reach out on any of the platforms!

@carolinegracecassidy

@CGraceCassidy

@authorcarolinegracecassidy